Annihilating Distance: Se

"Deftly written... An impressive anthology of original short stories... This multi-faceted literary treasury... is enthusiastically recommended." —Midwest Book Review

"Wonderful short stories... Very well written, very interesting, not your run of the mill stories." —Northeast Public Radio, Book Round-table

Siding with the Angels (novel)

"...Extremely polished..." "...Creative, yet frighteningly plausible..." "...A cast of memorable characters..." "...Intriguing elements at play..." —New York literary agents

"...An excellent book. Vigoda writes with a great depth of human understanding and a brilliant sense of suspense and action. His characters are vivid and compelling..." "...This suspense-laden thriller... provides excellent, believable character development... [It] keeps us wondering whose side we're on." "Vigoda... brings a deep understanding of current events to a fictional page-turner..." "This book has it all, an intriguing plot, well-defined characters, history, current events, an ethical conundrum, intelligence, and it is written well to boot..." "A virtuoso performance in print: engrossing, compelling, suspenseful. Compares favorably to Umberto Eco." — Amazon reviews

Skipper's Project (novel)

"...A massive plot that binds its strands like rope... The changing voices, tenses, time periods, and landscapes make it a richer story. That strategy doesn't always work, but it does here... Vigoda has gone for broke, especially in the medieval story, and the result is great... A talented writer, a completely enjoyable novel." — Sacramento Book Review

FROM *Who Gathers the Breeze*

...Margherita sat with Agnoletta... and suddenly began to sob. "*Madonna?*"

"It's just that I have never before seen such majesty..."

"It is very beautiful, *madonna*, but that is not all."

"Not all?"

She shook her head smiling as at a child and said, "You are in love, *madonna*."

They stared at each other for a long time. "Am I?" she finally replied... "Perhaps you are right, for I am quite certain I have never felt this way before."

"You are in love, *madonna*."

She thought, "Then after all I will not die without ever having known love..."

After a while [Tiffany] rose again to walk around but whenever she stopped he stood close and when their hands brushed he again took hers and they continued hand in hand until she led him back to a pew where he took her waiting hand again as they each pretended to look at the church and she said, "What are we doing?"

"I'm holding your hand. What are you doing?"

"I don't know what I'm doing."

"We can stop."

"That's just it, I don't want to."

"Have you seen it?" When he didn't answer [Margherita] concluded that he had. "[The preacher] told us a true story... about when a priest refused to bury an unrepentant usurer. His family insisted on burial so the priest said they would leave it to divine will and they loaded the body onto a donkey to see if it would take it to hallowed ground. But it didn't, it headed straight for a dunghill where robbers were hanged." Francesco said he didn't believe such stories but his face lost color all the same.

It seemed a fantastic world in which everything was possible no profit goal too high to attain with everybody scratching everybody else's back even as they competed fiercely; and exulting in his victory Bob threw himself into the firm's future with full confidence in his abilities and the almost unbelievable potential of the new securities in which his firm was a market leader and in which as he saw it he was one of the chosen insiders the elect of the elect.

"...I do not believe there is sin in our love. The poets assure us there is none and I cannot feel any. I could almost say my marriage is sin, because it is a lie..."
"Then again I say I'm confused. Your thoughts seem jumbled, mine certainly are... Perhaps we try to think too much?"
"Intellect is our gift. Surely one cannot reason too much, only incorrectly."
"I would have said love is our gift and that one cannot love too much."

I have a high-stress job with a lot of responsibility... and yet the prospect of walking for four hours over level terrain the day after tomorrow has me worried. About what, I don't know... I hope I'm as ready to be tested as I think I am, but I'm also excited. I think it's going to be beautiful. I think I'm going to meet interesting people. After seventy days of walking I'm going to be in Santiago de Compostela and I'll be able to look back and say, "I just climbed over the Pyrenees, I crossed deserts. I walked a thousand miles."

Who Gathers the Breeze

a novel

David Vigoda

Collioure Books
Albany, New York

Published by Collioure Books
21 Aviation Road
Albany, New York

Library of Congress Control Number (LCCN): 2014960032

ISBN: 978-0-9728250-8-5

Cover design and photographs by Liz Vigoda. Front cover: Facade (detail) of the Église Sainte-Marie in Oloron-Sainte-Marie. Back cover: The Pyrenees (close-up) from south of Bassoues, France.

All translations by David Vigoda.

Printed and bound in the United States of America.

1 3 5 7 9 10 8 6 4 2

Ieu sui Arnautz q'amas l'aura
e chatz la lebre ab lo bou
e nadi contra suberna.

I am Arnaut who gathers the breeze
and hunts the hare with the ox
and swims against rising tide.

—Arnaut Daniel, troubadour (twelfth century)

Preface

This novel is an extension of the previous two and has the same basic plan, to combine contemporary developments with historical origins. *Siding with the Angels* looked to the twelfth century, *Skipper's Project* to the thirteenth; when I started what became *Who Gathers the Breeze*, I looked to the fourteenth century for fundamental cultural ideas that have had a direct, pervasive, and important influence on life today. I knew I wanted to tell a story about the reverence for business in contemporary America and to do this, perhaps paradoxically (though the paradox was not created by me but actual events), through the mortgage crisis that triggered the financial crash of 2008.

Commerce and banking in modern form arose and achieved cultural prominence at the same time and place as romantic love, which does not strike me as mere happenstance, especially as they share the then new experience of individual autonomy. The challenge was to combine them in a novel that grips the reader emotionally.

Francesco di Marco Datini was a prominent businessman in Prato (near Florence) in the late fourteenth century who left an enormous cache of letters and business ledgers that formed the basis of a study called *The Merchant of Prato* by Iris Origo; happening on the book I found my character fully formed, though I have invented much of his story. Similarly, fictional Margherita is modeled on the real Margherita who was Francesco's wife, though her story is a complete fabrication.

The modern story is fiction except that the events of the mortgage crisis really happened and the story adheres to the actual chronology and details of events. The few quotes of public figures are verbatim. I relied heavily on *The Financial Crisis Inquiry Report*, which is an excellent presentation of facts corroborated in numerous other documents.

The story involves pilgrimage because I'm fascinated by it, though I am not religious much less a Catholic, and it provides a wonderful structure for stories, especially about what is most or truly important in life. My wife and I drove the most popular French route to Santiago de Compostela, via Arles in Provence, in an effort to discover the medieval route, a wonderful, beautiful journey that supplied the descriptions in the novel.

I have never worked so slowly and exhaustively on anything in my life. This enabled me to see deeper than ever before into the structure of story and how it's told; not any particular story, but any possible story.

One of our great literary myths is Dante's *Divine Comedy*, which I studied while planning the novel and saw how the structure of my story had parallels to his. As I delved into the poem I found more ways in which I could refer to it, which enabled me to show how evolving ideas about love might actually have worked on people in the fourteenth century and how that relates to us today. More is said on this in the postscript.

Like Dante I associate the physical features of the geography at each stage with the meaning of what occurs there, but whereas he was free to imagine his geography I was constrained by what is actually there. Thus my pilgrim must descend, not ascend, into Paradise, an interesting challenge; but I see drawing parallels to the *Divine Comedy* as more than an arbitrary exercise, rather an explicit attempt to show that my story, while fiction, is founded in history and in that way not an arbitrary tale about love but an exemplary one.

Dante was much indebted to the troubadours, whose poetry is the primary source of what we call 'romance.' Now the big debate about the troubadours is whether they meant what they wrote and if so, in what sense, because the poetry is not just scurrilous, in its time it was blasphemous, even heretical, and downright subversive. To me it seems obvious, especially since, whatever its initial position, romantic love became the dominant culture that is still with us almost unchanged. The question I have asked is what might have happened if a couple in love when the new ideas were still controversial actually tried to implement them.

I came to the decision early to write the narrated text in long sentences with few commas and later decided to eliminate all of them. This simple gesture soon revealed to me how it guided the flow of words and the structure of sentences which gave the story its particular sound and mood and tempo. Medieval prose, note, was written without commas. If you simply keep reading the flow will show you where the natural pauses are and the grammatical structures will appear.

Most medieval novels were written entirely in rhymed couplets and I thought it would be fun to insert bits here and there as a kind of narrative punctuation. A similar feature is when an otherwise distant narrator suddenly addresses the reader with an exclamation. I should also mention that among other sources I looked to Boccaccio's *Decameron*, for example his sexual euphemisms and the delicious tale about two students warring over a girl, and to Chaucer for his frankness about sex.

This book has been a marvelous journey for me, dare I say a pilgrimage; I hope it will be for you too.

PURGATORY

Chapter One

She'd found the first day easy ("glorious, wonderful," she said) the second hard the third painful and on the fourth day her legs were getting stronger but the doubts persisted and she thought, "What have I done, was I mad?" for she had covered all of fifty miles against a journey of sixteen hundred after which she would have to walk back and over Europe's two highest mountain ranges and she'd thought, "By all the saints in Paradise, what possessed me to ask for this, beg for this, demand this?" Her husband (when at last he'd consented) had urged her to ride but she'd said pilgrims didn't ride that even kings walked but he said that was nonsense that he'd heard of great lords including those of the Church going to Compostela in splendor with large retinues of retainers and servants and supply trains and preceded by fanfares and all mounted and she didn't doubt he was right but told him tersely that that was not how she wished to approach the sacred.

He tried to bite his tongue but failed as usual telling her that priests merchants artisans and craftsmen freemasons scholars even monks and mendicants all rode that the only ones who walked were those who had no mount that even peasants rode if they could and she noted that he'd omitted women in reply to which he screamed that women were not supposed to be on the road at all at least not without protection. She'd thought, "I know for a fact that women go on pilgrimage and in larger numbers than men will admit, and sometimes without their husbands, but I also know you can't argue with Francesco, not if you're his wife, his servant, his employee, even one of his partners," therefore she'd said nothing just stared and when he spoke his first words were that her escort would be mounted which was the first she'd heard of an escort and she replied, "A true pilgrim walks, ask anyone."

DAY ONE. To inaugurate her pilgrimage she had wanted to be sent off from the duomo the magnificent religious symbol of Siena but the bishop had more pressing business so instead she presented herself to her parish church where after confessing and taking communion her priest had her kneel before the altar and in a ceremony for her alone placed the staff and pouch before her and blessed them. Then partly from memory but mostly by improvisation he recited the insidious perils of the devil which could be repelled with the staff and the importance of mortifying the flesh represented by the impractical skinny pouch and when he had said enough he blessed her and presented her with her spiritual weapons the signs of the pilgrim which now marked her.

Though her husband was conspicuously absent (having made his goodbyes in his own way) her mother and sister were there as well as neighbors and friends and many women of the parish and Agnoletta her maid was beside her who was also blessed though she did not take up the staff and pouch. Lapo who'd said he would come unless detained by some unavoidable matter didn't appear but as a surprise the priest had arranged for members of the local Confraternita di San Giacomo to come who "like the souls arriving at Purgatory in Dante's great poem" sang *In exitu Israel de Aegypto* and marched her out of the church in an impromptu procession and when they reached the duomo steps Lapo came hustling up out of breath and embraced her.

Then however into the piazza came the caravan guards and porters with their weapons and their goads and even the pack animals which could not in any case be left unguarded each so laden that one more woolen bolt surely would have downed the beast and all there to be blessed men animals and goods as though the caravan's mission were as holy as hers. She knew how Father Naddino felt for they had exchanged many words on this bitter topic but he duly blessed them and then there was nothing left as weeks months of thinking and hoping and arguing and scheming and planning and preparing had come to fruition nothing left but to turn up the Via Banchi di Sopra and begin. Had there been a band of pilgrims the confraternity would have accompanied her to the city gate but inhibited by the presence of her husband's caravan it retreated when she joined it and left the square thereby presenting her with her first spiritual test which was not to be bitter against her husband who though he had let her go and provided for her safety in his own way had made her pilgrimage look like a pseudo-pilgrimage for the Way must be a spiritual test as only a spiritual test could justify a spiritual reward.

As she passed between fine buildings she saw her city with new eyes eyes that would not for a long time fall on familiar sights eyes that observed as if they wished to fix in memory all they saw and then there was the Porta Camollia and then trembling she passed through it and left it behind and she who had rarely been outside Siena's walls was now setting out alone but for her maid on a journey of unimaginable reach. She would have gone as a pilgrim among pilgrims and had tried everything to change Francesco's mind about such a bizarre arrangement knowing that no one changed his mind once he had fixed it which he did immediately at every turn an intransigence that marked him and she feared would one day destroy him.

It had taken half the day for the porters to arrange all the goods and provisions and load up the mules whereas had she been with pilgrims she could have set out at dawn in fact she could have set out at Easter as was traditional and appropriate instead of six weeks later six weeks during which she had waited with growing frustration for Francesco to complete his business arrangements so now it was summer when it could have been spring. Still she might have been thankful the first stage was short for she had no idea how well her legs would carry her or even if they would but for her if not the men who had done this before every turn in the road presented new marvels and this being the first day she paid no attention to her legs only her heart and the country was beautiful with enough rain earlier to raise hopes for a good year and banish memories of a terrible winter in which thousands had starved.

Walking past a cluster of peasant huts surrounded by a low makeshift wall of stones cleared from the field she noticed a little imp unwashed almost naked in the afternoon heat staring at her wide-eyed from the safety of the enclosure and on an impulse she waved but he didn't respond until suddenly he ran away but soon returned with a skinny girl of eight or nine whose eyes were dark pools of fascination who cried gaily, "Where you headed?"

"Compostela," shouted Margherita though the girl was nearby. "To the tomb of the apostle Giacomo! Beyond mountains and deserts, almost to land's end!"

The girl said nothing but her expression registered astonishment. "Where's that?" asked the boy tugging at her,

"Where's that?" She turned to him slowly wide-eyed and shrugged elaborately and for the next hour there was even more spring to Margherita's step as she thought regarding everything, "How interesting, how beautiful."

Though only nine miles from Siena Monteriggioni had centuries earlier been a frontier fortress to hold back the Florentines and still looked it with its crude high walls and many towers so when Margherita for her first night on the road was directed to a rough little church in the old Romanesque style she approached with some trepidation while trying to act like a poor pilgrim rather than a rich city-dweller. Predictably she didn't sleep well but one reason happily was the excitement at having seen on the wall of the sparsely decorated church a scallop shell the symbol at once of the apostle his sanctuary in faraway Spain and the pilgrimage there and though she knew she would see many more it gave her a jolt to see it for the first time.

DAY TWO. Though this stage was on easy terrain and at fifteen miles not a long journey she'd been told with only a hint of deference to the master's wife to be ready for an early start whether to set the pattern or try her she didn't know but when the caravan came for her having slept somewhere she neither knew nor cared they set off with barely a word and soon her legs ached and she was tired. Just north of town the road joined the river Elsa so called though at this point it was a brook which they followed all day through a shallow valley between gentle hills a pleasant walk despite the pain the fields and meadows and woods idyllic the temperature pleasant the sun invigorating so as heavy as her legs were her heart was light even though no man spoke to her beyond the requirements of courtesy and she was not in the habit of chatting casually with her maid so the day passed mainly in silence.

When a merchant caravan approached both stopped to exchange information since Francesco's agent the *fattore* was always interested in news about commerce and the count who was captain of the guards needed to hear any reports about attacks by brigands or military operations or other potentially hostile activity. The *fattore* maintained a headful of information about what was selling and what wasn't about unfair competition against foreign merchants about exchange rates political developments tariffs and tolls anything to cause delays on the road whether any inns were to be avoided and whether there were any reprisals against merchants or persecution for usury while during the whole exchange the count observed the other guards while his men however detached they might have appeared remained well positioned and alert.

While the *fattore* made manifest the mercantile character imposed on Margherita's pilgrimage she fumed at the rear of the caravan unable to comprehend how her husband could do business with a man of such greasy ways whereas the count she knew to be from the respected Sarteano family which though not of Siena had faithfully served it for generations and a man whose sternness like a hard seed was embedded in the sweet pulp of courtesy. His noble manners were designed to soothe not impress and if he had any disdain or contempt for merchants he concealed it perfectly so Margherita could see how such a man could survive the never-ending bitter and often violent intrigue of the commune's mercantile politics which her own father had not; so why was he employed as a caravan captain by a merchant who was neither noble nor despite his considerable wealth in the first rank of Sienese commerce?

While they were talking a priest rode up who seeing Margherita's pilgrim attire dismounted to chat and praising her for walking claimed (in a way that invited disbelief) that when he'd made a pilgrimage to Rome he'd walked every step and condemned those who rode for insufficient seriousness of purpose then whispering a second condemnation of 'usurers' asked how she came to be traveling with a merchant caravan. When she replied with an attempt at vagueness that this was the only way to obtain her husband's consent he immediately drew the correct conclusion and blurted out, "With a merchant for a husband, and a rich one at that, by all appearances, I can certainly understand why you seek forgiveness—and go all the way to Santiago to beg," whereupon unbidden he blessed her and quickly left.

By the time the caravan had reached the day's destination it had left the Sienese *contado* and entered the Florentine which caused Margherita to think, "I am already in foreign lands. It didn't take two days to cross the Sienese frontier," and indeed Poggibonsi looked like a frontier town having been razed by Florentine forces seventy-five years earlier and only partly rebuilt.

DAY THREE. The long distance albeit easy walking of day three made it an ordeal with her legs painfully sore her feet blistered and again she had slept poorly because her body ached and she was unused to sleeping anywhere but in her own bed and so she was scared not knowing if she could continue while knowing the men were itching to see her falter even letting her know the stage would end with a climb. Especially around mid-day beneath the sun's fire she was tempted to ride kept gazing at the horses which Francesco (ignoring her wishes) had provided for her and the maid saddled but sans riders and led by a porter but over and over she told herself that if her pilgrimage were to have meaning she must endure its rigors.

The scenery was just as calm and pleasing as the day before but when one's limbs shrieked it was harder to enjoy the loveliness of the broad gentle river valley and the Elsa cool and glinting in the sun inspired here and there by streams flowing calmly out of the low hills. The next day moreover she would cross the Arno a decisive transition into new territory though still Tuscany and it impressed her how each step took her farther and farther from home from everything she knew the comforts she enjoyed the security of home and family such as it was of neighborhood and friends even of church all abandoned in the foolhardy act of embarking on the open road open to every kind of new experience both the enjoyable and the frightening. San Miniato offered nothing but shelter a secure wall to protect the caravan at least from external thieves and both Franciscan and Dominican convents to accommodate the women who arrived exhausted for naturally Margherita's insistence on walking required her maid to do the same; and though she had no reason to prefer one convent to the other her discomfort was increased by a confrontation with a friar who insisted she come with him.

A non-stop talker the scrawny man with a skin condition informed her along with countless other useless bits of information that the lands she had just traversed were long disputed between Pisa and Florence and that the city had just consented to ally with the Florentines and he talked on and on taking no notice of her fatigue or interest in her journey until suddenly his demeanor changed and in a way meant to be portentous whispered that she was fortunate he had found her before the others. The others of course were the friars of the competing order and he launched into a dark commentary on their loose morals the risk a woman of her character would run spending a night with them and how she would escape in the morning only by delivering a purse of gold. Fearing she might have fallen into the clutches of one who possessed the faults he found in others (for he looked like one struggling with concupiscence) she looked for rescue and found it in the two caravan guards assigned to see her safely to her night's lodging who intervened and accompanied her to the other convent where she thanked them and they turned away with polite if cursory acknowledgement.

DAY FOUR. Out of sheer exhaustion she slept better and hoped she was getting used to strange beds knowing there would be nights with no bed at all unless one counted some cloth spread on a church floor and furthermore once off the mountain she discovered that her legs were getting stronger when she no longer felt a frightening weariness in every step but though the soreness was gone the blisters and the doubts which had arrived on just the second day had not. "Think of it," she thought, "I had all of one carefree day. The blisters will disappear, but what of the doubts? Not doubts, fears." Still she took satisfaction in frustrating the caravan which had been hoping she would beg an escort back to Siena and was disappointed to find her ready to walk.

As she reached the bridge across the Arno a man approached to say that this crossing had been bedeviled by brigands for ages but not for a hundred years thanks to his venerated order and though not dressed in a monk's habit he carried a wooden pail which he made a point of shaking so she could hear the coins making her ask if there were a toll.

"There is not," he replied, "but contributions to our saintly work are greatly appreciated."

"You are not a monk."

"I am not, but one of the order's many lay members. We rely on donations." A wizened little man with two teeth and a distorted smile she could barely understand him but not finding the *fattore* who was already across and not sure what to do reached into her purse that contained just a few coins and dropped one in his pail where it made a feeble clink as it joined the others and she smiled sheepishly. "Faith, hope, and charity, my lady," said the man. "As a pilgrim you know this better than most. Faith, hope, and—"

"I have only a few coins," she replied embarrassed then blurted out, "I am but a poor pilgrim, you know."

"So it seems," replied the man. "One who nonetheless travels with a rich man's caravan."

"You have your coin," said a guard appearing at her side the youngest of them and one who had rescued her from the repulsive friar the previous evening. "Kindly let the lady pass." He nudged her arm the man took a step aside and they mounted the bridge.

"Thank you," she said. "I don't know why..."

"There will be a thousand like this, *madonna*," said the youth. "Thousands."

"Thank you," she repeated.

They crossed in silence he leading his horse and when at the other end another man with a pail approached he waved him away but scarcely off the bridge they were accosted by yet another who exhorted them to visit a famous abbey directly ahead with its miraculous relics and Margherita having heard much about the precious wonders to be found along the pilgrim routes was anxious to go inside. After assuring the count she wouldn't linger and having the *fattore* refill her purse she entered the church and made her way to the reliquaries in the chancel where monks were positioned one of whom graciously received her coins a polite man about her age with the beginning of a paunch.

After telling the stories behind several relics he asked her destination and was visibly impressed saying with a sigh, "I have never been, but it is a dream I have," and when she reminded him that his life was already sacred he stared at her smiled sadly and nodded. Waiting in vain for him to speak she asked if she might inquire where he had originated to which he merely replied, "Here in Fucecchio," and after another silence conducted her to an elaborately jeweled reliquary where he said, "It is a great gift to find meaning in life. I think many pilgrims set out in search of it, even when they know the sacred is not somewhere else. But it is said the outward journey facilitates the inward. May I ask if you have found this to be so?" Reminded that she had been en route only a few days and was still adjusting to the requirements of travel he smiled gently and said, "May you find what you seek."

Margherita politely thanked the count and the caravan crossed the town and entered a vast swamp then a wild dense forest and later a remnant of the ancient Roman road still paved with an engraved stone marker that everyone passed without comment. When they reached Altopascio Margherita having walked five hours was ready to rest but wanted first to tour the renowned hostel complex following which she was disappointed to learn she couldn't stay because the beds were reserved for the ailing with those for the fit provided by a monastery outside town. Assured it was equally famous and nearby she proposed to go there but the *fattore* would have had her stay in a convent in town and a verbal tussle ensued that concluded with him sighing and the count agreeing without expression to assign the same two guards to escort her and they proceeded down the road but there was no monastery. With evening setting and no one on the road they walked and walked in complete silence until after a considerable distance they reached it whereupon the guards said they would return in the morning with the caravan and turned back to town without another word.

> Renunciation darkness sleep,
> But come the dawn a vow to keep.

DAY FIVE. It being Sunday Margherita had intended to rise before dawn to sing *lauds* with the monks but was sleeping too well to rouse herself when the bell was tolled her first good night's sleep and after *prime* at dawn she wanted to attend mass but the caravan arrived and the *fattore* said she could hear it later in Lucca. The route was flat and easy and they stopped for breakfast in the shade of a small rural church with a baptistery where upon entering a priest appeared to welcome her and when she politely complimented him on the attractiveness of his church he replied, "Ah, you are from Siena. May I ask your destination?" and then he was impressed saying, "You are to be praised, *madonna*. That is an immense journey."

She asked if he had been there but he was shaking his head before she'd finished the question saying, "I am needed here. It is good to be needed, no? I hope you will not think less of me if I confess I am content. I can't even remember the last time I went to Lucca—or wished to. Would you like to see the baptistery?" He didn't make her inspect every little thing or drone on with names and dates and who married whom he just held the door open while she politely scanned the fountain and pillars and in silence they returned to the nave where she was left to pray and afterward she rose to ask him to bless her pilgrimage. Returning to the bright sunshine she wondered how he could have known she was from Siena and was about to call out to her maid when she overheard conversation that made her halt.

"Does anyone here not agree our pay is at best grudging? And now we have this extra charge to slow us down."

"I agree. For the right fee I'd carry the pope on my back. But for nothing? Unfair, I say."

"Me too. The count should have exacted higher wages."

"Maybe he did."

"He would have said something."

After a pause a new voice was overheard: "Some of us were born noble..."

"There goes our young nobleman again!" This immediately provoked laughter.

"Yes, my sovereign lord, and what would you have us do?"

"Yes, please, highborn one, tell us, we tremble with anticipation."

"A noble's duty is to protect a lady," replied the voice.

"She's not a lady," someone barked then quickly lowering his voice added, "she's a merchant's wife."

"Who is in fact noble," admitted the *fattore*. "They say her father fell on hard times through political intrigue and was banished from the commune, but till then they were a respectable family. The master wished to marry above his station so as to raise it, while her mother, a widow reduced to penury, was forced to offer the girl. No one is more unhappy with this arrangement than me," he added without mentioning the extra fee he had negotiated on account of it, "but there it is."

"The lad is right," said the count approaching, "so as a knight I must protect her, since she is helpless on her own and in my charge. Those who are not gentlemen must strive to act like one. Those who cannot shall at least earn their pay."

"As generous as that is," added another and the conversation devolved into jibes and gripes.

Francesco's order to go with a caravan she found repugnant objecting vociferously to the very idea of commerce on a pilgrimage but she had no choice it was the price of his consent and though she had heard of women pilgrims banding together reflecting on it in calmer moments she had to question whether being together without an escort made them safer. Either she abandoned herself to Fortune or took precautions and Father Naddino reminded her that foolhardiness was not necessarily piety nor prudence automatically impiety, "but," she objected, "a caravan?"

"God will know your heart."

Still she continued to argue with her husband and even appealed to Lapo his notary but to no avail she would be the sole pilgrim among merchants the sole woman among men and "Is that what you want?" she taunted but Francesco insisted it was the safest way to make such a long perilous journey noting that she would be on the road a year or more.

"Pilgrims do not travel with armed guards."

"Those who can afford them do." She knew he would never furnish his men to protect pilgrims. "Unprotected women alone on the road," he continued shaking his head, "I won't even think of it." Having dispatched an escort over such a distance she knew it made no sense to him not to send goods for sale.

When he had gone on pilgrimage the idea of guards would have been absurd but she knew that was different for they had all been men and a huge crowd and they had only gone into the *contado* yet how would it be to arrive at a convent or monastery or hostel every day with a merchant caravan wouldn't she simply be turned away or at least have to explain herself? Alternatively they of course would stay at inns was she to join them? "Am I to stay at inns, a woman alone, surrounded by rough men? Is that your idea of safety?"

"If it comes to that I will make sure you are guarded."

"And who will guard the guard?"

"Don't be ridiculous, my men would never... There are women for that purpose, as you know. And don't give yourself airs." He apologized for that last outburst but patiently as patiently as a man could who lacked all patience assured her she would be fine saying, "God will protect you," and seeing she had no choice she accepted his terms with great reluctance.

At Lucca's gate the caravan was directed to the nearby customs warehouse where merchants deposited their wares in their own secure store-room and submitted an invoice to the officers in charge thereafter paying duties to remove merchandise and Margherita more than embarrassed to be standing in a pilgrim's robe during the lengthy process of itemizing and depositing the caravan's considerable supply of goods informed the count that when they were done they could find her at the duomo around the corner. He started to object but seeing her face instead made an offer to send two men with her which she declined but when she left with her maid he sent the guards anyway and later when the *fattore* was finally done he informed him that the master's wife had departed for the duomo and they exchanged looks.

"Two of my men are watching her."

"I gave my word I would look after her."

"So did I." Again they exchanged looks.

"Perhaps she doesn't require constant supervision. She is in church after all."

Though surprisingly the duomo contained little of interest Margherita was exceedingly gratified to find there what she most desired namely women pilgrims moreover women unaccompanied by husbands instead the group she met was part of a larger group traveling with a similar company of men from Lombardy south to Rome. How she wished they were going to Compostela! Asked about their motivations one said it was a chance to get away from an intolerable husband and daily life generally saying, "I want to see something else before I die," and another said she was curious to see a venerated holy place but interrupted herself to say, "Me too, I'd just like to see something new. Where I come from I know every chicken and cat." A third laughed for they all knew each other from before and said Margherita could be sure they weren't going out of reverence for the Church, "Not from what I hear."

Like Margherita they were all married to much older men as was the custom all unhappy with them and none particularly religious and were immensely enjoying their pilgrimage which had begun when a charismatic preacher swooped into town recruiting pilgrims for Christendom's holiest site after Jerusalem and a hundred had enlisted including couples and families but these women had contrived to leave behind their husbands as husbands had left behind wives. Though they carried their religion lightly they expressed a sincere interest in having an authentic religious experience saying they didn't know what to expect other than to be seized at some point by fervor but in the meantime were having the time of their lives. "We often sing as we walk and hold prayer meetings along the way, meeting people, inviting them to join us."

"It costs practically nothing, since we are fed and housed at every stage. The harbingers who precede us arrange this with hostels, confraternities, all kinds of religious institutions, even municipalities."

"Sometimes it doesn't go smoothly of course, we're a large group, but we manage, even if that means a dozen of us sleeping together on a pile of straw."

"A dozen? More like twenty!"

They were amazed to learn she was alone and wondered how it was possible asking whether in the convents she was not suspected of being a disguised prostitute at which point she admitted to being accompanied by guards but didn't mention the caravan but at that moment the *fattore* appeared marked by dress as a merchant standing at a distance and scowling at her which caused an extremely awkward silence until making excuses the women left.

"How dare you," she hissed in his face.

"Apologies, lady, I thought by remaining at a discreet distance..." He didn't appear apologetic.

"I am your master's wife. You have no..."

"I promised your husband I would look after you. As you know, he is not my master, we are partners."

"Very unequal ones obviously."

He shrugged. "I promised him."

"I do not need a chaperone, least of all in church."

"Alas, I must be the judge of that. A woman alone, after all."

As a woman alone she was well aware of their respective positions but reminded him that she was a pilgrim who carried almost no money and a married woman of a certain age to which he replied in a conciliatory voice that he would wait for her to conclude her business in the church.

"I am not here on business."

"You know what I mean."

"Unfortunately I do." Again he shrugged. "I am off to San Michele since, thanks to you, my *business* here is concluded."

"Excellent. I wish to go there myself, to confess and take communion, it being Sunday."

This was her intent too and though she doubted his sincerity she had no choice but to accept his company and when they exited she noticed the two guards.

The basilica of San Michele was located in one of the city's main squares which was still crowded with all sorts of people when she returned outside in the early evening including pilgrims and hawkers of every imaginable item as well as some unimaginable and her excitement would have been complete but for the *fattore* who was a visible challenge to the authenticity of her pilgrimage. She was contemplating another attempt to get rid of him when he called attention to the hour and she thought, "He wishes to go to his inn to settle into a fine supper and perhaps partake of other entertainments." He offered to accompany her to her convent if she was ready for supper or if not he would leave her with the two guards the same two who had been with her from the beginning the young man and his older companion whose names she didn't even know and with whom she had barely spoken. With the *fattore* gone she was free to enjoy the crowds meet other pilgrims and watch the vendors and the street performers and she found she didn't mind the guards who were smart enough and courteous enough to not interfere yet remain at hand besides which she didn't need Agnoletta to note that their presence wasn't a bad idea so when suppertime came she was not unhappy to be escorted to the Convent of the Augustinian Sisters by the duomo.

Chapter Two

DAY SIX. The men being entitled to a day of rest per week and enjoying Lucca's attractions the count granted them the day but for the *fattore* it was his first chance to ply his trade so when the count informed him that having engaged himself as Margherita's chaperone she was primarily his responsibility they agreed he would pay guards out of his own account to watch her. This arranged he immediately went to the customs depot where he had engaged a local broker to facilitate whatever commercial transactions he would make while also amassing information about the business climate in Lucca which rivaled Siena not just in politics but commerce (since in practice the two tended to merge). The depot was a metropole where merchants came and went all day and not just from Italy but all over Europe bearing goods from beyond and all eager for information which was as necessary to prosper as the right goods for sale and having it to exchange was as much coin in one's purse as the actual coins.

Margherita's goal was to be with other pilgrims especially women without their husbands and though the three women of Lombardy had departed at dawn the convent hosted many others whom she had no trouble meeting since everyone wanted to share experiences and to be at liberty in a city was a pleasure rarely enjoyed by women so they set out together to tour the religious sights. At the first church she confessed, "I am a pilgrim, father, I go to Compostela, but as a merchant's wife. He should go on pilgrimage too, a real one, not that walk in the meadow, especially since he lives in spiritual dread. At this very moment his *fattore* is at the warehouse, it sickens me, father. Pilgrimage, after all, doesn't the one contradict the other?"

"Child, are you here to confess your husband's sins or your own?"

"I do not know if it is a sin. I didn't choose my husband or his caravan..."

"Then let us leave both."

"But what about— I don't make loans but I receive interest as surely as if it went directly into my purse. Am I not a usurer once removed?"

"Is he a usurer?"

"*Luke*, six thirty-five, 'Lend, hoping for nothing again.' And in *Exodus* usury is condemned, I forget the... And *Leviticus* also. And *Deuteronomy* and... and the psalms that praise generosity and Ezekiel, who damned the usurers."

"Don't forget *Matthew* six twenty-six and *Luke* twelve twenty-four, but do you mean to say your husband does nothing legitimate?"

She caught her breath. "Father Naddino, my confessor back home says gain without work is shameful because man must gain his bread by the sweat of his brow. He calls it *turpe lucrum*, which he says means the vileness of gain. He says usury is like theft."

"The *Book of Sentences*, Peter Lombard, twelfth century. He is well taught, your priest."

"Then you agree and I am condemned."

"No one is condemned, child. Hence confession, hence pilgrimage."

"But my husband refuses pilgrimage, or rather that little stroll..."

"Again I ask whose sin you are here to confess. We can talk all day about how money must produce wealth by work, not time, because time is God's and therefore money created by time is stolen from God."

"But father, I worry about this, not just for... Is it true that receiving interest for a loan is wrong? Francesco says God does not condemn the profit of a loan when there is risk of loss, he claims to have this on good authority. He says even the Church does not condemn usury, only excessive usury. What am I to reply?"

"My child, you ask a question that, had we the time and I the knowledge, could keep us here till this great church crumbles into dust."

"It troubles me, father."

He sighed. "Obviously the Church condemns usury, but what

constitutes usury? In principle it is any interest at all, but there are important exceptions, risk, loss of use. And what if I loan you money without interest and you, in gratitude, freely give me a present? Interest rates not deemed excessive are widely accepted, even by many in the Church. So again I ask if your husband is a usurer and, if so, what confession you wish to make for your role in it."

The count did not socialize with his men or stay at inns instead he had approached a man in the street dressed as a social equal and politely inquired where he might present himself to request the courtesy of accommodation in return for news and good conversation. In this way he found himself hosted in a palace of the lesser nobility and had occasion to tell his hosts that he was conducting a noblewoman of good character but a merchant's wife to Compostela and that though he himself had not taken up the staff and pouch it was his intention once there to ask absolution for any sin he might have committed by assisting a usurer.

"A usurer you say?"

"In fact I do not know if the man commits that sin. I use the term generally."

"Yet you surely know that in your city as in mine many of the best families are extensively engaged in commerce, including the lending practices with which the Church seems to trouble itself so mightily—at least when it is pleased to trouble itself."

Feeling the ground go soft the count stepped back and said, "Of course, as you say. I only meant to state the commonplace that pilgrimage is in itself a meritorious act. We never know where we are in our journey toward Heaven, especially a knight such as myself employed as a man of arms, and I would like if possible to make myself worthy to enter that kingdom when I find myself outside its gate."

That night again Margherita didn't sleep well though after five days she had been toughened and wasn't exhausted so she wondered if she was too excited to sleep having had a glorious day or perhaps she was too anxious knowing that the past days had been easy maybe the easiest of the entire journey and that starting in the morning the stages would be longer and harder and in a few days she would reach the first mountains real mountains not Tuscan hills. Perhaps sleeping in a mass of women some tossing others snoring she was too uncomfortable in any case she dreamt of Francesco who didn't say anything but she knew from his expression that he was calling her a foolish woman.

DAY SEVEN. For the most difficult stage so far the youngest of the guards fetched Margherita from the convent and the caravan exited the Porta San Donato to follow a straight road to a river where there was a little wooden bridge flanked by a church and a castle and when a man there proposed a visit to a nearby hostel famous for serving pilgrims she waved him away casually. "Well done, lady. I see you learn quickly," she heard and turning to find the young guard nodding smiled. Steep hills came into view but the road followed a defile for some distance before starting to climb and there a solitary pedestrian approached an old man with a walking stick bareheaded and barefoot a peasant and when he reached them he blurted out without any greeting to beware the plague ahead. He spoke strangely and might have been demented nonetheless was questioned closely but either he knew little or would only say little claiming he had come from a village in which everyone was dead or dying of a terrible affliction but as to the name of the village he only shook his head and for its location gestured vaguely behind him.

Without dismissing the news out of hand which would have been too dangerous the count and the *fattore* agreed not to turn back since no one in Lucca had said anything. "We will ask as we go," announced the count loudly as he put his horse forward but the old man as he passed the line of mules and faced Margherita practically threw himself upon her with the guards nearby reflexively converging on him. "Pilgrim," he cried out hoarsely, "ask forgiveness for us where you go. We have sinned and God punishes us for it." His voice trailed off. "We have sinned... God punishes us." He shook his head sadly and fell silent.

"Who has sinned, old man? Where do you come from?"

"Come from?" He repeated his vague gesture. "I come from my parents and they from theirs. Where do you come from, if I may ask, pilgrim?"

"Come, lady," said a guard. "Clearly he is demented."

"Or a fool," said another. "Though he has not the clever look of a fool."

Margherita took his hands. "Where do you come from, old man?"

He stared at her. "From my village. It is near, yet far. I alone still walk. My family... Where do you go to see God, lady?"

"I go to the shrine of the apostle in Galicia."

"Santiago," he whispered incredulous and stared as she submitted to his gaze staring back. "You are not frail like me." He grabbed her forearm and gently squeezed it. "You are strong, lady. Yes. May you go straight to your holy destination."

After a silence she said, "If I could I would bring you with me."

"You will bring me with you."

After another silence she asked, "Have you eaten today, old man?"

"Eaten?"

Ordering that food and drink be brought he drank carefully so as not to spill a drop and returned the cup. "Bless you, pilgrim."

"Pray for me too, old man, for I too am a sinner."

He raised a hand in a way that might have been a blessing a wave a salute. "You are strong, pilgrim. Go to meet your fortune, just beware of the plague."

Soon they were ascending a fairly steep track and Margherita who was determined to keep pace looked only once at her horse but the young guard himself mounted said, "Do you think God would punish you if you rode?"

"From what I have heard, if God punished every pilgrim who rode, there would be few pilgrims."

"Then..."

"I do not walk just to please God, since apparently He is content to have his pilgrims ride, I walk to please myself."

"How so, lady?"

"I'm not sure. I know I want to feel every step. I want to know that if I accomplish this, that it was I who accomplished it. I want to touch the earth..."

"To touch the earth. Well said, lady. That's like poetry."

"I didn't mean to..."

"No, no, I like it."

"I don't know what made me say that. I guess I mean I want to be humble, not to play the rich merchant's wife."

At the bank of another river the count called a halt to break fast and water the animals and everyone broke into their habitual groups.

"So we're talking to the master's wife," kidded the guards.

"So we're talking to the guards," kidded the maid.

An older guard suggested that the lady might like to give her purse to the lad to help his beard grow unless he had a larger one to give her and everyone roared with laughter since purses symbolized not just anything to do with money but because of their shape and where they hung everything to do with sex. The conversation wandered and soon they were taking aim at their employer again with someone saying, "Would someone remind me why we risk our skins for a usurer?" and so fell into telling tales about usurers starting with the one that they were responsible for the recent droughts.

"It's burying them in consecrated ground that's the problem. A fellow at the inn told me that no sooner did they dig one up, this was near Arezzo, and get him away from the church, they got rain."

"I don't know if I believe that."

"Why not, it makes sense."

"Usurers! How do they live with themselves?"

"I bet if we saw the old man's strongbox, we'd see the devil squatting on the lid."

"That's no lie. Then answer me this, how does the old man not see it himself when he counts his gold?" and this developed into a pantomime with the greedy miser and the hovering devil. "If ever a man was born for burning, there's one. The wonder is he doesn't see it."

"See it? They say you can smell it, it stinks of sulfur."

The *fattore* sitting at a distance with the count saw the pantomime and the merriment and asked what was so entertaining.

Since only money exchange was tainted with usury rather than trade one of them reminded the group that they were involved only with the master's merchandise not his commerce in credit and loans and one said, "Thank God for that," and many crossed themselves.

"In Perugia a usurer was declared a heretic and had a cross branded on his chest and thighs."

"I heard in France Italian merchants can't receive the sacraments."

"I heard a preacher say that when a usurer dies, demons drag him straight to Hell."

"Nothing can save him."

"Unless he makes full restitution. I heard a priest say that."

"Fat chance of that happening."

"He might make a partial..."

"Partial's no good. The priest said so, and he was very emphatic about it."

"And yet the pope protects them."

"That's because... I heard he owes so much money to Sienese banks, he'll never get out of debt."

They continued west along the stream and through another rising defile before beginning a long gradual descent and where there was a break in the trees and a clear sightline Margherita's jaw dropped. "Have you never seen the Alpi Apuane?" asked the young guard and asked again and still time passed before she turned as if she had just heard him.

"I have never seen any mountains. My whole life has been in Siena."

"You've never been outside it?"

"Not more than a few miles."

"Then you shall see some amazing sights."

"I have already seen many."

"Where the quarrymen have worked, there are walls of white marble. You will have the Apuane before your eyes much, today and tomorrow—and tomorrow you will reach the sea." She could only nod for the peaks mostly bare rock sparkling white under the sun and surging upward as terrifying as they were magnificent could not have been imagined.

Now you know, lady, what Dante recalled when he imagined Mount Purgatory with sculpted walls of white marble and rising steeper than forty-five degrees so high "that it vanquished sight!"

There was an abbey in the foothills where they would rest and when the count inquired at the gate about plague and the monk shook his head everyone sighed with relief no one more than Margherita who was glad to rest her legs but she was also keen to continue and in fact as they covered the last two hours to Pietrasanta her wish to see more of those wondrous mountains was granted many times as they circled southwest around their base.

DAY EIGHT. Feeling fit Margherita no longer feared walking greatly encouraged that she'd been able to sleep on the stone floor of the church that constituted the town's only accommodations for women but in any case the road took them on an easy walk along the plain between sea and mountains mountains which seen again were no less astounding but the sea could be neither seen nor heard nor even smelled. The only town along this stage was on a slight rise against the face of the Apuane and when the caravan stopped there to ask again about plague and gather information about the route ahead the young guard invited her to follow him up a steep path and when they had climbed enough they sat on an outcrop and in silence gazed.

Not yet high the sun sent its rays glancing over the endless sea perfectly calm sheer as glass. "Have you seen this many times?" she whispered as though normal volume might disturb the harmony and after another long pause thanked him quietly.

"When next you see it, it will be no less moving." She breathed deeply as did he and came another long silence.

Asked how he had come to work for her husband he informed her that the men had left the municipal war captain's force the previous year when violence had erupted between the rival clans in the city or more precisely after the Truce of God imposed by the General Council had failed to stop them. "No one had much stomach for jumping into murderous brawls in the street between noble houses or a *vendetta*. So when our contract terminated... The count had good references but found few opportunities. The master was seeking more caravan guards."

"Yes, he feared for his warehouses in the city and sent out more caravans. Do you... Is it..."

"It's a step down for a *masnada* and not as well paid, but... At least we're mounted again. The count says we may be hired later by the commune."

"You don't seem angry."

"Angry? At whom?"

"At having to work for a merchant. I wish I could be free of anger. It's a grave sin and I am on pilgrimage after all." He glanced at her but said nothing.

She had gone to see Lapo her husband's notary to ask what he thought of her going to Compostela telling him the idea had arisen from a sermon and though she'd initially dismissed it found that with each unhappiness and here she slowed to make sure he caught her meaning with each unhappiness it returned. Still she dismissed it a woman first of all and one with heavy responsibilities, "But lately I've..."

"A pilgrimage is arduous, and such a long one. Mountain ranges, swamps, deserts, dense forests... And, as you say, how much more so for a woman."

"So you advise against it."

"I do not advise at all, I wouldn't presume." Though privately he liked the idea he felt duty-bound to Francesco and would choose his words carefully.

"But you do not presume, I ask you."

He pretended that some object had suddenly caught his attention then turned back. "What does Francesco say?"

"Nothing, since he knows nothing."

"You mean you haven't discussed it with him."

"Of course not. I already know what he will say."

"Is there anyone with whom you have discussed it?"

"Father Naddino, my confessor. He tells me what I already know, that without my husband's consent it is out of the question. He assumes that is the end of the matter, but when I press him, when I ask if pilgrimage is for men only, then..."

"So he blesses the idea."

"I believe I would have his blessing if I could assure him my husband does not disapprove. But Francesco will certainly disapprove unless you, unless someone, but you are the only one... I know you owe him a professional obligation."

"I also consider him a friend. I have been in his debt since he paid my schooling at the university, but more than that, as you know I am quite fond of the old devil."

"I do know. And I believe you are my friend as well, and I am forever in your debt for teaching me to read."

"Your friendship, *monna*, is as dear to me as Francesco's. As for the lessons, as there was no charge, there can be no debt."

"You are kind and generous. As my friend I come to you today, and as my husband's friend I am hoping... But I do not yet know your own opinion."

"May I ask if you have considered a more accessible destination? Rome for example, which is so much closer and less arduous. And probably safer. You would be there in a matter of days."

"Perhaps that is why Santiago is forever in my thoughts. I do not know why such a long journey seems what God asks of me, but I have come to believe that is the case."

He stared at her not harshly but carefully which she accepted knowing he was a deliberate man. "I believe that when we are called, we must answer. That when we search our hearts, in honesty and humility, and find that an act or deed is good, that it generally is good. And while most pilgrims of necessity will be men—especially on long pilgrimages—women are not unknown on the road to Santiago."

"Then you do not oppose the idea."

"It is not for me to oppose or not."

"But as my friend I ask it of you, for I value your opinion almost more than... Will you talk to him?"

Again he stared before speaking then unexpectedly smiled as if he might have been talking to himself and said, "I doubt I will ever be free to go, much as the idea attracts me. Not with so many responsibilities. But I have come to love a certain solitude, especially as I have grown older, and I believe I know the quiet that comes with long reflection. For me, my refuge is not the open road, but my little farm. I can be alone there and, make no mistake, every pilgrim walks alone. Have you heard me boast that I was a shepherd boy? I think those were my happiest days." Margherita waited patiently. "Have you been reading the book I lent you?"

"When I can, yes. It's not easy and Francesco doesn't allow much time."

"Saint Brigid's *Revelations* have given me much spiritual sustenance. Well, there are many books. If you prefer, I can give you a different one."

"No, no, I want to read it."

"If you go on pilgrimage, you can take it with you."

"Then you will talk to Francesco?"

"I will sound him out," he said at last. "If he does give his consent, and if you do not change your mind when the enormity of your undertaking becomes apparent, then I will ask a favor in return, if I may."

"Of course, anything."

"When you get there, make an offering for my mother—and for me too."

As the caravan approached the intersection with the road to Carrara it was met by a group of canons returning to the cathedral who as they approached warned everyone to pay no attention to the one following and while their greetings were courteous they hurried to get as far away as possible before the laggard arrived who when he did said, "Hail, brave knights of commerce, lords of coin and ambassadors of lucre! May your money crops prosper, your loan harvests be plentiful, your merchant battles rich in spoils. I salute you, I bow to you, I turn my arse to you and fart like a trumpet."

"Pay no attention to him, ignore him, you may kick him away if you wish," shouted the group from its distance. "He is mad, he is deranged, he knows not what he says."

When he saw Margherita he stopped as if struck. "A pilgrim! A pilgrim, by God! And a lady, if I see rightly. Well then, lady, I bid you good day and marvel at the company you keep. As I see that you walk when others ride, therefore a pilgrim true I say, therefore well met. Have you been to the sea, lady? I say, have you been to the sea?"

Realizing he expected an answer Margherita shook her head slowly.

"But you must, for it is right there, can you not smell it? A stone's throw away, yet I'll wager you purpose to walk some great distance." Her eyes widened. "I bid you go to the sea, noble woman, and toss a rock in it as I do. Come, I will show you," and as he reached for her hand armed men closed on him whereupon stopping still and looking around he quietly said, "Perhaps not. Ah well. What I meant to show you is that a pilgrimage is like throwing a stone in the sea, both being tokens of love. For is not life's creator like the sea? Immense yet intimate, as common as earth yet unfathomable, a mystery whose mystery cannot be adequately expressed, beautiful yet terrifying, and in every way fascinating, could you not sit before it for hours just staring? I love God as I love his creation, I love the idea of loving as I love the idea of being loved. I love the idea of being nothing yet everything, everything yet nothing. I love being a holy fool, dancing and laughing my way to Paradise. If God were a woman, I could fuck my way to Paradise." And without any transition he began to sing:

> Since [we] see new flowering
> fields and meadows to green return
> streams and springs to clear
> breezes and winds
> well should each the joy enjoy
> of which [one] is joyous.

(Guilhem de Peitieu, troubadour)

To everyone's surprise he had a good voice but he suddenly stopped at the verse's end to say, "When we sing of joy we sing of pleasure, pleasure in all its forms, generically as a scholar would say, but a particular species is that intimate pleasure a man and woman give each other when they join. Do I make myself clear, lady?"

"Too clear," said the young guard. "Perhaps it is time you moved on—toward Paradise."

To his surprise the man actually turned to look down the road as if to check if Paradise were there. "Thank you," he said politely,

"I shall. I love it that God has placed me beside a marble quarry so that I may the more easily find rocks for my throwing and so little by little toss this entire mountain into the sea without even beginning to fill it," and on he went. When they continued the young guard dismounted and walked beside Margherita and since again the only accommodations for women were a church floor (with an unsavory inn for the men) he left her at the church and wished her goodnight so when later they were lying side by side beneath the vault still searching for a comfortable position Agnoletta said out of the blue, "Don't pretend you don't see how he looks at you."

DAY NINE. Margherita awoke haunted by the two men crazy seeming yet not crazy who had confronted her on the road finding it impossible not to consider that they had been sent just when she'd started to accept the idea of traveling with a caravan therefore perhaps just for that reason which was why she hadn't slept well having had disturbing dreams. Realizing the mad canon was not mad it seemed almost sacrilege to leave the sea without having touched it but it was too late because the road which before had simply paralleled the shoreline at a distance was now separated from it by a broad mound of low hills and as the caravan proceeded along the foothills of the Alpi Apuane she had no choice but to follow and when they came to the Magra River they turned upstream into the Appennini mountains.

> Now gone the sea now come the hills
> Now Purgatory spirit fills.

The way however was surprisingly easy given the steep mountains whose base they had been traversing.

> This little island around its base its base,
> down there there where the wave beats it,
> bears rushes on the soft mud...
> The sun will show you, that rises now
> [where] to take the mountain by more gentle slope.

(Dante, *Purgatorio*, Canto 1)

As they followed the mumbling river up forested hills making the easy ascent Margherita found herself for the first time in vast wilderness uncontrolled savage listening for wolves while the caravan traveled in silence as if out of respect with only the clopping of hooves for comfort until without warning a mule started braying and broke free and ran down the embankment knocking its baggage loose in all directions. While the porters restored order and the guards rested comfortably in the shade Margherita took her book to the stream and when she had perched on a shaded boulder the young guard moved to where he could watch as she carefully settled herself removed her sandals and opened the book to the marked page.

Her finger slowly traversed the lines of text while she quietly voiced the words moving back up the page more than once to repeat a section until after a few pages she closed the book and regarded the trees and the hills and when a bird called she turned and as if in reply hummed the melody sung by the mad canon. Sliding off the boulder and taking up the hem of her long robe she stepped gingerly into the stony cool water now staring into it here and there as if to find a trout hiding in a sheltered pool now looking around at whatever might catch her eye and then she grabbed some leaves and tossed them one by one watching each go over a tiny waterfall swoop around a rock flow gently and disappear downstream. Stepping carefully she moved toward the middle into the sun removed the cap that confined her long hair which she shook loose and closing her eyes tilted her head to feel the heat on her face.

When they came to a town whose entrance required crossing a municipal toll bridge she said, "At this rate it will cost a king's ransom before we're done. Must every pilgrim carry a fat purse?"

"The town owes its existence to the French Road and must live off its travelers."

"How is it different from brigandage?"

"The toll-keepers are less polite," he said and for the first time they smiled at each other and when they left town having stopped to eat and seek information about the road ahead and found themselves confronted with another toll bridge she turned and they smiled again and then the count sent him ahead to scout. In two hours they reached the next town which seemed even more of a frontier post with something about it something in the air causing every man in the caravan to be unusually alert unwilling to depend on the municipal guard resolving to keep a close watch overnight on the merchandise and the animals for though the town was walled it would not have been hard for brigands to surmount it assuming they were not already inside or were not the townspeople themselves. The one reassuring item was that they were finally convinced the old man had been raving because no one had heard anything about plague everyone anxiously asking, "Where was his village?"

There was an inn but after inspecting it the count decided the caravan would stay together outside and he with it with even the *fattore* deciding he preferred hard ground to an inn where the carousing was disturbingly raucous and again there was no pilgrim hostel though the surrounding hills nestled their monasteries but as Margherita was asking about them a woman came forward to offer hospitality. She led the caravan to a grange where one could buy food and water for the animals straw for bedding and cramped but secure quarters but as for food and drink for the men they must make do with what they had and then as she led the women to her house she said not to worry about traveling with a merchant caravan. "They are on a different path than you. The path may look the same, but how could it be? They are simply going from here to there to turn a profit, whereas you are on a quest, and on that quest there is no here or there, for everyplace can be here or there. Do you see what I mean, have you thought about this?"

Margherita wasn't even sure she knew what the woman was talking about.

"They are traveling through the world, you through your own being. The land you discover exists inside you. It is the same natural world you know but has become spirit. I see I have frightened you, don't worry, I'm not crazy, it's just that I love to talk to pilgrims for I am a pilgrim myself." When Margherita asked where she had gone she laughed. "How long have you been on the Way?"

"Nine days."

"Long enough. Have you noticed how the worldly becomes otherworldly, the ordinary extraordinary, the usual unusual? Nature become miracle, meaning enlarged. Beauty appears everywhere."

Margherita's eyes lit up. "Indeed," she thought, "something like that has happened, have I not experienced it from the first day?"

"Sister, the sacredness you seek lies not at the end of your journey, it is everywhere along it, it is the journey itself. Everything you experience, fatigue, aches and pains, as well as what is pleasing, enjoyable, beautiful, for everything is there not a spiritual face? They have banished sacredness from their world, defy what is good in themselves, while yours is complete, undiminished. They move in fantasy, yours is the real world. And now you ascend. Now that you have begun, you must continue. You have left the muddy flats of the sea, the void from which we emerge, the mountain is our journey. Wisdom resides above, the greater beauty." She would have kept talking had they not arrived at the house where she immediately busied herself to provide a meal.

A strange woman, thought Margherita, who was she who could speak of such things with such authority perhaps a priestess of some secret cult that survived in this remote area but if so there seemed nothing threatening about it on the contrary it sounded quite wonderful and she would have had the woman say more but couldn't stay awake. Moments after closing her eyes she was asleep with Agnoletta beside her in the hosts' bed the woman sleeping beside them on the floor with her husband.

Chapter Three

Tiffany lived in a fifteen-room house in wealthy Short Hills New Jersey where she worked as an investment analyst for a boutique hedge fund lived with her husband Bob of four years and had a lovely three year old daughter named Kiley; she was comfortable pleased with her marriage relatively happy and quite satisfied with her career so it was unexpected for her to become obsessed with pilgrimage to Santiago de Compostela and have an affair with a tedious medieval scholar seventeen years older who made a fraction of what she did. Bob not only worked on Wall Street for one of the big investment banks he was lucky enough or as he told it shrewd enough to get assigned to an MBS desk because as he saw it this was the place to be as mortgage-backed securities had quickly evolved from stodgy products issued by quasi-governmental agencies into the hottest new securities on the Street.

Every weekday Tiffany got Kiley dressed and gave her breakfast before taking her to daycare and short of an office emergency was home for her supper which the au pair had prepared because it was important to her to spend time with her daughter and in any case she wouldn't have missed it despite the short sleep and the work time lost because the girl she called her little princess was the love of her life and she doted on her. With the au pair's prompting Kiley would tell her everything she'd done that day and show her the drawing she'd made and after supper Tiffany would give her her bath and brush her hair and read her stories until it was time to start the bedtime songs at which point hopefully Bob would rush in to kiss her goodnight; afterward grabbing some food she would finish whatever work hadn't been completed earlier and list the action items for the following day and only at that point which hopefully was before bedtime was she free to scan the many Compostela websites.

"I don't get it," said Bob, "it's all religious stuff."

"That's the point, it's not. Not all of it."

"But what do you see in it?"

Their jobs were demanding but lucrative and prestigious and since they worked in the same field there was inevitably a certain amount of competition between them with Bob impressed that he worked on Wall Street and made billion-dollar decisions and Tiffany excited to work for a small shop that gave her freedom to range wherever her nose took her to sniff out investment opportunities. Though she herself didn't work with mortgage-backed securities because despite all the dizzy math and computer crunching that designed constructed priced and traded the new securities and despite the high returns on investment what she saw was still ultimately just mortgages but her firm had gotten into them by contracting with a major house to manage some of its CDOs the new collateralized debt obligations that had come to dominate mortgage securitization. She preferred her own work which entailed searching from Silicon Valley to Kazakhstan for above-market returns not just packaging investments but finding and analyzing them filtering stocks one week for unrecognized opportunities the next identifying special situations where as the jargon had it investor value could be unlocked through restructuring so as far as she was concerned Bob could play with his mortgages while she looked at companies and currencies business plans and financial statements at trends and dead ends.

Preparing for bed they would recapitulate their days still talking as they lay side by side often competing to see who had had the more stressful day sometimes comparing investment notes sharing insights giving advice until finally settled enough they would have sex and go to sleep or if too tired just go to sleep. Once Tiffany said, "They recommend not carrying more than ten percent of your body weight."

Roused from sleep Bob asked what the hell she was talking about and why the hell she cared to which she replied that the first concerned how much weight you could carry day after day in your backpack and therefore how important it was to pare one's list of non-essential items and the second was that she was thinking maybe they should do a pilgrimage. "Not the whole thing, obviously, a lot of people just do the last sixty miles."

"Do a pilgrimage. You do know what time it is, because some of us have to work in the morning." He knew that the way to manage her unpredictable enthusiasms was to let her exhaust her interest but preferably not at midnight when Kiley was up at six.

"Do you think we could? Sixty miles, that's, what, four days? Do you think we could leave Kiley while we pop over to Spain?"

"Guess what, hon. I'm not interested."

"Not at all? It sounds really cool."

"Not at midnight it doesn't."

She let him sleep while she reflected that if he really wasn't interested (and she recognized that Bob had strong opinions about what interested him and what didn't) she could go alone but the next thing she knew Kiley was calling and Bob was groaning. It was not unusual for him to run for his train in a foul mood frustrated to have gotten so little sleep the night before something important had to get done at the office and so it was this morning that he jumped aboard the moment before the doors closed distraught at how much precious time he would have lost had he been a second later for this was the last day of a sales contest. Trading operations were not for the hesitant their boss was aggressive and to keep one's job one had to be the same so when he'd announced a sales contest Monday morning to clear out the mezzanine tranches everyone revved their engines. "Move them out, people! Shovel them out, I want them gone by close of business Friday. The one with the best numbers gets the brass ring, so what are we waiting for, let's hustle, people, let's hit those phones!"

In the seventies and eighties banks sold their mortgages to a 'government-sponsored enterprise' that issued securities against them a single bond-like security collateralized by a pool of mortgages and as homeowners made their monthly payments the lenders would remit them to the issuers who in turn would pay the owners of the securities. It was conceptually a simple arrangement and a lucrative one so the market expanded and by the nineties banks which since the eighties had been securitizing various types of loans began securitizing mortgages but with an innovation whereby they divided the single mortgage-backed security into slices.

In a pool of mortgages some homeowners might default so the innovative idea was that one investor could buy the first claim on the collateral another the second and so on the way creditors line up when a company goes bankrupt and each claim was a separate 'tranche' (French for 'slice'). Initially there was a modest number of tranches but by 2000 the number had significantly increased as had the complexity of contractual terms creating a large variety of tranches each with its specific risk and return characteristics with the senior tranches being the safest (and thus lowest-yielding) the junior the riskiest (and highest-yielding) with the mezzanine tranches in the middle. Where once there had been a single mortgage-backed security now there were as many as twenty; the reason Bob's group was under pressure to 'sell the mezz' was because the intermediate tranches proved to be the hardest to sell with the senior tranches so attractive the securities issuers often kept them for their own accounts while the most junior were sought by hedge funds seeking high-risk investments to produce high returns for their clients.

When Bob came through the door Friday evening Tiffany was waiting for him and he nodded.

"Yeah?"

"Yeah."

"All right! What do you want to say, Kiley?"

"I want to say... Good job, daddy!"

"There's champagne chilling in the fridge."

"Can't wait," he said but when she was done putting Kiley to bed she found him fast asleep on the couch.

The more she read about Compostela the more attracted she became to the idea of walking there from far away plodding five six seven hours a day with a heavy pack from hostel to hostel which no one online had ever described as more than adequate (and some as less) even though she had never hiked and had never stayed in anything but good hotels. It was a mystery to her as much as Bob, "I don't know," she said (to him or herself), "there's just something about it. I don't have to psychoanalyze it and I don't want to," though she knew that with her schedule she might get to walk sixty miles but nothing more substantial and only the more substantial felt right to her which she confessed one evening.

"Too bad you can't do it online, it would be so much more efficient."

"Virtual pilgrimage?"

"Just a thought. I don't see you going over there for a month or two or three."

To her surprise the idea she rejected as not just ridiculous but almost insulting began to grow on her because online she wouldn't be in a rush she could walk the entire route but still the fundamental idea of pilgrimage was authenticity and nothing seemed less authentic than pretending to walk; that was what gave her the idea of actually walking around the South Mountain Reservation logging miles furthermore the pilgrim routes were subdivided into daily stages so she could do a stage at a time and apply it to the pilgrim route. Virtual pilgrimage! If she were walking from Arles to Saint-Gilles which was the first stage of the most popular route called the Way of Arles (there were four official routes across France all converging in Spain) then she could go online to visit the places she would have seen in fact she could write a blog!

No sooner thought than done for the next night she was researching backpacks and hiking boots and started compiling her list of gear wondering whether that last was silly since she would be walking around the local watershed; it was already weird enough to be seen with a backpack and walking stick where everyone was walking their dog or taking a stroll but this was the only way to know exactly how much everything weighed so she proceeded to collect everything needed as if she were really going to Provence until one night she was deciding which was the best brand of blister pads.

"You know you might be crazy, don't you? You hate hiking."

"This isn't hiking, it's pilgrimage."

"I forget, what exactly is your pilgrimage about?"

There were seventy stages mostly ranging from twelve to eighteen miles with a total distance of a thousand twenty-four miles a thousand miles in two months' walking but if she could manage to get out every other Saturday (and it was hard to imagine finding more time than that) then she was talking about two and a half years to complete her journey and that assumed she walked right through the winter. "Well, why not?" she thought even as she couldn't help wondering whether she was serious about committing herself to walk a thousand miles when every report she had read talked about the ordeal of pilgrimage and how mental stamina was finally more important than physical; and what of the enormous time commitment not just the walking but researching the blog she'd already started planning and without the blog she asked herself what was the point of the whole project? And further she wondered what of the time away from Kiley when Saturdays and Sundays were the only days they spent more than an hour together; and would Bob be supportive could he take up the slack while she was occupied given that Saturday was the one day of the week when in principle his time was his own though even then as often as not he worked?

"How's it going?" he asked one night and she nodded. "Still going ahead with it?" She nodded again and he didn't mind because he figured the actual walking wouldn't last longer than the first try second at most and as for the blog she could do as she pleased he saw no harm in that though he still had no idea what she was thinking. "A pilgrim," he thought, "I married a pilgrim." He figured the blog too would no doubt be dropped when she saw how much time it took away from her job which like his spilled all over their lives something they both accepted as the price of success.

What came with his win were front row seats at a Broadway musical a night at the Plaza Hotel with a bottle of Dom Pérignon and dinner at one of the most exclusive restaurants in the city all of which he accepted as the reward earned by his ability to create wealth an ability he regarded as socially the most important; this view of his merit was confirmed in the regard accorded him not just by the waiters and hotel staff but everyone when they learned he was an investment banker. In the splendid dining room after beholding all the superb diners he said, "You realize this puts me a step closer to VP."

"Did he say anything?"

"He wouldn't. But he knows I want it, I think he'll take this win upstairs to get the okay. I'm not saying this isn't nice, but that's the real brass ring." As a vice president even without anyone reporting to him there would be a huge increase in compensation and the way would be open to millions more. "Watch out, I might make more than you this year."

"Never happen," she said smiling. "So when do we get serious about a second home?"

"How about right now? Where would you like to be?"

As he gazed toward their financial horizon he could see only blue sky though it was true that never before had house prices risen so much so quickly and consequently there was some question about the market being 'overheated' but no one was concerned neither market participants nor government regulators nor economists nor the public that was keeping the boom going. In fact Lehman Brothers one of his firm's major competitors had just announced a plan to increase its share of the market with a more aggressive strategy whereby the firm would remain active in distributing that is selling securities it underwrote but would now keep more of them for its own trading accounts; this made sense to insiders not just because demand for mortgage-backed securities was so great but because the main problem with mezzanine tranches had largely been solved a year or two earlier. The problem arose precisely because they were in the middle with risk and return characteristics that were not particularly attractive to many investors because they were not safe enough to be considered safe and not risky enough for the high returns expected by speculative investors which is what hedge funds were their deliberately obfuscating name notwithstanding.

The solution was to sell mezzanine tranches from existing mortgage-backed securities to those who would repackage them into new ones thereby causing the former middling credit ratings to be largely transformed into the highest a feat accomplished because the credit rating agencies shared the general belief that there was an increase in diversification that greatly reduced the risk. Repackaging however omitted the highest-rated mezzanine tranches whose ratings were high enough to be sold directly to investors as well as the lowest-rated whose ratings were too low to be reborn as triple-A and yet too high to interest the hedge funds; it was the latter that tended to accumulate on the underwriters' books and which the sales contest had been intended to remove. By reducing its inventory of the hard-to-sell MBS tranches his unit had not only protected itself against the possibility of rising interest rates which was another question the market was pondering but had liberated capital for reinvestment at even higher leverage.

They'd been operating below ten to one which meant for each dollar of the firm's own capital invested it invested nine more it had borrowed which was a risky strategy of course especially since the (constantly renewed) borrowing was as short as overnight whereas the investment in mortgages was obviously long-term; so for example a ten percent adverse move would completely obliterate the firm's investment but on the other hand (and it was the other hand which was expected) a ten percent move in its favor would double its investment. Lehman Brothers was moving to higher leverage which was what would make it possible to both sell more securities and keep more and thereby increase market share and Bob's boss intended to do the same because the third question was also dismissed which was whether the market in mortgage securities was distorting the market in mortgages.

Inside Bob's firm it was obvious that they could not sit still in the face of Lehman's challenge so soon his boss was guiding them into more highly leveraged deals using the very same mortgage-backed securities as collateral for short-term loans that they used as collateral for the CDOs they were marketing. In addition to creating CDOs for sale managing them for other underwriters and investing in them through their own trading accounts they were creating a second internal hedge fund open to large investors that was similar to the one they'd been operating since 2003 but more highly leveraged and no one had the slightest doubt it would be at least as successful. It seemed a fantastic world in which everything was possible no profit goal too high to attain with everybody scratching everybody else's back even as they competed fiercely; and exulting in his victory Bob threw himself into the firm's future with full confidence in his abilities and the almost unbelievable potential of the new securities in which his firm was a market leader and in which as he saw it he was one of the chosen insiders the elect of the elect.

At the same time Tiffany was also working hard on investments finalizing a couple of major deals while at night she was reading accounts of pilgrims pleased to be comfortable straddling such different worlds. It became evident how profoundly different were the medieval and modern experiences of pilgrimage for as she told Bob in bed one night she'd noticed that practically everyone talked about the solitude how it was an ordeal and how that ordeal gave profound meaning to the long repetitive days of walking. She said she very much doubted that that was what pilgrimage was like in the Middle Ages because she surmised it would have been too risky to travel alone and there was good evidence that pilgrims traveled in groups; furthermore the modern routes were hiking trails routed through isolated areas away from roads whereas formerly pilgrims preferred to be on the road especially since the wilderness was truly wilderness.

She said she'd also come to realize that today's pilgrims were focused on reaching their destination whereas heretofore there were pilgrim sites at many stops along the way in fact pilgrims would make detours to reach some of them as if they had all the time in the world as though time didn't exist then as it did now.

"And something else, it's so obvious you don't think about it, but I bet you today there isn't one pilgrim in a hundred who walks back. Once you reach Compostela, that's it, hop on a train, catch a plane, it's over. Having to walk back changes things, don't you think?" She also told him there was controversy about the routes through France which most sites assumed were official in some way and which were in the sense that the French government had established them as such with the general understanding that they followed the established medieval routes but some scholars were saying they didn't and even went so far as to claim that there weren't any recognized routes at all that medieval pilgrims simply traveled haphazardly. "It has to do with this guy who wrote a book in the Middle Ages, some are claiming he made it up."

"Remind me why you care?"

"Because it's interesting?"

There came the day when she was ready to walk her first stage and out she went with all her gear and a fair amount of trepidation and when she returned he asked her how it had gone and she replied, "I just walked from Arles to Saint-Gilles, thirteen point six four miles."

"How do you feel?"

"Fantastic. In three days I'll be in Montpellier."

"And what will you do there?"

"I can see you don't get this."

"Won't dispute that point, but you can try me." That evening she started her first blog post and though used to her onslaughts of enthusiasm Bob was shocked to hear her say later in bed that she was thinking about starting a foundation to support pilgrim studies. "Seriously? I don't get it." Not only did she assure him she was serious but it quickly became evident how much thought she'd given to the idea as she described the frustration of perusing websites that gave contradictory information about the historical aspects of pilgrimage. "Wouldn't that take a lot of time and money? Also a lot of money?" She said she'd saved enough from bonuses to get the foundation started and through its first year offering a substantial research grant. "And after that? I seem to remember discussing a second home." She said they could still buy one as he would soon be a vice president and she was working on a couple of deals either of which could turn out to be highly lucrative.

As far as she'd been able to determine her foundation would be the first specifically to support the study of pilgrimage through grants to scholars and in reply to the question she herself posed as to how much research there was to support she admitted she didn't really know but there seemed to be very little and thus one of the goals of the foundation would be to encourage more scholarship in this area. Disappointed to learn that the Way of Arles was just a hiking trail inspired by what was held to be the medieval Via Tolosana the Way of Toulouse and distressed to see the very idea of pilgrim routes debunked she had delved into the question and realized there wasn't enough reliable information to support a dependable answer. Thinking she might do some research herself drawing on her undergraduate major in classics and knowledge of Latin she had quickly learned that this was an esoteric field so she began to think about hiring a professor and then wondering how to convince one recognized the need for credibility and that was when it occurred to her to start a foundation.

A consultation with a lawyer convinced her that it was feasible and immediately she was devoting all her pilgrimage time to planning its mission statement and website how to make it known to the academic world and attract scholars to serve on its board of advisors while laboring over its name for weeks before finally settling on the Foundation for Pilgrim Studies. When she told Bob her intention to go ahead he objected on the grounds that by committing all her money she was effectively commandeering his for things they both wanted like a second home but she repeated her optimistic assertion that the money would keep flowing. Every business had high initial costs she noted but he objected that while he was as optimistic as her he believed it was poor practice to spend money before it was made.

"What could go wrong?"

"Nothing. I just think we should wait."

"Sure you just don't like me being a pilgrim?"

He didn't answer but turned away knowing it was too late to object berating himself that he hadn't tried to intervene earlier even as he recognized that once she got an idea in her head there was no dislodging it; he was shocked at how quickly and thoroughly this idea of pilgrimage had taken hold an idea he was completely unable to comprehend and one he never would have imagined could have any attraction for her and he recognized it was that not the money that disturbed him. She told the lawyer to file the papers hired a design firm for the website and began work on the call for entries.

The Foundation for Pilgrim Studies announces its fellowships for recognized scholars wishing to conduct research in the field of pilgrimage. Scholars may work in relevant disciplines including history, religion, sociology, anthropology, psychology, art, literature, medieval studies, or other interdisciplinary programs.

Pilgrimage is practiced in several major religious traditions where it is similarly regarded as an extraordinary experience outside habitual routines whose purpose is to put one in contact with the divine; at the same time it has served more mundane functions, such as respect for the institutions of worship as the agency of divinity and social cohesion around a set of shared formulations of the sacred. As a revered activity it has endured for millennia. In recent times there has been a surprising resurgence of interest in pilgrimage in Europe and North America where it might have been expected to disappear as anachronistic, moreover a significant portion of this interest seems to reside in those who profess no firm convictions of belief or adherence to a particular faith.

Are new formulations of the sacred emerging that do not require a specific theology, that are compatible with natural science and contemporary values? Does the paradoxical connectedness and isolation of modern forms of communication foster a desire to participate in ancient rituals?

Recognizing that to date little work has been done in this area, the foundation supports scholars pursuing innovative or unconventional approaches to fundamental questions about the utility and meaning of pilgrimage.

Why is geographical transposition an essential feature of pilgrimage?

Does pilgrimage offer rewards (in whatever dimension) unobtainable by other means or practices, and if so, by what modalities and to what ends?

How do features of the pilgrim's unique personal-social matrix interact?

Does the problematics of pilgrimage differ among traditions or is it universal?

Why is pilgrimage a valorizing feature of certain faiths while it is absent in others?

How does autonomy function in pilgrimage and how does it relate to practices or behaviors of solitude or other forms of ordeal such as deprivation and pain?

How does pilgrimage relate to other rituals of change and disruption versus continuity and confirmation?

How does the pilgrim utilize the imagination/ imaginary, especially its immediacy both as instantaneous and unmediated, for inspiration and a method for processing the uncertainties and ambiguities of existence? How may this enable the transformation of reality and the liberation of or from experience, thought or feeling?

As myth, metaphor, or narrative, how does pilgrimage empower ethical evaluation and decision-making, recovery, forgiveness, improvement and renewal generally?

How does pilgrimage function in the expression of love, fear, hope and wonder?

The stipend offered was substantial and expenses including travel were separately covered furthermore in certain circumstances it could be renewed so even though the call specified that "this year's grant cycle focuses on pilgrimage to Santiago de Compostela" she was confident it would attract a good number of applicants and so was disappointed even shocked when belatedly only one submission arrived which naturally made her wonder where she had erred. She had found no way to instantly create an academic advisory board but had hoped a compelling call for entries would be persuasive and the amount of the stipend sufficient to answer any questions about the credibility of the foundation and the application review process.

That the foundation was someone's pet project she doubted was an issue since she knew money created legitimacy; perhaps she should have hired a recognized figure as a consultant but she didn't know anyone and that would have eliminated a potential applicant also it would have slowed her down complicated the process when she was confident she had a pretty good feel for the current condition of the field. Perhaps, she reasoned, the problem was merely that the field was so small and being nascent had no recognized department which had made it difficult to disseminate the call for entries.

Despite her disappointment she was quite pleased with the submission she received not only because it came from a prestigious university but because it addressed at least in part her own interests for it began: "The central problem today in medieval Compostela research is or ought to be, not why people went there, which is obvious, but how, a terrain that has yet to be adequately explored. The pass into this broad valley of intriguing questions lies over the mountain of contention about the historicity of the French routes. First proclaimed in extant manuscripts almost nine hundred years ago, the simple yet unanswered question is whether these were in fact the traditional highways or rather the invention of the author, and if the latter, what his motives might have been. Complexitizing this problem is that we do not yet know for a certainty who he was.

"Solve that puzzle and we may know the routes. Know the routes and we can more effectively study how travel was effected, how necessary services were provided, by whom and at what cost. Know that and we can say with a higher order of confidence than has hitherto been possible who traveled and by what means. Thus for the first time could we hypothesize with some exactitude how many pilgrims there were, and of these how many were women and how many were not of the nobility. Was Compostela available to all medieval society or only the privileged and the desperate?

"But how are we to identify the author of a book whose very name has yet to be settled among scholars? Two and only two strategies are available in principle, either to search for evidence within the work itself or hunt for satisfactory external references. The latter is practically impossible, for where would one search? Possible documents, ecclesiastic and civil, are on the one hand vast and on the other fragmentary and dispersed, and otherwise problematic for a host of reasons. Thus must any research agenda hopeful for success look within the corners of the manuscripts. Twelve survive. They have yet to be compared."

"I found him," said Tiffany. "His proposal is wonderful. I think he might be crazy, but it's wonderful."

After a suitable delay she sent him a letter of congratulation an official acceptance and a performance contract that called for periodic progress reports in return for remittances of grant funds; but hoping for quick answers to some pressing questions (like the idea of a recognized route) and seeing no need to pretend the foundation was not her personal project since she knew projects more or less eccentric of successful entrepreneurs earned respect simply because of all the money involved she began to send him emails. At first he didn't reply then only briefly even cryptically but she would request clarifications and in that way communication between them developed formal at first and brief and restricted but gradually more expansive and casual and she told him about her plans to walk a thousand miles in virtual pilgrimage from Arles to Compostela and write a blog. Eventually she could email him impulsively about some thought and he would reply with one of his own until the exchanges became relaxed and strayed from research topics into personal items so when she asked if he ever had occasion to be in the city and proposed lunch to review his progress he replied that that was entirely possible.

Arriving first because her habit was never to be late for a meeting unless the intent was to insult someone she was waiting in the lounge when a middle-aged man appeared who was obviously the professor but when she discretely signaled to him he looked at her and looked away and in fact walked right past her. "Professor?"

"Are you..." He looked surprised in fact astonished and when later she asked him what he was expecting he said a woman his age or older because he confessed that was his prejudicial idea of who would be wealthy enough to start a foundation and have pilgrimage for a project; asked if blogging hadn't been a hint that she was younger he admitted that that had confused him but said apparently his prejudice ran too deep to be dislodged by contrary evidence.

Chapter Four

DAY TEN. On this day the caravan would reach the top of the pass in distance not excessive though with the steep climb the most difficult stage until the Alps but there was a hostel there for travelers which everyone was keen to reach so when Margherita thankfully refreshed arrived early she found the caravan ready to leave. They traveled upstream through the narrow valley now closer now farther from the river according to the terrain which though generally not steep was rugged and continually ascending through unbroken forest until in a few hours they arrived at Pontremoli a forbidding fortified town at the confluence of two rivers in fact with several torrents descending toward it from other passes it had considerable strategic importance. This explained the massive castle that dominated it from a hill perhaps also its condition for it had been destroyed several times most recently just eighteen years before the arrival of Francesco di Marco's caravan in 1347. It had been rebuilt (again) but the renovations though substantial were still incomplete which is what most gave a hostile appearance to the town which they entered across a fortified bridge.

Despite the thousands of pilgrims who transited there was not a church or holy site worth visiting in or around the town which was nothing but a way station with services for travelers (at a hefty price) yet fiercely contested by rival lords and even political factions for fifteen years earlier so bloody was the fighting within the town that a fortified wall was built through the middle a separation still needed. Margherita was told not to go off on her own while the caravan prepared for the more isolated stages ahead by replenishing provisions checking the animals' shoes and making any needed repairs to the many boxes and chests (for the bolting mule had caused damage).

A mile north of town just beyond a hamlet the ascent would begin in earnest but till then the route was almost level so after exiting past the looming castle and crossing the river one of the guards began to sing a popular song with bawdy lyrics and one by one the others joined even the porters and soon the hamlet was seen ahead. Though it had an entrance gate there was no wall just the houses abutting each other with the doors and windows facing inward a small tight cluster astride the road with an outlet at either end.

It seemed oddly quiet as they entered but they didn't realize they were in danger till the gate behind them closed and a heavy wagon was dragged across it and then the same thing happened to the far gate as handfuls of terrified villagers immediately disappeared. Bewildered they had stopped when the first gate was closed but after the second the count ordered everyone forward and several guards galloped ahead to remove the cart when a shutter opened on the second floor of one of the houses and a crossbowman fired catching one of the guards in the back and when it pierced his hauberk he screamed. The young guard dropped from his saddle and grabbed Margherita and a moment later the count arrived and they shielded the women between their horses then he remounted leaping into the saddle and drew his sword.

"Forward, forward," the count repeated as two of the guards forced the door and moments later the corpse of the archer was pushed out the window but other shutters were thrown open with archers loosing arrows and so a second guard was hit this one in the eye who landed with a thud and never moved. Using the dead sniper's crossbow a guard took aim at another who fell back into the shadow screaming and the count ordered guards to grab their crossbows and rush houses. Realizing there could be snipers in every window so that the more they advanced the more exposed they became and further that there could be a mounted force waiting outside the gate he ordered everyone back but it was no easy task to turn the caravan around with most of the mules rooted in place and the porters terrified and so a third guard was shot.

"Back, back!" he repeated. The young guard helped him get the women back to the gate which took them out of the lines of fire then kicked in a door to find men to move the wagon but found a pathetic family huddling in a mass on the floor in the corner gaping at him in terror. He tried another door but found the same so rather than lose more time he rushed up the street to help the porters move the animals as an arrow whizzed past him.

With guards providing covering fire the caravan clumsily made its way back to the gate where porters set to moving the wagon while the count still shielded the women with his horse meanwhile the young guard placing himself in the street before the porters took the crossbow from his saddle-loop and watched the windows and when one opened he shot and two guards rushed the house. When the porters had the wagon rolling the count whistled loudly and the guards gradually retreated while assisting the wounded the corpse having to be left behind then after a guard slipped outside to make sure there were no brigands the gate was thrown wide and they moved as quickly as possible back down the road goading the mules into a trot the women using their horses then turned uphill into the forest.

While the women attended the wounded the count sent out scouts to learn how many brigands there were also to discover where their horses were and how many were guarding them and when the *fattore* who had managed not to panic in the melee whispered about returning to Pontremoli he shook his head. "They were waiting for us. That means someone back there, a confederate or someone in their pay, alerted them that we were coming."

"You think we wouldn't be safe there."

Again he tersely shook his head saying, "We must defeat them or escape. And we don't have much time, they'll regroup and attack," indeed all the guards were on alert and had taken up defensible positions around the caravan with the women wounded and porters in the middle. They were in the trees just above the long narrow valley with the rocky stream running along one side and steep hills rising six to eight hundred feet behind them and across the valley; when the scouts reported that they could find neither brigands nor horses the count twirled his beard while the others watched until suddenly he said, "We stay put till dark and remain on high alert," wishing to avoid another fight because with a man dead and three wounded he had only ten effectives left and could not afford to lose more.

If he tried to move in daylight he wouldn't get far before being spotted given his lumbering pace slowed further by rough terrain for he couldn't use the road which would expose him to another ambush by unencumbered brigands meanwhile his current position was pretty good. Their crossbows were much less effective when he could shelter behind rocks and trees so the advantage of numbers assuming they had it was diminished and he doubted they would have much stomach for close combat once more of their men had been felled. To go on the offensive however would likely cost more men therefore much as he hungered to exterminate them he needed a plan of evasion and for that he needed information which for the present there was no way to get so he had no choice but to sit and wait even though he was not well hidden for the forest was not thick enough for complete cover while a single sound could give him away.

The porters were huddled beside the mules and one of them said, "Have you heard the one about the lion, the wolf, and the fox? They had caught a bull, a cow, and a sheep, and the lion told the wolf to divide the spoils. The wolf said, '*Signore*, you take the bull, I shall take the cow, and the fox can have the sheep.' The lion angrily raised his paw and ripped the skin from the wolf's head. Then he told the fox to divide the spoils. The fox said, '*Signore*, as our king you should have the bull, your wife our queen should have the cow and your children the sheep.' The lion said, 'Who taught you to divide so well?' 'The wolf did,' replied the fox, 'when you gave him a red cap.' If this business were left to me, I should let the brigands have it all and go home."

"But it will not be left to you," said another, "which puts me in mind of another tale. A man condemned to death was taken out into the forest to be hanged and the executioner said, 'We have been ordered to hang you, but we will grant you this favor, that you may choose the tree.' They led the man to one tree and then another and another, and this went on and on, but no matter how many trees he inspected he could never find one to his liking. In this entire forest I do not see a single tree to my liking. If we get out of this alive I will walk to Santiago with the master's *donna* to find the one on which our Savior was hung."

Said a third, "Whether we will or no is not up to us, but God, and so I sit here thinking of a joke I have heard many times but, as I see now, never properly understood. A certain woman was used to swearing. Her priest exhorted her at confession to renounce the foul habit and she said, 'By God I shall not swear again.' 'But you just did,' said the priest. The woman was shocked. 'By Lucifer, you are right. I shall cease at once.' 'But you have just done it again,' he said. 'You must confine your exclamations as the Lord has commanded by saying "yes, yes" or "no, no." More than that is wrong.' 'Father, I will do as you command and you'll never hear me swear again. If you do, by God, you may punish me as you see fit.' If I am delivered from this peril, I too will follow the lady and, promising never to swear again, beseech the apostle to put in a good word for me above."

"If you are delivered," said a fourth, "may it be as you say, by God!" and everyone laughed.

If neither brigands nor mounts were to be found they must be in the hamlet and unless they had given up which the count figured was highly unlikely they must come out furthermore their biggest fear must be that he was scurrying back to Pontremoli and would leave them empty-handed and humiliated after losing so many men. To avoid falling into an ambush themselves however they too would need to send out scouts and no doubt had done so already given their need to move quickly and sure enough down the road came a single man unarmed moving with trepidation yet as swiftly as he dared and the count whispered in the *fattore*'s ear, "They think I took your advice."

"I don't understand."

"They're worried we have turned back for good and cost them their booty," and seeing the road otherwise deserted he signaled to two guards the first of whom surprised the man from the rear the second from the front after he'd turned a tactic that proved unnecessary as terrified he immediately fell to his knees and began to wail pitifully. Practically carried before the count he was answering questions before they'd been asked saying the brigands for clearly he was not one of them were in fact massed inside the hamlet some twenty of them all mounted and awaiting his return.

"And if you don't return?"

At this the man fell to wailing again but eventually they understood that if he didn't return soon with information about the caravan's whereabouts his family would be slaughtered and again the count twirled his beard; after more questions and a promise of help the man was released with specific instructions and an explicit threat and went bounding up the road as fast as he could manage.

"Do you trust him?" asked the *fattore*.

"Of course not. We shall soon learn whether he trusts us. What is certain is that we will never be safe so long as the brigands run free." A short time later they appeared armed to the teeth at full gallop.

Very clever, count! To make them hurry so, not looking either right or left or listening for a telltale sound!

When they were gone the young guard and his mate ran to the hamlet where they quickly found the rope placed for them at the far end and pulled themselves up to the roof of the barn then the younger carefully crawled to where he could see each gate where sure enough a brigand stood guard; meanwhile the older had found where the thatch had been parted and they let themselves drop to the straw pile below and went to the door.

"No," whispered the older pulling his friend back, "I go."

"Let me have him."

He shook his head then reluctantly nodded and the youth raced for the near one whose neck was slashed before he'd drawn his sword and for good measure the youth buried his sword in his chest then turning in time to see the other guard disappear through a door he yanked his sword and took after him. "Tuccio!" snapped his friend but it was no use he kicked in the door and as his eyes adjusted to the dark he could see his man across the room with a sword against a child's neck.

"Fool," he sneered, "do you think I care about a villein? Slaughter them for all I care, but when you have done we will hack off your arms and legs piece by piece. Or you can use your head and help us." The brigand dropped his sword and roughly pushed away the whimpering child and as he headed for the door the young guard followed and with a fierce blow severed his head which hit the dirt floor with a dull thud before his body. "I told you you could use your head to help us," he said as he stepped over the corpse past his silent friend and went outside to open the gate.

The older guard shouted for the captured villager who tentatively emerging from a doorway was told, "Get everyone out and hurry!" and immediately he called on others by name to come out but no one did.

"By all the saints in Heaven," he pleaded frantically, "come out, come out or we are lost!" and when a few showed he screamed, "Be quick, by God, get everyone out, we have precious little time to save ourselves!" and though still not comprehending they ran from door to door and finally the men of the hamlet were in the street more dazed than afraid whereupon the guard set them to work and bid them make haste.

The caravan meanwhile moving as soon as the brigands were out of sight had been heading for the hamlet as fast as possible coming into view moments after the gate was opened approaching at what seemed an agonizingly slow pace so by the time they arrived the village women were on hand to hide the women wounded porters and animals while the count positioned his men and just minutes later could be heard the sound of horses.

When the leader saw the gates open he halted his band with a raised arm and stared and was still staring when some ten villagers on command came running out of the hamlet crying and beseeching 'the great and brave but merciful lord' to have pity on them for they had done no wrong. Prostrating themselves in the dirt they reported in plaintive cries that the caravan had overwhelmed the two good men protecting the hamlet and had continued up the road taking one of them along and leaving the other in a ditch on the far side of town his head cruelly severed from his body.

"And that fool of yours said he saw no sign of them. I'll gouge his eyes out with my bare hands. When did this happen? Speak, damn you all, when, I say!" It just happened, they wailed, the caravan couldn't be but a short way up the mountain, hearing which the leader immediately spurred his horse while a guard on a rooftop kept him in his sights so that if he smelled the trap and stopped it would be the last thing he did before going to Hell. He didn't stop though instead the whole band sped forward and no sooner inside the hamlet than the prostrated villagers running up behind them pulled the gate shut from the outside while the same thing was done to the far gate and the slaughter began.

No sooner begun than almost ended for the first volley left a third of them dead dying or disabled the second sent more to join them and then the guards raced down the street to assault them with lance and sword the young guard disappointed it wasn't his arrow that had felled the leader. Leaderless and with most of the band down the remainder quickly surrendered pleading for mercy and the count would have had them bound and leashed so the villagers armed with their weapons could march them to Pontremoli for arrest but blinded with fury they had their own idea of justice and beat them to death on the spot. "Well," said the *fattore*, "you were wrong when you said we must defeat them or escape. We have done both."

Tired as they were they couldn't stay in the hamlet because

there was no food for the animals the villagers having barely enough for their own besides the wounded needed medical care so though pressed to accept hospitality they had no choice but to climb the mountain their goal however no longer the pass but a monastery they were told was closer. No sooner beyond the hamlet than they could see how it was perfectly situated for brigands with steep mountains on three sides leaving them free to control the approach as the caravan had learned to its loss; furthermore the route beyond the hamlet ascended a series of switchbacks making travel especially slow for any caravan thus easy pickings for robbers even on foot while there was an alternate route beside the torrent too rugged and narrow for most travelers but perfect for those wishing to hide. After crossing a narrow torrent on a rickety bridge it was more or less a continuous climb often steep for eight miles for all of which Margherita suffered not just from exertion but fear primarily the fear of falling off the pace thereby retarding everyone especially the wounded who were suffering badly but the greater fear was surrender because having surrendered once what would stop her from surrendering again?

How many times did you gaze longingly at your horse, nobly born lady! How many times did you almost surrender to the desire!

The young guard urged her as much as he dared to use her mount but she resisted reminding herself that the porters also walked she need only keep pace with them but they of course were used to it and what of Agnoletta who was struggling stoically for how could a servant ride when the mistress walked? She could if the mistress insisted which she did thereby giving both of them some comfort but when at the top of the switchbacks the count paused to rest the animals and she tried to catch her breath only one guard looked at her sympathetically then after what seemed but a moment they started again and from there the road mainly followed the ridge but there was still a lot more climbing. It occurred to her that what had happened to her earlier almost being killed (or worse) would not have happened had she been on a proper pilgrimage therefore so much for Francesco keeping her safe which no sooner thought than she recalled his face distorted with rage screaming at her loudly enough for the whole house to hear, "You are not to tell me how to run my business! Do you hear, woman?"

She had not given ground she never gave ground she wasn't afraid of him for he had never once struck her though many times had come close which was perhaps one of his better qualities he never struck the servants either but when his anger was aroused no tempest ever raged with more fury; it made no difference how many sermons he attended how many pious declarations he made with some measure of sincerity the man could not or would not control a violent temper it was as if a demon possessed him perhaps one did. The sin of anger was not foreign to her either as she acknowledged but argued it was only Francesco who could provoke it as if the demon possessing him also held her. "A caravan! You would send me to God with goods for sale?"

This particular argument was fueled by a sermon she had just heard in the piazza delivered by a friar recently arrived in the city for purposes of exhortation; speaking as was customary for such open air preachers in the early morning to catch the men before work and the women before errands people poured into the square from all over the city to be moved frightened entertained he even had remedies for ailments. On this day as on many days he thundered against usurers asking portentously, "And who bears the greatest burden of risk to their immortal souls, the greatest risk of eternal damnation, who offends God the most, no less than if they spit in his eye and cursed his name, than they, they"—and here he pointed in the direction of the grand palaces of the city's wealthiest merchant bankers—"those whose corrupted flesh daily pollutes those marble halls, as well as those who would live there, whose practices though smaller in scale are no less despicable, no less anathema to the Church."

He could go on like this pointing to someone whose dress was too splendid to please God or another who had allowed his attention to wander saying, "You there, yes you! You let your attention wander when I speak of Lucifer's pit? Take heed you don't fall into it!" He would tell jokes exemplary stories parables fables horrifying tales filled with stench and demons and bags of gold of richly deserved hair-raising punishments he spoke of strange portents frightening in their suggestiveness and then he could pivot to the most pitiful of stories one he claimed he had witnessed with his own eyes that would bring the crowd to tears men no less than women. Francesco and this was most astonishing to Margherita astonishing and infuriating did not deny his guilt even admitting to her, "I have sinned as much as a man can sin," making her jaw drop he always said something like this whenever this topic arose but the next day nay the next hour the very next minute he was back to his old ways he never changed it was all but impossible only faith remained to see how he would ever change; if he was to be saved others must intercede on his behalf.

"You have been to Pisa I believe," and she told him what the preacher had said about "The Triumph of Death" a famous fresco in the cemetery building which depicted the rich merchants and usurers in their fine robes recoiling in fear from the horrors of damnation. "Have you seen it?" When he didn't answer she concluded that he had. "He told us a true story, it happened just a few years ago in Umbria, I forget which city, about when a priest refused to bury an unrepentant usurer. His family insisted on burial so the priest said they would leave it to divine will and they loaded the body onto a donkey to see if it would take it to hallowed ground. But it didn't, it headed straight for a dunghill where robbers were hanged." Francesco said he didn't believe such stories but his face lost color all the same. "So many stories, you think they're all lies? What about the family of a usurer who opened his coffin to find demons filling the dead man's mouth with red hot coins?"

It seemed interminable but finally the monastery was just ahead at the top of yet one more climb but thankfully the last; there was a bell hanging beside a massive wooden door and when the peep-hole finally opened the count explained their circumstances emphasizing pilgrim and wounded and after a pause the door creaked slowly open. "Let us look to your wounded. I fear, however, that we haven't food enough to feed such a large group, nor beds." The count assured him they could look after themselves it was the wounded who needed tending and they would all be thankful to sleep in security after the day's ordeal though he did wonder if accommodations might be found for the women to which the monk nodded and bid everyone follow.

DAY ELEVEN. Saturday was the customary day for women to wash their hair and with that and a good night's sleep during which she hadn't even heard the bells calling the monks to prayer Margherita felt refreshed and sought the guards to thank them and especially the youngest for saving her life. "If I did that, lady, and I doubt I did, you are certainly most welcome."

"If you didn't do that, you were certainly valorous."

"Nay, lady, I did no more than what was—"

"You were brave, as were you all. I am extremely grateful."

"You too were brave. Not a single cry of fear, and brave also on the road in keeping up with us."

"You are kind, but as to all that, I guess I'm just too stubborn to submit."

"Then we are most impressed with your stubbornness, lady."

"Nevertheless... To all of you, thank you. I regret if my presence exposed you to additional danger. Our arrangement was not my wish." Looking at each of them she nodded gratefully and the hardness of their faces softened and the guards replied at last their anger hollowed.

When Margherita left the young one followed and when they were out of sight she waited for him to reach her and they continued in silence until she said, "May I ask your name and where you are from?"

"My name is Bertuccio Bovattieri di Giunta but everyone calls me Tuccio. As to the second, before I reply, would I be too forward to dry the tear on your cheek?" Lacking a handkerchief he used his sleeve.

"Do you do this often?"

"As often as you like, lady." They continued in silence until he said, "I was born in San Giovanni d'Asso, of noble birth. Of course you never heard of it. We are noble in name only. My father has neither arms nor armor nor horse. His only vassals are a few serfs, his only holdings a house and some fields. I've seen peasants better off."

"Forgive me, but where is this town?"

"Town? A hamlet like the one we just visited. It's in the Deserto di Accona, that unblessed region southeast of Siena. Who knows what ancestor condemned us there. When we were boys, my father's highest hope was that my brother might be taken into service as a squire, as much in hope of gifts, maybe an income, as to learn the arts of knighthood. As for me, as the younger son it was to be the Church, where, he kept assuring me, there were many paths to riches."

"The Church!"

"No ragamuffin could have been less suited. I liked only the outdoors, roughhousing. I hated letters, couldn't sit still a moment."

"Your mother taught you?"

"She never learned herself, though she tried to pierce our leathery heads with a few rudiments, anyway she was too sickly, still is, poor thing, it's a wonder she holds on. No, it was my father. He tried, but he was laboring all day as hard as his serfs and anyway it was hopeless. My brother did better than me, but not much. We just wanted to wrestle, run around with the peasant boys. And then we were old enough to work and that was it."

"What about the village priest, surely he could have provided a few lessons."

"He's illiterate. You know what they say, 'poor land, poor people.' The earth's all red clay, you see, you can barely do anything with it—except come spring you can get your wagon mired."

Oh-ho! What each doesn't know about the other! She that he is illiterate, he that she was illiterate till recently. What they know however is what they see in each other's eyes.

"You may call me Margherita," she said and they parted he to his weapons and his horse she to confession and mass after which the abbot was curious to understand the odd pairing of his guests and she dissembled neither the facts nor her views such that he sought to reassure her. "Who is to say, *madonna*, what God has in mind for you, that he puts you on the Way thus freighted?"

"So you think there may somehow be wisdom in it?"

"Is wisdom in a thing or in what we make of a thing? I would counsel less anger and more patience. Open your heart as well as your mind and who knows what you may discover."

"Thank you, father. I will consider your words."

"May they be of help. Further, if I might..."

"Please."

"Have you considered how many have trodden this same path? I mean to ask if you have meditated deeply on this fact, for in my time"—his pepper beard was well salted—"thousands have arrived at our little sanctuary. Not all are pilgrims, but many are, not all bound for Santiago, but all bound somewhere, to ask something, in hope of something. On this path, this very road that you tread, so many have gone before and will follow. Is that not wonderful in itself? I have always found it so. I see in that a mystery all to itself. A chain is forged, is it not? We each stand alone before what is holy, alone we approach the sacred, yet never alone. Never alone. Alone each tries to leave the mundane, but never alone. Alone each tries to be simpler, more considerate, more compassionate, more aware, but never alone! Alone on the road, alone in nature, but not alone. Are we even alone with our most private thoughts, for how many others have thought the same? Alone on the Way yet constantly meeting people and so not alone.

Walking for oneself yet walking for others, others who can't, even those who won't, and thus not alone. Have you noticed how many ask why you are on the Way so they can tell you why they went themselves or wish they could go? The desire to confide, to share... You see suffering. It is hard to share suffering, but not so hard to alleviate it. Wish them well, take their requests with you, pray for them, for everyone craves nothing so much as not to feel alone. And then there are those who step forward to help, this wonderful impulse we have. We know that true charity is love and true love is charitable, and in all of it never alone, never alone."

Margherita vowed to meditate on the abbot's words and not to fret so about her husband and succeeded more or less and felt uplifted but in the lesser parts her thoughts strayed whereas Tuccio's thoughts never strayed.

Chapter Five

DAY TWELVE. At the request of the count who had made it understood he would thank the monastery generously for it as for all its care and hospitality the mass included a requiem for the slain guard and as for the wounded the condition of one was poor the others would recover if their wounds didn't fester but they were in no condition to travel let alone return to duty and everyone visited them including Margherita. The one who would not recover asked in a failing voice if she would beg for him at the tomb of the apostle but, "Not for me," he whispered, "for my poor wife," and as she nodded he explained in halting phrases that his wife had never been the same after their child died. For years she did not get pregnant though they tried everything the midwives suggested but finally a miracle a little girl! And when she died... If the good lady would beg the saint to see that her spirits were lifted... Margherita took his hand her eyes blinded with tears.

Later book in hand she went out to the fields among the laboring monks to open it beneath a shady tree and read aloud as best she could which was haltingly while Agnoletta who was playing aimlessly with a stalk of grass was roused only when she saw Tuccio approaching and said, "Look, *monna*, what a coincidence."

"What makes you think he's coming here?"

"Could it be because he has been staring at you for days?"

"He has not."

"Don't tell me you haven't noticed. 'You may call me Margherita.' I thought he would faint."

"Don't be silly, he's just a boy."

"Quite a handsome one, and old enough by the look of him.

What? It's good, a woman should have an admirer to keep her husband in line. During the requiem this morning, I don't think he took his eyes off you for a moment."

"Ridiculous, the mass was for his friend."

"When a man wants a woman, he'll stare at her while his saintly mother is lowered into the ground."

After Tuccio explained that he'd been on some errand when he happened to notice them Agnoletta excused herself saying she was bored and would go play with the cats and Margherita watching her leave said, "She's going to flirt with the guards."

"Good, it will relieve their sadness and boredom." He asked the subject of her book.

"Not one to interest you, I'd guess."

"It will if you read it."

She confessed that she read only haltingly having just learned and hiding his surprise he said he didn't mind but she was too self-conscious and left the book closed saying, "Have you ever wondered why nature is so beautiful, so rich to the senses? They say God made it so for love of Man, but why such beauty, if we are only to leave it, and so quickly? They say Heaven will be that much more beautiful, but I don't see how. They say God, being perfect in beauty, could make nothing less; but they also say He is perfect in power and thus could do anything. If ugliness and misery and evil do not come from Him, yet He suffers them to exist—they say it is for our benefit, so that we may seek salvation."

"Why then such beauty?"

"So you see it too?"

"I do now, lady. Margherita."

"Perhaps, like life itself, beauty must forever remain a mystery."

"So too, love."

"Yes, I think you are right. Why do you think God did not grant us sufficient intelligence to understand what most moves us?"

"Perhaps so we could be all the more moved. Margherita."

DAY THIRTEEN. In a monastery the liturgical process from death to burial could be lengthy especially when a nobleman requests full rites for one of his own who died during the night and was to be buried in the afternoon so this occupied everyone's full participation for much of the day with any scorn for clergy and church and any lackadaisical attitude toward religious observance set aside though this did not guarantee everyone's full occupation with pious thoughts. Margherita was still trying to meditate sincerely on the abbot's words but the services inflamed her anger for she couldn't help thinking that this man would not have died leaving a widow already undone by the death of a child (every time she recalled his deathbed plea especially when the monks were singing tears welled up) if her husband had not insisted on sending out this caravan and even as she recognized the unfairness of this charge she could not forgive him his dubious financial transactions.

Yet she acknowledged that a merchant seeking to avoid a charge of usury was able to do so with considerable assurance if not certainty while lending money or granting credit for she had to admit that the Church had twisted itself in moral knots to find financial arrangements that were not deemed usury though they looked like it of this she kept reminding herself to try to put the matter in perspective. The world was full of merchant bankers many of them noble families with extensive operations not just in Siena but as she had seen in Lucca and elsewhere and they did business with popes and kings so who was she to judge her husband who was of middling size compared to those giants and in this way she tried to calm herself but the memories and thoughts were no less bitter.

"Consider the friendly loan," said her priest who clearly couldn't abide the hypocrisy of a Church that condemned commerce while benefiting from it. "Its terms signify that the lender expects nothing in return. This respects the Gospel if it is as it seems, but it is not. How can it be, when the one who has borrowed five little *soldi* pretends to have borrowed six? Or the one who has borrowed five hundred gold florins repays five hundred fifteen, claiming the addition is a gift? If I told you who took out that big loan, you would call me a liar."

"Father, how could I call you a liar?"

"Yet you would not believe me. You could not, if I said it was the pope. See, I told you. The pope himself, yes, I have it on good authority from a church emissary who had it himself from the one who made the loan. And the repayment, including the so-called gift? Made from the Papal Treasury."

"How can you endure such hypocrisy?"

"Even when the Church is not the Church, God is still God."

"But surely the Church must..."

"Faith cannot be based solely in the messenger, but in the message and the message's Author."

"But what of the messenger?"

"Everyone is a sinner by nature. Forgiveness is always good."

"I try to forgive, father, but... Such cynicism! How do you do it?"

"I am still trying, trying and failing, for I too am a sinner. 'I will lift up mine eyes unto the hills, from whence cometh my help. My help cometh from the Lord, which made Heaven and Earth.'"

Tuccio was trying to meditate on death and the loss of a friend and succeeded up to a point but beyond that point all he could think about was Margherita and all he could feel was desire especially with the object of his love constantly before his eyes.

> For thus it happens to me, lady most noble that there be
> that desire [for] you, which deep in my heart burns,
> counsels and tells me that I you love and you serve and you court
> and wishes that I renounce seeking other company
> for you in whom all good quality resides...

(Arnaut de Maruelh, troubadour)

He was not the only one with ideas far from death however for one of the monks a good thirty years his senior had his eyes where they would not have been had age and circumstance taught him discretion but so entranced was Tuccio he didn't notice however to Stoldo his friend and protector there was no mistaking that unblinking stare. Between the obsequies and the processional he pointed out the offender and advised Tuccio if he cared about the lady (for he had seen the look in his young friend's eye) to keep an eye on him; sure enough the monk approached on some pretext and monopolized her attention but more infuriating to the lad he stood close and touched her more often than could be explained by chance.

He was offering to help her fulfill the current stage of her pilgrimage by showing her a very special holy relic.

Agnoletta asked, "Will my mistress be able to touch this holy relic?"

"To her heart's content."

"I fear she might break it."

"I can assure her it will be quite firm. And then I can teach her how to sing lauds."

"You are generous."

"I do the work of salvation with pleasure. I find that when married women go on pilgrimage without their husbands, either they suffer for lack of that which makes the hell of marriage a temporary paradise or they seek a destination they know but rarely visit."

"And you take it upon yourself to minister to such needs?"

"I am a servant of God."

"Do you find women who seek union with the divine in this way?"

"Most certainly."

"Those who, in their zeal to reach Heaven, begin on Earth?"

"Exactly. The relic has performed miracles."

"Women who, having received communion during the day, wish to receive it again at night?"

"As you say."

"Who wish to be visited by the angel that flies without wings?"

"Just so."

"Who wish to light a candle at the holy altar?"

"Those especially."

"Excellent. *Donna*, this is the man we have sought. Tonight we shall show him our leper's bells."

The blood drained from the monk's face as he suddenly found a pressing reason to be elsewhere nonetheless Stoldo warned his protégé to keep an eye on his lady if he didn't want to see her starting to fatten in a few months.

"With him? What could he be to her?"

"She's God-bitten, that one. Watch her, I tell you."

"How am I to do that once everyone retires for the night, they inside we outside? Must I really fear?"

"Remember that tale about a randy monk who entertained a farmer's daughter in his cell each night? I seem to recall it was said to be right here in this region."

"But that one was complaisant."

"What if he forces her with threats?"

While Stoldo informed the monk he would rather kill him and burn in Hell than see his master's wife fattened with his bastard Tuccio beseeched Agnoletta to scream bloody murder if he tried anything.

DAY FOURTEEN.

[I] marvel how I can endure
that I don't show her my desire
when I see milady and look at her

her beautiful eyes so well become her
little restrains me yet I toward her don't run...
(Bernart de Ventadorn, troubadour)

By evening it was clear the wounded would not be able to travel anytime soon so the decision had been made to continue without them they to convalesce till they could return home meanwhile Tuccio was tense as a bowstring till he determined that 'that pig of a monk' hadn't spent the night 'rooting in my lady's bed' but even when Agnoletta assured him they had slept like babies and he could see in Margherita's face that nothing had happened he was frustrated by the count's order to scout the road ahead. As they were still in the wild they were still in danger and the count was determined not to repeat the mistake for which he would not soon forgive himself and to this end he also had Stoldo lag behind should brigands attack from the rear and ordered the *masnada* to stay by its horses whenever the caravan stopped.

This it did at the top of the pass near the hostel that had once been its day's destination but Tuccio stayed forward as Stoldo stayed back and breakfast was a tense meal as everyone scanned the trees for hiding marauders rather than enjoy how the leaves shimmered in the light and shook in the breeze. When they reached the first settlement the count sent half his men forward to make sure the place was safe and did the same again at the next but at least the traveling was easier with the trend now downward and one of the guards began to sing but it was halfhearted with no one joining and it dwindled and then Tuccio appeared at a gallop to say a caravan was approaching. "A caravan?" asked the count.

"I thought it best to alert you, *signore*." The count nodded and had him stay with the group in case some subterfuge were at work but instead the most jovial of merchants appeared with a few wagons and a half dozen guards who shouting his greetings from a distance approached with a fat smile elaborately wishing everyone good day and seeing Margherita exclaimed, "Ah, there it is, an excellent ploy, and one I use myself, but in my case I too wear the robe. No sense wasting opportunity, I have gone hither and yon to more sanctuaries than I could recall, plying my trade. An excellent plan, you are to be commended," he said to the *fattore*, "may your ruse prosper and I wish you good fortune, have your men keep a sharp eye for thieves and robbers, this world being what it is."

Returning to his position Tuccio managed to pass Margherita and lock his eyes on hers but then alone again on the narrow road he talked to himself wishing and complaining frustrated and angry as well as tender with transports of emotion he even talked aloud as though someone were heeding his words even prepared to carry out his wishes hour upon hour of this his horse plodding till by the time he approached the night's settlement he was sure he was going mad. Again the count sent men to investigate before entering *en masse* to find a pilgrim hostel run by the municipality which looked safe with a place nearby where the caravan could camp and a feeling of relief settled on the group even when shifts were assigned through the night to guard both the caravan and the hostel but all Tuccio saw was an evening without Margherita which now stretched before him like a desert followed by a cold night to stand outside thinking about her in bed.

While he helped set up camp he sulked with nothing before his eyes but the picture of her disappearing into the hostel without so much as a glance which caused Stoldo to whisper, "You have the sickness. That's it, isn't it? You're in love."

"Thank you for figuring that out!" he hissed. "My closest friend in the whole world."

"But..."

"But what, she's the master's wife?"

"That and twice your age." Awaiting a response that didn't come he thought, "The illicit kills the little passions but augments the great."

Tuccio speaking at last said, "The wind snuffs out candles but fans fires," and described how beautiful Margherita had looked reading on the boulder her fingers moving slowly across the text her sandals beside her the light the whole scene, "My God, how beautiful she looked. Something struck me in the eye, and from there to my heart, it was like being shot."

"Love's arrow."

"I'm sure I flinched as if it were an arrow. Even now I can see her, and each time it's like being shot. It hurts. I feel it in my chest. I have never experienced anything like this before. Have you?"

"My friend, you are not the first to spy a bit of female flesh."

"It wasn't just that."

"I know, it is real love and not just desire."

"So you have felt it?"

"Never. Ah, you wish to pity me, well we shall see which is the greater blessing, to be seized with love's intensity, overwhelmed by that madness, or to be spared."

"Better to suffer it. I have heard people say of visions that they are too beautiful to describe, that's what this was like."

"Except it was not God you saw."

"No, but it was an angel."

"Perhaps. But this angel pulled up her robe and that is a different kind of vision."

"I admit it, when she raised her robe and stepped into the stream, my breath stopped. And when she shook her hair loose... My God, how beautiful she looked as she waded, the way she dropped a leaf in the stream, then another, watching them—and before when hearing a bird she began to sing. Surely this is different. How she drifted off into contemplation. Sometimes she was lost in reverie, other times gazing at the scene. Do you know she has barely been outside Siena?"

Such a discussion could not escape the notice of others who had the courtesy not to intrude while lacking the serenity not to be curious and all that was required for gossip to circulate was for Stoldo to say, "He has seen the lady in her garden," that potent symbol of feminine sexuality and pleasure beauty and allure mystery and purity inaccessible unattainable so when the guards were free to relax the raillery began.

DAY FIFTEEN. A desert truly a desert no less than the one from which he came in fact more so because the Deserto di Accona was filled with farms and villages albeit poor whereas here there was nothing nothing not one settlement just wilderness and a narrow snaking path descending steeply out of the mountains easy going but Tuccio cared nothing for easy beautiful but he was sick of beauty desolation was what he saw.

> "...because the place where I was put to live
> from day to day more of good is stripped
> and to bleak ruin seems disposed."

(*Purgatorio*, Canto 24)

He had implored Stoldo to ask the count if someone else could scout so he could travel beside her but when Stoldo did he learned what might have been predicted that the count was not happy to hear that one of his men was trying to get inside the master's castle; that it should be Tuccio he found ludicrous given the disparity in age and concluded it was infatuation.

"No doubt, *signore*. But you know what they say, 'no water quenches love's fire,'" and the count made sure Tuccio spent the entire day nowhere near the woman.

In good faith and without deceit
[I] love the most beautiful and the best.
From the heart to sigh and from the eyes weep,
for so much I love her, for which I have sadness.
What else can I do if Love seizes me
and the prison in which it has put me
no key can open but mercy
and of mercy I find none at all?

(Bernart de Ventadorn, troubadour)

It was during the night standing guard in the street outside the room where she was sleeping sleeping naked that the desire had arisen to serenade her and having arisen loomed and having loomed possessed and when in the morning he blurted out his idea in a frenzied whisper Stoldo said, "Now I know you are mad."

"A young man is expected to sing outside the house of the young lady he courts."

"Young lady? By what reckoning is this one young?"

"It's a rite of betrothal."

"What betrothal? My God, man, think what you are saying!"

"Think? How can I think?"

Said Bruno to Calandrino, "Well I say to you that you make her melt like ice in the sun. By the body of God, if you bring your [three-string] rebec and sing a little to her from those love songs of yours, you will make her throw [herself] to the ground from the window to come to you."

(Boccaccio, *The Decameron*)

Nothing could dislodge this grappling hook of an idea not even the problems he himself itemized as, "One, I know no suitable songs, two, I have the voice of a crow, and three, I can't even strum a lute," and when Stoldo pointed out that his intent was not to marry the master's wife but cuckold the master he replied, "I want to declare myself."

"Do you not see that love's sickness has addled your wits?"

"She is unhappy and wishes to be consoled."

"This you know by watching her read a book?"

"She's on pilgrimage. Why else does anyone endure such a thing?" In his mind he could see his wonderful performance making her swoon with pleasure...

"...Love
kindled by virtue always another kindles
provided that its flame appear outwardly."

(*Purgatorio*, Canto 22)

...but when it became apparent that he was to spend another day with no chance to speak to her he returned in loneliness and despair to talking to himself out loud like one insane such that when they had descended to the town at the base of the mountains beside a small river where they would spend the night the fleece of his hope had been shorn of all joy and he found it the most desolate place on earth because ahead lay the vast plain of the Po.

> We went across the solitary plain
> like a man who returns to the lost road,
> who until [reaching] it seems to himself to go in vain.

(*Purgatorio*, Canto 1)

Margherita had something else on her mind.

"The *damnum emergens*, the *stipendium laboris*, the *lucrum cessans*, the *periculum sortis*, the *ratio incertitudinis...*"

"Ser Lapo, you know that I—"

"I give these terms only so you will know Francesco does not lie when he claims not all interest is usury. But are these legal concepts valid? I myself have consulted the bishop's canon on this very question, an erudite man."

"What does he say?"

"He speaks as long as one will listen. And when I have come away I try to recall what he said."

"But surely..."

"Of course. There is the practical answer. I am a notary in service to a merchant, not a canon who may theorize in his cloister, and if there is to be commerce it must be facilitated with legally binding contracts. I have used these..."

"Subterfuges?"

"May we not say 'exceptions sanctioned by the Church?' What choice have I? I owe everything to Francesco. So I write the contracts and then I go to confession and make acts of contrition and give alms and walk the fields of my farm—and I urge him to do the same."

"Is your soul at peace?"

"I hope one day it will be. Our merchants know very well that canonical interdictions of necessary practices will turn to canonical justifications. The expansion of trade creates a growing diversity in the forms of credit. Which in turn engenders increasing complexity in commercial contracts. We are in a new world, *donna*."

"But surely there has always been trade, money-lending—"

"Of course, but not like this. Over the last two hundred years, say, but especially in our time, an economy has emerged that is based, not just on the productive capacity of land, but also of money. Money itself! Not just exchanging wealth, but producing it. Small loans have become gigantic. Once they were local, now they cross borders and long distances. Where they were made at market stalls, now there are banks, with branches in every major center. New forms of credit, accounting systems. It is we Italians who have brought this to the world. And we Sienese have been in the forefront from the beginning, and we can be justifiably proud of this. But, because it is new, we understand it poorly. Our intellects struggle to catch up with events and it clashes with our deeply held convictions."

"Are you saying our convictions must give way?"

"I hope not. I hope not. Well, shall we turn to something more pleasant? You must taste the oil I have just brought from my farm."

She saw an old man in a pilgrim's robe limping toward her leaning on his staff with each step who seemed in no hurry and when he saw her he exclaimed, "A solitary pilgrim, moreover one who walks, and a woman! I greet you, who have descended from the high wild. I go toward it. I shall sleep there tonight, for many nights till I too emerge. May I ask where you go? Myself, to Rome. They say a cesspit of vice, yet a holy place, I go in hope. For what? you ask. Closed was my life, small. With the very first step, opened. I accept the test. I do not mind rain or bad food, fear not wolves or robbers, only that this lame leg will defeat me. We shall see. The mountain passage is long but in a week I, like you, shall emerge onto the splendid plain as if to new life. I shall think new thoughts, have new feelings. Fare well, *madonna*, may your going be full of hope and joy."

She turned often to watch the old man recede into the distance and disappear around a bend and found her step was lighter as if he had lifted a weight from her back.

> "*Signore*, let us go with greater haste
> for now I do not tire as just before
> and you see now that the hill a shadow casts."

(*Purgatorio*, Canto 6)

DAY SIXTEEN. Finally clear of the mountains though still beside their base crossing a river that flowed north to the sluggish but mighty Po they passed lush cultivated fields like the ones seen in the first days an easy walk with the land more or less flat and the visibility all around made the threat of brigands seem small which freed Tuccio to travel beside Margherita; and this caused the tension of the past two days to release like a crossbow discharging so even the unmistakable looks from the count failed to dispel their calm pleasure. When he asked why she was on pilgrimage she stared at him surprised and had to think long before saying, "I came to believe the time had come to do something decisive," and there was another silence until she asked if he found that ridiculous.

"Not when I hear you wondering about the world as you do. You have a certain appreciation of things. And to learn to read! Books are such difficult, impenetrable things, though no doubt there is wisdom there. Such a mind would be poorly contained by the price of capons. I think of the falcon, which no matter how subdued by captivity or submitting willingly, has in its nature to soar."

"And you?"

"I am a boy who wrestles in the dirt, a youth who dreams of knighthood, a man whose prized possession is his horse. I have never sat still."

"Your heart is large."

"My mind is small."

"It seeks in its way, like mine."

"Then we share a way of seeing. But, unlike you, I have not thought much about weighty matters. Though now I find myself curious."

While their conversation continued without speaking she was struck above all that neither her husband nor her relatives nor her friends or neighbors nor her priest nor even Lapo had ever asked why she wanted to go on pilgrimage.

Fidenza was located on the great trunk route from Torino in the Alpine marches along the north side of the Appennini to the Adriatic connecting with another to Venezia and points beyond which made it a great catchment area for pilgrims not just from Italy but northern and eastern Europe so what Margherita discovered were large diverse crowds and the stir of the most popular pilgrim sites with hawkers and preachers of every description and providers of every service from blacksmithing to prostitution. Above all she shared the palpable enthusiasm of so many assembled seekers all dressed in the uniform of pilgrimage the robe of a certain rough woolen cloth that ironically her husband imported from Romania.

To select a hostel from all the alternatives was a bewildering pleasure that became her tourist round presenting her at every turn with languages she had never before heard and strange coiffures with friendly looks and greetings. As usual she was accompanied by guards but not Tuccio and Stoldo who had been assigned to guard the caravan rather two others who were polite though still strangers and she led them on a meandering tour until entering a small square they found themselves facing some two hundred flagellants dressed in long white woolen robes with large hoods carrying the staff and pouch and chanting in unison as they whipped their own backs.

Some circulated among spectators with exhortations to repent or failing that to contribute and one of them suddenly appeared before her to ask, "Have you repented, woman? Have you forgiven? Only then is your burden lightened." Flagellants were common in Siena but never had she been confronted with one in this way and they stared at each other until she smiled glad she too bore the sack and staff and then she nodded and nodded and smiled again thinking, "As he says, so it is," and a great desire filled her heart as she thought, "I forgive you, Francesco. Now I am free to travel my own way."

> "Therein light of Heaven made us wise
> so that repenting and pardoning out
> from life we went to God reconciled,
> who with desire to see Him stirred us."

(*Purgatorio*, Canto 5)

The guards however were repelled by the sight of whips rising and falling the awful sound of it mixed with chanting and here and there someone shrieking in pain or beseeching the first pilgrim who had walked not for himself but for everyone else and fearfully one whispered, "They are heretics, no?"

"*Madonna*, we think you had best withdraw," said the other anxiously but she and the hooded man were staring at each other until she reached into her pouch and handed him a coin.

"Bless you, *monna*, you are kind. May I ask your destination?" As she told him she was looking at the scallop shell attached to his robe at the shoulder and when he exclaimed, "But you don't wear the shell!" she said she thought it proper not to display one until she reached Compostela since it was intended to signify that accomplishment. "I commend you for your modesty, *monna*, for surely you know many wear the shell as a general badge of pilgrimage."

"I did not know. Still, I'd rather show it as an accomplishment than an aspiration."

"Have you considered that aspiration becomes accomplishment when one actually becomes what one aspires to become?"

"I don't think I understand."

"You are already there if you are there in your heart and mind."

"What do you mean?"

"When you forgive, you have arrived. When you repent sincerely, you have arrived. Do a good deed, arrived. To ask for forgiveness, which can be harder than to forgive, arrived again. Yes, you are on a journey and that journey has meaning in its destination. But what happens when you reach it? You turn around and repeat the entire ordeal in reverse! Is the second half without meaning? Surely each step you take is an arrival if you place yourself where you aspire to be, which is to actually be what you wish to become." She was stunned into silence and surprised when she looked up to find him still there and they both smiled.

In the evening after Tuccio had learned from the guards where she was staying he told the severe woman who opened the locked door that he was her protector and must speak to her about an urgent matter and when she appeared with a worried look and saw who it was a look of pleasure replaced it.

Seeing this he too smiled saying, "I had to see you."

"There is no urgent matter I hope."

"There is. I had to see you."

"For what purpose?"

"For the purpose of looking at you." Hearing this the old woman rose from her chair to move between them and turn the young man out the door but he took her elbows gently and said, "It's all right, grandma, I just needed to make sure my lady had not been harmed by my absence. Then you are well, lady?"

"Quite well." She was staring at him as if for the first time as if they were living one of those courtly romances in which he was the hero lover and she the beautiful queen.

> I turned toward him and looked at him intently.
>
> Fair-haired was he and beautiful and of noble aspect.

(*Purgatorio*, Canto 3)

Chapter Six

As soon as he sat down Tiffany felt comfortable with the professor for being so professorial which allowed her to feel like she was again a serious student where the economy was of ideas the currency facts and the value in truth; and he having expected someone completely different also felt comfortable for he was taken with her sincerity and poise in short each was unexpectedly charmed by the other. He ordered a scotch to keep her chardonnay company so they could perform the obligatory exchange of pleasantries at the bar with its glassy elegance and the gratifying clink of ice cubes adding sophistication to the most casual comment and this initial phase completed they moved to a table where they performed the ritual of menus and only then were they free to engage the purpose of their meeting. "You'll want to know the status of my research," he began.

"I'm interested, I'd love to hear about it."

"Of course at this early stage there isn't much to report. I could tell you where I stand—where we stand I guess I should say—with the manuscripts. Would you..."

"I would, because that's where it begins, right?"

"Indeed. So... Do you know about them?"

"Feel free to begin at the beginning. If you'll be the teacher, I'll be the student." He smiled in a fatherly way and launched into a lecture on the manuscripts that began with the admonition to keep in mind that what many called the *Pilgrim Guide* was only one of five so-called 'books' that comprised the total work and that it was not a travel guide in the modern sense. "But it asserts the four routes."

"It does. And there lies the root, if you'll pardon the pun, I guess even if you won't, of the controversy which we propose to resolve. When I say 'we' I refer to your largesse and my penchant for immersing myself in the most arcane of investigations."

"But surely not picayune."

"Surely not, most surely not. On the contrary, for precisely here lies the problem and the solution to this issue hanging over the thousands of pilgrims who now trudge across France each year in full belief that they trace the ancient ways."

"Which in fact they may, correct?"

"Most correct."

"Do you..."

"Not yet. I prefer to keep an open mind, or to put it another way, let me spend a vast sum of your money before revealing my opinion. And as long as I'm being completely gauche, might I ask how you come by this money? I'm thinking, if you haven't robbed a bank, you must own one."

When she told him what she did for a living he nodded knowingly which encouraged her to describe her work in considerable detail ending only when their artfully laden plates arrived to initiate a brief silence of appreciation after which he let her know he had successfully arranged for facsimiles to be made of all twelve manuscripts.

"What do you call them, by the way?"

"That in itself is interesting, that we lack even a satisfactory title. We cannot call it the *Pilgrim Guide*, we must reserve that title for Book Five, which is in fact the guide for pilgrims. We could call it the *Liber Sancti Jacobi*, which being in Latin will hopefully impress somebody."

"The *Book of Saint James*."

"You know Latin!"

"I majored in classics."

"Did you now! Might I ask where." Grinning she told him she'd gone to Yale at which he sat back and stared at her. "So you studied with..." and he named several of his colleagues in the Classics Department while she nodded or shook her head and commented on what she had loved and what she'd found difficult and he noted the huge debt classicists owe medievals. "They copied the ancient texts, the monks did, including the most profane, not to say bawdy and even pornographic, which is interesting to think about, which none of my colleagues do, and if they hadn't we wouldn't have many of them. But of course this is not a sufficient reason to pursue medieval studies."

"What is?"

He smiled. "The culture was so rich and beautiful. Invariably it's presented as squalid and ignorant and yet in our millions we take ourselves with considerable effort and expense to gaze at its unsurpassed monuments."

"I have a confession to make. I almost took your 'Medieval Saints' seminar." He stared at her. "Well, I considered it."

"You got cold feet."

"Could we just say I had a scheduling conflict?" He was still staring at her. "You were saying about the *Book of Saint James*..."

They made small talk for a while until he said, "And here you are, you returned to the Middle Ages, and with a foundation no less. I still can't believe it. You've done very well for yourself, my lady. You've made me very curious to know what brought you back. When were you at Yale? You're what, twenty-something?"

"You're so kind. I'm Class of '96, do the math."

"I'm no good at math."

"I'm thirty-three."

"Married? Single? Divorced?"

"Married, five years. We have a daughter, Kiley, who's four, my little princess. The sweetest little girl on earth."

He smiled. "I remember when my Morgan was that age."

"So you're married too."

"Widowed."

"I'm sorry."

"Cancer. It's ten years now, but..."

"I'm sorry. She was young."

"Very young. Much too young. What does your husband do?"

"He's an investment banker on Wall Street."

His head snapped back. "You're quite the couple, aren't you? Now, I know this is silly, but I must confess I don't know what an investment banker is, does. Aside from working at a bank and making investments."

"He puts deals together."

"Sorry. Nothing registered."

"Do you really want me to explain?"

"If you'll be the teacher, I'll be the student."

She smiled. "The whole thing starts with mortgages. Banks make mortgages. So some bank, in California say, borrows money, say a billion dollars, overnight loans, renewed daily, fully collateralized, so it's very low risk, very low interest. They borrow from a whole bunch of lenders. The money is used to make mortgages, like four to five thousand of them. The deal is to sell the mortgages to a bank or securities firm that will use them to underwrite securities. That firm could be one of the lenders or another firm, makes no difference. So the borrower writes the mortgages, which takes a couple of months, and then sells them, using the proceeds to pay off the lenders. They also take a two and a half percent fee, which is what they get out of the deal. Okay?"

"Not sure, but keep going."

"Okay, so now some Wall Street firm, say it's Bob's, has bought a pool of mortgages and it's going to use them as collateral against securities it'll create. It's called 'underwriting.' They could just issue one security backed by the whole pool, which is what used to happen, but different investors have different goals and there's a whole lot more money to be made if they issue a lot of securities, all collateralized by the same mortgage pool, but with a hierarchy of claims against it, should there be any defaults. You don't look like..."

"Keep going."

"So they create twenty different tranches, each a separate security they can sell. They range in credit quality from triple-A to junk, but more than three-quarters of the deal is triple-A. Almost all the rest is still investment grade, and then there's a little junk at the bottom, maybe three to four percent."

"I don't understand."

"What part don't you get?"

"I don't think I get any of it. It sounds awfully risky."

"How risky can it be when eighty percent is triple-A?"

"I have no idea. It just sounds risky. If I understand you correctly, the same firms are playing multiple sides of these deals. Isn't that like playing poker with yourself?"

"No, it's nothing like that at all. Everything is fully collateralized, they're large pools so there's plenty of diversification, and the odds of something going seriously wrong are vanishingly remote. In case you haven't noticed, house prices are going through the roof."

"And people buy these things? By 'people' I mean..."

"Are you kidding? The top tranche the underwriter usually keeps for itself, because it's as close to risk-free as you can get and still pays better than Treasuries, so it's like free money. All the triple-A tranches go to institutional investors. Bob packaged a deal that went, I think, to three foreign banks, a couple of US government agencies, a state retirement system, a hospital... So what little risk there is gets spread around the world. Most of the other tranches get repackaged into new securities, which raises their credit ratings, and there's a little piece at the bottom that hedge funds gobble up. Not my firm, by the way, it's not our thing, though we do manage some CDOs for underwriters."

"CDOs?"

"That's what they call them. Collateralized debt obligations."

"Why would anybody buy the worst piece?"

"To make fifteen, twenty, maybe thirty percent."

"Wow. This is what you do."

"This is what Bob does. He puts deals like that together, finds buyers. But you're right, I'm in that world too."

"And to think you could have been in my medieval saints class. What did bring you back, I'm so curious. This is just amazing."

It was eighteen months since she'd become interested in pilgrimage a year since she'd bought gear and yet she had walked only five stages five out of seventy but it was not for want of trying though she had taken the entire summer to work up the nerve to start rather the problem was that the experience had not been gratifying. The South Mountain Reservation all of three miles on its long axis hosted strollers and dog-walkers not hikers so first was to overcome embarrassment to be seen in full hiking gear including a water bottle she needed not to slake her thirst but calibrate her load because she was determined that her experience be authentic; it wasn't unlikely she'd be seen by someone she knew and while not shy she thought it could be awkward to try to explain to those known only casually or (worse) through work that she was virtually on pilgrimage to a holy site in Spain. Of course she could have said she was exercising but anyone who saw her blog would know she hadn't told the whole story and that bothered her as it bothered her to be unsure how pilgrimage mixed with business. To be safe she would have kept it private but that seemed improper as well as impossible and the fact was that she would have welcomed attention because it would help validate what she was trying to do; so she developed a short explanation in the event of need and finally set out from the house for the reservation a mile away to pick up the path that followed a little brook called the Rahway

River.

In barely a mile she confronted South Orange Avenue the heavily trafficked county road that bisected the reservation where she turned back onto another path and so on back and forth within that enclave until her pedometer told her she had walked the requisite distance to have completed the first stage; though it had hardly been a hiking experience and as pilgrimage none at all she felt it had been a satisfactory start and even managed to feel optimistic enough to believe it was more exaggeration than lie to tell Bob it had been fantastic. By evening she was convinced it really had been at least in the sense that after so much thought and preparation she had finally walked; and with that excitement she wrote her first blog post about arriving from Nice by fast train to Arles a wonderful city studded with treasures like a perfectly preserved Roman coliseum and the incomparable facade of a medieval cathedral as well as being the home of Van Gogh when he painted his most famous works. Nonetheless whenever she thought of going out again she remembered the actual experience and stayed home to find greater reward in researching pilgrimage and developing her foundation.

Among the reasons for this procrastination might have been that she felt the enormity of a thousand mile commitment or was too distracted by negative thoughts about spending precious time away from Kiley while leaving Bob to take care of everything or that instead she could be doing something useful like the weekly shopping or even work. Maybe she'd been waiting or hoping for an insight or feeling that never came that would have validated her obsession with this strange activity; and when there was no experience when nothing happened she felt foolish or assumed she had missed something or was simply squandering valuable time. She herself did not know whether it was any of those or perhaps all of them but what she did know was that she would go out again once she had decided where to go a debate that took weeks during which Bob never said a word happy that her interest seemed to be waning at least for the walking part of the project now that she had sampled it a development he had predicted.

In that however he was wrong because what happened instead was that in thinking about where to go she began to think more deeply about the purpose of walking for she had read enough to know that there were only a few reasons to become a pilgrim and she knew she wasn't searching for God or trying to expiate some shameful behavior nor did she seek deliverance from some affliction. If she was searching for the purpose of her life or the meaning of life generally there had been no insight nor did she expect one because if she was seeking in this way she was doing it unconsciously; and that left the final possibility that she was hoping to meditate to have dedicated quiet time to set aside the cares and distractions of life to see what happened. If that was it nothing had happened no wonderful insights no insights at all just a flurry of distracting thoughts concerning everything she could be accomplishing were she not pretending to be on pilgrimage; if she was seeking simply to participate in something inherently beautiful she had found nothing beautiful about walking in the South Mountain Reservation nor inspiration much less some type of call nor a glimmer of transcendent reality or sacred presence nothing.

The conclusion that she was not really a pilgrim she refused to accept because what contradicted it was that she couldn't get the idea out of her mind and in that refusal realized that she had violated the first rule of pilgrimage which was to leave home and go somewhere else; virtual pilgrimage was a great idea even if Bob had been facetious when suggesting it but had this inherent problem she called inauthenticity whereby she needed to pretend to be where she wasn't which made it hard to do what she was supposed to be doing. She had naively hoped the problem would automatically resolve itself; now that she'd learned it wouldn't she needed to find a solution and it came to her immediately that since she couldn't change her surroundings she must change her state of mind in other words the commitment to pilgrimage must be more than logging miles in order to have fun online.

Furnished with that insight the only one she could claim she wrote her second blog post describing the first stage from Arles to Saint-Gilles. *This morning I was really nervous. I couldn't believe I was actually setting out—on foot!—on a journey of one thousand twenty-four miles. Alone. I'm going to cross deserts, hike through rugged mountains (still inhabited by wild boar), cross the Pyrenees... Also like today, I'm going to spend many hours trudging through industrial zones, crossing highways and railroads... This morning I walked for too long within hearing—and even sight—of a super highway.*

When she went out again it was back to the reservation but she also walked through neighborhoods hoping to find that more pleasant less boring hopefully more conducive to thinking about pilgrimage but found herself actively trying to ignore her surroundings to make herself available to what might come but again nothing did. She consoled herself that her experience would probably have been no better had she traversed the actual stage for the flats around Saint-Gilles were notoriously boring as were the two that followed through a sparsely settled agricultural industrial zone. That in fact became the theme of her blog post that pilgrimage sometimes entailed boredom which inevitably caused pilgrims to question or even doubt the value of their ordeal but the feelings were as transitory as the geography and more interesting stages would soon arrive.

That was the optimistic version of having found it impossible to have some kind of authentic pilgrim experience while walking the comfortable uninteresting predictable streets of suburban New Jersey the entire time thinking about work while trying not to think about work to make room for an idea or feeling that would be inspiring. It was just Short Hills after all and beyond it was just Millburn and Livingston and South Orange which could not have been further from Provence and the Middle Ages and questing for something that couldn't be bought in one of their ten thousand stores; it was clear she had to find someplace more conducive to her purpose but it wasn't obvious where to go also that would involve travel time when time was so scarce.

Finding it impossible to motivate herself to go out again she concluded that if she were going to continue she had to find a place where she could be alone the alternative being to give up walking a thought she hated but one that kept returning because it would solve so many problems; but then of course she would never actually experience the ordeal and that made her fear her pilgrimage would thereby become not just virtual but a sham. Again she experienced the need for authenticity which so far she hadn't found but she was not ready to concede defeat so when she went out again it was to the Morristown National Historical Park which was a short drive provided walking trails and was historical (the revolutionary army had wintered there) which she thought might be helpful.

Also this being the shortest of stages only seven point four miles she could be there and back quickly and not having to worry about lost time could try to focus on what she was trying to achieve but as she walked through the calming woods of Jockey Hollow she had to admit she didn't know what that was; or was it, she wondered, that she knew but wouldn't admit it? 'To admit,' she mused, meant 'to confess' but also to 'let in' so she asked herself what she wasn't admitting and driving home realized with some satisfaction that that reflection was the first pilgrim-like experience she'd had and then she couldn't wait to return for the next stage which at twenty-two point three miles would be three times as long.

The historical site was linked to a longer trail that would easily accommodate the required distance as it picked its way through an Audubon Society wildlife refuge a private estate open to the public the Historical Park a county park a former railway route an arboretum and a town park; even that involved a number of streets the center of Morristown and crossing main roads but she knew that was not unlike sections of the GR653 the modern Way of Arles in fact she probably had a better experience than she would have had there. When she returned to her car she had virtually reached Montpellier and resolved that that evening if she didn't fall asleep from exhaustion she would write about the interminably annoying walk between a highway and a super-highway where the most pleasant sight was a barge-filled canal whereas the next stage would be one of the most exciting and beautiful though also the longest.

"I'm guessing the fifth stage would be the detour to Saint-Guilhem."

"Why do you say 'detour?'"

"Have you looked at a map?"

"I wondered about that. So you think the route is incorrect there."

"Not at all, I haven't the slightest doubt that pilgrims even en route to far away Compostela detoured for such a famous monastery. It had a piece of the True Cross, after all. Founded by a cousin of Charlemagne and as you say in a profoundly beautiful and stirring location. They had no interest in efficiency, you see. The distance added, the time, didn't matter. Pilgrims are on God's time and God has all eternity." He also noted that it was one of the sites specifically mentioned in the *Pilgrim Guide* as a place that must be visited.

"Are you... I know I shouldn't ask this..."

"No, I'm not. It might seem strange that the man who gives a seminar in medieval saints is unshakable in his atheism. I still teach it, by the way, it's a fascinating subject. I'm guessing that was your breakthrough stage."

"I haven't gone out since. That was in the spring. I stayed home all winter and then I went out a total of once."

"The problem being...?"

She shrugged. "The last one I did in the fall, I felt pretty good about that. And it was beautiful outside, the colors were at their peak. I don't know. What do you think?"

"Maybe you're expecting too much? Are you hoping to see Jesus standing beside a tree in the middle distance?" She assured him she was as non-religious as he. "And yet you're on pilgrimage."

"Is that...?"

"Not in the least," he replied and they both smiled. "But I think we can say that people go on pilgrimage in quest of something. Any thoughts?"

She shook her head. "I could not be happier with my life. Do you think I'm just playing?"

"Look how much work you're putting into it. And you say you hate to hike!"

"I do, isn't that weird? What am I doing?"

"As I said, I'd guess you're looking for something. That you don't know what it is doesn't shock me. In fact it suggests an authentic search."

"Really? Authentic?"

"And for what it's worth I bet you'll succeed."

"Why do you say that?"

"Because you strike me as a person who doesn't fail at important tasks."

"And yet I've only done five stages in all this time."

"You're on God's time, remember?"

"I thought we agreed there is no God?"

"No, only that we don't believe in Him! Tell me about your long walk to Saint-Guilhem."

When autumn became winter she'd lost all motivation and then it snowed and she decided it was all right to postpone her pilgrimage till she could learn more about it meanwhile the foundation's application period was open and she had high hopes and maybe it was also a factor that Bob had run into problems at work; but then spring worked its magic and she awarded the grant and started writing to the professor and began looking for a good place to walk her stage. Since she would be (virtually) traversing a sparsely populated region to a wilderness area she decided she needed a relatively remote location as scenic as possible and settled on Stokes State Forest but at twenty-four point eight miles it was an eight-hour hike plus travel time which meant it would be an entire day away from Kiley and by the time she got home exhausted she didn't know whether to exult or cry.

"It seemed to be working," she told the professor. "I was close to nature, undistracted. 'Conducive to reflection,' as I wrote in my blog. I just wish I could tell you one thing I learned."

"That's not how it works. You don't put in the coins and out comes a candy bar."

She asked whether he thought the very concept of walking equivalent miles was a gimmick or an authentic attempt to go on pilgrimage in the only way available given the demands of her life and tried not to be offended when he pointed out that the defining feature of pilgrimage was a full rupture with the mundanity of daily rounds. "But," he added, "don't be too hard on yourself. Pilgrimage ain't easy. Did you mind the solitude?"

"I wish I could say I experienced it. If anything I was fighting it the whole time."

"Who wouldn't? It feels like drowning, doesn't it?"

"It sounds like you've done pilgrimage yourself."

"Actually I have not. Of course I have visited many a pilgrim site. But I'm generally on much too tight a schedule to think about walking from one to another."

"There it is again. We just don't have the luxury of being on God's time."

"Thanks to people like you, no we don't. It was the medieval merchant banker who invented modern time in the calculation of his interest. Monks gave us the clock but it was the investor who enslaved us to it."

"So it seems I'm my own enemy."

"Who isn't? But what you're correctly suggesting is that pilgrimage is an attempt to find something important."

"Which is?"

"Which is whatever each pilgrim seeks," he said smiling.

"I don't know what I seek, that's my problem."

"Maybe discovering something worth seeking is what you seek. You can't force insights or repose."

"It's so hard to find repose."

"That sounds like a pretty big insight right there."

Despite having effectively made the professor her advisor in matters of pilgrimage and on that subject had been unexpectedly frank in her confessions and declarations Tiffany remained mindful that she headed the foundation that was funding his research and so had refrained from indicating the problems Bob had been encountering. In the heady months after his triumph he had been put to work to create a second internal hedge fund like the one the firm had been successfully operating for three years but more leveraged that is with more of the CDOs in its portfolio bought with borrowed money in order to further increase the expected investment returns; at the same time he had the all but explicit promise that upon its successful launch he would be promoted to vice president and in September he had his second triumph of the year when it was successfully launched. As talk continued of his promotion he brought investors into the fund such that by year end it was worth nine and a half billion dollars a billion from investors the rest borrowed; the 'enhanced' fund had attracted in four months what the original had in almost four years a point he emphatically made at the Christmas party when he used the excuse that they were both drunk to tell his boss he expected a promotion 'like soon.' In the new year talks continued until the funds 'ran into head winds' and 'went south' which was jargon for the market turning negative causing securities prices to drop.

"What's going on?" asked Tiffany.

"'Worried about housing.' What are they kidding me? A few points down and they're worried? Ninety percent of these funds is triple- or double-A," but the same leverage that multiplied the funds' gains when prices rose multiplied their losses when they fell and in February they fell twenty-five percent.

When investors started to redeem their investments Bob's boss sent an email urging them to 'double down' by investing more at current lower prices and wrote, "We see a prudent opportunity here. I am putting in additional capital, I think you should as well," and a week later on a conference call he again touted an increase of his own investment as evidence of his confidence while assuring them both funds had plenty of liquidity. Privately he told Bob to sell securities to raise cash but in the current climate he couldn't find buyers and a few weeks later he learned that his boss had redeemed a third of his own investment but what he couldn't determine was whether he had sold just before or after they'd heard that JP Morgan would be asking the hedge funds to post additional collateral against their loans.

As was typical for hedge funds they obtained their leverage

with repurchase ('repo') agreements which were collateralized short-term loans where each night the lender would 'roll the debt' and the collateral consisted of mortgage-backed securities purchased from the lender. With the decline in value of the securities the amount of collateral had fallen well below the required five percent so JP Morgan had telegraphed that it would be 'requesting' more securities to restore the total with the implied threat of course that if they didn't get it they would decline to renew the agreements. This naturally sent Bob's group scrambling especially since if one lender was doing this the others were likely to follow which would put both funds out of business so he went to work on a new deal that would repackage a quarter of the funds' CDOs into new CDOs with refurbished credit ratings; when the bulk of them were sold as very low-risk investments to money market funds they received desperately needed cash but still had to face the repo lenders and for the time being Bob's promotion was off. A week later Tiffany met the professor who while she was paying the bill after a polite negotiation asked if the foundation had received many submissions and upon hearing that she was happy with the response thought, "My God, I was the only applicant."

Chapter Seven

DAY SEVENTEEN. If he had known this song he would have been thinking:

> Ah, 'fine love' coveted.
> Body well made, slender and pleasing
> fresh face rosy
> which God formed with his [own] hands.
> All the time you I have desired
> for no other at all pleases me,
> other love I don't want at all.

(Bernart de Ventadorn, troubadour)

If she had known this song she would have been thinking:

> On joy and on youth I feast
> and joy and youth sate me
> for my friend is the most gay.

(Comtessa de Dia, troubadour)

If yesterday's stage had had a few bumps today's was as flat as earth could be and straight and Margherita awoke with a joy that didn't fade so as she walked she loved everything she saw finding it beautiful like the sky even the peasants in the fields and when a bird sang her heart jumped. The road was crowded with travelers of every sort pursuing every destination and every purpose a parade a procession a march to ends with no need to hurry because there was no place to stop but the town where everyone was headed a journey of at most five hours which left plenty of time for the camaraderie of the road.

The hostility between the caravan and her had softened considerably with the common ordeal of the mountains dispelling much of the distrust the men counting in her favor that she had not lost her head during the ambush as well as having kept pace overall while she had come to see them as genial men who unlike her husband were not indulging the excesses of commerce but merely toiling for wages not gruff as they had seemed to her initially. The *fattore* was another matter but Tuccio was beside her and the time passed pleasantly in conversation and when they stopped for breakfast at the crossing of one of the streams draining into the Po there was time for the men to sit on the bank and tell stories and for her to take out her book while Tuccio sitting at her side embarrassed her. "I can't read with you watching me."

"Do I disturb you? Good. Get used to it, because I'll always watch you."

If they had known this song he would have sung,

> Beautiful sweet lady dear,
> to you I give myself and grant myself.
> I will not have my joy complete
> if I do not have you and you me.

...and she would have replied,

> Fair knight, so dear is
> your honored lordliness
> that each day I am amazed.

(Raimbaut de Vaqueiras, troubadour)

Reader, must I say more? Use your imagination!

In the evening after everyone settled into the accommodations of the large town they joined the townspeople and their children in the square where a *giullare* was to perform. Open-air performers ranged from jugglers magicians and acrobats to actors and musicians the latter ranging from the crudely entertaining to sophisticated artists who sang and played the songs of the poets even poets themselves who sang their own compositions; the *giullare* a minstrel welcome at many courts had a prodigious memory for love songs whether of the old troubadours or newer lyric poets like Dante a sophisticated repertory that might not have held the audience but for his mastery as a performer taking everyone from tears to laughter and back at will.

For Tuccio who had never before heard serious poetry whose sweet melodies captivated him with the languid strumming of the lute and the clear-toned singing of the flute the lyrics exploded in his mind for in them he discovered himself the noble supplicant seeking the love of a high lady who while gazing up at her sought to elevate himself to become worthy of her attention for she was clothed in virtue and beauty. He was daring in his unbidden advances she supremely modest and if he won her favor which sometimes he did sometimes he didn't and sometimes the song ended unresolved it would be because his merit had become worthy of hers and she was always married always.

The lyrics were not discreet whether in descriptions of her body or the love-making that was always the poet's goal for if his amorous quest was idealized its fulfillment never was for example there was a whole genre in which the lover spends the night with the lord's wife until morning separates them and when the poem was written by a woman the roles were reversed and the lyrics were particularly frank.

> Well would I wish my knight
> to hold one evening in my arms naked,
> for he would consider himself overjoyed
> if only for him I made [myself] a cushion,
> because more by it am I made beautiful
> than made Floris of Blanchaflor.
> I give him my heart and my love,
> My mind, my eyes, and my life.
>
> Dear friend, gracious and gallant,
> When will I hold you in my power?
> And may I lie with you one evening
> and may I give you an amorous kiss!
> Know, great desire would I have
> that I hold you in place of my husband,
> provided that you to me have pledged
> to do all that I might want.

(Comtessa de Dia)

Margherita was struck by the figure of the exalted lady object of intense desire even if she didn't feel exalted and wondered who could be her lover if somehow she became that lady no one back home to be sure not that her daily passage from kitchen to confessional allowed her to meet anyone but on the road even on pilgrimage there was a certain freedom. She was sixteen when she'd been married to a forty-one year old workhorse who was neither handsome noble attentive nor charming not even ardent in bed merely one who needed a noblewoman to elevate his social status wanted a dowry a mother of children to create his 'house' and carry his name in short neither loved the other nor was attracted to the other. For him there were mistresses in other cities servants and slave-girls for her nothing and though like everyone she had heard the bawdy tales of wives who brazenly cuckolded their husbands they bore no relation to her life.

Addressing the pilgrims in his audience the *giullare* discussed the basis of all the poetry which was *fin'amor* ('fine love') taking purification as his main point interpreting 'fine' to mean 'refined' and noted that purification was mostly a process of divesting not acquiring therefore pure love which he called the only true love was philosophically simple possessing a single unitary nature not mixed not composed of parts and as the philosophers taught the more simple the closer to the sacred source of being. Thus was *fin'amor* holy and he said this in all sincerity after having sung song after song with frank expressions of sexual desire saying, "You pilgrims who have made yourselves destitute in divesting yourselves of all you have left back home, does not this purposeful poverty leave you tingling with spiritual impulse? We poets sing of desire, a desire that is fine and good because it is pure and is not fulfilled until we are worthy both to love and be loved. And in becoming worthy, are we not most vulnerable?"

FRANCESCO. Dressed in what he considered his most impressive outfit Francesco entered the Palazzo Pubblico the huge government building of the Commune of Siena at the base of the vast hemispheric bowl known as the Campo to deliver a letter intended to further his prospects of acceptance into a commercial campaign of the city's leading (and mainly noble) merchant bankers which would further the commune's political ambitions. Despite his best effort he got no farther than a chamberlain who promised to deliver the letter and in consolation offered a private viewing of the recently completed frescoes he called 'the glory of the commune' which Francesco who was utterly indifferent to art was yet desirous to see because appearing pressed for time seemed inconsistent with being distinguished.

The hall of the governing council was larger than he expected and more magnificent with elegant doors and high ceiling of the finest carved wood and walls and floors of gorgeous inlaid marble with three of the walls above door height filled with frescoes lit from a large window and it was to the one at the head of the room that the chamberlain directed him with a tap on the elbow. It personified government in a dominating king-like figure dressed in the city's colors flanked by women personifying prudence fortitude and peace on one side magnanimity temperance and justice on the other while a second series of figures personified wisdom justice and concord this last at the level of the commune's affluent citizens a procession of whom faced Government and brought to it the cords of justice that Concord had intertwined. Opposite them below a figure of justice (displaying a decapitated head) soldiers guarded a group of bound prisoners behind whom was a group of poorly dressed unshaven figures who according to the chamberlain were the peasantry and the city's 'little people' who not being citizens were excluded from participation in government.

Francesco cared little for any of this and sensing his impatience the chamberlain omitted a recitation of the fresco's lengthy inscription directing him instead to the long wall that depicted the commune both city and *contado* under good government a crowded bustling panorama of characters eagerly and fruitfully engaged in daily activities urban and rural. He walked alongside noting how well it depicted the city's architecture and the dress of its people and then turned to the opposite wall where the effects of bad government were depicted in personifications of war treason fury discord fraud and cruelty (strangling a child) presided over by a devil-like figure above whom sat Avarice Pride and Vainglory while to the side was a town engulfed in fire violence and rape. "Thank you," he said, "most edifying," and regaining the Campo felt pride in his city and the contribution he had made to its welfare (and the further contribution he proposed making) but could not avoid a sense of irony created by the murals whose image of unity stability and prosperity was belied by actual events especially in recent years.

DAY EIGHTEEN. To Tuccio's delight the count had given the *giullare* permission to travel with the caravan to Piacenza and no sooner were they en route than he brought his horse alongside in search of counsel he being an expert in affairs of the heart as to how best to win the love of his own (married) lady. Again the terrain was almost perfectly flat and the road straight but the stage was half again as long as the previous one and the June heat unusually hot so they took advantage of the streams draining out of the mountains to quench their thirst and refill their gourds.

Assuming he was talking about some servant girl the *giullare* framed his advice with some condescension putting Tuccio at pains to demonstrate his seriousness about *fin'amor* clarifying that the lady in question was truly above him married to his employer and twice his age and that both she and he appearances notwithstanding were noble. Careful not to reveal his surprise because he realized the lad was utterly serious and seeing him avid to learn the *giullare* made it his project to instruct him in some of the fine points of courtship taking for his texts his considerable repertoire of love poetry but first he appraised Margherita carefully with a professional's eye and questioned Tuccio closely asking was she virtuous had she responded to his approaches were any other men pursuing her did she already have a lover.

He mentioned the name Petrarca as the greatest living poet in Europe heir to the troubadours and Dante and a reincarnation of Cicero and in a certain way Saint Augustine and spoke of him in reverential almost mythical terms describing how he had steeped himself in the ethos and lyrics of the troubadours, "as did Dante himself, who even discussed them in a work on language, and of course they appear in his *Divina Commedia*. One, Sordello, was an Italian who wrote in the troubadours' *lenga d'oc*, that's how greatly they have influenced us. Dante made himself fluent in the *lenga d'oc* as can be seen from his use of it in *Purgatorio* twenty-six. But back to your situation..."

They reached a large stream where Tuccio drank as eagerly as he was to drink the knowledge pouring from the *giullare*'s lips excited at what seemed to lie ahead in every sense for at Piacenza only two hours away the caravan which had so far been heading northwest on the ancient route would turn west onto another which Hannibal had used to invade Italy in the third century BC and Julius Caesar to invade Gaul in the first and he thought, "Everything is new because now I am in love, and I have discovered *fin'amor*. My lady knows something of my love, I know little of her feelings, now we enter new territory, amply charted yet for us not at all." While thus ruminating he absentmindedly hummed one of the *giullare*'s tunes a sweet melody he had used for one of his most plaintive songs and the *giullare* asked if he would like to learn the words assuring him there was no surer way to a woman's heart or her bed than to sing for her and to substantiate this claim he cited no less an authority than Heloise who declared that a man who knew how to sing could instantly draw the heart of any woman.

"So I was right!" thought Tuccio.

"But as Eloisa correctly noted, the melody must have an amorous meter and rhythm and the lyrics an exquisite sweetness.

Of course the lady must know that the love of which you sing is for her alone. In that way she will declare, as did Eloisa writing to Abelardo, 'What married woman, what girl has not burned in your presence? What queen, what great lady has not been jealous of my joys and my bed?'" This made him question whether he had been right after all because while believing that to serenade a woman helped win her favor he'd always imagined that what most made a nobleman attractive was his prowess his deeds of valor and bravery in combat but surely the authority of Heloise and Abelard must be correct for like everyone he had heard of their famous love.

Across the plain the city walls were visible from a considerable distance but the river near one of whose many bends it was located not till they were almost at its bank where Margherita discovered a powerful attraction in the seeming lazy meandering of this languid but terribly flood-prone river. While he accompanied the *giullare* as he announced his evening performance she visited a thousand-year-old basilica but dutifully inspecting the revered relic of the city's fourth-century martyred bishop she decided that tomorrow she would go to confession and mass but this evening she would hear the *giullare*'s love songs; it was while standing in the large crowd waiting for him to appear that a nearby drunk loudly commented on the 'odd sight of a single woman in a pilgrim's robe.'

"What can she be up to, waiting for a *buffone* to sing his dirty ditties and juggle? Care to wager she's one of those who go on pilgrimage to frolic? Remember that bunch that went back and forth from the tavern to the church? Dancing in the church, I heard. And I heard there was a woman there got a bunch of young men talking about having her all together because she was said to be quite willing. Fond of it, the way I heard." Tuccio was immediately before him but flanked by several ruffians as big as him he offered sneers instead of apology and as the crowd backed away they began to encircle the youth; but not retreating rather looking like a cat ready to spring he said he would obtain an apology one way or another and it was only Margherita's guards appearing beside him and the timely interference of the local constabulary that prevented bloodshed. When he returned she could see his chest heaving and thanked him with a touch that lingered longer than necessary the performance began and a short time later she felt the pressure of his arm then his fingers seeking hers and she let him find them.

Tremendous land, loosed river flowing
Unknown what place brave Love is going.

FRANCESCO. One day at Lapo's insistence Francesco allowed himself to be caught up in a crowd rushing to hear the latest insurgent preacher a thin man with a strident voice who took obvious pleasure in thundering against his favorite sins lending at interest and profiting from time. Himself a Sienese merchant and a contemporary of Francesco to whom he was not unknown he had abandoned his fortune to serve the poor and sick and after being banished for incitement despite belonging to a magnate noble family he preached throughout Tuscany and Umbria until recently he had been allowed to return. "I tell you," said Lapo, "there has never been such a sermon. You will think you hear Saint Francis and will be born again."

To warm up the audience he said that to the three godly orders laborers knights and clerics the devil created a fourth usurers who do not participate in Man's work usury being the absence of work because money works alone with time. Ascending to a higher register he continued, "Did not Saint Augustine say, 'Commerce is of itself an evil?' And Saint Jerome, did he not say, 'Man the merchant barely if ever can please God.'" Shouting: "Did not Thomas Aquinas, recently sainted say, 'There is something disgraceful about trade, something sordid and shameful?' And Saint Francis, did he not repudiate his family of wealthy merchants to 'follow naked the naked Christ?'" Thundering: "I say to the merchant, 'Do you buy goods wholesale and sell them unchanged at a higher retail price? If so, you defile the precept of the just price and stand condemned, and your soul rots before the eyes of God.' I say, 'Do you lend at interest? If so, you stand condemned by all good men and the fires of Hell lie before you.'"

The crowd was suitably responsive with loud cries of condemnation Francesco involuntarily recoiling since it was obvious by his attire what he was and he thought, "Was it this to which my friend wished to subject me?" Yet he was not displeased there was actually a certain relief in being publicly vilified for it made it easier to live with himself indeed the sermon encouraged him to continue his good works imagine greater ones perhaps decorate an entire church alcove and so thinking he returned to it with as much interest as everyone else.

The more to inflame his audience the preacher had retreated to a lower pitch knowing everyone would expect another assault saying, "The usurer is a unique sinner, for he sins constantly, because his money earns interest constantly. He sells time. Worse, he steals from time. And how do our poets treat the merchant, the banker, those who traffic in money? The poet Dante puts them in Hell, in the seventh of nine circles, on a fiery desert beside the sodomites and others who commit crimes against Nature, for so he regarded usury." As he described Dante's vision of their torment his voice rose again until concluding he shrieked, "Do the saints and angels in Paradise not cry out against the usurers, 'To Hell, go to Hell?' The myriad stars and all the planets, do they not cry out, 'To the fire, go into the fire?' The very elements of nature, do they not rise up and exclaim against the usurer, 'To the executioner, send him to the executioner?'" Francesco left quickly lest anyone take the preacher literally but all the same he was moved.

DAY NINETEEN. It was a standing order of the count that at least once a week everyone in his *masnada* would confess and hear mass it seeming prudent not to tempt Fortune but afterward Tuccio was free to resume his lessons and the *giullare* who had become fond of him and whose great love in life was to immerse himself in songs of love who to gain his living had to travel constantly was thrilled to have such an avid pupil. So rather than throw dice at the inn which normally he would do on a day of rest he was happy to lecture on the symbolism of *fin'amor* and the structural complexity of its poetry in meter and rhyme; afterward they threw dice joined by Stoldo and another guard which especially on Sunday also tempted Fortune but which even the count was powerless to prevent.

While they played the other guard Nico kidded Tuccio about his newfound passion for love saying, "God only knows what you see in that one, but I applaud you for trying to put horns on the master." Having grown up in the *masnada* Tuccio was used to such treatment which Stoldo soon joined and which was facilitated by a large jug of wine but the *giullare* defended him saying, "Why this woman and not another need not concern us. Love has pierced him with its arrow, leaving him to suffer its delightful pain, and no mortal may withdraw it save the lady herself. This puts me in mind—this and the dice—of a *cansó* that says, 'May I never win at the gaming table if I ever pursue another woman besides you,'" and he sang it.

Afterward Nico said, "Then let's see if young Tuccio here empties our purses or his own."

"I, an authority in such matters, am convinced, especially as I have undertaken to instruct the youth in some of the fine points of seduction, that you had best close your purses now, gentlemen, for he is certain to possess the lady's heart in short order."

"But will he stay true?" asked Nico. "Otherwise it is we who win. Isn't that what the song said?"

"He will stay true, of that I have no doubt. You have only to look at him to see how steadfast he is," and they all made a show of staring at him as if to judge his faithfulness.

"Tuccio is steadfast to a fault," said Stoldo, "we all know that. Therefore his purse will not be emptied here. The question is, will it be emptied tonight?" His broad smile made clear that from one symbolic meaning of the purse he had moved to the other.

"Enlarged with the proceeds of ours, it will soon be bursting with coin and begging to be emptied."

"Quick, someone go tell the lady what is in store for her."

"She will learn soon enough."

"Learn? What's to learn? She will empty it herself."

"All at once or a little at a time to last all night? You've seen the lady, Sir Expert in Love, which do you think she'll prefer?"

While the *giullare* pretended to think Tuccio said, "The next to speak shall feel the edge of my blade."

"The lad is serious," said the *giullare*.

"The question is whether the lady shall feel the edge of his blade," said Nico.

"That assumes she hasn't felt it already," said Stoldo.

"Judging from the look on his face, I'd say she has not." Tuccio jumped on him and they wrestled. "You know you can count on me as a faithful friend," shouted Nico. "If your blade is not sturdy enough for the task, mine can be placed in service!" Tuccio punched him. "Ow! That hurt."

They ended up laughing and when it became quiet Tuccio said seriously, "She holds my heart in her hand. That's the simple truth."

"Excellent," pronounced the *giullare*, "you are learning well. There is a sonnet that turns on just that image—Dante, recall I spoke of him—where Love feeds the lover's heart to his beloved. You should know, though, it's meant to be frightening, and in that case, to lighten our mood, I must tell you all a story. Have you heard the one about Saint Peter and the *giullare*? The moral of this tale is: Love is a game of chance, but if you play it right you will attain Paradise. Once there was a poor *giullare*, his name I couldn't say. When the wind blew, he shivered in his shirt because his three loves were dice, the tavern, and the bordello, but there wasn't a nicer guy in the world. Still, the hour of death came. Now, devils are always looking for souls to snatch, but one poor devil who'd been down on his luck, no sooner did he see a *giullare* die than he grabbed his soul and, throwing it over his shoulder, ran back to Hell.

"His colleagues had made some great finds. This one had brought back a bishop, that one a wealthy merchant, another a monk who'd fathered half a village and they all rushed into Hell seeking Lucifer. When he saw such prizes, he cried out, 'Be you welcome, my good devils! Your charges shall be poorly lodged,' and he tossed the wretched souls into a cauldron. Just then arrived our devil, who dropped the *giullare* at his hooves.

"'Vassal,' asked he hopefully, 'what were you on Earth, a bawd, a traitor?' 'Nah, just a *giullare*. Since I'm lodging here now, I'll sing if you want.' The lord of Hell had no need of songs and put him to work keeping the fire under the cauldron. 'Lose one damned soul and I'll rip out your eyes, hang you by your tongue and eat you alive. Do well and I'll serve you a roasted monk in pimp sauce. I'm off to Earth with my devils for some entertainment.'

"Well, the *giullare*'s keeping the cauldron at a steady boil when who should arrive but Saint Peter, bearing a gaming table and three dice. 'Friend,' he says, 'care for a friendly game?' He pulled out a fat purse, but the *giullare* explained he hadn't two *soldi*. 'Not a problem, you can bet souls.' When he explained what would happen if he lost even one, the other waved. 'Who's going to say anything? Look at these fine pieces of silver. Brand new.' 'One soul a throw,' bid the *giullare*. 'Two,' countered Saint Peter.

"You can guess what happened. Soon the *giullare* was playing double or nothing to recoup his losses until he had lost everything. He accused Saint Peter of loading the dice. 'Liar!' he shrieked. 'Cheat!' screamed the *giullare* who leaped on the coins, but Saint Peter grabbed him so hard he had to let go to pull his beard. They beat each other up pretty well, but in the end there went Saint Peter, marching back to Heaven with all the souls in Hell.

"Back comes Lucifer with his devils and finds it awfully quiet. He looks in his furnaces, looks in his cauldrons, and says, 'Oh *giullare*, pray, where are all my souls?' 'I'll tell you, sire. Some old guy came in here and showed me his purse and I thought to empty it, so we played. But the business turned bad because he had loaded dice, that hypocrite, that deceiver.' 'Giullare, you have cost me dearly. Damned be the devil who brought you here. By God, he will pay!' That poor devil they slapped around pretty good and made him promise never again to bring a *giullare* to Hell. As for the *giullare*, Lucifer said, 'Damn you too, since you have lost me my guests. Get the hell out of my hostel. God loves pleasure, let him take care of *giullari*!' He ran off as fast as his legs would move, with the devils on his heels, and went straight to Paradise where Saint Peter gave him rich lodging. Since then *giullari* may amuse themselves to their heart's content, because for them the gates of Hell remain shut."

"Not a bad story," said Nico, "but for my taste the sauce could use more pepper. Have you heard the one about the beautiful blond virgin who every man wants but she insists on becoming a nun?"

"Not that one again," groaned Stoldo.

"Shut up, he hasn't heard it. It's a great story, a monk convinces her to join his order disguised as a man and she becomes his partner in more ways than one."

The *giullare* nodded in polite appreciation. "I could tell a few tales along those lines myself."

"How about— A priest is dying to fuck the young daughter of a merchant woman and offers a sack of florins to spend the night with her. The woman agrees and he can hardly wait, his dick is stiffer than a rampant stallion's and he swears by God to serve the virgin as she should be, but the woman has hired a prostitute to—"

The *giullare* was nodding. "Heard it, my friend. Heard it in more variants and—"

"He shakes the lemon tree nine times thinking—"

"We know, we know."

"How he says he'll teach her the *Credo in unum*?" Nico was disappointed to see the *giullare* still nodding. "Well somebody else tell one then."

"All right," said the *giullare*, "I will tell you 'The Three Ladies of Paris'" and looked around to see if anyone had heard it but Tuccio asked if he would sing another song instead.

Margherita went outside the city to sit beside the Po where she spent more time reading the river than the book in her lap while the guards kept away beggars and thieves and sitting beside her Agnoletta thought, "I sit here twiddling my thumbs while my mistress stares into space with a holy book in her lap, but she doesn't fool me, I know what's on her mind. Fortune has favored her, that's for sure, she'll receive excellent service from one so young, and I don't begrudge it to her, that's how it is, the young ones seek highborn ladies while the randy old goats chase servant girls. Ah, now she opens her book—but see, she looks away. It's impressive, the river, I wouldn't believe it were I not seeing it with my own eyes. Those were beautiful songs the *giullare* sang. It's quiet here. Well here I am sitting on the banks of this great river outside a city I never heard of, where they eat strange foods and speak an Italian I can't understand. I made it over the wild mountains, walked every step of the way, sometimes exhausted, once in fear for my life. It's nice here. Nice and calm. The world looks pretty good from here. In the beginning I was frightened about how far we were going, how many months we'd be on the road—and my mistress refusing to ride. Now I know why she wanted this pilgrimage."

Chapter Eight

DAY TWENTY. The *fattore* informing the count that he would stay in the city another day to take advantage of the commercial opportunities that abounded (which had been difficult on a Sunday) left everyone the pleasant task to devise a day's recreation and letting his master go alone this time to announce his performance Tuccio raced to find his mistress and having convinced her guards to remain outside the duomo they closely scrutinized the artwork in the unlit side chapels. In the evening they heard the *giullare*'s performance of course which seemed particularly sweet and as they returned to her hostel by the most circuitous route she asked him if he had not noticed the disparity in their ages, "And so," he thought, "the test begins. What would a troubadour reply?"

"When a woman is beautiful, a man notices above all that she is beautiful. Her age doesn't matter, unless it contributes to her beauty, which is the case with the fair lady whose vision is before me now." With that reply he thought he had done rather well flattering but within the bounds of truth flowery (the part about the vision) but within the bounds of poetry.

"You do not prefer women your own age?"

"What could they offer that you do not? Whereas you offer more, the wisdom of experience. I dare say you are surely more experienced." After their eyes locked they continued in silence a very pleasant silence. "In any case, what is age? You are a woman, I a man, how could it matter what age we are, if we are attracted to each other?"

"You are a man, but a young man, whereas I, alas, am... shall we say mature. Worse, I fear middle age has caught me."

"Nonsense."

"A woman of my age... Approaching middle age, then."

"Nonsense, you retain all the beauty of youth."

"You are kind to say so, though we both know you lie."

"I do not lie. I do not know how to lie, I would say I despise lying. But to lie in service to love, that is not really lying."

"See how young you are! You are, what, fourteen?" She said that deliberately to taunt him.

"I would say I am twenty-five, lady, if that would please you."

"It would not please me, for then you would be old."

"Then I am nineteen."

"Is that the truth?"

"Of course not, I seek only to satisfy your wishes."

"I wish to know the truth. Do you fear the truth?"

"There is not much I fear, lady, of that you may inquire of any of my fellows. I am sixteen, and that is the truth."

"Sixteen."

"Sixteen, yes."

"I was married at sixteen."

"Then you know it is a mature age."

"I know nothing of the sort, for at sixteen I was a virgin."

"Fear not on that score, lady."

"But I do not. Why should such a thing concern me one way or the other?" Again they walked in pleasing silence.

"I do not ask your age."

"A wise decision, for I would not reveal it."

"That is of no consequence because I do not care what it is."

"You would if you knew."

"On the contrary, if I knew I would know it was of no consequence. Good night, Margherita."

The hostel was supervised by a frail old prioress a tiny woman inexplicably endowed with a firm voice and the gentlest of smiles who made it her practice to meet every woman who appeared in her doorway to seek shelter by inviting them to sit across from her where she would take their hands and gaze at them. Margherita did not mind the gaze nor the grip of such dry bony fingers nor the quiet nor the elimination of all distraction and this is what the old woman said: "It is hard to live joyfully in transcendent love, perhaps even to feel it, when human love is absent. One may come to fear that she is incapable of love, that she lacks the gift, because she lives bereft of it. On the contrary, love does not need to be learned, for the ability exists in all, love is natural if anything is and all that is needed for love to be expressed is for it not to be suppressed. But we often do suppress it and thus feel loveless, neither receiving nor giving this most extraordinary treasure. And so we take to the road, embark on a journey toward love in hopes of discovering it. And we may, we may, not because it is in fact ahead of us but simply because some accident has released it from its prison."

DAY TWENTY-ONE. Again the road was straight and flat and cut by streams but for Margherita a new day a beautiful day with a scent of liberty in the breeze and enjoyment of Tuccio's fascination in the heat but in the dustless air clear to all that something was between them and oddly though the caravan was tracking the nearby Po River it was always out of sight. They wanted only to be beside each other warmed by the sun but so many watched them and while he didn't care she had no choice but to care for these were the *lauzengiers* about whom he had been warned by the *giullare* (while she needed no warning) they of the bitter tongues whose spiteful gossip would crush love no matter how pure and deserving who appeared wherever *fin'amor* appeared and had to be defeated or else resisted or else ignored were fine love to triumph.

> Barons, out of my suffering I invite to a joust
> false disloyal *lauzengiers*,
> for such a lady have I chosen
> in whom is noble, natural merit...
> No more than can without water live the fish
> can be without *lauzengiers* the gallant love of a lady.

(Peire Vidal, troubadour)

As the poem implies the *lauzengiers* would make true love impossible but on the other hand did they not make it possible? Perhaps our pair sensed this however unlikely—call it bizarre if you must—this particular pairing of souls might appear to those who would imagine love easily understood easily contained.

See these two a young man of arms on horseback a would-be knight noble by birth if not by life protecting with that life if need be a load of goods yet always dreaming and a woman walking beside him not quite old enough to be his mother noble herself yet living as a housekeeper to a husband old enough to be her father uneducated without expectations yet with an inchoate longing for something she herself could not identify. See them as would a falcon swaying on heat currents high above symbol of love forever wild yet submitting willingly to captivity and see them as the river flowing contentedly along an ancient dusty track with no thought for the history beneath their feet occasionally for the gazes of those around them but always for each other. Wherever Margherita looked someone seemed eager to banter or snicker or gossip at her expense so she said, "These people who press on us are many." (*Purgatorio*, Canto 5)

Tuccio who agreed but would not be deterred replied, "What do you care what's whispered there? Come behind me and let people talk," (*Purgatorio*, Canto 5) and noted that the guards were all his friends and the porters no doubt supported him too because resentment toward her had all but disappeared while no one liked her husband so it was just the *fattore* and the count but she said those were the two with power.

"You are troubled."

"I don't know if I am troubled."

"That means you are." Having seen the heavy looks from both of them she did not yet know whether it was her duty to do their will she knew only that when she had set out on pilgrimage she had had no idea no idea what thoughts would be filling her mind three weeks later.

"Nothing is the world's noise other than a gust of wind, that now comes from here and now comes from there." (*Purgatorio*, Canto 11)

Tuccio's farewell to the *giullare* had been regretful for his words had been like drops of precious liquor and oddly for a man who sang of love without ever experiencing it there was real affection and sorrow in their parting for he had been greatly entertained by Tuccio's passion not for a woman which many men shared but for poetry which most men did not; and to dispel the mood he clapped him on the shoulder with a final word of advice: "Never doubt yourself. You're a fine-looking man with all the vigor of youth and she is unhappy. Make yourself worthy of her favor as I have instructed and you shall have it."

"Are you bothered," asked Margherita, "that no one but us is happy to see us conversing?"

"And yet, excepting the count we are the only ones nobly born."

"Yet what has it gotten us?"

"Gotten, lady, I cannot say, but what might we not earn

thereby? I believe myself capable of a noble love. I believe you are too for I believe I see it in you."

"You believe much."

"Did the *giullare*'s songs not move you too? I felt they did."

She thought, "Whence comes this belief in me?"

Agnoletta thought, "Any woman can see she is stirred that he felt her. Of course she is, when was the last time a man felt her? Possibly never, poor thing."

Tuccio thought, "Every day I improve and refine myself, because I serve and revere the most noble woman in the world." (Arnaut Daniel, troubadour)

Margherita thought, "Never before have I listened to poetry. How moved I was! To think that I..."

Agnoletta thought, "Just look at her."

Margherita thought, "He is generous and nimble and knowing, in him is good sense and knowledge." (Comtessa de Dia, troubadour)

Tuccio thought, "She is so excellent, and of the richest merit." (Arnaut Daniel)

Margherita thought, "You are excellent and well-bred, and you recognize all fine merit, for which your friendship pleases me." (Raimbaut de Vaqueiras, troubadour)

In the distance they could see a party approaching and at a certain point could make out that two walked in pilgrim robes while others rode and there was a pack mule which made Margherita's heart leap thinking, "So I am not the only one." The guards were alert as usual but there was no danger and greetings were exchanged followed by information while Margherita approached the pilgrim and his servant to ask why he walked when so many rode.

"I always walk so my pilgrimage will be authentic, for I have seen enough hypocrisy in the Church to last till the end of days."

"Always?"

"I am returning from Compostela for the third time, I have been to Rome five times, and many other places besides. I have never been to Mont Saint-Michel though, some day I should like to go there. And Jerusalem of course, but no one has yet requested it."

"I don't understand."

"You don't? I go for others. *Madonna*, have you not heard of the proxy pilgrimage? My clients pay me well, I insist on that."

"But who are they?"

"Who? Once I walked for an aging countess in ill health, once for a dying man afraid of Judgment, but mostly for those who have the means yet lack the will. I assure you it is honorable, the Church sanctions it." He said he traveled with his brother who was a dealer in holy relics and indulgences and insisted she meet him since he'd noticed right away that her robe lacked the emblem of her journey. "For a suitable sum, he can furnish you with a rare item indeed, not just a shell of San Giacomo but one taken from the sea where his boat came ashore." When she politely declined he offered indulgences. "You need only whisper in his ear what sin requires absolution and he can provide a pardon signed by a bishop. I can personally guarantee your donation will be turned over to the Church. One hears of abuses."

FRANCESCO. There were those who said Siena had more flagellant confraternities than any other city and that they were a refuge for merchants and bankers in fear for their souls; what is certain is that they were known for their public displays and that Francesco was not immune to guilt. When he said, "God give me grace, if it be His pleasure, to lead a better life, for it is a dog's life, and all through my own fault," he was as sincere as the commune's governors who swore when reciting the oath of office not to confer an office or honor of the commune on anyone known to engage in usury or make an illicit contract. In the presence of colleagues publicly scourging themselves Francesco could express his own repentance but privately wondered what he could or even should change for example was it half as blameworthy to make half as much profit was he supposed to sell his goods for less than their value or give up commerce entirely?

Of the half dozen men involved from the local confraternity he knew them all as minor tradesmen and recognizing that their self-denigrating spectacle (which he'd noticed while on an errand) displayed not just repentance but sympathetic suffering in imitation of Jesus a kind of sacrifice to become more worthy he considered himself free to choose a different form of sacrifice and told the nearest, "My wife wishes to go on pilgrimage."

He was advised to go with her.

"She would go all the way to Compostela."

"The better to gain merit. She does well to fix her eyes so far. As would you."

He said he would go with her.

"You will be praised for it. We merchants must prove ourselves no less than anyone else."

He said he would certainly go said it sincerely.

He was encouraged to join the confraternity as it followed the Via Dolorosa.

He said he would certainly think about doing just that and that he would take his wife to Compostela and that he was thinking about undertaking some major improvement to the church and that he might send someone on pilgrimage on his behalf which as the other knew was approved by the Church and had the advantage of saving two souls with one journey.

"You should go with your wife to Compostela."

"I shall. I fully intend to. You are right, of course."

DAY TWENTY-TWO. The caravan was well on its way when riders could be seen galloping toward them who when close enough shouted that mercenaries were coming and the count shouted back, "How many?"

"Many!"

"Close?"

"Too close!" They were gone before he could ask more and he didn't deliberate long; fortunately the land that had begun to rise to the south of the route the previous day now amounted to hills high enough to slow a charging horse and forested if lightly and he ordered the caravan to disperse so as not to make a single track and regroup in the hills. They faced confiscation of the animals and weapons looting of the goods even abduction of Margherita for ransom also the porters and maid could be pressed into service and if the men were considered hostile even if they weren't their lives could be at risk. Though none of the other travelers were so much exposed no one would dare to be on the road when a band of soldiers came through who supplemented their pay with loot and fleeing they naturally followed the *masnada* even the penniless for anything could happen especially to women.

The count wished to get several miles away but with the mercenaries possibly close and the land relatively open he needed to hide quickly; fortunately the road generally followed the outline of the hills so being less straight than before the range of visibility was less and there were still streams coming down from above which created covering noise for those hiding while slowing the advance of those pursuing and his hope was to find one. "How is it we had no knowledge of this in Piacenza?" asked the *fattore*.

"Apparently no one knew. I thought I had identified hostilities yet heard nothing about a moving army. I conclude we're not in hostile territory."

"Meaning they're headed elsewhere."

"Still, we will take every precaution."

"What about returning to Stradella?"

"We have no assurance of being allowed inside. And we may not have enough time, we don't know where they are, they could appear any moment. And who knows, that might be where they're headed for the night."

"I wonder where they're going. Could be almost anywhere, I guess. But why didn't we hear? Those criers were local, how could they know what's afoot in Milano, say? They've been caught by surprise, and us with them, in the middle of a vast arena."

If the army were transiting the area they could return to the road as soon as they were gone but if they happened to bivouac nearby they would have to remain hidden all night; if they attacked no one could say what might happen and Tuccio who had been ordered to stay behind to watch the road but had appealed wordlessly to the count who relented and sent Nico and Stoldo told Margherita he would stay at her side no matter what happened.

"What might happen?"

"We don't know how many there are. There could be a hundred or more. Maybe five hundred, maybe a thousand. If they come for us and there are too many, I will die here. But I will not leave your side."

Luckily a change in the terrain covered them from the road letting them continue cross-country a few miles but though they found a stream it wasn't sufficient for protection so the count opted instead for the far side of a mound with scouts deployed on top and there everyone waited and waited and Margherita asked if this was what it was like working in the municipal war captain's force, "facing uncertain danger."

"Did you know that when the war captain was dismissed two years ago for conspiring against the governing council, the entire force was too? It was the only prudent course to take, since you couldn't be sure who supported the plot, but that left the city in immediate need of replacements. We were among the first to be approached, I think that's when our loyalty to Siena received its greatest acknowledgement. The count answered the call at once."

"That was a frightening time. To think that you..."

"There was no serious fighting."

"But the threat."

"Of course. We patrolled the city twice a day looking for prohibited weapons. We had to guard at night too."

"Was that... How did that..."

"I didn't mind, though it proved impossible to prevent men from bearing the weapons. The count advised us to choose our interventions carefully."

Among the travelers who had followed the caravan into the hills was a man who in his pilgrim robe was of indeterminate social status carrying nothing but staff and pouch and alone and who in contrast to everyone else was utterly calm a strange man one might have thought demented and though people eyed him carefully he threatened no one and suddenly he began to talk quietly but loud enough to be heard. "Why should I try to be better on the Path, am I not always on it? Wasn't I on the Path before I started, and won't I still be on it after I have finished? Whatever I want to bring forth out of myself on the Path that I deem good, whatever I strive to produce, whenever I succeed I must strive to express it always, wherever I am, for I am always on the Path, I never leave it. It is impossible to leave, because obviously the Path is my life. And if I do succeed in doing good, I grieve for the opportunities I wasted. Why did I have to come here to do good, wait till now? And when I behave well, I fear that I won't always. But if something good comes out of me that I didn't know was there, something new, only then am I truly happy, for that is a gift."

Nico reported that the mercenaries had appeared and were continuing down the road and later returned to say they were gone though Stoldo was still watching just in case so with cries of thanksgiving everyone arose and the count led them northwest to a point on the road that would put them well away from the army and heading to the next town which was not far. As was typical in such situations it had thrown open its gates to the surrounding country so when they arrived villagers were entering in droves their animals before them and carrying whatever they could but with so many seeking refuge not everyone could be sheltered and among those failing to find lodging was the caravan which couldn't even find stabling for the animals. To address the situation the city had proclaimed that the public square could be occupied overnight but could not enforce controls on the suddenly outrageous prices for food fodder and even bedding straw so the men faced an uncomfortable (and watchful) night in the square while Margherita did only slightly better to persuade the prioress of an Augustinian sorority to squeeze her inside.

FRANCESCO. "The question is whether you prefer to limit your risk or increase your potential return, since you cannot have both. Now, since I will be furnishing most of the capital... During the years you will be abroad, I cannot be worried about your commitment to the enterprise."

"Francesco, you need have no—"

"If you were simply to receive a fixed rate of return—never mind for the moment how it would be characterized—I find myself wondering what incentive you would have to see the enterprise prosper. You are paid in full either way, you see."

"Francesco, I certainly—"

"Furthermore, what induces you to devote yourself to careful management when so many pleasurable distractions beckon?"

"I assure you—"

"On the other hand, were your capital fully at risk I would not want you afraid to venture it out of fear of loss. No risk, no return, after all."

They were on the rim of the Campo watching a hundred workmen pave the vast hollow a project begun twenty years earlier and now approaching conclusion.

"My reply is simple. I wish to be a full partner as I must see my capital grow rapidly or face extinction; but I wish to protect my capital against total loss as I simply would not have the resources to recover. Therefore I propose a hybrid arrangement, part full partnership, part limited."

Francesco walked along the rim pretending to watch the workers and asked, "What form would you say our Campo has been given?"

"A shell, of course, an upturned shell."

"Like the pilgrim shell, would you say?"

"Very like."

"Yes, I think so too. They say the upturned shell indicates the palm of the hand which symbolizes good works," and he fell silent again in a way which allowed no interruption then suddenly said, "So my dear friend, do I understand you to say that you seek profit where it is easy and a guaranteed return where it is not?"

"Not at all, that is not— I must have a way to control my exposure. You do the same yourself."

"Yet you ask me to increase my exposure so you can reduce yours."

"Not at all. You do the same. It's just that you have many partnerships, whereas I would have only this one. I simply cannot afford—"

"Of course not. Nor would I have you take undue risk, even had you proposed it, and it pleases me that you have not. We must, then, find middle ground where we are both pleased. What did you have in mind?"

Now it was the turn of the prospective *fattore* to fall silent knowing the crucial stage of the negotiation had finally arrived so he too discovered a consuming interest in how the ground was prepared for the paving stones a ploy Francesco would not have allowed but which this time suited him since he had already achieved what he needed namely a way to off-load substantial risk while characterizing the arrangement as a partnership to avoid a charge of usury. The issue was whether the investment constituted a loan or ownership for if the return was a fixed rate of interest the enterprise had received a loan whereas if variable and subject to commercial risk it had gained a partner and while partnerships were approved loans were not but the disadvantage of partnership was unlimited liability hence the impetus to provide loans but disguise them as partnerships to avoid clerical censure.

The would-be *fattore* younger than Francesco and with considerably less capital could not afford unlimited liability for so hazardous a commercial undertaking as the proposed caravan while Francesco needed equity partners to diversify his risk though not the kind of young merchant foolhardy enough to risk everything on a single venture so the middle position suited him best. This hybrid arrangement moreover gave Lapo what he needed to satisfy his conscience while designing the contract to look more risky than it actually was without disturbing the *fattore* who understood the importance of how a commercial arrangement appeared to clerical authorities.

DAY TWENTY-THREE. After a mostly sleepless and entirely comfortless night the caravan set off early as much to get out of town as distance itself from mercenaries but at the first opportunity the *fattore* ducked into a primitive little church to pray while everyone ate breakfast. He had done well in Lucca and Piacenza and escaped danger twice and believed he would not have if God were displeased with him but thought it best to let Him know he was thankful also that he had sent word back to Francesco to reassure him the caravan was doing well and that his wife was well and he was watching over her.

He assured God he was being diligent in his bookkeeping looked forward to many profitable engagements and would never forget that Messer Domeneddio (Sir Lord God) was a partner in the enterprise entitled to one percent of all profit which he promised to be scrupulous to see that He got; and he noted that in this it was he who had prevailed on Francesco who though diligent in paying alms had not until this joint venture created an account for Messer Domeneddio to be maintained like any other. Indeed he had been insistent with Francesco on this point because he did not believe it was enough to write something pious on the first page of one's accounting ledgers such as, "In the name of God and of profit," or, "In the name of our Lord Jesus Christ and of the Holy Virgin Mary and of all the saints in Paradise, may they grant us possessions, multiply our wealth, and save our souls," no he assured God he was setting aside the money and that once settled in Barcelona His full share would be distributed to the poor and charitable institutions.

The entire night he had not been able to get out of his mind how the mercenaries had appeared from nowhere that not a word of their existence had been heard though the count and he were always diligent in seeking information that could affect their security; also that strange pilgrim who had appeared out of thin air were these warnings they seemed so but then why, he asked, "Have I erred, Lord?" He didn't believe so but after he finished praying he left a large offering and returning outside admonished himself to always be on guard against practices that might offend God because whether or not those were messengers he had been reminded that one could never be too careful about one's salvation especially a merchant.

It was an easy stage a beautiful day and gradually the fatigue and ill humor dropped like dried mud off clothing for everyone but Tuccio and Margherita from whom it had fallen with their first look at each other. The hills that had protected them the day before were gone the land again flat in all directions and the road straight and though it was a long stage their journey floated like a small boat on a stream of earnest conversation both of them eager to be known to reveal to make gifts of intimacy.

What they said shall not be told, no, not the intimacies which you are most eager to hear!

You may hear that when Margherita said she found the idea of living by plunder repugnant Tuccio confessed that when he was starting out his goal had been to become just such a mercenary saying, "Who would take a ten year old boy with no family, nothing to show for himself, undisciplined, a vulgar ruffian with a slim claim on noble birth, and make him a squire in a fine household, clothe him, teach him, train him to become a knight? Squires are made to forge alliances, acquit obligations or create them, but who would offer to us, who had nothing to offer in return? That question robbed my father of sleep. I, meanwhile, slept soundly with the most delightful of dreams. Like the unknown foreign knight who enters the lists and defeats all, so would I enter a tournament, a tournament somehow for boys, such being the way of dreams, and no one stood long before me until, like in the romances, I faced my greatest adversary. I even said to my father one day when he looked particularly vexed, 'Don't worry, father. His name and finery don't matter. Let me at him and I will knock him down.'

"I didn't lack for confidence. Now, as you must know, there are always *condottieri* who seek to hire their mercenary bands to one city or another for this or that campaign. The campaigns don't last but the bands do, moving from one employment to another, and this requires, not just fighting men, but everything fighting men need including young men to care for their arms and armor and lead their second horses. True, I was young for this, but I thought to falsify my age and, as for the rest, brazen it out, though there was one problem, which you can readily see: My slight size would not easily support my lie.

"Still, that seemed the only way open to me. But, true knight or not, I sought honor on the field as much as the next dreamer, and not every *masnada* was honorable. Let me ask you, why would Siena hire men of its own *contado* who are already obligated to volunteer in its militia?"

"I imagine that otherwise they might ravage farms and towns until the commune thinks again about the arrangement."

"So do I. And I had no wish to join such a *masnada*. I was not about to hold my neighbor at knifepoint while my comrades took his chickens."

"But do not men become mercenaries as much for the spoils as the pay?"

"The knight's code of war recognizes legitimate spoils. A defeated man's horse and arms, a prisoner's ransom. For one in my circumstances the attraction was obvious, the more so as my father assured me there was no dishonor in it. But how to tell which *masnada* engaged in honest service and which in brigandage? The Sarteani, with whom I serve and who have served Siena for generations, have never to my knowledge threatened it. But how I came to join them is a tale for another time, for I wish to know more about you."

By the time the caravan reached Alessandria in the evening the men were ready to eat any food even if burnt raw stale or tasteless and sleep in any bed provided the straw were not foul but Tuccio and Margherita found a tower to climb where after ascending the spiral staircase they emerged onto a parapet with a clear view of the Alps arrayed in the distance and in silence gazed at the stupendous vision as he slipped his arm around her waist and said, "I will go with you to Compostela."

"Yes, I know. So will you all, as my husband has directed."

"I do not go for your husband, I go for you, Margherita."

When she asked whether he would go for himself he said, "My father went to Assisi to pray that I would be delivered to the life he believed I deserved. I am not known for prayer, Margherita, I tell you that frankly, not because it speaks well of me but because I will not lie to you, even to inflate my merit."

"Isn't that what men do?"

"I would have you love me as I am, Margherita, because I cannot be what I am not. But you have inspired me to seek within myself, to see if there is not some holy spark there that San Giacomo might inflame."

She confessed that she was not very devout herself saying, "I would not lie to you either, I too could use the apostle's help. Do not the rules of love dictate that we strive to improve?"

"So did the *giullare* instruct me, Margherita."

"In that they do not contradict the gospel."

"Do they in some other way?"

"I have not heard in the gospel that it is meritorious to pursue another man's wife."

After a silence he replied, "Yet our greatest poets all sing of it. It seems a difficult question, perhaps we should go to the apostle's house near Spain's faraway coast for an answer. What do you say, Margherita?"

Chapter Nine

The next time they met he made sure to arrive first but he didn't wait for her at the bar he waited outside waited a half hour and when she was almost upon him and asked startled if he'd just arrived he said, "More or less." At the table he told her the good news that he had already received manuscript facsimiles from London Barcelona and Pistoia where they were excited about the project saying, "The British Library, always efficient. There are two there, one is late fifteenth, the other 1325, copied right at Compostela as were two others, Salamanca and Vatican one twenty-eight, which is interesting. So there we are, on our way. Barcelona houses Ripoll, which along with Compostela was the basis for Vielliard's 1938 translation, I presume you know it."

"I know of it."

"Of course. That's where the modern interest is rekindled. Still in print, though other translations have appeared, and of course voluminous secondary literature, Melczer, etcetera etcetera. Pistoia is interesting. Sixteenth-century copy of a thirteenth-century copy, probably based on a twelfth-century original sent by the archbishop of Compostela to the bishop of Pistoia. And if the account given there is true, Pistoia also received the jawbone of Saint James, a priceless relic. This would be 1138, when the CC was almost certainly compiled circa 1137 to 1145."

"CC?"

"*Codex Calixtinus.* You're familiar with that name? I prefer it because *The Book of Saint James* sounds definitive but isn't. Since we know Pope Calixtus was not an author of the work even though the prologue attributes it to him, it has the virtue of being vague in meaning yet precise in reference. Also his name is used to identify the work in the few medieval inventories where we have found it recorded. So, how are you, my lady? How's the world of high finance?"

"I'm fine. Very high. Well, not entirely."

"Can I ask if you walked since we last... I didn't see a new blog post."

"No. I was going to. When I left you I was really fired up, you know. But then... What I decided is that I wanted to hang onto Saint-Guilhem. It's such a revered pilgrim destination and once I leave it I walk several stages through a wilderness area, so I wanted something to happen first."

"Didn't?"

"Didn't."

"Don't worry about it."

"I am worried about it."

"You shouldn't. I think... Here's my prediction. I think your pilgrimage is going to be amazing."

"What makes you say that?"

"I think I said it last time. I don't see you as the kind that fails. Your post was interesting."

"Thank you. Coming from you, that's..."

"I wish you had taken my seminar."

"Thank you. Gee."

"Did you enjoy classics?"

"I did."

"Classics gets most of the glory. Anyway, your blog..."

BLOG POST #6: Montpellier to Saint-Guilhem-le-Désert. Stage: 5. Stages remaining: 65. Distance: 40.0 km, 24.8 miles. Cumulative distance: 127.0 km, 78.7 miles. Remaining distance: 1,524 km, 944.9 miles. (This is a virtual pilgrimage in the sense that I'm not really en route to Compostela, but I am really walking the miles.)

While Arles was a wonderful city to visit and the basilica at Saint-Gilles was really interesting, the stages were pretty boring and even annoying at times. (See posts.) What a relief this one was!

[Description of Montpellier. Little or nothing survives that's medieval.]

Since this was the longest stage, almost twenty-five miles (ouch!), I set out early. Although my guidebook recommended taking a tram and bus to Grabels, which is the first town outside the city, I walked from my hostel so I could say I did the whole thing. [Difficulties finding the correct route out of the city. Importance of asking more than one person for directions because people try to be helpful even when they don't really know the way.]

When you get past Grabels you're in what's called the garrigue, *which is an astonishingly beautiful semi-arid environment with all kinds of colorful plants and flowers and dramatic sharp-edged boulders. Check out the images. I walked through this amazing landscape for miles, over rounded hills and around curves, so new vistas kept opening to view. The air was perfectly clear. The heat was intense but being dry it was quite bearable. I was alone most of the time, which is amazing when you consider that this is high tourist season (and high pilgrimage season). There weren't even many cars.*

Whatever the reason, I enjoyed the peace. Before my pilgrimage I hated hiking, and I'm not sure I like it even now, just walking for the sake of walking; but I have to say there's nothing like the peace of quiet. Granted this was only my fifth stage, but for the first time I felt like maybe I was getting a taste of what pilgrimage in the Middle Ages might have felt like. What my own pilgrimage might feel like. And I liked it. I liked it a lot. I felt like I could walk through garrigue *for another sixty-five stages and never get tired, never get bored. As for being alone, well it was only for a few hours, so I can't really talk about solitude—not yet. I continued like this for five hours till I got to the town of Aniane (22.6 km, 14.0 miles from Grabels).*

It occurs to me that this was the first stage where the modern and medieval routes are the same and have the same qualities of isolation and rugged beauty. From Arles to Montpellier it's more difficult to compare because the geography of the Camargue has changed so much since the Middle Ages and the area is so much more developed. Today I could legitimately feel like I was walking on the path of countless pilgrims over a thousand years. That affects you. At least it affects me. I can't say exactly why, but it does.

[Description of Aniane and the historical link between its monastery and Gellone the original name for Saint-Guilhem-le-Désert.]

After Aniane the landscape transitioned quickly to gorge country, not unlike garrigue *but mountainous and craggy. Instead of rolling hills, I was confronted with my first gorge, the Gorges de l'Hérault. Just as beautiful, more dramatic. (See the images.) Right away I could see why a monastery would be in a place like this and why pilgrims would make a point of going to see it, even if it didn't have a three-inch piece of the True Cross (which it supposedly did) and was founded by a cousin of Charlemagne. But to reach it I had to cross the gorge.*

The river that runs through it is about twenty feet wide and boulder-strewn. Even now there was enough water to make crossing dodgy, it must be something in spring. So you would want a bridge and fortunately there has been one for a thousand years, called the 'Bridge of the Devil' (Pont du Diable). I couldn't stop taking pictures.

Saint-Guilhem is gorgeous! [Description of the village crowded with tourists.] *I must be careful, though, not to imagine that this bears any resemblance to the medieval town it reincarnates. Too perfect, too rich for that. The tourists may not care, but I'm a pilgrim!*

The church is quite beautiful in its severe primitive way, but it didn't stir me and I've been wondering why. I've decided it's because it's new. What's odd about that is that if I were arriving in the eleventh century, when the original church was built, it would have looked as new to me then as it does to me now. I think we can't help being conditioned by our conception of the Middle Ages as ancient. So I look at the church and think some of it may be medieval, but a lot of it is obviously recent reconstruction. The building stones don't look aged. The edifice is too perfect, like a new car. I want it to be old, the older the more impressive. I want it to look used, even worn. I want to see small imperfections that somehow make the totality more perfect. To me, that seems more authentic. Authenticity seems to be allied with truth. What is truth when applied to individual experience?

As I try to make sense of my feelings today, I don't know whether to exult or cry. I find myself inclining one way, then the other, and it's not just fatigue. I admit I wanted so much for something to happen, to have a meaningful experience. When I say 'meaningful,' maybe I should say 'spiritual,' but lack the courage, I don't know, I wouldn't describe myself as a spiritual person. I think I'm walking to find out why I'm walking.

Can sheer beauty inspire a spiritual experience? The entire stage today was amazingly beautiful and dramatic, the scenery, the village, the church. If the church isn't stirring, its spectacular setting against craggy calcine mountains certainly is. And there's almost a party atmosphere in the town, even joyous. Surely this is sufficient to make one's heart leap. Is that (or can that be) the beginning of something more? Can awe become spiritual?

On a cliff across a ravine, high above the village, maybe three hundred feet up, are the ruins of two chapels, one on top, the other perched on the side. If I am not in awe of the chapels, I am in awe of those who built them.

Is there not something literally grand, big and wonderful, about beauty? In its presence do I not feel small? But not in a bad way. I feel privileged to be there, to be able to receive it. One might even disappear in such grandeur. Might one not possibly feel the presence of something huge?

If one is seeking and says to oneself, "I am on pilgrimage, therefore I must be profoundly stirred," then does not the experience vanish? It can't be forced. It seems to come of its own volition, exist in itself. That's very strange, I think. A mystery.

"Can you guess what I found most interesting?"

"I have no idea. I can't believe I said anything that..."

"I really wish you had taken my seminar. You're something of a mystery yourself, my lady."

"I don't feel like a mystery."

"You straddle antithetical worlds. And you seem to do it without losing your balance, which I find..."

"Professor, I'm dying here. What did I say?"

"You adumbrate a fundamental question about the redemptive possibility of beauty. That is very interesting. There's a lot to be said about that, a lot."

"Wow. I wish we had more time to talk."

"Me too. Neo-Platonists saw two fundamental traits in existence, intelligence and goodness, and beauty was closely allied with goodness. So closely allied that it wasn't always obvious whether the world was beautiful because it was good or good because it was beautiful. Plotinus, for example... Well, here I go, stop me before I bore you to death."

"No, no, on the contrary, I..."

"In your blog, you said you're walking to discover why you're walking. That's why you need to keep walking."

Tiffany was not giving any hint of Bob's frustration with his job which was affecting their home life with the predictable forms of stress mostly his but inevitably hers such as when he angrily accused her one night in bed of having jumped precipitously into her foundation without sufficient thought and committing money they could have used for things they both wanted like a second home. Her response was to ask what the odds were of his not getting promoted to vice president and he replied that the odds were nil but that that wasn't the point. "That is the point. You'll get it, so what's the problem?"

"When is the question. He's been jerking me around over a year now." He knew he could probably force the promotion by threatening to jump ship but it didn't seem like a great time to do that when the market waters were as choppy as they had become; he knew that once he started shopping there was the possibility that his own people would find out with the consequence that if he didn't land another position his chances of a promotion could greatly diminish.

The essence of the tranche structure of claims on a collateral pool of mortgages was that the lowest rated tranches which had the last claims would suffer first from defaults and the way CDOs were structured it didn't take a high level of default to affect them; but this concern was all but universally considered remote if not theoretical which was why these tranches were avidly sought at ever higher prices by hedge funds. In April 2006 however home prices had peaked nationally and that summer mortgage loan defaults had spiked such that by early 2007 a significant percentage of mortgage borrowers *never made a single payment*; these developments naturally caused declines in the value of mortgage-backed securities and questions about their high credit ratings in fact CDOs with high concentrations of lower quality ('subprime') mortgages were suddenly facing severe downgrades. Because of these developments new accounting rules came into effect that required financial firms to price their mortgage-backed securities at current market prices a requirement that posed two great problems the first that for a large number of securities there was no active market or even none at all and the second that this required large reductions in the reported values of assets on the books of financial institutions.

The reductions also reduced the value of collateral which triggered calls for more and with the multi-trillion dollar market entirely structured on a high proportion of collateralized borrowing such calls were inherently destabilizing. All house purchases are leveraged to the extent of the mortgage but by this time the mortgages that underlay most of the MBS industry were highly leveraged with low down payments and high loan to house value ratios; the securities were themselves financed at high leverage ratios and CDOs made from other CDOs were financed with another round of debt plus investors many of which were the same firms creating these securities typically bought them with yet another round of debt at ratios normally fourteen to one and often higher. Three quarters of all subprime and other substandard mortgages were securitized into CDO tranches initially carrying triple-A credit ratings.

All this was happening when Bob's hedge fund was facing investor redemptions and a call for more collateral and what particularly irked him was that asset value reductions were required on many securities even if there were no actual losses and in some cases even if the firm did not intend to sell them though of course he might have seen that these objections were irrelevant so long as the securities were reported as assets. Investors suddenly learning that their investments had been mispriced and disturbed by rising mortgage delinquencies and not knowing how much worse the situation could get would naturally worry about their ability to sell at a reasonable price and so decide the safest course was to sell immediately; but those who were already out had little desire to get in and ratings downgrades only exacerbated the concern which made selling more difficult.

This was enough to keep Bob awake at night and generate tirades about how stupid the new accounting rules were. "They created a problem that didn't exist. They claim that securities are overpriced which inevitably spooks the market so prices decline and then they say, 'See, you're reporting inflated prices, you need to mark them down to the market.' So now we've got prices driven down by forced sales thanks to the bean counters who don't know a damn thing about the business. We literally have to go out and raise capital to cover losses that were never there." Tiffany would watch his chest heave and figure he was calming himself but then there would be another outburst. "The problem goes away as soon as everyone calms down. Housing isn't going away. Most mortgages are fine. The rating agencies never knew what they were doing anyway. And don't get me started on the regulators—who are mostly out to lunch anyway. Why make us go out and raise capital to cover losses that don't exist? Get out of our way and everything will work out just fine. Do you know the stock market fluctuates more in a day than the entire value of all subprimes?"

Nonetheless it was at this point that analysts at Bob's firm reported to his boss and the lead manager that by their calculations the value of both hedge funds had declined sharply causing the lead manager to write in a confidential email that if the new valuations were 'anywhere close to accurate' the funds should be closed. Three days later on a conference call however he told investors, "The key sort of big picture point for us at this point is our confidence that the market has not systematically broken down. We're very comfortable with exactly where we are." Bob learned this later as he heard from investors and information circulated surreptitiously among his colleagues but he still wasn't concerned only frustrated that this would slow him down on his career path; and a short time later he was relieved when his boss circulated an email to announce that the Enhanced Leverage Fund the one using higher leverage with which he was more closely associated was only down six point six percent in April. It soon became known however that the Pricing Committee was revising this figure and then the fund announced a nineteen percent drop and froze redemptions meaning it would not allow investors to sell.

Bob went home that day in a bitter mood and as soon as he opened the door started fulminating again at the bean counters as well as irresponsible journalists who reported information out of context; he barely said hello practically ignored his daughter and spent the evening on his computer with the door closed gathering information dependable or not from contacts. "Do you want to say goodnight to your daughter?" asked Tiffany who opened the door just enough for her head.

"Good night, princess," he said.

"What's wrong, daddy?"

"Nothing's wrong, princess. Daddy just had a hard day at work."

"Why?"

"I just did."

"But why?" He kissed her again and returned to his computer and when he arrived at the office the next day he was ordered to sell collateral at whatever prices he could get to raise cash because what he hadn't discovered the night before was that his parent company had met with all ten of the hedge funds' repo lenders (who provided the overnight repurchase agreements by which the funds operated) to forestall a demand for more collateral. Some of these firms had sold to the funds some of the very CDOs that were now collapsing in value nonetheless all ten refused the appeal and when this became known to the funds' investors their requests for redemptions accelerated.

Knowing redemptions could not be frozen forever impelled the firm to act though it had no legal obligation to rescue either the investors or the lenders and had little of its own capital in its funds; but the lenders were the same large investment banks with which it did business constantly while news of the failure of one of its investment subsidiaries could raise concerns about the firm itself. While it conducted a review of each fund which had Bob's group working feverishly to gather statistics and endorsements to enhance their image the calls for more collateral became a barrage that affected not just the funds but the entire firm's ability to conduct business with some in management complaining privately of chaos. Finally the decision was made to repay the outside lenders in full and become the sole lender but only to the High Grade Fund;

Enhanced Leverage the fund on which Bob had pinned his hopes for advancement was to be left on its own.

Said the professor, "I have this vision of your world as vicious and glamorous, a gladiator sport in which the weak perish while the strong are crowned. Yet here you sit, calm, relaxed... I have no doubt you move confidently in this world of which I have only a murky image and obviously you're successful. I keep trying to picture the young woman who might have sat in my class and made a presentation about the valorization of miracle. I'm trying to grasp how someone from your world finds their way to mine."

"It wasn't that hard really."

"But in its own way a kind of miracle, no? My world is so... Yours in contrast is everyone's darling, a glittering new city on the hill, prestigious for its innovation and outsized ambitions and high stakes and huge rewards and above all its staggering success in creating wealth, if mainly for the privileged."

"I won't dispute that. But it's your world I'm visiting. I don't pretend to live in it like you do, but I'm glad somebody does. So if you wouldn't mind, I'd love to hear more about the manuscripts."

"It's interesting that there are so few of them. We have evidence that seven or eight others have been lost. It's possible that many more were lost for which we haven't found records, but that seems unlikely. Book Four, which recounts the mythical exploits of Charlemagne driving the Muslims from northern Spain, exists today in about two hundred copies and was translated into many vernaculars, whereas we have no evidence of a single copy of the *Pilgrim Guide* by itself. Just three of the twelve are twelfth century, when the cult was in full swing, and none from France, even though it was definitely written by a Frenchman."

"And Compostela was so popular."

"Third only to Jerusalem and Rome. Yet this so-called *Pilgrim Guide* that today we find revelatory of the entire cult of Saint James was more or less unknown until the mid-twentieth century. No accounts left by French, Italian, or English medieval pilgrims indicate any knowledge of it."

"What do you..."

"I hate speculating. It's just odd. When the original was written at Compostela the cathedral had just been rebuilt on a massive scale, with monumental sculpture and precious metalwork. There would have been large crowds of pilgrims. We know for certain that by that time the pilgrimage had been established for two centuries."

"Do you think when we find out who wrote it, that that might help explain..."

"How nice of you to say 'when.' Possible. I wouldn't count on an incontrovertible attribution, though I believe my research will help us move closer to a reasonable conclusion." Suddenly he looked at his watch.

"Am I keeping you? Sorry, I had no idea what time it is."

"On the contrary, I don't want to keep you. If you..."

"Not at all. I've got time, I'm enjoying this."

"In that case I might mention... Before you leave Saint-Guilhem for your next stage, I don't know if you're aware that you can actually visit it in New York." She looked at him quizzically. "I see you trying so diligently to have an authentic pilgrim experience, I'm thinking you might like to know that part of its thirteenth-century cloister has been erected right here in the city."

"Where?"

"At The Cloisters Museum."

"I never heard of it. I have to go there."

He paused before saying, "I was thinking that, if you're free now, I'm free now..."

"Oh my God, that would be wonderful. Would you really?" They jumped in a taxi and headed uptown and when she saw the medieval recreation on top of a tall hill and inside practically ran from one gallery to the next she kept repeating, "Oh my God, I don't believe this!" while the professor followed and watched. "This is amazing," she told him, "I had no idea."

"Would you like to go to Saint-Guilhem?" From the large central hall he led her into a room that was set up like a cloister with arcades around all four sides surrounding an open courtyard with a large basin at its center a skylight giving the illusion of open air. "The sculpted columns are original. You're in the south of France." He let her wander around the room.

"Thank you," she said returning to him.

"The original cloister was rebuilt in 1206. It had two stories, these are from the upper story," and he led her to several of the columns noting the sculpted treatment of acanthus leaves an artistic motif taken directly from Roman models that at the time would have existed throughout southern France. "You must be tired," he said smiling, "since you walked twenty-four point eight miles to get here."

She smiled back saying, "I don't feel tired because I'm so excited to be here. Or there. I'm really there."

"You can feel it?" She nodded. "If you really were there, you'd be in a reconstruction not unlike this. The difference is that that one is completely rebuilt. And of course it's on the actual site."

"How much of it is original?"

"Not much. You'd have to do the same thing there, use your imagination."

"Oh God, I love this. Thank you so much."

"You're very welcome, my lady."

"Why do you call me that?"

"I'm sorry, I..."

"No. I like it."

They walked around together. "A monastery church would be open to the public for mass and other services, but the cloister was the private domain of the monks."

"So I'm seeing a monastery as the monks would have seen it. Silly question but were there women monks?"

"Not many, not at this time. Later they became more common, including some famous ones like Saint Brigid of Sweden. Who founded a monastery, by the way, after a pilgrimage to Santiago de Compostela."

Again she walked around in silence and returned. "This helped. I'm ready for the wilderness."

"Word of advice?" She nodded. "Pilgrimage is more in the head than the feet. If your head never leaves home, your feet will never take you anywhere else."

"Thank you, that's... You're pretty good at this, you know. I can't believe you've never gone yourself." He shrugged. "Maybe you have in your head. Maybe it's none of my business. Do you come here often?"

To her surprise his face changed. "I haven't been here in ten years. Not since my wife died."

"Oh, gee, I'm so sorry for asking."

"Don't be. How could you know? Besides, it's ten years, I need to be able to at least talk about it." He fell silent but seeing he was preparing to speak she waited. "In your Saint-Guilhem post you made interesting comments on other themes besides beauty. Authenticity, meaning, awe, spirituality. Don't those really come alive here? I discovered this place when I was in college at Columbia and I didn't get here often, but each time I did, something special happened. I brought my wife here when we were dating. May I show you something?" He took her to one of the tapestry rooms and planted her before "The Unicorn in Captivity" where she stared rapt. "This was one of her favorites."

"It's so beautiful—but not just beautiful."

"Exactly my point. Aside from anything else it's an iconographer's dream, because everything in this crowded field of images is symbolic."

"Of?"

"On the superficial level, sex. At a deeper level, procreation. Deeper yet, vitality. Ultimately, I'd say the mystery of life. And celebration of it, enjoyment. The composition could not be more exuberant and yet the overall effect is one of ineffable calm, isn't it? The sweetness of life, the goodness of life, the love that is possible because of life. Do you see how it touches those weighty topics you mentioned?"

"But I was just raising questions, I wasn't claiming to answer them."

"You have sixty-five more stages." She turned to see if he was joking and smiled. "I'd like to tell you why I haven't gone on pilgrimage." He paused she waited. "We talked about it, my wife and I. After all I was writing my dissertation on it. But of course I was busy, and she was busy, and then we had kids, and then she got sick."

"You mentioned a daughter last time," she said after a pause. "How many..."

"Two. Louis is twenty. He's at Penn. The funny thing is... Not funny, something else. As the cancer took hold, she became more... more something. Spiritual I guess. More sensitive to the deeper layers. But by then she was too sick to go."

Tiffany put her hand on his arm and rubbed it gently. "You must have loved her very much." He nodded eyes tearing; all the way home and afterward she wondered at the fact that he had brought her to the museum.

Chapter Ten

DAY TWENTY-FOUR. Agnoletta was stirred by Tuccio's calm declaration when they were hiding from the mercenaries that he would die where he stood to defend Margherita she couldn't get it out of her mind the sight of them together how he said it; but why Margherita and not her when she was younger and prettier and Margherita had barely reacted whereas she was thrilled? Only a day earlier she'd been feeling pity now she was jealous of her who was getting the attention who had a lover whose long days were passing like minutes while she was forced to trudge mile after endless boring aching mile. "Just look at them," she thought, "talk talk talk, oblivious of everyone else, yet don't I minister to her needs, wasn't I the one who pointed out to her what she couldn't see herself, that the handsome young guard was staring at her in that way of men that can have only one meaning?"

"That look is now in her eyes too," she continued, "but what does it amount to, is she going to give herself to him, not likely, not that one," and the more she thought about this the more reasons she found to take her mistress's place, "and why not, what's she got to give?" But how, she wondered, could such a result be brought about and would she really do it? "What do I do, walk up and say, 'My mistress will never give you what you desire, why not take me?' A little pleasure during this ordeal would not be unwelcome, but it won't come from that quarter even if I could find a way to be alone with him, not when he has eyes only for her."

Thinking about it more she acknowledged she wasn't in love with him didn't even really desire him what inflamed her was his passion for Margherita and what a passion it was. "When did a man ever..." she asked herself and realized that it was the very impossibility of having a chance with him that made him seem so attractive and inflamed her jealousy.

As the caravan was watering the animals a young pilgrim approached on horseback with a servant also mounted evidently from the horses' caparisons and the servant's livery a nobleman who as he drew closer hailed everyone most heartily Margherita in particular. "Hail, *donna*, I bid you good day, indeed the best of days, why not, since such wishes cost nothing. A fellow pilgrim I see, or rather sister pilgrim," and without pause he asked if he might water his horses beside theirs to which the count quickly judging his face and manner agreed with equal courtesy. Seeing that everyone was eating the young man asked if he might do the same and graciously offered to share whatever he had, "though be warned it is not much, though sufficient for a pilgrim seeking forgiveness." There was something about him Tuccio liked at once and he invited him to sit beside them and after his servant had set out food and drink for all to share he used the occasion to tell his story.

"Several years ago I went to Padova to study philosophy and lodged in the home of a fellow student who in no time became the closest of friends. After his father died, leaving him an orphan, I persuaded him to marry and went so far as to find him a suitable wife of marvelous beauty and the most noble parentage, and when he was going to meet her he invited me to come along since I had not yet seen her. She sat between us and as assessor of the beauty of my friend's wife, I began with the utmost attention to look her over. I found every part of her to be extremely well qualified and I found myself silently praising each of them in the strongest terms. When we returned to the house I made an excuse to retire to my room to think.

"There I found that the longer I reviewed her qualifications the fiercer became my desire to give her the diploma myself, and this disturbed me greatly. 'Ah, Tito,' I chided myself, 'what misery! Will you let yourself be carried away by love's illusions, by hope's deceptions? Open the eyes of your intellect, give place to reason!' And so I resolved to do what was proper and, feeling much relieved, went to bed.

"No sooner there, however, than the vision of her beauty filled my mind and I found myself discovering excellent reasons to reject my hasty resolution. The laws of love, I reminded myself, are more powerful than any other, supplanting not only those of friendship but even of the divine. Besides, who, having seen her, could honestly reproach me? In fact, I concluded, my dear friend should be overjoyed to learn that his wife would be loved by his best friend and not some stranger.

"In the morning I returned to my senses, but in the course of the day—and the next and the next—my senses came and went many times, until I was forced to take to my bed in a state of exhaustion. Gisippo was naturally concerned, refusing to leave me for a moment, and repeatedly urged me to divulge the reason for my sudden unaccountable infirmity. I put him off as long as I could but finally confessed everything. I reassured him that he need have no fears because death would soon bring me the reward I had earned, but what was my astonishment when he replied, 'Have I not till now shared all my possessions with you?'

"His fit of generosity, however, quickly passed. Well, to make a long story short, we came to blows and would have drawn our daggers had not the commotion we caused quickly landed us in jail. The judge, learning what fast friends we had been till love had intruded, sentenced us to separate pilgrimages, he to Assisi, me to Compostela, so that we might become reconciled."

"So you have been there," said Margherita.

"I am on my way back, prepared to reconcile."

"And she?" asked Tuccio.

"Betrothed to another."

The caravan resumed its journey across land that began to rise ever so gently on both sides until the rises came almost together to form a shallow passage at the end of which lay Asti cradled in an upturned palm of land as if the terrain were subtly nudging Margherita and Tuccio to notice that the open plain was ending.

DAY TWENTY-FIVE. Imperceptibly the land was rising mile by mile its flatness in fact a slight incline until the caravan reached a spot that gave a nearly unobstructed view of the Alps some thirty-five miles away and everyone naturally took the measure of it thinking, "I must climb over that," for it confronted them as a vast impregnable wall in fact it seemed to curve around them jagged craggy soaring insurmountable and Margherita staring at it lost her confidence. As they continued to the next town a monk approached to whom she immediately confessed where she was bound but that now seeing the enormity of the task she was afraid; out of small round eyes he stared at her without expression his face wrinkled beard grizzled until he said that a long pilgrimage and a high mountain were the same in that both might seem impossible yet people found a way. "They are motivated by a superior principle, imposed by an intense desire to succeed by force of will. Do you feel an intense desire? Can you identify the principle that moves your pilgrimage?"

"I don't think I understand," she replied disheartened.

"Did you promise God? No. Do you seek grace then?"

"I don't know," she whispered.

"You must ask yourself why you have struggled to get this far, why you would even contemplate ascending that," and gesturing toward the Alps he departed.

As she continued in silence Tuccio dismounted to walk beside her and later said, "I know you to be determined. Perhaps you resolved to surpass yourself, to do something you would have thought impossible."

For a long time she stared at him before saying, "You have asked to hear about my life and I have said nothing. That's because there is nothing to tell."

"You do not go alone, Margherita. I have pledged to go with you. If it is your wish, we will go together."

"Like every wife I maintain the household, there is nothing to say about that. Unlike many wives, my husband dictates everything I must do. Each morning, each evening, all day long if he is around, he orders me about like a servant, treats me like a servant, scolds me like a servant. In fact a slave, since servants receive a salary. Nothing is left to my discretion or judgment. If anything is missing he is certain it was stolen. Once I lost a ring. I looked everywhere, even had the street swept, went to the pawnbroker in case it had been stolen. Distraught, I sought comfort from him. Instead I got a cold reply about his distress over the loss of a valuable object."

"I am sorry to hear that."

"He told me I vex him mightily whereas the wife of one of his friends has caused no vexation in thirty-fives years."

"Margherita, if I could..." To his surprise she smiled.

"A few years ago I left him. I waited till I knew he would be gone all day, packed my things and went to my mother." She laughed. "Agnoletta can tell you all about it, can't you, Agnoletta?"

"Indeed, *madonna.*"

"He was kinder for a while after that, wasn't he?"

"For a while perhaps."

"Margherita, I can see why you determined to go on pilgrimage. Why you walk. Why so far."

"I do not go to get away from him."

"Whatever the reason, what you're doing is... You see how few women are on the Way. We shall climb the Alps together. I've heard it looks less daunting the closer you get to it."

"Please tell me more about your life. How did you come to serve with the Sarteani?"

"An interesting tale, and I will tell it, since you insist, only because it reflects well on my father, who struggled so hard on my behalf. To find a place for me he was making inquiries wherever he could, traveling hither and yon, leaving early, returning late. Somehow he obtained a letter of introduction to the count of Sarteano, of an ancient family, with much experience in arms, for seventy-five years in defense of Siena. My father went to Assisi to beg for me and on his return we made the day's walk to the castle, he still dressed as a pilgrim, partly for effect, partly because he had no finery, having already borrowed to the hilt to get me outfitted."

"At a ruinous interest rate, no doubt."

"No doubt, though he would never say. The pilgrim robe also eliminated the need to buy horses. We waited in the courtyard for what seemed the longest time, no one offering any refreshment, until at last my father was called. I waited again. I was hungry, but paid no attention. People stared at me, including a boy my age, dressed as I prayed I would be. He stared at me, I stared at him, then he walked on without a word.

"Later, the servant returned for me. My heart leapt. I followed him into a room. Of course I had never seen anything like it, but tried to look as though I had. The count questioned me and I replied as best I could. Then he asked what made me think I was apt for a life of chivalry. 'With respect, my lord, may I say I am poor in means, but not in spirit. If you will but test my prowess, I would gladly show you my aptitude.' This was more or less what my father and I had worked out, except for the word 'prowess.' I was supposed to say 'ability,' but it just came out and everyone smiled—everyone but my father.

"'Prowess, you say?' repeated the count. I bowed my head, afraid to look up. At last he said, 'Why not? A test of prowess it shall be.'

"To get to the point, when at last I stood in the courtyard with a wooden sword, facing the boy I had seen earlier, who attacked me with all the ferocity he had been taught, I stabbed him in the heart. The second time I knocked the sword out of his hand

and the third time I knocked him down. Later I learned he was the count's son. Fortunately I hadn't hurt him. Next was another squire, quite a bit bigger, but it didn't change the result. The count stared at me, then turned to my father. 'Your boy has done well. May we see how much he has learned?' My father of course agreed. 'Can he ride?' The count might not have seen his worried look, but I did. 'He is a nobleman's son, my lord. Of course he can ride.'

"They put me on a mare and handed me a wooden shield and a bludgeon, a stout stick wadded with cloth. I had never sat in a saddle before, only bareback. They placed me at one side of the courtyard and the big squire at the other and at the signal we charged. I came at him from the left instead of the right, which caught him completely unawares and he went down.

"This time when I stood before the count, I could barely stand still. Never before had I felt like this. I felt invincible. My final opponent was a youth, four, five years my senior, old enough to be using real weapons and of course much bigger than me, and they had us fight with sword and dagger. Wooden ones, fortunately. All I remember was seeing his strikes and thrusts and parrying them, one after another, as if everything was happening slowly. I would attack furiously, like a wolf. I couldn't defeat him, but I may have driven him back. We stopped fighting only on command. I wanted to keep going. I was angry, whatever had possessed me earlier still did. I challenged him, but he nodded in courtesy and fortunately I instinctively did the same and then the count called me.

"My father never would tell me how much he gave for my clothes, weapons, and horse. Whatever the amount, it simply added to his debt. Only last year when I started earning money was I able to help him. I pray that damned loan is over now."

FRANCESCO. Every chance he got Lapo Mazzei would ride out of Siena on his old mare to his little hill farm nearby where his mother still lived where he would work in the garden care for the sheep supervise the birthing of the lambs and the farm's modest production of wine and oil enjoying nothing so much as breathing the air of his modest fields not even reading the pious tales of the *Fioretti* of Saint Francis to his children by the fireplace. In the evening he talked to his mother and the conversation usually turned to his life as a notary in the city sometimes his work for Santa Maria della Scala Siena's preeminent hospital and charitable institution more often his work for Francesco di Marco like him of humble beginnings and one day looking distracted his mother asked, "You look tired, are you getting enough sleep?"

"Yes, mother."

"Then what?"

He told her there was a commercial case pending before the ecclesiastical court disturbingly similar to a new undertaking of Francesco's with direct implications for him since he wrote all his contracts and that he had left the city directly after a meeting to discuss it; a quite large undertaking even by Francesco's standards in which he was effectively acting as broker for a large quantity of raw wool originating in England and transiting to Siena to be turned into cloth before further shipment. This complex transaction would involve several parties and take well over a year to complete with numerous technical details to be specified including of course the timing location and amounts of payments as well as the currencies in which they would be made and therein lay the notary's anxiety but Francesco said, "Why do you worry, we have done this before," and when he told him about the court case and noted that the size of his transaction would inevitably attract attention he was no more concerned than usual asking, "You're handling it in the usual way?"

This entailed writing separate contracts for each stage so there was no easy way to directly link purchases with sales thus no way to compare prices thus no way to infer that interest was involved in markups however surreptitiously even unintentionally thus no way to find the transaction usurious. Francesco would purchase goods from a supplier while buyers would purchase goods from him which together created a series of purchases but not sales because the contract stated that he was paying for the goods on behalf of the buyers hence the claim that there was really only one purchase and sale with the buyers merely reimbursing him for his outlay of cash to the supplier.

How then to explain that the amount of reimbursement would be higher than the amount of outlay? In addition to the usual ways in which an otherwise usurious markup could be deemed acceptable such as demonstrable risk of loss was the fact that this series of transactions was conducted in multiple currencies which required rates of exchange rates that were nowhere specified furthermore the raw wool would be improved in various workshops in Siena some belonging to Francesco. Further still the various letters of credit involved could be purchased by third parties which inevitably entailed discounting for perceived risk and while the Church took a dim view of trading in securities it had to recognize the importance of diversifying risk among investors even if that entailed a gain to the seller.

Lapo's problem with all this was that at its heart was credit and credit was without question a form of lending and if the price paid on terms was higher than the cash price which of course was always the case then interest was involved however disguised or hidden and interest was usurious unless an exception applied. In fact credit was at the heart of practically every commercial transaction even small local ones implying that practically all commerce was inherently usurious yet everyone acknowledged that commerce was essential and required lending and profit so the final question was whether Francesco's transaction was legitimate or attempted to dissemble his schemes to profit from unjustifiable markups and of that he wasn't sure. "We must distinguish between what is blameless and what shameful. The doctors of the schools, versed in theology, and the canons of the church, versed in law, have put their minds to it. And they have instructed us notaries who must apply this knowledge to our contracts."

"Then what's the problem?" said his mother. "No one is more capable than you in the law, nor wishes more to walk in the straight path."

"That's the problem, there is no straight path. The path of commerce today could not be more sinuous. Nor is there just one. Wherever one turns, more paths, all twisting constantly, turn here, turn again. We notaries make them turn, to avoid the risk of condemnation. How then is one to distinguish between the twisted path that is proper and one that is not?" It occurred to him that these paths were like the pass routes over the mountains and further that commerce could be likened to a high mountain range which from a distance appeared implacably hostile with no possible means of ascent yet from close up ways were found past every obstacle using tortuous routes that followed the courses of water running downhill sometimes dangerous sometimes easier than one would imagine but always ultimately successful. "What do you think, mother, is my salvation not at risk as much as Francesco's? And how do I know if I am on the right path?"

She touched his cheek and he sighed and sighed again.

"There's something else. Today he tells me he's going to be a father. When my eyes widen he says, 'No, not with her, she is still barren. With a servant.' 'Does she know?' I ask. 'She will,' he replies, 'I need her to raise the child. Pray this one survives.'"

DAY TWENTY-SIX. "Why, walking on this flat plain, do I feel like I am on a high ledge? I do not know why I am here, Tuccio."

"Margherita, please do not fear the Alps."

"Do women walk over the highest mountains?"

"This one does."

"I would not displease you."

"I would not have you walk for my pleasure."

"Twenty-six days, Tuccio, and what do I discover but that I do not know why I go."

"If that is true, perhaps you went to discover why you must go."

"If I feel this way now, how will I feel when I really am on a high ledge?"

"It will seem as nothing compared to the ledge in your mind."

"I wish I could see, Tuccio."

"See what?"

After a long silence she said, "Tell me more about your life."

"Only if that would please you."

"It would."

"Then for your pleasure you shall hear how I decided to become a man of arms. I was six years old."

"Six years old?"

"I went out alone as I often did, probably ran away from my lesson, when I stumbled upon a band of armed men and a line of pack mules."

"A caravan?"

"I was impressed, though they were probably not well furnished. 'Knights!' I said to myself. I'd never seen any before. They were resting in a field and I came forward, I don't remember being scared, and called out, 'Good day, knights!' Some of them startled and others laughed. When I got up close I could see their weapons beside them. I took their boredom for concentration, in my mind they might as well have been knights of the Round Table and I had no doubt each was contemplating the great test of arms he was about to undergo on the field of honor, so I didn't mind that they ignored me. One of them bid me approach. 'Ever swung a sword before?' I shook my head solemnly, staring into his eyes. 'Go ahead, pick it up.' My eyes must have bulged as I turned to the sword, which was about as long as me. 'Be careful though. Don't kill any of us.' I grabbed the hilt with both hands and soon had the thing swinging around my head. Everyone laughed. 'Mercy, Sir Knight,' shouted one, 'please spare us, for the love of God!' Then I was shown how it was done. I ran all the way home and told my father with the last of my breath that I wanted to be a man of arms. Never wavered, not for a moment."

"Is that a true story?"

"Why wouldn't it be?"

"Thank you. I have decided why I shall climb the Alps. 'From here I go up to be no longer blind.'" (*Purgatorio*, Canto 26)

"I don't understand."

"I'm not sure I do either."

At that moment the caravan was surprised by the sounds of horns and the count ordered everyone off the road they were not far from Torino where they would cross the Po and had begun to climb having entered a low pass between mountains that rose fifteen hundred feet an odd formation on an otherwise vast flat plain. Before long heralds came into view followed by a large retinue of knights and ladies in resplendent dress mounted on beautiful palfreys the former with fine armor and weaponry and trailed by squires leading high-spirited caparisoned chargers; they were led by an imperious lord who despite his advanced age sat very straight in the saddle and as he approached one of his heralds cried out, "Make way for Count So-and-so, lord of..." at which the men of the *masnada* doffed their hats and bowed.

"If I may ask, *signore*," Nico called out respectfully to the last of them, "whither and whence?"

"On pilgrimage," was the entire answer from a man who barely turned his head in deliberate discourtesy.

Trailing this parade of finery was a considerable caravan of carts and pack animals servants and porters drivers and grooms even minstrels and other performers and the caravan had to wait till all had passed before resuming its own journey and said Nico, "In different circumstances I should like to have had a further word with that gentleman."

Stoldo shook his head saying, "Our fine horses bear no comparison to those magnificent beasts."

Tuccio chuckled saying to Margherita, "There you have it. I need say no more about my life."

"Nor mine," she replied smiling. "At least now I know what I must do. 'From here I go up to be no longer blind.'"

"I still don't understand." A short while later they reached the Po which they had not seen since Piacenza on the other side of which was Torino formerly a Roman military outpost at this strategic entrance to two of the principal routes across the Alps and Tuccio thought, "She contemplates crossing the river as though it were a wall of fire."

DAY TWENTY-SEVEN.

> "Put down now, put down every fear,
>   turn you this way [to the fire] and come, enter confidently."

(*Purgatorio*, Canto 27)

This was to be a day of rest in anticipation of the more difficult stages ahead though the men had to prepare for scant services and for Tuccio there was an additional task meanwhile Margherita would have visited holy sites but what there were were scattered among the Alpine hills so she met pilgrims at the hostel run by a confraternity whose chapter head had insisted on washing her feet when she'd arrived. He had washed them with care as though his salvation depended on it which in his mind was the case as he was of those who took the virtue of charitable love with the utmost seriousness saying, "Did not Jesus wash the feet of his disciples at the Last Supper? So do I kneel before you. May you be washed clean of sin and purified. There is also Hebrews thirteen two, 'Be not forgetful to entertain strangers, for thereby some have entertained angels unawares.'"

Asked if he washed the feet of every pilgrim at the hostel he sadly replied that while that was his goal it was not always possible and asked why this was so important said, "The feet I wash carry pilgrims to their holy destinations, thus they are themselves holy. By cleaning them I hope that some of that holiness may come upon me. Your feet, for example, shall take you all the way to the distant shore and in a certain way will take me with them. For me who never leaves this place, that is my pilgrimage, and so I am sometimes heard to remark that, through the feet I wash, I have been on countless pilgrimages."

"Could you not go yourself?"

"Pilgrimage is far. This is my place."

The day passed in pleasant conversation and after supper when all the pilgrims were at the hostel musicians were heard in the street and people gravitated to the windows the better to hear; when Agnoletta saw Tuccio standing among them she ran to fetch her mistress shouting, "*Madonna,* you must come to the window at once!" He had hired three musicians who between them played numerous instruments and going from one to another sounded like three times their number; one glance out the window and Margherita's heart leapt.

Near the end of the introductory instrumentals they signaled to him to get ready and despite himself he could not hide his fear positively terrified for once in his life. He had practiced in secret whenever he could ever since the *giullare* had taught him the song (by Jaufré Rudel, troubadour) and after racing through his chores had scouted the city's inns for musicians to hire then they had practiced; fortunately they could easily fit the song to a melody and one of them a quick study had learned most of the lyrics a feat that astounded Tuccio who had memorized them with such difficulty.

"Remember the rhyme scheme," the *giullare* had instructed him, "'ay, onh, ay, onh, is, is, atz.' It repeats the same way in each stanza. There are seven stanzas and each one has seven lines, with a three line closing *tornada.* Don't roll your eyes, it's not that complicated. Every second and fourth line ends with the word '*lonh,*' 'far' or 'far away,' usually '*amor de lonh,*' 'love from afar,' which is what the song is about. Keep this in mind and it will help you remember. Note the theme of each stanza. Give each theme a name you can easily remember, better a string of names that together form a sentence. For example, 'In May/ the Lord/ shelters me/ far away/ to enjoy love/ made by God/ which I desire.' Do you see? First stanza: the month of May, thus the sweet song of birds, the scent of flowers, but this is love from afar so I am sad and these do not please me. Second stanza: The Lord is true, through whom I shall see love from afar. Again I am sad to be so far away, if only she could see me standing before her as a pilgrim with staff and robe. And so on. And the *tornada* is just a variation on the last three lines."

"Please, keep going!"

"All right. Third stanza, very important, 'shelters me:' I will ask her '*per amor Dieu*' to shelter me where I am far away and thus I shall dwell close to her though I am far away. '*Per amor Dieu*' means both 'for love of God' and 'by God's love.' Never forget, *fin'amor* is complete love, spiritual as well as physical. Fourth, 'far away:' When will I see her, we are so far apart, separated by so many passes and roads. Yet we are not separated from each other. It shall be as she pleases. Fifth, 'to enjoy love:' Never again will I enjoy love if I do not enjoy this love from afar. Sixth, it was God who created this love from afar; and seventh, I desire this love from afar, for no other joy pleases me as much, but what I want is kept from me because I was cursed at birth to love but not be loved. Do you see?"

"God help me! And how many songs do you remember?"

"I don't even remember how many songs I remember, but this is how it's done. Sometimes I take the first letters of the names for each stanza to form a word. Remember a single word, I remember the whole song."

Tuccio began to sing at first weakly but the musician who had learned the words joined him and soon enough he was on his way with the voice he had been given and whatever courage he could summon. During the instrumental refrain between the first and second stanzas he was reminded to look up at the window and smile for earlier he had been warned, "Look down and she will think you contemplate Hell; look up at her with beaming joy and she will know you place her among the angels in Heaven." Fortunately it was a relatively simple melody with a slow steady long-short rhythm so by the third stanza he was completely immersed in the song conscious of nothing but the amazing singing poetry-spewing voice coming from his mouth.

"*Madonna*, you are blushing!" said Agnoletta after the third verse; "*Madonna*, you are crying," she said after the fifth; and after it was over she said, "*Madonna*, I have never seen you tremble so."

Stoldo stood down the street astonished while more guards were secretly listening from around the corner meanwhile inside the hostel everyone was crowded around Margherita and Agnoletta would have run to Tuccio when he was done but the chapter head scandalized had locked the door and kept the key.

Chapter Eleven

FRANCESCO. In the Via Banchi di Sotto above the Piazza del Campo where merchants and bankers of the city congregated to discuss commerce Francesco overheard a conversation about an arrangement he found extremely interesting and not long after asked Lapo to draught a contract of sale but the situation became complicated when he was asked what he was selling and he said he was not the seller but the buyer and Lapo asked why the seller's notary didn't draught the contract as was customary. "Because I wish to control the terms of purchase," was the reply.

"And the seller has no objection?"

"The seller has no choice. Without me there is no sale."

"You are the only one interested in purchasing this item."

"I have initiated the purchase."

"Of an item no one else wants or for some reason cannot buy. Perhaps you could explain how this could be."

Francesco explained that after he bought the item in question which was a parcel of land he would agree to sell back the usufruct.

Confused Lapo asked, "What is the purpose of owning land when you don't own its usufruct?" The usufruct would give the seller of the land the right to use or enjoy or keep whatever the land produced even though Francesco would own the land. "I don't see the point of this."

"He will pay me for the usufruct."

"Then why not just keep the usufruct?"

"I prefer to have the payments."

"Payments? Plural?"

"Rental payments. I am not selling the usufruct, I am renting it."

"For more than its worth."

"Of course not."

"Well then, if the rental payments equal the value of the usufruct, again I ask why you don't just keep the usufruct."

"And again I answer because I prefer the cash."

"Which you would have in any case from the usufruct directly. Francesco, I know I have no head for commerce, but until this moment I didn't doubt my ability to reason."

"It's a temporary arrangement."

"Until when?"

"Until the seller repurchases the property."

"And why would he do that?"

"Because he wishes to own it."

"Then why does he sell it?" Lapo strongly suspected something was other than it appeared but didn't know for certain until he learned that after he drafted the contract of sale another notary would draw up the usufruct and a third the repurchase contract each having no knowledge of the others (or so pretending). "Let me ask you this: How does a sale of land immediately followed by a repurchase of its usufruct against rental payments and after an agreed term the repurchase of the land, how does that differ from a mortgage loan?"

"Completely different."

"How so?"

"I am not taking collateral, I am making a bona fide purchase."

"And bona fide re-sale."

"Exactly."

"With rental payments in between."

"Exactly."

"And the parties agree to the contract of repurchase at the same time as the contract of sale?"

"What difference does that make?"

"Simply that the repurchase contract nullifies the sale contract. My friend, we are dealing here in appearances."

"Nonsense."

"Need I point out that the supposed renter never in fact enjoys any use of the property supposedly sold? In that case, what could the payments be for, if not for the use of the purchase money received? And in that case, how could the purchase money in fact be for a purchase? Furthermore, a sale in contemplation of annulment is on its face not a bona fide sale."

"Why not? I can think of any number of reasons why a buyer would need to re-sell a purchase."

"Reasons known and agreed upon at the outset?"

"Who is to say they are known and agreed upon?"

"Please do not ask me to be a party to this." What he found forever inexplicable was what men thought to gain by trying to hide usury from the authorities when they (presumably) knew that from God nothing could be hidden as it was written in Hebrews four thirteen, "all things are naked and opened unto the eyes of Him with whom we have to do."

DAY TWENTY-EIGHT. They were traveling straight up the middle of the Val di Susa which at this stage was more or less flat but felt completely different from the Po valley because mountains rose steeply on both sides and everyone knew that soon enough they would be in front as well but at only fifteen miles the stage was not difficult and with clear visibility and much traffic there was no need for the count to send Tuccio forward so he called him to ride at his side.

He disliked Francesco as much as his men did believed he paid like a miser and was not used to taking orders from a merchant but recognized that were it not for his offer to hire the *masnada* (albeit on the cheap) he would have had a hard time keeping his men profitably (and legally) employed; further he hoped to return to more suitable employment and for this he might need the merchant's recommendation hence his concern when he saw one of his men trying to bed his wife. That Tuccio was the one he found astonishing and would have been amused if he weren't concerned though in fact he was amused for like the rest of the men he couldn't fathom what had possessed the youth why not the lady's maid who was closer in age and probably easier?

"Do you love the lady?"

"I do, *signore*, with all my heart."

"What is your plan?"

"I wish I had one. I would fly to the moon with her if I could."

"There to live in eternal bliss, no doubt." Tuccio said nothing. "You have the madness."

"*Signore?*"

"You have the madness. Anyone can be afflicted with it. It passes. I speak of love."

"Yes, *signore*, I concluded that you were."

"Be warned. Once love's madness takes hold..." But he knew it had already taken hold.

Think not that this be mere metaphor! Are not love and insanity both seen as a kind of possession with common features? "What has come over that one? He (she) is distracted cannot think straight forgets to eat laughs and cries on the slightest provocation feels intense pleasure and pain can't work or sleep..."

"Now that we enter the mountains again I have need of scouts, not just up the Val di Susa but all the way down into Provence and beyond. Is it unreasonable to wonder whether a man stricken with love sickness is dependable?"

"You know I would never fail you, *signore*. I owe everything to you."

"That you would not I do not doubt. That you will not is another matter."

"I will not fail you, *signore*. I give you my word."

"We shall see." They rode in silence until the count said, "I could order you to have nothing further to do with her. I also know I might as well order you to stop breathing. The only remedy is to send the lady off, which is impossible, or send you off, which I cannot bring myself to do. I must hope that the madness soon lifts." He counseled Tuccio to remember who the lady was and who he was and where his duty lay and then added, "Remember, if you fuck her, there will be consequences for everyone." Again he fell silent then said, "Go. Go back to her. Any fool can see she is as crazy for you as you for her. I might as well try to separate one side of my hand from the other." Privately he freely admitted it would not fill him with regret to see Tuccio cuckold the old miser.

Margherita was in a panic never before in her life had she felt the way she did now unsure of her feelings her skin now flushed now pale unable to find a safe place to rest her gaze nor a safe expression to carry on her face; she craved the opportunity to speak with Agnoletta but with so many men around there was no opportunity and though Tuccio rode beside her neither could find anything to say besides banalities to which silence was preferable but silence was misery.

"O soul," I said, "that seems so eager
to speak with me, do so that I may hear you."
(*Purgatorio*, Canto 24)

Down the road came a Franciscan friar on horseback who

being a mendicant was forbidden to ride which of all sights was the most demoralizing to Margherita who had been steeling her resolve to walk over the Alps while fighting the desire to ride. "Friar," she blurted out, "I am shocked and dismayed to see you mounted. Pray tell us how you justify such egregious behavior."

Faced with her anger he wasn't the least embarrassed saying, "Your implication is correct, *madonna*, that *Il Poverello*, our dear saint, may he rest in peace, would never sanction what I do. Yet I consider myself a good adherent to my order. 'How is this possible?' you ask, and I reply, it is possible because times change and we must change with them. I am called here and there over vast distances, vast distances. How could I possibly fulfill my duties at the speed of my wobbly legs? Dante here has twice as many and so much stronger than mine. I have asked God for guidance and he has told me many times in no uncertain terms, 'Fra Falduccio, you must ride so as to fulfill the many tasks I require of you.' If I may ask, where you are bound?" Embarrassed at her own discourtesy and unsure whether to despise the man or thank him she stared tongue-tied but Agnoletta told him and he exclaimed, "May the Lord bless you, ride, *donna,* ride! Mount up at once! To horse, I say! Let me see you astride the beast!"

At this the men (except the count and *fattore*) who had had smirks on their faces all morning laughed heartily for a woman riding was a ribald euphemism for copulation; indeed there was a story everyone had heard about Alexander the Great and Aristotle in which the great general is shirking his responsibilities having taken up with a local girl of breathtaking charms and Aristotle his teacher and the greatest philosopher of all time rebukes him until the girl parades before him in an orchard cavorting flimsily dressed and picking flowers while she sings. Seeing her a thought comes to him namely that he should close his book and he says, "Oh my God, if only that marvel would come closer," and when she does he grabs her.

She pretends to cry out then says, "Oh, is that you, Aristotle?"

"It is, sweet lady. Hush now and for the love of God come inside and appease my desire."

"Master, before I give myself to you, you must grant one wish, because I suddenly have a great desire to ride you like a horse around the orchard. Let your back bear a saddle for that way I will ride more honorably."

The friar who had no idea why people were laughing was

noting that the road ahead would not be easy but when Margherita blushed he knew he had stepped into something so before another word was spoken he exclaimed that he was late and spurred his horse which only caused more laughter until Agnoletta sympathetic toward Margherita's plight and with no affection for her husband who had tried to bed her confronted the men.

Two miles before town they came to an abbey beside the road to serve pilgrims and the count saw Margherita deposited for the night before continuing to the walled town dominated by a castle but when Tuccio learned that that evening there would be a performance of a famous love story he rode back to the monastery.

"I brought horses, since this is not part of the pilgrimage, but if you prefer to walk..."

"What of the count?"

"In the castle for the night."

"And the *fattore*?"

"Do we care? At the inn and unlikely to leave. By the way, I passed a beautiful old church on the way here."

People were heading to the square where the actors would be performing and when Tuccio arrived with the women Stoldo said, "You should have had me go with you," but he shrugged. The entertainment began with some clowning and juggling then with a form of popular farce known to Italians from Bergamo to Napoli for its use of stock characters such as the Venetian merchant the pedantic scholar the clever servant and of course the lovers; and played broadly and mostly improvised the crowd was soon roaring with delight in fact when it ended another was demanded and only afterward did the actors begin 'the tragic history of Abelardo and Eloisa.'

The leader of the troupe stepped in front of the makeshift curtain to tell the essential facts of this true story that two hundred years earlier there lived in Paris the greatest living philosopher whose nickname was Abelard, "renowned not just for the force of his intellect but the eloquence of his speech and the beauty of his person. At least according to him he was. 'I can have any woman I want,' he boasted. Attracted to a certain girl by her strong intellect, he was engaged by her uncle to tutor her privately, but it was not toward her intellect that his body inclined and it was not long before they abandoned the lessons to taste all the pleasures of unrestrained passion. 'There were more kisses than explanations,' he confessed. 'My hands returned more often to her breasts than to the books.' When the girl's middle begins to swell he abducts her and sends her to his family, but when the uncle finds out what his fifteen year old niece has been doing with a thirty-six year old man, he goes almost crazy.

"Abelardo offers to marry the girl, whose name is Eloisa, and her uncle agrees but in the interests of discretion she lives with him and he beats her so Abelardo abducts her again, this time sending her to a nunnery. Enraged, her family gains entrance to his house by bribing a servant and while he is sleeping punishes him with the most cruel and shameful form of vengeance, amputating the part of his body with which he had committed the crime. In the morning, says Abelardo, all of Paris is filled with cries, complaints, lamentations, trembling, and compassion. He runs away to a monastery and Eloisa takes vows. It is this terrible true tale that our little play portrays."

Hardly begun than the audience is roaring with laughter and it is easy to see why! Two actors appeared behind the curtain and could be heard to say:

"Open the book till you see a big section."

"Why it is big, master, yet seems to grow as I observe it."

"Do not fear, young lady. You must learn to seize knowledge and make the most of it. Seize it with both hands, as if to say, 'This shall I put to good use.'"

"Such is my fervent wish, teacher. If only you will instruct me."

"I shall do as you ask, but do not worry if you do not master the lesson right away, for some lessons must be repeated over and over again."

"I shall repeat it as often as you wish."

"Remember, your uncle has urged me to punish you severely if you do not perform your lessons satisfactorily."

"How am I doing so far, master?"

"Excellent. You certainly have a firm grasp of this subject." And so on.

DAY TWENTY-NINE. When before setting out Margherita casually gave orders for horses to be saddled no one was foolish enough to say anything for this was a challenging stage twenty-one miles following a river uphill but with unimaginably spectacular scenery whose majestic beauty caused her mind to swoon her heart to swell. Stirred by grandeur too amazing to believe too overwhelming to contain one stirring merged with the other and

Tuccio was equally stirred.

> Such soaring peaks beyond all measure
> Who wouldn't yearn to share such pleasure?

After returning from town the previous evening Agnoletta had said, "He excites you, and why not? Your husband is an old man, he has never satisfied you and you have never loved him. Did it not excite you to feel Tuccio's arms go around you? I doubt your husband ever looked at you the way he does. He is bursting with youth's vigor, says he dreams of you every night, anyone can see he's in love with you, it's only natural to feel as you do. And this 'fine love' of which you two speak, it sounds almost holy. Has anyone else ever approached you this way? As for him, you are his first, I would wager on it. Not the first in bed, but the first in love. You are free for the first time in your life, naturally you are susceptible to new experiences."

> Free, upright and sound is your will
> and mistake would be not to follow its judgment.

(*Purgatorio*, Canto 27)

Three monks suddenly emerged from the steep mountain beside the road surprising everyone before they explained that they had descended from an imposing three hundred fifty year old monastery perched on the very pinnacle of the mountain two thousand feet above them and everyone looked up but nothing of it could be seen. When they urged Margherita to make the climb assuring her her pilgrimage would not otherwise be complete and she courteously declined one abruptly asked, "What is the purpose of your pilgrimage?" and she stared.

"Your manners," said Tuccio, "I find them wanting."

"You must have a purpose," they said ignoring him.

"No doubt she does," he said pushing his horse another step closer. "How is that your concern?"

They were young not much older than him. "True pilgrimage," said one, "requires the utmost seriousness," and the others nodded energetically. "You must suffer."

"You must cry," said the second.

"You must reflect," said the third.

"What she does is her own affair. It is time for you to resume your journey."

"We stray and fail. You go to learn what is right and gain strength."

"We do not live simply. You go to leave behind the

inessential."

"We never look into ourselves. You go in order to inspect."

"Be gone. Now."

"You go to be on the right path."

"You go to find courage."

"You go to learn patience."

"Be gone I say."

"You go to help and be helped."

"You go to be simple."

"You go to become equal to others and yourself."

Tuccio nudged his horse against them and they ran away with a blessing on Margherita's pilgrimage and an hour and a half later she was importuned to climb another mountain whose summit contained a world-famous monastery.

The road was dotted with hamlets and churches with castles and fortified towers on overlooking hilltops and monasteries out of sight on summits but no towns until they came to Susa a city already ancient when Julius Caesar conquered it on his way over the Alps to Gaul; at the approach was a triumphal arch built a few decades after his campaign and fully intact the first complete Roman structure they had encountered. They passed through glancing at the bas reliefs then a short distance farther passing beneath what remained of an aqueduct that had once served the nearby half-ruined amphitheater they crossed a narrow river to the walled city where they were scrutinized by a large contingent of heavily armed guards before being gestured through the arch of a massively tall but crudely built medieval gate.

Margherita and Tuccio visited the twelfth-century *duomo* but found to their surprise that they were conspicuously followed by the *fattore* who when it came time for her to go to the convent abruptly dismissed him and insisted on walking her there himself causing Tuccio to think:

> Julius Caesar conquered the lordship
> by his effort of all the world completely...
> Since one single man without fortress and without tower
> conquered the world and held it in his control,
> thus well should I, according to the best opinion,
> of your love by right be emperor...

(Arnaut de Maruelh, troubadour)

As soon as Tuccio was out of sight the *fattore* turned on her to say he had been slow to approach her on a certain subject because of its delicacy that denying the evidence of his eyes he had refused to believe his partner's wife was flirting shamelessly with one of the guards and a youth at that; but eventually as their behavior became more brazen it was apparent to all that an embarrassment had developed and unfortunately it fell to him as her chaperone to take action. He insisted he would not be speaking were he not compelled but as it was he had no choice but to inform her that her husband had engaged him as part of their financial arrangement to be her chaperone.

"Are you saying he is paying you to..."

"I tried to refuse, but he insisted."

He was angry at her for having created such an awkward situation and at her husband for having taken advantage of his weaker position to force this role on him for while he had grudging respect for the man's success and wealth they were not friends much less family simply partners because each had what the other needed. The cost of the goods strapped each day on the mules was enormous and the expenses of travel were considerable if all went well there was much money to be made but the risks were huge; "and now," he griped, "the man's wife, in front of everyone, decides to take up with one of the hired men," a situation he knew he must stop because he would be held responsible and it would end his partnership.

Livid Margherita noted that besides her maid Tuccio was the only one willing to converse with her.

"We are not talking about conversation."

"You are not my lord, you're not even one of my husband's principal partners. I owe you nothing beyond good manners, not even that, if your own don't merit it."

He bit his tongue then changing his tone said, "I beg you to consider the difficult situation in which your husband—for whom I have the highest respect, let me say, as I do for you—in which your husband has placed us. 'A merchant caravan is no place for a woman,' I told him, but he was concerned for your safety."

Later he weighed his options thinking, "I could demand that the youth be dismissed, but that would worsen the temper of the men; and once gone what prevents the woman from taking up with another? Personally I don't see the attraction. Why aren't his desires directed at the maid? But if that's how it is, then that's how it is, as the saying goes, 'Nature does what nature is.' When a man wants a woman he'll do everything in his power to possess her as everyone knows, and when that happens what chance does a woman have, fickle by nature and weaker in will, against the flattery and cajoling and so on?" and the more he thought the angrier he got and that started him to wonder whether there might be a way in which his knowledge of her infidelity could be of value.

FRANCESCO. Not being one for quiet or solitude which only tended to make him anxious it helped Francesco think to watch men work especially on construction sites so when he had occasion to visit Lapo at his office in the hospital he preferred to step outside into the busy piazza where expansion work on the *duomo* (which if ever completed would make it the largest cathedral in Europe) had been continuing for years. Lapo usually tried to coax him into the *duomo* where a quiet corner could be found but on this day Francesco seemed especially needful to stride around the square until he had fully vented his dissatisfaction with a mason he'd hired when Lapo raised a subject he'd raised before but without success which was to encourage Francesco to slow his frenetic pace and enjoy life more.

"Forgive me, my friend, but it is that very friendship which compels me to speak to you once again about this. Whether it is seemly for you to be so driven to accumulate ever more wealth is for you to decide, though eventually it will be decided by a higher power, but for the sake not just of your soul but your health I must urge you to take more pleasure in your good fortune. Must I remind you that the wealth you have acquired is merely a loan that must eventually be repaid to its divine source?"

Unusually Francesco listened making no attempt to rebut the argument or turn it to his advantage rather he put off the notary by promising to consider his advice which saddened more than upset Lapo knowing that (hopefully) Francesco still had time to make testamentary plans for his estate and as for how he lived that was his choice. Oddly Francesco who sincerely respected Lapo's piety and found in him the closest he had to a son agreed on both points that he had time and that it was his life but came to the opposite conclusion Lapo's that therefore action should be taken his that it need not for if he was not living his life as he wished it was certainly the only way he knew.

DAY THIRTY. They had left the Val di Susa but the river they'd been following since the Po yet flowed beside them steeply downhill as they ascended the grueling incline they would endure for three days and where it was especially steep they had to dismount a fact Margherita found bitterly ironic. She would have said so if Tuccio and she hadn't quarreled over what had happened the previous evening and if he weren't ahead scouting and fuming at what he deemed her refusal to see the simple fact that the *fattore* had no authority to interfere; for her it was complicated because she acknowledged that he was right on the facts and whether he possessed the authority might or might not be beside the point which was this: Now that her behavior had been placed before her in stark terms how should she respond? At first she'd been enraged at him for having dared to talk to her as he had but later was overcome with embarrassment confusion and guilt and lying awake in bed couldn't dispel the concern that he was right and thought, "What madness and folly is love!"

That *fin'amor* had sounded lofty, full of wonder;

And how *giullare*'d spoken, sung, oh how he'd sung!

Convinced was she. The dream to which she'd joyous clung

Now seemed illusion; what was whole now torn asunder.

She swore she would not ride again but quickly learned she couldn't keep up without exhausting herself so when the caravan stopped to rest and eat by a village she slipped away unseen to find a little rustic church but it was empty so she wandered through the narrow lanes asking for the priest whom eventually she found at his lunch which he reluctantly left to hear her confession at the altar. Fearful she withheld nothing surprising even herself while he was barely able to believe a tale about a woman pilgrim alone who is no sooner on holy mission than she publicly cavorts with a caravan guard what's more a youth half her age; as she confessed he was reeling fighting to maintain a serene expression in case she should look up while asking himself, "What penance do I impose on a woman who claims to be alone and a month into a pilgrimage of over three thousand miles, having walked, walked, if she is to be believed, all the way from Siena?"

Finding it shockingly lenient she urged him to deal with her as she deserved so he quickly doubled everything issued a stern warning about staying on the straight and narrow path and led her to the door where she thanked him profusely and wandered half dazed around the hamlet till Tuccio suddenly grabbed her arm saying, "Where the devil have you been!" Roughly she tore her arm loose. "Where have you been?" he repeated more gently but still distraught.

"What is it to you?" she hissed.

"But it is...!" he began to scream but caught himself. "But it is everything to me."

She looked at him shook her head said, "It should not be. It must not be."

"Never. Never. Where did you go? As my master's lady whom I am duty bound to protect I ask you... Margherita."

"To church, that is all."

"Please... Do what you will, feel what you will, cut out my heart and stamp it into the mud, but please do not frighten me like that again."

"You, frightened?" she said with the hint of a smile.

"Only of you," he said his voice breaking. "Please."

They walked in silence back to the caravan where she asked the count if he was aware that they were now in French lands saying this was what the priest had told her though as far as she could tell the village seemed as Italian as the others. In the afternoon the stage was less strenuous though it did involve crossing the boulder-strewn river which for the animals was always risky though fortunately the water flow was less agitated due to a leveling of the grade immediately upstream; meanwhile Margherita allowed Tuccio to ride near her if not quite beside her both less distraught though still alone with their most private thoughts in which Tuccio imagined deeds of great valor to win her heart...

> Many [a] fine tourney have I decided
> with blows I land so deadly
> that no place I go does man not shout,
> "This is Sir Peire Vidal,
> the one who upholds gallant love and love-making
> and acts with prowess for love of his lady friend."

(Peire Vidal, troubadour)

...but he could not banish despondency.

> Fallen I am in bad grace
> and have well and good done like the fool on [the] bridge
> and do not know why this is happening to me
> unless it's because I climbed too high against [the]

mountain.

(Bernart de Ventadorn, troubadour)

For the rest of the stage he followed her blind to the wonder of the forests deaf to the enchantment of the cuckoos seeing nothing but her back hearing nothing but the clop-clop of her horse while

Margherita's most private thoughts concerned the look on his face when he'd found her in the village.

Two riders appeared a man and woman obviously a married couple he about forty of robust build she slender no more than eighteen a most handsome couple even in their pilgrim robes whose accoutrements fine horses and stately style showed them to be high nobility as did servants squires and knights following also splendidly dressed and mounted; as they approached formal greetings were exchanged but nothing further and to the shock of some they passed in silence and disappeared around the turn with their proud satisfied looks.

The caravan continued to a large fortress containing a hamlet strategically located along a relatively level stretch of the route whose function seemed to be to regulate traffic through the pass and there was a pilgrim hostel operated by monks with an adjacent church whose bell was ringing as they approached; all but two were relieved that the stage hadn't been as difficult as expected the remaining two incapable of relief.

> It was now the hour...
> that the new pilgrim with love
> pricks, if he hears [a] little bell far off
> that seems the day to mourn that is dying.

(*Purgatorio*, Canto 8)

The *fattore* negotiated with the officials at the gate shocked not that he had to pay customs but at the amount assessed yet pleasantly surprised that everyone was allowed inside having half expected to spend the night in the wild; meanwhile Margherita and Tuccio waited in silence not even looking at each other until just inside the gate she entered the hostel without a word or glance while he pretended to be distracted.

Chapter Twelve

Her enthusiasm rekindled by the visit to the Saint-Guilhem cloister in the museum which encouraged her to exercise her imagination to the utmost she set out the following Saturday into the wilderness except she was actually walking the homogenized streets of Livingston which could have been any suburban town in America but she clung to the idea that each building was a rock formation each intersection a new vista as her mountain path came around a bend or over a summit. When she reached the end of the stage fourteen point nine miles later and started her car she found that the greater challenge was not to imagine she was somewhere she wasn't but to bring home more of the experience than soreness in the shoulders from the backpack. Trying to discover what she had learned or felt she reminded herself that a pilgrimage was not a transaction though many hoped it was nor a mechanical transmission from sore feet to yearning heart or questing mind though many hoped it was and so she advised herself to take home that faint glimmer of insight she thought she might have seen and see if it grew brighter see if she could blow on it gently to fan the flame.

She tried to express it to the professor in an email but found she couldn't and as the week slowly moved through one distraction after another despaired of retaining whatever there might have been and was thus impatient for the weekend when she hoped in person and with his help she might recover it; but when she was at last sitting across from him she realized she couldn't put the glimmer into words because it was not a thought but a feeling even the feeling of a feeling.

"It sounds like you're on your way," he commented.

"I hope so. It's a lot of effort, you want it to be for something."

"Uh-uh. Transaction."

"You're right, thank you. I could never do this by myself."

"That's one reason few pilgrims ever walked alone, at least that's a likely assumption. Being alone is a modern feature. Have you thought of asking a friend to join you?"

She said she would give that some thought though no one came to mind. "Frankly, I'm not hiding my pilgrimage but I'm not trumpeting it either. Especially since I'm so confused about what I'm doing."

Of course he didn't know her friends, he said, but as to the uncertainty regarding her motives he took that as a promising sign that her quest was sincere. "Not that there's anything necessarily suspect in knowing one's motives. The pilgrim who walks in hope of forgiveness, for example, or to gain clarity. But the one who intrigues me the most is the one who doesn't know why they go, only that they must go."

"I think you'd be wise not to make too much of my doubts."

"I wasn't referring to you necessarily. Think about the hardships of the medieval pilgrimage and imagine those who endure it for reasons they know not. I recognize that your journey, being virtual, could end any time. As you said, you turn the key in the ignition and your quest vaporizes like exhaust. Which makes the journey that much harder, no?"

"I hadn't thought of it that way."

"You tend to be hard on yourself."

"Not really. I'm just competitive."

"Good for you, I say. That's why you're where you are and I'm where I am."

"You're a tenured professor at Yale."

"I also devote my academic career to paddling the backwater of a backwater."

"I admire your devotion to an obscure field. I find it admirable."

"No you don't."

"Must I remind you that you are the first grantee of the Foundation for Pilgrim Studies?"

They stared at each other and he eventually nodded. "You see, we can all use a little boost now and then. Thank you for that, my lady. Mine, alas, is a stodgy world but one that interests me greatly."

"It's a wonderful world. The more I learn about the Middle Ages..."

"Yes, but you see I exist professionally in a narrow academic field in which all the players are known and whose positions are fixed, we argue incessantly at conferences and write papers attacking each other's positions. The books we publish are read only by each other."

"Have you ever thought of writing a book for a general audience? Ride the wave of enthusiasm for pilgrimage? You don't see it as a fad, do you?"

"I think there's a good chance it isn't."

"That it's not a fad, right? Did I get your grammatical locution right?"

"You did. Being the bright student that you are. I do wish—"

"I took your seminar, I know." He smiled again and she said, "It could be a marvelous book."

"Even with my grammatical locutions?"

"That's what editors are for."

"You're very good for me, you know."

They talked half seriously about what his book might be and ended joking about hosting a popular television documentary with him walking to Compostela touring the cathedral and displaying the priceless *Codex Calixtinus* and that reminded him to tell her that more facsimiles had arrived so he had plenty to keep him busy; in reply she asked if he considered himself spiritual.

"I don't think so. I wouldn't describe myself that way."

"I wouldn't either. Myself, I mean. And yet you devote your life to pilgrimage. You were going to go on one."

"True enough. But I also study saints and monks and I can assure you I am not the former and have no interest in becoming the latter."

"Do you think we might be spiritual without knowing it?"

"I would say rather that we're curious about religious experience. Who knows what you might discover about yourself? It does seem a bit at odds with your line of work. Still, who can say? As for me, at the risk of making you think less of me, I fear I am not very interesting. I'm a stodgy old professor—"

"You're not old."

"I'm waiting to hear about 'stodgy.'"

"You're not stodgy either," she said smiling. "It's amazing the stuff you get into. Just being able to decipher those manuscripts is amazing. It's this whole disappeared world you get into. Like a cave with marvelous formations that very few people get to see, or even have any idea about."

"Feel free to continue."

"I think I'm done for now. I'm just wondering... You read about people having awakenings."

"Entirely possible. Something like that happened to my wife, after she became sick. We don't understand as much as we like to think. We appreciate even less. You might surprise yourself, you've already surprised me."

"Meaning?" He looked like he was going to speak but in the end only shrugged and they each looked away. "So if I understand you," she said later, "I can hope for an awakening but there's no way to encourage it."

"On the contrary, there's an entire apparatus at your service. It's not guaranteed to work but its purpose is to facilitate such experience, it's called religion." She made a face. "But of course we're not religious, we're just possibly spiritual."

"You don't see a difference?"

"I do, but... Have you ever been to a medieval church?" When she said the short answer was no he said he must have visited hundreds and while never once feeling the urge to pray had found them marvelous environments for reflection. He said he wasn't suggesting prayer or confession or hearing mass or taking communion or even lighting a candle but he said, "Just to be in a really beautiful church, especially if there's music..." When she said she wasn't aware of any medieval churches in New York he said that in fact there were several if one were willing to accept a facsimile. "Ever been to one?" She shook her head. "These are the big Gothic cathedrals everyone knows, whereas I personally prefer the smaller, less gaudy Romanesque variety that is typical of southern France. Still, it's the next best thing to being there. You did express a desire to get more into the spirit of pilgrimage. I seem to recall you even expressed some..."

"You're right, I asked you here and it was very kind of you to come into the city again so soon and I should take your advice."

"Just a suggestion."

"Your museum suggestion was perfect." She said she would do it and sheepishly asked if he would accompany her. "As my tour guide. If you wouldn't mind."

"I wouldn't mind."

In the taxi he said he recognized her commitment to walking but noted how difficult it would be in New Jersey suburbs to imagine oneself on a pilgrim route in the south of France much less in the wilderness and that's why he suggested Saint Patrick's Cathedral but warned that as a modern recreation it wouldn't bear close scrutiny rather it was the ensemble itself he found most impressive. When they arrived he followed her in silence as he had at the museum and watched as she gazed at first the facade then the vast interior which was richer in materials and more redolent of an original than she'd expected. "Thank you again," she whispered in his ear and after walking around the vast nave led him into a pew where they sat in continuing silent observation she looking at the cathedral he discreetly looking at her and when he heard her sigh he took her hand that had been resting near his.

After a while she rose again to walk around but whenever she stopped he stood close and when their hands brushed he again took hers and they continued hand in hand until she led him back to a pew where he took her waiting hand again as they each pretended to look at the church and she said, "What are we doing?"

"I'm holding your hand. What are you doing?"

"I don't know what I'm doing."

"We can stop."

"That's just it, I don't want to. Did you come here with your wife too?"

"Yes."

"After she got sick?"

"Yes."

"Why am I doing this?"

"You're a pilgrim, you're searching."

"For this?"

"I don't know. What is this?"

"Did you hold hands with your wife too?"

"Here? I don't remember."

"How did you meet?"

"At a party. No great story. How did you meet Bob?"

"We were at Wharton together. May I ask how old your wife was when she passed?"

"She was thirty-nine when she died. Morgan was six, Louis was ten."

"How old were you?"

"I'm fifty, does that bother you?"

"I've never done this before. I mean it, I never have."

"Neither did I."

They gently retracted their hands and sat in comfortable silence. "You're right, it's very restful here."

"There's also the Church of Saint John the Divine, which is near my old haunts. Also Riverside Church, another Gothic recreation. They're pretty convincing."

"What do you think about in church?"

"You mean me?" She nodded. "I don't know, whatever's on my mind. I think I like it best when I don't think about anything."

"That's what I'd like to do right now."

"Go ahead."

"You're not pressed for time?"

"I'm quite content to sit here beside you, my lady."

"I don't know what to call you."

"You could call me 'Mark.' People do, you know."

"How many women do you call 'my lady?'"

"Just you."

"What about your wife?"

"I called her Jessie or Jess."

"What did she do?"

"She was a nurse."

"I like that. She took care of people."

"She had a way with people. She was a good mother, too."

"I try to be a good mother. I think I'm a good mother. Would you hold my hand again?" After he gently squeezed it she asked if he knew this was going to happen.

"I don't know what's happening."

"I don't either."

"Does it frighten you?"

"Frighten? I don't know what I feel, but frightened isn't it."

"I'm glad. You're a remarkable woman."

"You think so? Bob's humoring me. He thinks I'll drop this whole pilgrimage thing soon enough. Who knows, maybe I will. I tend to get enthusiastic, you see. I know myself that much. I discover something and then I jump in with both feet and sooner or later I'm on to something else. I went through a whole pasta thing once. All you hear about is northern Italian, northern Italian, I discovered southern Italian. Simple recipes, really delicious. I have a confession to make. During my last stage I thought about you. About how attracted I was to you at the museum."

"Then I have a confession to make too."

"You were?"

"I could have kissed you." Later he said, "Maybe pilgrimage will mean more to you than pasta."

She said she'd just had the idea to play music while walking to distract her from her surroundings and he agreed that would be a good thing to try noted that concerts were held at these churches asked her what kind of music she liked and when she confessed she didn't listen to much classical music asked whether she was familiar with the great church music of the Renaissance. She said maybe virtual pilgrimage wasn't a good idea after all and that if she was serious she would find a way to really walk even if only the last sixty miles which in fact had been her original idea but Bob hadn't been interested and while she couldn't blame him especially since the idea had come as a complete surprise perhaps she should have pursued it on her own; then she asked how he had gotten into pilgrim studies and he said, "When I was in grad school, there was no such thing. I saw a chance to open up a new field."

"What was your dissertation on?"

Its subject, he said, was the role of a certain monastic order in promoting the Spanish pilgrim route to Compostela in the late eleventh century and explained that a prominent monastic order centered in Burgundy France in a place called Cluny had become interested in Compostela and influential in its promotion for example having it declared a bishopric and had acquired or gained influence over a number of monasteries in northern Spain some of which were along the route which became known as the French Way or Camino Francés. Asked why he picked that subject he said that the Cluny order did much to establish and promote the route using abbeys and various types of hostels to serve pilgrims and the two abbeys he studied were active in that regard as well as being important in their own right and also had the advantage of still existing.

"So you went to Spain."

"More than once. And elsewhere to find pertinent material." The problem, he said, was not just that information was scarce but that research materials were scattered besides being fragmentary and far too often obscure or subject to interpretation; and then he faced the larger issue of trying to remain within the limits of what was accepted as the academic practice of history as opposed to sociology or religion or literature and art criticism. "Sometimes I had to defend my methods more than my findings."

"What did you find?"

"I was able to show how the monasteries actively promoted the pilgrimage, but in the near absence of data, numbers of pilgrims for instance, each fact must be carefully added to the building of knowledge. Perforce there has to be much speculation, which I find particularly unfortunate when so much of it is passed off by certain of my colleagues as if it were established truth."

"Did you ever think of giving up? Picking a different field?"

"I'll tell you why I didn't, because it was exciting. I wasn't studying an abstraction called history, I was studying people and their activity, with all the complexity and ambiguity and contradiction and change. It's marvelous work, but don't expect much reward beyond the joy of discovery."

"Wow, thank you, I really want to do this."

"You keep thanking me, but it's I who should be thanking you."

"My role is easy, you're the one doing all the tedious work."

"May I ask if Bob is a problem?"

"Oh no, no problem at all. I'm free to do anything I want, I could go to Spain."

"I guess I'd like to know more about your marriage."

"There's nothing much to tell, really. It's pretty conventional, no particular problems. If you're thinking that's why I'm hooked on pilgrimage, that's not it." After a silence she raised their hands which were still intertwined and said as far as she could determine her marriage had nothing to do with that either. "Really, I'm pretty happy. I guess this is the moment when I ask if you do this kind of thing often."

"I've never done this."

"I mean since your wife..."

"I've never done this. Not during, not after. I hope you can tell I wouldn't lie to you."

"So this is us being attracted to each other."

"This is me being attracted to you. What it is for you... Possible it's just infatuation with pilgrimage? The exotic allure of the Middle Ages? If that's what it is, maybe I should remind you I'm just a stodgy old professor."

"What if it's more than that?"

"Can you live with that? More to the point, can your marriage tolerate it?" When she shrugged he asked if he could make a suggestion. "I'm going to let go of your hand now so we can spend the little time we have left today talking about your next stage or your blog. Or my research, which you haven't asked about today. Which you should, since you're my employer."

Instead she suggested they walk around the cathedral again and maybe he would talk to her about why he thought people went on pilgrimage in the Middle Ages given all the hardships and even dangers and he said, "Saint Patrick's is right in the middle of the city and yet the moment one enters, one enters another world. You don't need this church to enter that world, but notice how much easier it makes it. And that's true whether or not you consider yourself religious or adhere to the church's particular faith. Why is that?

"Now, in some ways pilgrimage is like that. You break with your normal life and take to the road. No longer in familiar surroundings, among strangers... A different world. Now it's fair to assume the vast majority of pilgrims didn't do that. Most pilgrimages were local and lasted a day or week and were often mass social occasions, with the trappings of devotion but the feeling of a party. But the latter is not necessarily antithetical to the former, in fact it can facilitate it. It also introduces us to other aspects of pilgrimage which were also important. The first was simply the desire to get away, to take a vacation. Vacation: to vacate, leave where you are to go somewhere else. See something else, do something else, try to feel something else. Why do we want to do that? Any and every possible reason. Often we say we need to 'recharge our batteries.' What does that mean? Rededicate ourselves? Recover our vigor, our sense of purpose? Release tension, clear our head? Pilgrimage as vacation. Pilgrim destinations as holiday resorts.

"Consider your own pilgrimage. You're here on a Saturday, a million other things you could be doing with your free time, but all of them tend to keep you inside your world, inside your head. This is another world, isn't it? And something is on offer here unavailable in any shopping center or website. And you meet people you would never meet otherwise. Because their occupation is different, their social class is different, their gender is different, or they come from another land. Not long ago you and I were not only total strangers, but inhabited different worlds, even antithetical worlds, yet here we are. And yes, people seek on pilgrimage what they always but pilgrimage facilitates it. Affection, friendship, love... and frankly, for some, sexual adventure. I'm not implying anything about you and me, I'm not that foolish. But from total strangers we have become friends in a short time, and pilgrimage brought us together. It's not just a common interest. It bypasses a lot of distraction. It's a way to become close."

He handed her a handkerchief and she giggled. "Believe me, I have no idea whatsoever why I'm crying."

He shrugged. "Tension. We all have it. I once had a massage and started sobbing, out of the blue. Jessie said it wasn't uncommon. 'We store emotions in the muscles,' she said. It's too bad they haven't played any music, these places are amazing with music. I think I mentioned, they have concerts sometimes."

"Yes," she said, "I'd like to. That would be nice."

The moment they stepped outside they were of course confronted with a big city's clutter and clatter and she said, "You're right, it's amazing how jarring it is."

"And that's your challenge, you see. You're walking out here, but you want to be walking in there. That was much easier in the Middle Ages."

"I think music will help."

"Suggestion? Don't resist your environment. Embrace it, see what happens. Because the paradox is that, while they're different worlds, they're obviously the same world."

She asked if he had time to walk a little and they strolled up Fifth Avenue in silence gazing here and there at shops and people until the time came to part and after shaking hands awkwardly she hailed a cab and got in and drove away and he watched it stop farther up the block and saw her get out and when she reached him she put her arms around him and turned her face up toward his. When she got home Bob asked how her meeting had gone but before she had a chance to answer Kiley came running up shouting "Mommy!" and threw herself at her whereupon she began a recital of everything she'd done that day while Tiffany listened and went to see the drawings she'd made and looked inside her dollhouse to see something she didn't quite understand and put on her favorite music so she could be a ballerina and dance around the living room. By this time Bob had disappeared and she started making Kiley's supper and then sat with her while she ate and afterwards took her upstairs to start the long bedtime process so it wasn't till later when they were eating Thai take-out that she got the chance to ask him if he'd had a rough day.

He shook his head saying, "Kiley kept me pretty well distracted. And then, while I was sitting with her, I got an idea that just might turn things around."

"Turn things around?"

"At least stabilize things, our funds I mean. We're so far down, we're a screaming bargain to anyone with half a brain. My God, if I had ten million about now, I know what I'd do with it. If we put in ten mil, in a few months, once this indigestion works itself through the market, we could be at fifty, in a year at a hundred. A thousand percent in a year! How often do you see that kind of return?" He said he'd been asking himself all day why lower prices weren't bringing in buyers until finally he'd realized that what he had to do was persuade her to convince her boss to make a substantial investment. "It wouldn't take much, we don't even need a billion. It's all psychology, everyone's sitting on their cash. But if I can make a few calls to let some folks know a new investor has just come in with, say, a hundred... Which you could do easily, right? I know I could talk them into staying pat at least, and I bet I could even get them to move some of their cash back in. Then I just keep working my list. 'Guess who just got back in? Sure you want to stay out?'"

She tried to tell him there was no way she could recommend that to her boss and even if she did he'd never act on it. "You think he doesn't know I'm married to a player? He'd laugh me out the door."

"Laugh you out the door?"

"Or he'd hit me with, 'Look, we all sympathize with Bob, but he knew the risks.'"

"What risks? That's my point, this is a no-brainer. We're a screaming bargain."

"I don't know, Bob."

"You're worried he'll put you down. But what if instead you make him a hero? I'm not saying prices have bottomed yet, but we have to be close, right? In a month he could look like a genius. Come on, Tiff."

Of course he knew full well that lower prices were attractive only if potential investors didn't fear they would go lower and he had to know that no amount of hopeful talk about prices having hit bottom let alone cajoling was going to change that. The fact was that it had become known for the first time that many firms had large exposure to the very securities that were becoming hard to sell and this made potential investors reticent which made the market less liquid which made them even harder to sell and the harder they were to sell the harder they were to value and since valuation was the primary concern hanging over the market this made the situation even worse. Of course the firms might not have had to sell if the valuation concern hadn't led to calls for more collateral but even this might not have been so destabilizing had the loans not been so short-term; as it was huge amounts of cash had to be raised quickly very quickly with the predictable effect on prices and psychology both; worse when Bob's investors saw the funds selling they wanted to sell too to get out of the funds and that required raising more cash which meant even more selling with each sale depressing prices more.

Tiffany was not just sympathetic she agreed that the problem had been artificially created with an ill-conceived rule change by the accounting board and while she didn't agree with everything he said she had no doubt that on balance he was far more right than wrong. "If the market's saying that MBS risk is higher than previously thought, that's no big deal, that's how markets work," she told herself; risk didn't bother her since she worked with high-risk investments every day especially since here the risk was fundamentally low even if investors had magnified it with leverage and consequently she had no doubt the market would correct itself a view that was entirely consistent with what the regulators thought. Officials of the Securities and Exchange Commission had recently concluded that the exposure of the investment banks to subprime mortgages would not have a significant impact on their financial performance while the chairman of the Federal Reserve Bank had testified in Congress that the impact of the problems 'seems likely to be contained' and the Secretary of the Treasury testified the same day in almost the same words.

Nonetheless as information had become available from required company reports journalists had been writing about the situation which naturally had created anxiety among investors who vacillated between wanting to sell before prices fell further and holding till prices improved and the more they vacillated the fewer trades occurred which made setting prices that much more difficult which was why Bob described the journalists as hungry sharks smelling blood as he railed against them during dinner. "And for icing on the cake, the credit agencies have chosen this moment to downgrade securities." He apologized for having lost his temper during the week to which she replied that since the market was fundamentally sound she was confident it would recover as soon as investors adjusted to the new disclosures and reminded him that he was a survivor and would get through this, that she was not worried and he shouldn't be either.

"You know me, Tiff. It's just so frigging frustrating, that's all. To have these jokers who don't know what they're doing get in the middle of something..."

"I know. Don't start again, okay? I don't want you having a heart attack over this." She knew however that he couldn't really calm himself because despite his best efforts and that of the others in his group who'd been working frantically for weeks both hedge funds had collapsed to a small fraction of their recent value especially his more leveraged one whose value had shrunk to almost nothing.

"So," he said later, "how was your meeting?" Later as she was falling asleep she recalled with displeasure how she had instinctively tensed when he'd asked that question while she recalled with a pleasure she couldn't deny the picture of how her meeting had ended.

Chapter Thirteen

DAY THIRTY-ONE. In the morning Margherita looked even more haggard than the previous day causing Tuccio to avert his gaze unable to see her so distraught and so was surprised to feel her hand on his arm; their eyes met briefly before she led him down an alley and turned to look at him her face glowing with happiness inviting him to embrace her saying, "The *fattore* is a fool. Worse, he's one of those... I forget the word..."

"*Lauzengiers!*"

"That's it."

"But what..."

"To Hell with him. He's bound there anyway."

"But what..." She shrugged shrugged so irresistibly he kissed her again. "Tell me."

Again she shrugged. "I was up most of the night, at least it felt like most of the night. I don't remember how many hours I heard tolled, but the sun was up before I was ready to sleep. That's why I look so... I must look..."

"Beautiful. You look beautiful," and again he kissed her.

She thought, "So this is *fin'amor*. In fact it is ennobling. I love everything. I even forgive the *fattore*. Is *fin'amor*, then, true Christian love, holy, as Agnoletta suggested?"

"What?" he smiled at her stare but she shook her head.

> Anyone is mad who blames me
> for loving you, since so nobly does it please me...
> All other love I hold as nothing
> and you know well that no longer does joy sustain me
> except yours which gladdens and restores me.

(Castelloza, woman troubadour)

The level section around the fort soon ended and the climbing resumed a steep climb then more gradual then steep again gradual again while on both sides peaks rose a mile and more above them.

"Am I dreaming?"

"Yes. We are both dreaming."

"I feel no fatigue, even when we must lead our horses."

"I feel I could carry you on my back and run to the top."

To this sexual innuendo she made no reply their conversation continuing in silence with blissful looks until near mid-day they came to the confluence of a second torrent necessitating another crossing where the count called for food and rest before trying the ford; while Tuccio cared for the horses Margherita sat with Agnoletta in silence looking up and suddenly began to sob.

"*Madonna?*"

"It's just that I have never before seen such majesty."

"Truly it is wondrous."

"To be here... I feel like I am face to face with... My God it's beautiful here. I never knew. I never even suspected. Agnoletta, isn't it wonderful? Who could explain this? Who could even describe it?"

"It is very beautiful, *madonna*, but that is not all."

"Not all?"

She shook her head smiling as at a child and said, "You are in love, *madonna*."

They stared at each other for a long time. "Am I?" she finally replied.

"Half the time you are blushing. Your eyes are lit. You sigh often without noticing."

"Perhaps you are right, for I am quite certain I have never felt this way before."

"You are in love, *madonna*."

She thought, "Then after all I will not die without ever having known love," and said, "How wonderful it feels, Agnoletta. We must find you someone so you can fall in love too. Do none of the others...?" She fell back into the swirling rapids of her thoughts loving that she was in love that it had come at her like a torrent sweeping her downstream surging over boulders; and love she noted was everywhere in Christian devotion it was the essence of pilgrimage. "How very beautiful it is," she marveled. "It is like a spring flood, swollen with melted snow from above. I am not in it, no, I am the flood itself, I have become a torrent," and seeing

Tuccio thought:

> [A] *donna...*
> must dare to love him openly,
> for [a] lady, once she loves openly,
> from then on neither the worthy nor the valiant
> will speak of anything but graciousness.

(Comtessa de Dia, troubadour)

Though the crossing was again eased by leveling of the land only care and luck prevented injury but Margherita smiled at how shockingly cold the water was and Tuccio smiled because she was smiling and they came to a hamlet where a few ragged children were gleefully playing taking for granted whatever they had and everything they lacked who paused to stare but only briefly.

"Is that all we rate?" Tuccio called out playfully.

A few children turned and one the oldest perhaps eleven asked, "Going far?"

"Farther than you can imagine."

"Don't think so."

"How far can you imagine?"

"Far enough never to see this place again."

"But it's so beautiful here," said Margherita.

"What it is is lots of work and little food." These were the children of foresters whose work was always backbreaking often hazardous and never well paid even the children working long hours gathering the heaviest pieces their scrawny frames could carry.

"How come everybody wants to go someplace else?" asked a younger boy.

"Because, stupid."

"When I grow up, I want to go someplace else," chimed in a third.

"Where do you want to go?" asked Tuccio.

"I want to go to Camposella," he answered proudly without hesitation.

"Compostela?" asked Margherita aghast and the boy nodded a scrawny little thing whose age was hard to tell. "Why there? What have you heard?"

"I know things."

"Would you tell me? I'm going to Compostela."

The boy's eyes grew wide. "You are?"

She nodded. "What do you know?" The boy stopped to

gather his thoughts looking about as though they might be scattered in the grass then returned to stare. "What do you know?" she repeated quietly.

"It's very far away," he proclaimed.

"That it is."

"There's all kinds of people there."

"Do you know why they go there?"

"Because they want something."

"What do you think they want? Do you want something?"

Again the boy went into his thoughts came back looked at her his eyes suddenly lit up and said, "I want... I want..."

"Me too," said Tuccio.

When Margherita returned to her horse she ordered Agnoletta to feed the children.

FRANCESCO. Though not especially religious and like so many scoffed at priests and monks Francesco regularly went to confession observed all fast days and often attended sermons especially during Lent; and though not generous he made monthly payments for alms paid his tithes regularly and gave to Christ's Poor; also he contributed to hostels for orphans pilgrims widows the elderly and the sick provided dowries for poor girls and gave additional alms to common criminals political prisoners heretics and debtors in prison who would otherwise have starved.

He planned to provide in his will that much of his wealth go to the Church in restitution for any ill-gotten gains and was reconciled to the thought of his soul repenting for its sins and undergoing purification in Purgatory; but how long might he be there and how much of an ordeal might it be? Of course so long as he died with sincere repentance on his lips everyone agreed it would go much easier for him and he fully intended to do that but that did not eliminate his anxiety for he was not known for his patience and did not well endure pain.

He had vowed to go on pilgrimage would pay for masses many masses but as his confessor had warned, "Fail not to pay your debt to God, else the Creditor demand of you an interest rate too heavy to bear," but how much was that debt? This was what he longed to know for one could speak of holy ledgers with God as creditor and the like but how in fact was the calculation made some said one percent of profit but no one knew for sure no priest or monk could tell him how many prayers he must recite how many indulgences he must buy for each percent of interest; therefore though it had not been a great year for profit for his soul's salvation he decided to adorn a church maybe even build a chapel.

DAY THIRTY-TWO. After two nights of little sleep between three days of hard travel Margherita had slept so soundly that Agnoletta had to wake her but the moment she awoke she recalled how she had said goodnight and couldn't wait to get started though the day's stage would be the longest and steepest of the three from Susa the hardest so far possibly the hardest of the entire journey; they started up the steep-sided river gorge in the saddle but soon had to lead their horses.

"I keep thinking about the play we saw."

"What about it?"

"You know what about it."

He shrugged. "I know people make fun of it, but theirs was a great love story."

"Do you really think so?"

"Everyone focuses on the seduction and punishment, but that was not their love, their love was what came afterward. For the rest of their lives, though they could never be together, yet they remained true to each other. Is that not a tale of great devotion?"

"You don't mind that the caravan was laughing at us as much as the play?"

"Have no fear," said my lord,
"be confident, for we are at a good point;
be not tight but broaden again every strength.
You are now to Purgatory joined."
(*Purgatorio*, Canto 9)

"Some of it is good jest, some envy. So long as we are true to each other, why dignify it?"

"Because a woman's reputation—"

"Is only enhanced by attracting a lover."

"Being attractive is one thing, what one does another."

"This is Purgatory."

"What is?"

He gestured vaguely. "You and I are headed for Paradise, and the way to Paradise, as everyone knows, is through Purgatory, where all souls must be purified."

"Do you desire me as Abelardo desired Eloisa?"

"You know I do. Everyone knows I do."

"Here one should use a little skill,"
began my guide, "to approach

now here now there the side that parts."
(*Purgatorio*, Canto 10)

"We seek our way up through a twisting cleft in the rock. We must use care, even skill, if one can speak of an art of loving. Otherwise we may find the way blocked or lose our grip," she said even as she would not deny her own desire.

He said, "Come, here are close the steps
and easily now one goes up."
(*Purgatorio*, Canto 12)

"No one is more headstrong than me, but I would love you as the *giullare* described, not the way the old romances tell it. Tristano risked his life to leap into Isolda's bed, Lancelotto bloodied himself to get at Ginevra in her chamber, but that is not our way. Let us ascend to the heights of our love. As we have seen these last days, not every step is difficult."

We were going through the evening, watchful
ahead as much as our eyes could extend
against the late bright rays.
(*Purgatorio*, Canto 15)

"Can you see the way up? I cannot."

"Let us go one step at a time."

"We will not reach it soon."

"I don't care how long it takes, so long as I am with you."

"Sometimes we won't be sure of the way ahead. We may stumble."

"The more reason to go together."

"The light may fade before we have reached safe haven."

"I would grapple in the black of a moonless winter night if only you were with me."

After hours of mounting and dismounting they came to a place where they must leave the river they had been following for so long so after resting they crossed again and headed up a long steep winding ascent a difficult and at times dangerous climb where in places even the horses had difficulty walking.

And he to me: "The love of the good, missing
from its duty, here is restored."
(*Purgatorio*, Canto 17)

"I have never loved before. Is love always good?"

"I feel certain that our love is good. We will make it good."

"I hope so. I hope so."

"Do you doubt that love is good?"

"I don't know what to think."

"Perhaps about such matters it is wrong to think, rather we should let our hearts speak."

"That is passion only. What of duty? What of expectations and the judgments of others?"

"I believe that love is good. And I believe it is our duty to seek the good. Is pilgrimage not about love?"

"Are you on pilgrimage?"

"I already told you that your quest has become mine. My pilgrimage is toward you, you are my destination."

"Have you never hesitated?"

"For a man of arms, hesitation is likely to be costly."

"And if a lady hesitates?"

"She becomes only more desirable."

> And I, whom [a] new thirst was still searching,
> outside kept silent and inside said, "Perhaps
> too much questioning that I do burdens him."

(*Purgatorio*, Canto 18)

"But," she thought, "what kind of love is ours to be, if we do not do what lovers do? Yet he freely confesses his desire," and though dying to ask she held her tongue saying, "I must trust you."

"Then love me. For love is trust."

"Is it?"

"Isn't it?"

They continued up the steep road in silence.

> "Truly, many times appear things
> that give rise to suspect something false
> because the true explanations are concealed."

(*Purgatorio*, Canto 22)

"I cannot think about this anymore, it's too complicated."

"Let us make it simple. If we love each other, we should love each other. Do you believe that what Love wants must be?"

"I want to believe it."

"I did not choose to love you."

"I tried to love my husband, but failed. But is love a prison?"

"In that it has made me its captive, perhaps it is. But as it makes me free, how could it be? Do you not feel free?"

"I do feel free. I pray I am not deceived by false appearances."

When at last they reached the top of the steepest part of the climb the count declared a rest during which the two sat beside each other in silence not quite holding hands though periodically they would touch as if by chance; around the bend down the slope came a small contingent of horsemen in front two armed men behind them the leader of the group a man of about sixty but still vigorous well dressed and sitting erect in the saddle followed by three younger men in similar dress but identical hats with two more armed men in the rear. Greetings were hailed in the customary way as the leader passed but a short distance away the group stopped suddenly on his command and waited while he first sat stock still in the saddle lost in thought then dismounted and walked back uphill to where Tuccio and Margherita were sitting where he again offered greetings and asked if he might join them seeing that they were such an interesting couple.

"Couple, sir?"

"Only in the superficial yet strict sense that there are two of you, though if you will permit me, I would note the obvious, that you form a couple in the evident regard you have for each other."

"Is that so, sir. And this you observed just now as you passed?"

"That and not just that. But let there be no concern on your part, seeing that you two have not yet committed any impropriety."

Tuccio rose saying, "You presume too much, sir."

The man nodded with an appreciative smile. "Excellent, most excellent. You need have no concern for me, young sir, for I assure you that I approach in perfect amity and the spirit of charity, which motivates all pilgrims," and here he paused to bow again to Margherita, "for I do believe I can help."

"Help? With what, sir?"

"With your predicament, of course." Tuccio stared at him hard as did Margherita then the two could not resist staring at each other. "Please, young sir, lady, let not my years be wasted any more than they already have. You seek guidance, of the Church yet in a sense not of the Church, and as it happens, for this meeting must be counted an extraordinary coincidence, I am well qualified to offer it. As you might tell from my headwear I am a canon lawyer, and though not one to boast, I should mention, because it is germane to your assessment of what I have to say, that I am employed at the papal court in Avignon, from which I have been dispatched to Rome on the most important business, that is to say a matter of no consequence whatsoever."

The two continued to stare at him then exchanged another look until at last Margherita nodded slightly. "Excellent, most excellent. Now, to the matter at hand, since we have less time than good will, may one stipulate, since it is plain to any seeing eye, that you two are in love but unsure as yet what to make of it? Believe me when I say no verbal reply is necessary, so let us move immediately to facts in evidence numbers three, four, and five, that you lady are married, but not to this young man, whom you have met since commencing your pilgrimage." Margherita's jaw dropped the lawyer shrugged. "Obviously only one of you is on pilgrimage. Of course you had no intention of falling in love. No doubt you wished to travel with other women, but your husband, a merchant of considerable consequence, insisted that you go with one of his caravans. Facts, what, six through ten."

They were aghast. "But how could you possibly..."

"Simple. No woman would have chosen this arrangement, therefore it was imposed. But by whom? Obviously by a merchant who had a caravan such as this at his disposal. And who would this be but your husband? He is considerably older than you, I presume, since that is the custom. Now, when both of you have sufficiently recovered from your astonishment we can proceed to a consideration of remedies—in light of what the Church has to say on this matter but also what the Judge might say, were He to speak directly." His arms crossed before him he waited patiently for them to regain composure then nodded.

"Shall we proceed? Do you know, this is not the first but the second incredible coincidence that has befallen me on this journey, for no sooner did I leave Avignon than I met a most engaging young man, with whom I spent many pleasant hours arguing as we rode. Relevance, you ask. Well, this young man, a philosophy student if you will, had been sentenced to pilgrimage for having tried to kill his best friend over a girl."

"But this is extraordinary," said Margherita. "We met this young man a week ago!"

The lawyer held out his palms as if to say, 'There it is, case closed.' "Yes, a week, I was detained a week."

"You said 'arguing,'" said Tuccio.

"Like any philosopher he possessed an inquisitive and subtle mind, two qualities also present in a legal theorist such as myself, but he also possessed a third quality, all too rare in both professions, namely imagination. My own acolytes, whom you see waiting below like mules to be led, are complete strangers to it, but I digress. And this philosopher being so young was quite certain everything could be known and that he was well on his way to knowing it; whereas I, being so old, was equally certain that little can be known and that I am well on the way to discovering how little I really know. A delightful young man, of course he told me all about the circumstances of his pilgrimage."

"He told us, too," said Margherita.

"Then let us not waste time repeating it. The notion he wished to argue, and did so admirably, was the idea of a necessary act, in his case a pilgrimage required by judicial order, as one of personal freedom." Both of them stared at him blankly. "Do you see? Love is a necessary act, we are called to it by both nature and God. And when Love's arrow pierces our heart, we are wounded. We did not shoot the arrow, we did not aim the arrow, but we have been struck. Now we must act. What will we do?"

The two were still staring but now not blankly and Tuccio stammered, "You referred to something about court, a judge..."

"Excellent, most excellent. As I must be off, you can see my assistants awaiting me, let us... Now the Church condemns adultery and many a Church Father, starting with Saint Paul himself, Galatians five-nineteen, has condemned the acts that lead to it, as a canonist I can assure you there is no ambiguity here. So much for speaking to our nature. But I have often wondered, as I have perforce spent countless hours reducing the Church's wisdom to its regulations, how well we retain—or have even captured—the rulings of He who is both ultimate Judge and first Lawgiver. You may guess my wonder has led to doubt. And here we may note that beside this vast corpus of writing we have another, that of mystics, poets, who speak of Love differently, a love that is larger than the mere promptings of our senses. Curse me, I speak too circumspectly. To the chase, to the chase! Adultery requires a prior marriage; but what is marriage, is it made by the Church or by Heaven? By the Church, mainly; but what if, as is so often the case, it contravenes Heaven, even violates Heaven? Do you see, do you see? I hope so, because I must— You can see, the mules grow restless."

"Please don't go yet," said Margherita. "What do you...?"

"My dear lady, your husband would not have foreseen that he was pushing you into the arms of one of his caravan guards, one full of the youth and joy of which all our poets sing. Yet, as surely as my right hand now touches my left, he himself has shot the arrow into your heart. Now, since neither of you has any love for him but much for each other—fact in evidence number eleven if I have not lost my count—does he not bear direct responsibility for the acts he has set in motion? But how to convert this necessity to a possible freedom, the freedom of the will directed by the intelligence that is also claimed without ambiguity by the Church— and, more importantly, by God Himself, we know this with certainty because it is certain that we have this capacity."

"So you advise..."

"You are both on a path. It has a definite direction though not a certain destination. That latter depends on your intelligence and will. This in a sense is true of all true pilgrimage, is it not? As lawyer and as man I advise you not to avoid the acts that establish your freedom. Now freedom is not the right to do whatever you please, it too must be subject to law, that was the remarkable insight gained by my young philosopher. We submit to life's obligations, but willingly, not coerced. But in your case—this, may I say, is my insight—the question is where exactly one's obligations lie. Only by answering that question can we say of ourselves that we truly and fully exist. Farewell, lovers, I must be off, my mules will soon be braying—and by the way, the caravan is not so hostile as you both suppose. Fact number twelve!" he called out over his shoulder.

A short time later the count recalled the caravan to the route which was now much easier.

> "Do not make me speak while I am marveling
> for ill can speak who is full of another wish."

(*Purgatorio*, Canto 23)

"By all the saints in Heaven, I hardly know where to begin!"

"If we could be alone now I would know where to begin."

"Tell me what you are thinking, Tuccio, please."

"Thinking? Thinking is a thing I do poorly."

"I too. Yet now we have need of it more than ever."

> ...Discussing we went strongly
> like a ship driven by a good wind.

(*Purgatorio*, Canto 24)

The way seeming even easier than it was the two seemed to float atop their horses gazing at each other more than the scenery and so reached the top of the pass the final stage of the first part of their journey from which they would descend into Provence first transalpine *provincia* of ancient Rome now the territories where the *lenga d'oc* was spoken the home of *fin'amor*; first however would come a day of rest but more immediately food drink and shelter were needed and this they set to acquiring.

FRANCESCO. One day Francesco barefoot dressed in a long robe of coarse white cloth and a monk's cowl with a Franciscan cord for a belt set off on a nine-day pilgrimage at the head of twelve of his employees in the company of a thousand men. For the duration he would not take off his robe or lie in a bed or eat meat though he need not stint on fish or eggs vegetables or fruits cheeses or breads in fact he had two pack animals laden with all sorts of preserves biscuits and cakes both savory and sweet.

From his house where his band assembled he set out in early morning for the convent church of Sant' Agostino where he received holy communion then the men organized themselves by neighborhood and each group behind its crucifix proceeded three by three with lighted candles through the city. Punishing themselves with rods and accusing themselves of their sins they exited through the Porta Pispini to traverse the Sienese *contado* by an easy route that would take them fifty miles in four days to the western shore of Lake Trasimeno.

Mostly he walked and talked rested and ate but there were sermons and prayers especially at local shrines and beside the lake he heard mass; when he arrived back at Siena he again heard mass was blessed and given a fish then witnessed the reinstallation of the parish crucifix and only then back at his house did he remove his robe telling everyone, "May God make it profitable to our souls if it be His will."

DAY THIRTY-THREE. When Tuccio greeted Margherita this Sunday morning his first words were that he had dreamt of a young and beautiful lady seen to go through a meadow gathering flowers and singing (*Purgatorio*, Canto 27) and said he was certain this augured well for them; but unlike the prior night she had not slept like an exhausted well-fed goat protected by a watchful shepherd in the high mountains (Canto 27) rather her sleep had been troubled by what the canonist had rightly called their predicament. "Augurs? What future do you see for us? It is rare if we get even a moment alone."

"Yet here we are with an entire day in this remote place. We have only to go into the woods. All the joy of the world is ours, lady, if we both love each other." (Guilhem de Peitieu, troubadour)

"Into the woods? For our pleasure, no doubt, and then what?"

"We must go through the fire." He explained that in his

dream he had to go through a wall of fire before he could see the woman in the meadow who obviously symbolized the joys of love and when Margherita asked what the fire symbolized said, "Since our love occurs in full view, we must dare to face the caravan. Farther we do not go if first the fire does not bite our holy souls." (Canto 27)

"The mere thought of it terrifies me."

"I confess its heat will seem to sear us, but once through we will find no injury. So it was in the dream."

"But why must we do it?"

"Because the meadow is on the other side. What? Are you wishing us to stay where we are?" (Canto 27)

Did Tuccio refuse to acknowledge their predicament? Yes! Did Margherita? She was older and as a woman wiser in such matters but he took her reflection to mean she didn't love him. Like so many lovers' quarrels whatever one said only angered the other more and so the rhetoric escalated and the hurt and the fear alas had they had any perspective they would have seen that this escalation was the first open acknowledgement of what each meant to the other but what angry hurt fearful lover can do that?

"Would you push me into the arms of another? Am I that unfit for love, that you cast me down that way? Then speak to me no more, lady, stay with your rich husband and trouble me no more."

"You speak of fire and meadows as though you are still dreaming. Can you wake up and tell me plainly what you would have me do?"

"*Madonna*, my need you know and what is good for it." (*Purgatorio*, Canto 33) To this she made no verbal reply but her look was sufficient to make him exhale so deeply his shoulders sank as he said softly, "Margherita, we are at the top of the world. May we not act as the canonist advised?"

"No," she softly replied pointing to the peaks that yet soared above them, "there is the top of the world. We are caught in its hold."

"If we are caught, it must be because we have so chosen. Because you thrust your mind still into earthly things, from true light you gather darkness. Is our love not good? There is a good there above..." (*Purgatorio*, Canto 15)

"When you say 'there above' you tell me you are still dreaming. This is our life, Tuccio. I am on pilgrimage."

Again he sighed saying, "Good lady, nothing of you do I ask, but that you take me as servant, that I may serve you as a good lord, whatever the recompense may be." (Bernart de Ventadorn, troubadour)

And she sighing said, "Please do not judge me so harshly. You have captured my heart, I confess this to you freely and gladly, and would do so before the world if only I believed..."

Silent he remained eyes locked with hers thinking, "Never had I power over myself, nor was I mine from the moment she let me see into her eyes," (Bernart de Ventadorn, troubadour) and looked around as though for someone to intervene with a miracle but what he found were people watching from a distance including Stoldo and Agnoletta. His gaze encompassed the grass-carpeted prairie the forested hills rocky outcrops the naked peaks a plummeting stream whose ripples caught sunlight which made him say, "Tell me you don't feel it, Margherita! How high we are! The mountains may go higher but people do not, we are at the top, the very top, the peak, the summit, the pinnacle. Surely what might not be possible elsewhere can happen here. I love you, does that mean nothing?" He watched till he judged her answer clear before saying, "Well then, when you will have returned to the world and rested from the long road, remember me." (*Purgatorio*, Canto 5)

"How dare you say that! Did I invite you to love me?"

"You did not. I reproach you with nothing and blame only myself, for it is my foolishness that has brought us to this impasse." To himself he said, "Alas, so much I was thinking I knew of love and so little do I know. She has from me all my heart and has taken from me all of myself and her very self and all the world, and when herself she took from me, she left me nothing but desire and a yearning heart," (Bernart de Ventadorn, troubadour) and Margherita began to cry.

With new love comes the need to feel loved constantly in every little way when every look word gesture or absence can provoke instant doubt instant grief that says, "Am I mad? A fool? Please confirm for me again, as you did only a moment ago, that for loving you I am the most wise person imaginable." So Margherita who had never sought love nor expected it cried out just as Heloise reproached Abelard, "You alone are at the origin of my pain, and thus you alone must be at the source of my consolation. Since you are the only one who could bring me unhappiness, you are the only one able to make me happy," and

Tuccio rushed to enclose her in his arms.

A bent old man leaning heavily on a stick approached hatless and barefoot with extreme slowness and they relaxed their embrace to stare at him who had eyes so deep-set one could believe they looked inward as much as out and a shock of unkempt curly hair not one strand missing from his youth yet all turned white with a white beard and the biggest ears they had ever seen and fascinated they waited for he was evidently approaching them. When he was close he greeted them with a slow nod and would have continued on his way had they not hailed him, "Good day to you, grandpa," said Tuccio and the ancient nodded but instead of reply observed them in silence for the longest time as if his eyes progressed at the speed of his legs. They assumed he was unable to speak but nothing suggested dementia and there was something comforting in his placid gaze so they waited patiently until he nodded slowly over and over as though he had finally come to a conclusion when Tuccio asked, "What is it, grandpa?"

One would never have predicted the strength of his voice so utterly opposed to the desperate frailty of a body barely able to support its threadbare clothes as he said, "You will conquer fear when you accept the limits of your circumstances. Exhaust your frustration and let love fill that emptying space. Pilgrims always seek to become, but what is the desire to become if not the desire to finish with becoming and instead be? Pilgrims want to see clearly what has been murky, but for this, acceptance is required, and acceptance requires abandonment, both of what you have left behind and to which you submit. Nothing requires abandonment and acceptance more than love," and as abruptly as he had begun he fell silent and they waited but he was indeed finished.

"Grandfather, what of the will?" asked Margherita.

"With intelligence you may trust it."

"Are you a pilgrim too, grandfather?"

He took each of their hands and slowly raised them to his lips smiled and to their considerable surprise simply returned in the direction from which he had come; they stared at his figure receding ever so slowly and at each other with alternating smiles and looks of astonishment until they stopped looking at his halting gait and looked steadily at each other.

"Oh Tuccio, if only..."

He shook his head. "Remember what the aged said, no more 'if only.'"

"Can you be patient with me?"

"Patience is notably absent from my short list of virtues, but for you, Margherita, I will discover a way to add it."

The Durance River which they would follow in the coming days had its headwaters above them somewhere in the heights and they were clambering uphill beside it until when they were well out of sight they picked flowers and placed garlands on each other's head as tokens of love and as they embraced Tuccio said, "In my mind, Margherita, we are all the way up there, in the highest meadow. See the sun that on your forehead shines brilliantly, see the new grass, the flowers and the saplings." (*Purgatorio*, Canto 27) "Can you feel it?"

"I can, my dear. Now let us enter the stream as you promised," whereupon they descended into the cold rushing water squealing like children and when they emerged he said he felt like he was in church and she said, "From now on, when we are alone, you may call me 'Mita.'"

"Is that your nickname?"

"It is, but no one uses it but my mother's family."

"Mita," he whispered and kissed her and they returned hand in hand.

> I returned from the holiest water
> remade like new plants
> renewed with new leaf
> pure and ready to climb to the stars.

(*Purgatorio*, Canto 33 conclusion)

PARADISE

Chapter Fourteen

DAYS ONE THROUGH FOUR. Margherita had thought she didn't know how to love and that she had missed her chance for though Tuccio insisted she was beautiful she didn't believe him since when she walked in the street men didn't turn as she passed like they did for certain others yet she could clearly see the yearning in his eyes. "Of course he is sixteen, his blood runs hot, but why for me?" This she believed must be accounted part of love's mystery and wondered if God might have sent him for though she could not imagine a love less spiritual she felt for the first time that she could truly love God and wondered if the content of her pilgrimage was to discover love. "Before I was bitter, angry, confused, now my heart feels open to the world and its mystery and its redemptive possibilities, surely that has some significance because is that not how the sacred is revealed?"

Thus she believed Tuccio 'my dearest, my young tutor, my unlikely hero' was correct to call their love 'fine' for she felt chaste so long as they did not consummate it physically though she did not deny her yearnings because she knew that one achieved salvation by overcoming temptation perhaps God had even blessed women with such desire so that by the exercise of will they could resist it and so go to Paradise. "In fact, am I not already in Paradise?" for it was through her desire that she felt saved from the damnation of anger and thus blessed and never before had she achieved such sincerity in her devotions besides which she could find no better name for the country of awesome beauty into which she was descending beside a sparkling river.

She thought: "He loves me and I love him, though we are an odd pair. If I had conceived when first my husband crawled on top of me, a man already two and a half times Tuccio's age, and I, his age, dutifully spread my thighs, I would now have a child two years younger than him. Were it a girl he would no doubt fall in love with her instead of me, but I don't and I don't care that his beard is still wispy. He assures me I would not be his first and I have no reason to doubt him, given the confidence of his embraces, but of course our love must be directed elsewhere."

"Direct your grateful mind to God," she told me,

"who has conjoined us with the first star [of Heaven]."

(*Paradiso*, Canto 2)

"How easy it was to fall in love with her," he thought. "When I saw her at the stream I heard a clap of thunder from out of a sunny blue sky and with my eyes glued on her failed to see Love get a clear shot at my heart. Fortunately the *giullare* taught me well about the meaning of true love." He knew he could not agree when Margherita called it chaste but did believe it was refined pure elevated noble; but the poetry's sentiments the gazing and the longing the loving at a distance there came a time when the concepts of *fin'amor* became a present physical love that desired satisfaction and a future for as he told himself, "That she loves me I have no reason to doubt, given the fervor of her embraces."

In his enveloping joy he felt like the falcon depicted in images of love without missing the ironies that unlike the falcon he could not see ahead and was ascending to Paradise by climbing arduously down an Alpine pass (though hardly noticing); as for Stoldo's question ('why her?') Stoldo being the only guard he would allow to ask such a question because he was like an older brother the answer was, 'because she is so beautiful,' an answer he didn't understand. Tuccio pressed explained he hadn't chosen her Love had and as for her age, "I love it as I love the birth mark on her neck," and queried further replied, "She has freed me. I sometimes wonder if God sent her."

I replied: "*Madonna*, as devoted

as to be is possible, I thank Him

who from the mortal world has removed me."

(*Paradiso*, Canto 2)

As the count had taken all security precautions on the way up the pass so did he on the way down and with no patience for one of his men mooning over a woman he sent Tuccio forward to scout reminding him sternly to keep a sharp eye for though the river protected them from sudden attack on one side and the terrain on the other was usually too rugged even for brigands there were still places where they could be at risk. Ahead lay the vast valleys of Provence and Gascony between the Alps and the Pyrenees creating a general sense of anticipation even excitement over their attractions and possibilities albeit unspecified except for the lovers.

Margherita now rode as a matter of course it no longer seeming important to walk as the sincerity of her purpose she reasoned must be found in her heart not her feet and while public displays of affection were discreet everyone could read her heart on her face as well as Tuccio's which they both knew and therefore made no futile attempt to hide it which would only have brought more attention. Were Francesco present she would have argued that since he had never loved her another had naturally filled that void yet she had not betrayed her marriage vows therefore had not sinned and need carry no guilt; when Tuccio and she were alone however their feelings were given more frank expression.

How did she justify this? And the awkward questions that sooner or later could not be ignored—you know the ones!—were they getting asked? Much would you like to know!

Though switchbacks eased the steepest section much of the first stage entailed a continuous steep descent so for the safety of the horses they walked much of it arriving at Briançon after only a few hours yet deciding to stop there partly because it offered the best accommodations partly because it was fascinating. A Roman settlement this was the capital of the 'French lands' of which Margherita had reported lands which just four years earlier in 1343 had been purchased from the French dauphin by a federation of fifty-one communes; however in addition to land came (against a large payment and annual rent) political and economic rights including liberty of person and goods freedom of assembly and the election of representatives hence the name 'the Republic of the Escartons.'

The communes were called 'free' (*franc*) because their inhabitants were exempt from feudal service levied their own taxes and held the right to bear arms and hunt; they could also legislate their own rules for policing elect their own judges and were responsible for their own defense making their political and economic situation far superior to that of all their neighbors. Of course it helped to be on a principal trade route a situation exploited with three annual trade fairs one of which was international drawing merchants from as far away as Holland for which extraordinary measures were taken to assure the security of travelers. The charter bearing the dauphin's seal that constituted this republic was proudly displayed to anyone interested which was the entire caravan who all stared at it even those (which was everyone but the count) who couldn't make out a single word not least Tuccio.

DAY FIVE. As they rested on the bank of what was now a wider and tamer river with the Alps in the distance they watched monks manage a flotilla of logs they had floated down from the high country a job that in principle seemed easy but in practice was difficult and dangerous; they were sitting apart discreetly holding hands but unable to resist stealing kisses as they spoke softly in each other's ear so Agnoletta wouldn't overhear though the message could be read plainly from their faces. They were now in the County of Provence a new land with new wonders and new possibilities which they named Paradise.

> "Here the high creatures see the mark
> of the eternal value..."

(Paradiso, Canto 1)

Their talk flowed easily from sweet to serious with their tongues tickling each other's ear one moment and the next their expressions stern as one intimacy bumped into another beginning, "How lovely it is here, how content I feel," and almost immediately, "I must have somehow sensed that I must leave my husband, if only for the duration of a pilgrimage, to express my love of God."

"Is that what you were doing a moment ago, expressing your love of God?"

"In loving you I love Him. I truly believe that, so long as our love remains fine, for that is how I understand *fin'amor.* We love each other, our love is obviously not physical, therefore it is spiritual."

"Not physical?"

"You know what I mean," she whispered.

"I do, Mita, but I cannot agree. If fine love does not embrace physical love, it embraces shades, appearances, empty forms. I feel certain that were the *giullare* here he would first laugh at us then scold us for refusing to confess the desire that all lovers naturally feel."

"I do confess it, you know that. But I choose to distinguish between what I would do and what I will do."

"Therein is great merit on your part, for which I love you all the more, even as my frustration increases," and as if to demonstrate his frustration he nuzzled her neck. "Had you known the hardships, uncertainties, and dangers of the road, would you have remained determined to forsake the comforts of home?"

"Yes. You recall I left him once before, though I merely went to my mother. He wouldn't give an inch. I even thought of entering a convent, have I told you that?"

"No."

"It wasn't an idle threat, though how serious I was I don't know."

"But a convent..."

"I know. But every time I was close to gaining some stability, he would knock me off balance. He sees and hears only what he will, even if that is what he most fears. It doesn't matter what one says or does."

"Mita..."

"I began to ask why God was putting me through this trial. I came to believe He wished me to find my own spiritual path. Why else would he prevent me from getting pregnant? Do I shock you?"

"Of course not."

"After fifteen years, surely a trial must come to a resolution. Not just to endure it, but to emerge victorious."

"Like a knight in combat."

"Perhaps. Yes. Very like."

"Exactly like, I think. Has there really never been anyone else for you?"

"How could there be? Oh yes, one hears tales. In the tales there are never pesky servants or nosy neighbors." She laughed suddenly. "In one a woman is abducted by a pirate and after he enjoys her she decides she prefers him to her husband and refuses to be returned!" She continued, "I believe God sent me a message—twice, and I ignored it both times. Two children He gave my husband and I failed both times to..."

"I don't understand. You said—"

"—that the marriage was childless, it was. But my husband fathered two children of his own, the first with a fifteen year old servant in the house, that baby died in a few months. That alone should have told me something, but I didn't understand. I didn't even know I should be listening. The second was a year ago, also with a servant. Agnoletta knows all about it, of course. Everyone does."

"The baby?"

"She lives with her mother's family. My husband importunes me to raise it as my own, but I refuse. What good could I be to her, who would see only anger in my face, not the mother's love a child deserves. It is for her mother to love her."

"Where is she?"

"Still in our employ. As I say, he wishes the baby to live with us, to be raised as if it were my own and yet somehow with the real mother playing her natural role. But enough," she said nestling further into his embrace, "I was wrong to talk of such things, which remind me of how sad I have been instead of how happy I am. Let us talk only of love. How lovely it is here." Unable to restrain himself he embraced her unable to resist she responded.

"Let's never move from this spot. I wish to remain forever as I am now, with my arms around you, my hands stealing their way to your breasts, my lips to yours."

"The work of those monks with the logs would seem easy, but it is not, is it?"

It was a beautiful day in early July with high heat but dry air whose clarity presented in brilliant outline the alternately lush and stark beauties of the land as they proceeded along the river; a girl sitting on the side of the road watched the caravan intently as it passed to whom no one paid any mind since this was not unusual though some children would shout something but after it passed this one got up and followed. To follow more than around a bend or two was unusual enough but to keep following hours later was very strange for though vagabonds were seen on the road they were not children whereas this girl looked at most thirteen; barefoot dirty unkempt dressed only in a shift that was little more than a sack with arm holes cut in it which didn't even cover her knees she was too young to be adrift on the road and while the guards initially ignored her increasingly heads turned.

She seemed to pay this attention no mind in this way seeming content but everyone wondered where she could be going given that for a girl her age to walk alone even to the next village was not advisable especially clothed as she was yet they passed village after village and still she remained a short distance behind them. She seemed to entertain herself apparently talking to herself from time to time or quietly singing occasionally she looked inside her shift all while keeping to the caravan's pace thus eventually becoming the caravan's center of attention an object of fascination.

When they stopped to eat she stopped too sitting a short distance away making no attempt to come closer and she dropped from attention as food was distributed but as they ate a few of the porters looked to see if she was eating and saw she was not; they returned to their meal but from time to time turned to look and she returned their gazes but without expression until one of them went to her with a gourd of water and a hunk of bread. Without a word she took them and to his astonishment placed them carefully on the ground yanked on a leash he hadn't noticed and when a kitten appeared carefully poured a little water into her palm and watched it lap it up then broke off some of the bread into little pieces; only then did she greedily swallow the bread and empty the gourd and only when it was all gone did she look up to find the porter gaping at her.

As she continued to follow the caravan Margherita thought how odd it was that a waif should appear in such a remote section of the route where settlements were scarce and then like the others paid her no mind until they stopped at a hamlet that would shelter the caravan with a little church for the women which seemed the best hospitality they were likely to find. Everyone set about their tasks but when they sat down to their open-air supper the porter looking around found her just visible at the turn of the path and without a word put a chunk of roasted meat between two slabs of bread and took it to her with a gourd of water telling her to eat and then return to her village. "Where is your village?" he asked but she said nothing. "Be gone, then. You can't stay with us." He stared at her with bewilderment mixed with repulsion and she stared back inscrutably neither anxious nor calm until taking the food she fed the kitten as before and then fed herself consuming the huge sandwich with ravenous bites.

DAY SIX. When everyone awoke to find her rising where she'd eaten repugnance became hostility because such a filthy creature could not be allowed to attach herself to the caravan nonetheless some lacked the heart to chase her away on an empty stomach so when breakfast was apportioned she too was fed but the porter warned her this was the last and she'd better not try to follow anymore unless she wanted to risk angering the count who would set the guards on her. In reply she only stared and wondering if she might be deaf insane or an idiot he said, "Where is your village? Why are you alone on the road? Do you understand me?" but with no reaction he had no way to know what language she spoke or if she understood anything.

Sharing the general reaction Margherita couldn't understand why the count didn't make her leave or why the *fattore* wasn't concerned she might have gotten into the valuables during the night. People certainly fed beggars even disgusting ones since even they deserved charity for they too were God's children one need not even feel pity because alms-giving benefited the donor as much as the recipient; but this child was not like the others encountered along the way for this one was on the road herself which was unthinkable no one had ever seen such a thing it seemed wrong even sinister with one of the porters suggesting she could be a devil for why else wouldn't she leave them alone. Despite shouted warnings and threats the girl was seen in the distance as they continued along the river; Agnoletta convinced she was evil suggested that Margherita ask the count to get rid of her but she wished to forget about the waif for it was impossible to concern oneself with everyone encountered who was hungry when poor harvests the previous season had caused thousands in the Sienese *contado* to starve and not for the first time there having been a string of poor harvests in recent years.

It was among the porters that sentiment began to change during the day moved by the comportment of the girl who didn't seem to expect charity much less sympathy had made no attempt to beg yet had been thankful for what had been given and who hadn't requested more though clearly half starved; whether or not acknowledged this had ingratiated her if only a little with some of those most likely to appreciate her hunger so that at lunch she was well fed and by afternoon had won their sympathy. The *fattore* who in fact was concerned about her thieving during the night was more than once inclined to chase her away and finally expressed his concern to the count but the latter noted that the porters were in the *fattore*'s charge therefore it was for him to order them not to help the waif who after all had caused no harm or delay and was surely at least as deserving of charity as anyone else while he had larger security concerns than the threat posed by a child.

The guards were either too busy to bother with her or affected to be so with Tuccio sharing the general attitude having grown up among those who went hungry when harvests were poor; if the child turned out to be a thief and wasn't caught they would look bad but chasing her away was beneath them unless the count ordered it so if the porters wanted to feed her that was their affair. Meanwhile the waif seemed indifferent to everyone's reaction speaking only to her kitten and apparently content to play with it as if her precarious situation were a secure environment where her hunger was of no more concern to her than anyone else; being near a caravan however must have reassured her because she didn't mind that occasionally she had to run to catch up. When they reached Sisteron dramatically situated on the river beneath a sheer cliff she stayed close to some of the porters who fed her (and the kitten) a good supper and provided a place for her to sleep nearby in the barn though not without a stern warning. "If you try to steal anything, it will go badly for you, do you understand?" said one with a harsh expression pointing to the guards nearby but as usual she responded with a blank stare which they found amusing.

DAY SEVEN. In the morning they crossed the river on a stone bridge the only one along its entire length and passed into scenery no less spectacular than before but now in the hilly country to the west they saw the semi-arid meadows known as *garrigue* strewn with flowers and flowering shrubs and small trees with twisted trunks amid craggy limestone boulders which under brilliant sun and clear air was breathtaking and Tuccio said it reminded him of his homeland southeast of Siena.

"How do you live in a place like that?"

"With difficulty. Not much water."

"Water is a problem in Siena. Do you know the city is fed with underground aqueducts?"

"I do. Remember, I've lived in Siena."

"Did you meet many women there?"

After a pause he said, "I did have occasion to meet women."

"Did you form liaisons with these women? Remember, you have sworn never to lie."

"I did have my share of liaisons."

"How many?"

"Mita, if you are asking how many women I have loved, I can count them easily, for you are the only one."

"You would not—"

"No I would not."

"You are my first love too. For a woman of my age, that is..."

"Have you no idea how it affects me to know I am that one?"

She asked why he loved her and he replied because she was

beautiful.

"What is beautiful about me?"

"Everything."

"But, my age."

"I would not have you younger. Please believe that and be content."

> Love's beauty bold's exciting, rough
>
> That like *garrigue*'s all's not enough.

For a third day the waif followed the caravan at a distance but now with a degree of security and perhaps in consequence spoke for the first time (to someone besides the kitten) but unfortunately the porter didn't understand a word though she repeated it. As the caravan continued beside the river a monk appeared who invited Margherita to his abbey and she had difficulty declining because a pilgrim she'd met in the cathedral at Sisteron who had pointed out its twelfth-century Italianate features had urged her to visit the Abbey of Ganagobie saying the mosaics alone justified the climb and she was curious to see why.

The caravan however had over three miles to reach shelter which meant seven extra miles for Tuccio and Stoldo to fetch her in the morning but when the monk pledged to deliver her she agreed and at that moment a porter touched the waif and gestured to her to ask if she could go with the lady but she shook her head and urged again even took a step back. He couldn't understand why the girl would pass up a chance for a hot meal and maybe even a proper bed until he surmised she would prefer to stay with those who had been kind rather than try to attach herself to one who had been cold—and whose maid was openly hostile; for he had no way to know that the girl had been refused admittance to more than one holy sanctuary because she looked more like an evil spirit than an innocent child.

DAY EIGHT. "Isn't it amazing how far we've come?" she said describing how from the monastery's nine-hundred-foot elevation she'd been able to see the last of the Alps just above the horizon and she also reported that she had seen the mosaics. "It's not enough to look, though, one must know what things mean," and said the monk had explained how everything expressed more than first appeared.

"I don't understand."

"The animals symbolize things. There was a deer, a dragon, exotic birds, even an elephant. I have to say, it didn't seem like it had much to do with religion."

"Strange to have it in a church then."

"That's what I was thinking."

Where the road turned west from the river between hills Margherita had met the caravan which then continued through the winding easy pass heavily wooded on both sides a touch of coolness in the morning shade which eased her into a contemplative mood as she rode alone for Tuccio was scouting; but when they stopped for breakfast he was relieved and joined her in comfortable silence until she said, "She eats with the porters now, I see. For myself I don't care, but I'm surprised the *fattore* suffers her to stay, and the count. Do they not worry about the merchandise?"

"Apparently she is harmless."

"Filthy, though."

"I thought you liked children."

"I do like children."

They continued their simple meal of bread dipped in wine and afterward he took her hand almost absentmindedly and caressed it saying, "I missed you last night."

"I wish I could have understood the mosaics. I wish I knew more."

"You know how to read."

"Not well."

"You could, though, if you read more."

"I suppose."

"You rarely take out your book. Why not do it today?" She shrugged. "It is a great gift to know how to read."

"Indeed," she said and suddenly stared at him.

"What you suspect is true. I am illiterate." He told her he had never learned either from his father or the tutor at the count's castle in Sarteano and had never cared till he met the *giullare* but since then had wished he could read 'our greatest living poet.'

"'Our greatest living poet?'"

"That's what he called him."

"You love poetry that much?"

"I love you that much. If I knew poetry I would be able to express it. I would become more refined, more worthy of your love. A nobleman should be refined. Why else is it called 'fine love?'"

Soon they came to a town the first since Sisteron equally

fortified and apparently struggling to attract commerce with diverse purveyors beckoning as the caravan passed through its narrow streets beneath a crudely formidable citadel and when they exited she said she would teach him to read warning however that the only book she possessed was the pious volume he had seen not poetry.

"Perhaps it will squeeze a drop of piety into my withered soul."

"And better," she thought, "to first fix squarely in one's sight the love of God before turning to the love of woman."

When the caravan next stopped she had Agnoletta fetch the book saying, "Francesco was not pleased that his notary was teaching me to read."

"I'm surprised he allowed it. I wonder why the notary did it. I bet he was secretly in love with you."

"Don't be ridiculous. He hoped that by making me more pious it would inspire Francesco."

"I bet he was in love with you."

"You're wrong. If he loves me, it is as a sister, as to me he is a brother."

"It was watching you read that loosed Love's arrow."

No sooner had she begun the lesson (using Lapo's method) than catcalls began from guards clustered a short distance away which he stopped with the usual harsh affectionate banter calling them a bunch of illiterate louts; only later did they happen to see the waif standing at the same distance unabashedly gaping at them transfixed plainly fascinated by what she was seeing and Tuccio asked, "Are you surprised to see a grown man at his lessons?" but as usual there was no reply. The fact was she couldn't believe her eyes not just to see a woman reading but a woman teaching a man and as the lesson continued Margherita could not help but look and always there she was in the same spot with the same rapt look and when the caravan continued it was Margherita who stared and they stared at each other.

What most fascinated her about the girl was the kitten which she always fed first no matter how hungry she might be but also that for four days she had kept pace with the caravan and on such skinny legs walking all day and never even seeming exhausted her face unalterably calm even passive. By now some of the guards had joined the porters in remarking that she had never begged and always received politely but for them too above all it was the kitten which sometimes she pulled on a leash a tiny little thing beside which the horses and mules looked gigantic but which mostly she kept in her shift where it could be seen peeking out with two little round black eyes and a pointed little nose watching and sniffing the world as if it hoped to understand it.

For the rest of the stage Margherita watched her fascinated puzzled eventually concerned thinking, "Look at her, she's barely clothed," and when Tuccio next returned she said the same to him adding, "I should have taken her with me to the abbey. I know the porters mean well, but a girl does not spend the night surrounded by rough men."

Agnoletta however speaking out of turn said, "If you ask me, *madonna*, you did right not to take her with us. For starters she's filthy, no doubt verminous. And who knows what else?"

Although from time to time she muttered a few words just above a whisper in reply to a repeated question so little did the girl say that no one could tell what language she was speaking yet it was clear by now that she understood well enough.

Chapter Fifteen

Given how their meeting had ended the professor couldn't wait to see Tiffany again whereas she resolved not to see him at least not till she could understand what had happened to be sure it wouldn't happen again and as the following Saturday approached and she was mentally preparing for the next stage of her pilgrimage she could see she was going to be thinking more about him than Compostela. Surprisingly however that wasn't the case but the very fact that the stage had been the first she deemed successful made her want to tell him about it an urge she resisted until she received an email asking how she was and hoping the stage had been successful; soon emails were oscillating between them so when he said he had to be in the city soon she accepted another meeting and when they had taken their usual places at the table and were exchanging pleasantries she asked why he had to be in the city and he said, "To see you."

"You said you needed to be in the city soon."

"I did. To see you."

Seeing her reaction he immediately clarified that since she had posed so many questions in her emails he thought it would be helpful if they discussed them in person and since he was enjoying their meetings very much especially their excursions he was looking forward to seeing her again; she replied that while she too was enjoying their meetings which she found extremely helpful he shouldn't draw any conclusions from what had happened the last time which she dismissed as a one-time thing. Thus clarifying that neither was attracted to the other they launched into a discussion of the last two stages she had walked both successful she believed because she had taken his suggestions first that she embrace rather than resist her actual circumstances second that she listen to music.

"I think the music was your idea."

"It was?"

He nodded. "What did you listen to?"

She confessed she didn't know much about classical music and so had simply bought a collection called "Sacred Music of the Renaissance" without knowing what it was but which she found beautiful and listening to it as she walked through suburban streets was like being in a foreign film.

"That's great," he said.

"Some of the music was really stirring, which created this odd juxtaposition. I tried to do what you said, not fight with the reality of where I was, and that was interesting because it almost started to seem kind of beautiful. I watched a guy mow his lawn. I watched some kids running around. I can't put it in words."

"You don't need to, I can see it in your face."

"It was amazing how something so ordinary... I kept thinking, all these people... Everyone cares about somebody, everyone has worries, pleasures... I want to say it was beautiful, but that seems so..."

"Strange?"

"Trite, maybe?"

"Hardly trite. Not if you really felt it."

"I did, I just can't say it. Which is a problem when you're writing a blog."

"You're doing very well, my lady."

"You'd give me a passing grade?"

"I'd give you an A."

"You realize how distracting everything is. I still don't really know what I'm trying to get in touch with. We say, 'get in touch with our feelings,' but do we? Do we know how? How did we get out of touch?" The professor laughed. "Seriously. And our thoughts. So much talk. Talk, talk, talk."

"Well well, listen to you."

"Pretentious?"

"Not at all."

"At least I've realized the importance of quiet."

"That is much. I can't say I've learned when to shut up." He made a point of not saying anything and when she realized what he was doing she laughed and he chose that moment to say he had brought her something reached into his shoulder bag and handed her a small gift with a card that read, "For Tiffany, if only she had taken my medieval saints seminar." Removing the wrapping she found a five-disk set of sacred music of Palestrina and he said, "I think you'll like it. No doubt some of it is in the collection you were listening to."

"Thank you, Mark. What?"

"Nothing."

"Anything you'd care to tell me about this?"

"Not really. It has a medieval feel, or at least what I imagine medieval sacred music was like, which is mostly lost to us. Do you know there's music in the *Codex Calixtinus*?" She said she'd probably read that but had forgotten. "Talk about precious relics. Twelfth-century music. I'm afraid I can tell you very little about it, as music is my weakest suit."

As he had alerted her to expect he still had not received a facsimile of the *Codex Calixtinus*
but on the other hand he now had them for all the others so he had plenty of work although the Compostela manuscript was the oldest and the one against which he would be collating all the others; it was stored in the archive of the cathedral he said and the canons were very protective about letting anyone near it whereby even scholars who presented themselves in person didn't always get to see it but rather were granted access to a good facsimile.

"If it doesn't arrive you can always go there."

"It'll come. I keep badgering them, in a polite scholarly way."

"No interest in going there? The foundation covers travel."

"Tempting thought."

"If it doesn't arrive, maybe the foundation can send over a delegation."

"Meaning you?"

"I'd love to see it."

"Tempting thought."

Later she said there must be some kind of irony in the fact that her pilgrimage was just starting to feel like one during the section that had the least claim to being a pilgrim route for surely pilgrims en route to Compostela who had detoured to Saint-Guilhem would have returned to the road rather than strike out through the wilderness which was not just rugged but dangerous given the presence of wolves bears and wild boar. "Even today the risk of meeting a boar is not trivial. Do you agree?"

He said he agreed entirely adding that a true pilgrim carried nothing but some bread and water and thus was unable to survive away from a road where one could obtain food and shelter and anything else they might need including care if they became sick or injured. "There is also the important requirement generally absent from modern pilgrimage that the route be sanctified with holy sites or at least made interesting with places to visit. Why else make the considerable detour to Saint-Guilhem when you're bound for Compostela?"

And surely, she added, the wilderness would not then have held the attraction it did currently but rather the opposite.

"Agreed again in the sense that no one would deliberately shun built-up areas as we do now." The only reason he could imagine for avoiding the highway, he said, would be if word had spread that a section was in the control of brigands or marauders or if an army were known to be on the move.

"Then they would not have seen what I saw," for the wilderness route, she said, had taken her past the Priory of Saint-Michel de Grandmont in the highlands far above Lodève known today for its uranium mines but in the Middle Ages for its fortress-like cathedral dedicated to a venerated tenth-century warrior bishop and housing his miraculously uncorrupted remains. Given that Lodève was already a detour she doubted pilgrims would have made a lengthy climb into the mountains to visit a monastery that apparently had no particular attraction except the Neolithic remains that dotted the fields next to the monastery buildings. She described the tall narrow boulders carved into long rounded shapes standing upright in the fields the horizontal boulders lying nearby carved into elongated ovals with long slits cut into their length and the chambers created by upright boulders roofed with capstones and concluded, "What they signify is unknown."

"Unknown?"

"That's what it says online."

"Then whoever wrote what it says online should visit The Cloisters Museum and look at the unicorn tapestry."

"That's what I thought."

"Never underestimate the ability of scholars to find great ambiguity where there should be none and none where there should be much."

"It seems obvious, doesn't it?"

"To be clear, the images are plainly sexual, but their symbolic meaning extends far beyond what we today call 'sex.' 'Life force' suggests the meaning, the mysterious power that creates the miracle of life."

"That's what you said about the unicorn."

"Alas, I tend to repeat myself."

"No you don't. Anyway, you've taught me so much. Sex is never just sex, is it?"

"Indeed." After an awkward pause he added, "And I would suggest that there's something very modern in the discomfort we both just felt. Despite all our candor and sophistication and all the rest."

"Not in the Middle Ages?"

"Hard to say with certainty, but it seems so."

"That's so strange. I mean Christianity was so..."

"Which begs the question how deep its influence was. But to answer my own question, I think its influence was profound and thus the deeper insight is that the chthonic experience of a life force expressed through sexuality was as alive among Christians as pagans."

"Did you just say 'chthonic?'"

He shook his head sadly. "At last you see what you're dealing with. The wise course would be immediate evasive action."

"I can't believe you said 'chthonic.'"

He shrugged. "Get out while you can." They looked at each other. "I'm hoping you'll stay, though." Still they looked at each other.

"Okay, but don't say 'chthonic' again."

"Granted."

"Or 'hermeneutics.'"

"Promise."

"What does 'chthonic' mean, anyway?"

The professor reached across the table to touch her hand while she watched and their eyes danced together and apart; asked what he thought of siting a monastery in such a location he replied that it was not uncommon for Christian installations to be on or near Roman or other pagan sites which in turn might be on Neolithic ones either because the successor believed the ground had been sacralized or found it sacred for more or less the same reasons. "When there's only one hill in town, you don't need much of a theory, but a monastery in a remote mountain valley you can reasonably ask, 'Why this spot precisely?'"

Her face darkened staring until she said there was something she should tell him. "I feel like I've been sitting here under false pretenses. It's no secret that I feel comfortable with you and I... I don't know where that was going, I just know there's something I want to tell you."

"Please do."

"I've told you about Bob's work, but not the whole story. Things haven't been going well for him lately, for his group I mean. They've got a couple of hedge funds and Bob's been working closely with one of them. Anyway, long story short, they ran into trouble and last week they declared bankruptcy."

The professor sighed with relief then to mask his reaction nodded sadly and said, "Obviously not good news, but I'm not sure I understand, is he okay, are you okay?"

"For now, yes. A whole bunch of people were let go yesterday, which everyone knew was coming but Bob was reasonably sure he wouldn't be one of them and he wasn't. But of course he couldn't know for sure, so he didn't have a great week. And of course he can't be sure it's over, though it probably is." The professor nodded. "It's the uncertainty that's the hardest part. Things haven't been going well for weeks, months actually. That's the part I wish I had told you. I was trying to impress you and..."

"You have impressed me. This doesn't change anything. I feel bad for your husband of course, but it's you who impresses me. He's not the one I'm interested in."

"Mark..."

"What does bankruptcy mean exactly?"

"It was a classic run on the bank. Basically the investors lost confidence at the same time and wanted their money back. But there wasn't enough to go around because the value of the fund's securities had declined so much while the market had dried up, which is what caused the loss of confidence in the first place. So they had no choice but to seek protection. Weekend before last Bob came up with this plan, last-ditch attempt to save his fund, which included me, he wanted me to get my own fund involved, but I couldn't do that. Still, he thought there was just the outside chance, that's Bob, he's nothing if not determined."

"So are you."

"So he went in Monday all psyched for the final battle, but everyone else had had the same weekend to reflect, so while he's trying to pull in new money or at least stop the bleeding the funds are being swamped with redemption calls. Not a good day, not a great night either, and when he gets to the office Tuesday he's told the funds won't open for business."

"Meaning?"

"The decision had been made overnight to declare bankruptcy."

"But what does that mean, they don't answer the phone?"

"They answer the phone, but they tell people everything's frozen while the funds seek bankruptcy protection."

"I guess I don't know how a hedge fund files for bankruptcy. It's like a mutual fund, right?"

"No, it's not. I mean in some ways they're alike, investors pool their money and so on. But mutual funds are generally held in trust. Bob's fund was a corporation and it was incorporated off-shore. So it's not just a pooled investment, it's also a business operation like any corporation. And when it gets in trouble, it's entitled to bankruptcy protection like any corporation."

"I had no idea. My investments, such as they are, are not with hedge funds."

Tiffany nodded. "That's Tuesday. Friday a major rating agency comes out with a report highlighting the bankrupt funds and puts, get this, the parent company on negative outlook."

"Meaning?"

"Means what it sounds like, not good. They cite the bank's 'relatively small capital base' I think is how they put it. And its exposure to 'mortgage-related investments.' That afternoon the CEO calls Bob's boss's boss into his office and asks for his resignation. He's the guy high up in the parent company responsible for the two hedge funds."

The professor nodded as he watched thinking, "Why is she telling me this? Should I be flattered or worried?" "So," he said, "the firings were yesterday?"

"People went in one after another. It started after lunch and went all afternoon. That's why Bob can't be sure whether this was just the first round or he survived."

"He's worried Monday..."

"No, they wouldn't start again Monday. If you're going they want you gone. But two weeks from now, two months from now? In the meantime he needs to find another home in the organization, like ASAP. I think he'll be okay. Bob's a survivor, that's why I married him. Well, one reason."

"So," he thought, "she doesn't really love him."

"He's working his contacts right now. Come Monday he wants to have internal job interviews lined up back to back."

"He sounds like quite the dynamo. Thank you for telling me this."

She thought, "Why did I tell him? It won't impact his stipend."

"Tiffany?"

"Yes, Mark?"

"There's something I want to tell you too. The... I'm telling you this because we're no longer strangers. Tiffany, the claims I made in my grant application are exaggerated. By that I mean... May I ask why you're smiling?"

"I'm smiling because you're so cute when you get serious. You think I don't know that? It's a grant application, of course it's exaggerated."

He stared at her. "My God, what a relief."

"Silly man. You're still going to do the work, right?"

"Of course."

"Well then there's nothing to worry about, is there?"

"I guess not." He stared at her. "You're kind of marvelous, do you know that?" She stared back. "Let's go somewhere. I don't want to sit here all afternoon. Can I take you to the Metropolitan Museum?"

"You haven't let me down yet. You can take me anywhere you like."

"In that case let's go to a movie theater."

"Let's go to the Met."

No sooner had the taxi pulled away from the curb than they embraced and kissed and Tiffany said, "You like it when I call you 'Mark,' don't you?"

"Each time you say it a shiver goes up and down my spine." They kissed again.

"I wasn't going to see you again."

"Oh?"

"I came today to demonstrate that I wasn't attracted to you."

"I came in hopes that this would happen. All the time you were talking about your husband, I confess all I could think about was kissing you. That's terrible, I know, but it's your fault, my lady, for being so lovely."

"I wish I had a name for you. Anybody can call you 'Mark.'"

"There's 'my lord.'"

They kissed again and she thought, "His awe of my world and my ability to flourish in it is so refreshingly naïve. It's endearing, as is his disregard, even disdain for its goals. I love that he finds me amazing while caring nothing for all the money I make, and I find his obsession with picayune detail endearing, the mark of his dedication. The passion I encounter in my own life is for wealth and glory whereas his is fascination with his subject, with no possibility of reward beyond the hope of finding a student to share it. I am happily that student."

Asked to discuss his research the professor said that the author of the *Codex Calixtinus* was alleged to be Pope Calixtus II but this claim has been rejected by all scholars since around 1600 so attention had shifted to others mentioned as authors; among these Aymericus the Chancellor was named in the *titulus* to chapter nine of the *Pilgrim Guide* (which he reminded her was book five of the *Codex*) as co-author beside Calixtus but there was no more reason to believe one the author than the other. The *titulus* to the '*Ad honorem*' song which was in the same manuscript quire as the *Guide* attributed it to 'Aymeri Picaud, priest of Parthenay' and he was named elsewhere as well probably including the reference in the bull attributed to Pope Innocent II; now Parthenay was west of Poitiers and unlike most of the others encountered along the way by the author of the *Guide* the people of this region were praised. In addition chapter five of the *Guide* was attributed to a certain Aymericus and yet a fourth possible Aimeri was a monk named in another source called the *Historia Compostelana* as having been in Compostela at this time on a mission from the Latin patriarch of Jerusalem.

Could it be, he continued, that all these Aimeris were the same person and the author of the *Guide* even of the entire *Codex*? Some scholars had tried mightily to justify this conclusion but alas the evidence made this extremely unlikely; worse there was no sufficient set of reasons to conclude that any of them was the author or an author that last because the *Guide* was written in more than one style suggesting more than one author and finally other Aimeris were candidates for the identity of the 'Aymericus' of chapter five such as Aimericus of Angoulême a grammarian and Aimeri or Almerich the archdeacon of Antioch. "One conclusion we can draw with confidence is that the author or compiler of the *Guide* was French and probably from the region of Poitiers. We can point to several passages in the *Guide* in support of this thesis, for example—"

"Thank you, professor, that is sufficient for now," said Tiffany who then stopped his mouth with hers. Afterward he thanked her saying he was not unaware of his obsessive personality having been that way since childhood when he'd had an obsessive interest in stamps but she said she liked that about him and that as an undergraduate majoring in classics had had no idea how tedious was so much research on old texts ascertaining provenance authorship authenticity dates of composition besides identifying textual references addressing problems of translation even creating a reliable text. Reassured he agreed noting that all that and more preceded addressing standard questions about a work's purpose and meaning its merit and how it related to other works and she said, "So you see, you do important work," but could see by his face he didn't believe her.

As they started up the vast entrance to the museum he asked what a young beautiful woman like her could see in a man like him whom he again described as a stodgy old professor and when she asked why he kept describing himself that way he said it was in hopes that it would be contradicted. She replied that she had already done that more than once and repeated that he was neither old nor stodgy adding that he didn't need to pretend she was beautiful to which he immediately replied that she was beautiful and as they strolled through the galleries they looked at each other as much as the artwork and walked arm in arm and when they found themselves alone kissed and embraced and their faces shone.

As Tiffany had correctly reported Bob a survivor par excellence though stunned by the knockout blow to his career advancement prospects got on his feet cleared his head and returned to the fight for success on Wall Street by finding or even creating a new position for himself if possible within his organization otherwise elsewhere within the bank which had numerous operations where as he put it his skill set could be profitably deployed. Legally a wholly owned subsidiary capitalized with a small amount of parent company equity and a large amount of debt his organization had been created as an investment management operation to engage in activities from which the parent company wished to be protected in the event of loss. As it happened this plan had been unsuccessful but despite the demise of its hedge funds the organization survived with operations in all aspects of the MBS industry including the underwriting (creation) and distribution (marketing) of securities the management of securities and their underlying collateral (which was often more of the same securities) and active trading in the securities for the bank's own account.

Bob knew his strength was in deal-making and that his boss who had already said he didn't want to lose him just because they had hit a bump in the road saw his greatest contribution in that area so he methodically surveyed his group's operations to identify places where sales prowess could use bolstering whether this meant adding him to a team or replacing someone currently on it. Having done that he needed to identify the decision makers and devise strategies for getting in front of them with multiple strategies necessary because their ways of doing business varied and his network of contacts especially with opinion makers was not uniform throughout the organization and most important their loyalty to him was not uniform. In the amazingly brief period of not quite two weeks he convinced one of the team leaders that his machine had a broken part and that he was the replacement which explained why he came home one evening with a good bottle of wine a big smile and the announcement that he had been engaged to add new sales capability to the CDO management team.

Tiffany relieved at the prospect of life in the house returning to a less stressful level congratulated him but asked why the CDO manager needed new sales capability and was told, "Everybody needs new sales capability, especially now when operational lines are more blurred than ever. Everybody's in everybody else's back yard." The rating agencies were not as complacent as before, he said, so the successful CDO manager needed to create and maintain securities they would approve and investors would buy. "We have to meet industry standards and that means staying light on your feet, and that means having Bob in your corner." He also said, "Want to know the best part? Everybody says the bank leaves us alone to do our thing. Which is what they should have done with the hedge funds instead of pulling the plug, but don't get me started." In bed he said, "Do you need to do your pilgrimage thing this Saturday? Because I was thinking, if you won't be too tired, we could do something Saturday night. Get a great dinner?"

"We haven't been out much since I started this thing, have we?"

"Seems like every Saturday you're either too tired from your pilgrimage thing or you rush in from meeting your professor guy and all you want to do is eat take-out and watch movies. Remember when we had a life?"

"It must have been before I got pregnant."

"Come on, Tiff."

"The answer is yes, I need to do my pilgrimage thing and the next pilgrimage thing is seventeen miles so yes again, I'll probably prefer take-out and a movie to a blow-out dinner. But if you really want to go..."

"Not enough to wreck our marriage."

"You won't wreck our marriage."

"Is that yes to dinner?"

"I think you've earned it."

What Bob didn't mention was that the CDO management operation was hampered by the loss of the hedge funds because the firm had been using the first to buy securities from the second which could either pump up the value of the hedge funds if a higher price were paid or the expected return on investment to the manager if a lower price were paid; since the firm was positioned on both sides of the transaction it fully controlled the terms. With that capability lost it was entirely reliant on a similar relationship with outside underwriters whereby the underwriter would create a CDO consisting primarily of securities owned by Bob's firm which would then buy the lowest-rated tranches of the CDO thereby becoming the owner of a new security derivative of other securities it already owned and so increasing both its fee income from the increase in assets under management and its expected return on investment thanks to the leveraging that accompanied each new derivative.

This arrangement eliminated the appearance of a conflict of interest that was possible when the transaction was done internally and was lucrative so long as prices remained buoyant but that was precisely the problem because with prices under downward pressure investment returns were well below where they'd been a few years earlier when they were as much as ten times higher than management fees. Bob who considered himself a visionary was looking beyond the consensus expectation for an opportunity that wouldn't evaporate in a bit of heat and he kept his eyes open because if he could find that opportunity and bring it into the organization he'd be the hero he always wanted to be.

When the professor returned home after his meeting with Tiffany his sixteen year old daughter Morgan noticed a spring in his step she'd never before seen and asked who the woman was.

"What woman?"

"Come on, father. Out with it."

"Out with what?"

"Nice try, daddy, do I have to beat it out of you?"

"You realize of course that you're living proof of the proposition that one can be too perceptive. You're right, I'm seeing someone."

"I know that, father, I'm asking for the who what where when why. Actually I know the why and the what goes without saying, so maybe we should focus on the other stuff."

"Her name's Tiffany..."

"Tiffany? Who named their daughter Tiffany fifty years ago? Oh no, father, please tell me she's older than me."

"Rest easy. Quite a bit older."

"Named Tiffany? Can't be too much older."

"She's thirty-three."

"Thirty-three. I'm starting to like this. Father's seeing a younger woman. So before I ask what she sees in you, since I already know what you see in her, maybe we should start with innocent details like occupation, last known address..."

"She works for a hedge fund. She's some kind of investment analyst."

"Come on, how would you meet someone who... I don't get it, what aren't you telling me?"

"She's the one who's funding my research. Her foundation. So we met to discuss the grant and one thing led to another."

"So it seems." When she asked when he was going to bring her home to meet the family he told her she was already married. "Dear me, what have we gotten ourselves into?" Curious to see the one woman who had conquered her father's affections after the great loss in his life she asked if he could bring her to New Haven anyway.

"May I ask why you're so anxious to meet her?"

"Obviously, father, now that I know what you see in her, I'm dying to know what she sees in you."

"Am I that much of a paunchy old windbag?"

"Of course not, daddy, you're a sweet old teddy bear who chooses to devote his entire existence to picayune details about medieval monasticism and related topics no less fascinating to the general population. Besides, I want to make sure she isn't just using you."

"We're not going to marry, Morgan. I told you she's already married. Please don't jump to conclusions, we're not even seriously involved."

"Maybe she's not but you are. Just in case you didn't know that."

"Not really. I admit I'm quite taken with her, but..."

"'Quite taken,' I like that. Do you wish you could marry her?"

"Please listen carefully, most favorite daughter, I do not wish... Do you wish I would remarry?"

"Not for my sake."

"Do you worry about me? You shouldn't. I'm not unhappy."

"But you're not happy."

"I am happy. Especially now. But I wouldn't be happy if I knew you were unhappy."

"I'm happy too. And I hope your affair with a young married Tiffany works out, though I've never been able to figure out how those things work."

"You mean in all your sixteen years?"

"Yes, most favorite father, in all my sixteen years."

Chapter Sixteen

DAY NINE. After three days descending the Alps and three more in rugged upland followed by a day along a gradually calming river and another to leave it the caravan now traveled a long lane that gradually widened into a valley between high hills along the north relatively low and irregular whereas to the south much higher rounded and densely forested forming a continuous line like a curtain uniform and smooth and green. The road was level and straight and from what the count could learn that was how it would be all the way to the Rhône river and then south and west through the vast marsh lands and this was good news to no one more than Margherita and Tuccio who could anticipate being together all day who as they rode side by side in perfect weather thought, "May it always be like this."

Of the waif who was now an expected part of the caravan Margherita was still suspicious and felt repulsion despite her sympathy having been aroused so it was with mixed emotions that she found the girl staring again during another reading lesson with those unblinking long looks in which she admitted she saw nothing but gentleness. When one of the porters made yet another attempt to converse the girl unexpectedly pointed to her saying 'pilgrim, pilgrim' and then she pointed to herself and repeated the word which there was no mistaking.

"Pilgrim? You?" She nodded. "But you are a child. I say, you are a child." The girl stared. "Pilgrim where? Where do you go?"

The girls' eyes widened into the beginning of a smile and proudly announced, "Compostela."

The porter snorted, "But that is..." and gestured to indicate a great distance. "Land's end," he added. "Finisterra. Far beyond the

Pyrenees."

When the girl nodded energetically he pressed her to find out why she was set on such a distant goal wondering how she could imagine she could walk there by herself without money or food or even clothes; he managed to learn or was confident he had learned that she wanted to beseech Saint James and maybe the Virgin Mary to protect her but protect her from what he didn't learn still he delivered the information to Agnoletta who promptly relayed it to Margherita.

"Santiago! Are you sure?"

The maid shrugged. "That filthy little thing thinks she's going...?"

Everyone was astonished also fascinated as the mystery of this girl only deepened and sympathetic to the point that no one (excepting Agnoletta) could find it in their heart now it was certain she was neither a thief nor insane to thrust her back out by herself where no one doubted it was only a matter of time before some calamity befell her. The count let it be known she could join the caravan providing the porters took responsibility an invitation she accepted in grateful silence though still sat apart and barely spoke and after some discussion one of the porters rearranged some bundles and helped her onto one of the mules.

Margherita who suspected the girl simply had no idea how far away Compostela was or how difficult and dangerous the journey said, "A porter must have told her that's where I'm going."

"Then now there are three of us."

When they reached a small but important city two days from Avignon Tuccio joined her in the convent church to hear vespers and formally declare, "Mita, I have said that I will go to Compostela out of love for you, and that is still true and I confess I would not go without you, but I will go now for my own sake too. For obvious reasons I cannot take up the staff and pouch, and I say in all honesty that I would not if I could, nor can I wear the robe so long as the count desires my service, but I say to you in this holy place that I now commit myself to pilgrimage to better myself, so that when I arrive at the shrine I shall be worthy of it and worthy of you, that I may beseech Saint James to bless us."

DAY TEN. The caravan was proceeding without a rest day because everyone preferred to take their leisure in Avignon where the *fattore* would immerse himself in the luxury commerce for why languish in a wilderness outpost like Sisteron a fortification with something desperate about it when a metropolitan city boasting a prominent Italian colony glistened with attractions of every sort? The curtain of mountain became a range of much lower hills rocky and irregular more interesting but just as reassuring for the land seemed open and harmonious making everyone feel welcome in some inexplicable way as if they approached a great celebration; but for Tuccio who was attracted to the form of fine love called 'love from a distance' because it seemed most noble even if not the most satisfying in an obvious way this excitement provoked a specific urge and as Margherita and he became progressively more intimate the other side of fine love increasingly asserted itself the one in which love was consummated.

Their exchange of garlands and ritual bathing in the source of the Durance at the summit of the Alpine pass had expressed their love while seeking to contain the sexual urge that was threatening to escape but that beast could not be permanently subdued and now it was attempting another escape thanks to Nico who opened the cage for whenever Tuccio was teased he was generally the one who initiated it. He took as his theme the question of why the youth hadn't yet jousted with the lady and continued, "Have you performed any feats of arms at all? Have you even drawn your sword? How she must be pining away in her garden. 'Tuccino,'" he said in a falsetto voice, "'Tuccinello, as you have touched my heart, won't you touch other parts of my body? Don't worry, my dearest, I do not fear wounding, indeed I sigh for it. Even if your sword is only a knife, dearest, I am dying to see how it pricks,'" and Tuccio leaped on him more than half in earnest and they needed to be pulled apart.

The problem he confessed afterward to Stoldo was that Nico was right and he didn't know what to do to which came the succinct reply, "You have won the tournament, why not take your prize?" so later when he was alone with Margherita he reached for her.

"What are you doing?"

"Don't tell me you don't want it too."

"Stop." By the time he stopped both of them were panting. "We can't do this."

"I can't stand it any more."

"You have to stand it."

After a troubled silence he confessed that he had been thinking more about the troubadour songs dedicated to consummated love than the others.

She sighed and warned, "Once we start touching each other..."

"We already touch each other."

"Once we touch each other more intimately, there will be no going back. Whatever step we take we will take again and again."

"I'm waiting to hear the terrible part."

"Each step urges a further step. Once we go down that road..."

"That road too is fine love."

"The poets may claim so. I doubt my confessor would agree."

"Mita, we have discussed this."

"We have, and I thought we agreed to pray for guidance at the saint's tomb."

Later when Stoldo asked him if he had claimed his prize he shook his head saying, "She wants to give as much as I want to take, but..."

"Is it not driving you mad?"

"Of course. I am afflicted as the count said. But of all the arrows with which I could be struck..."

"Since you enjoy the pain so much, you would not want to seek relief from those whose profession it is to assuage such pain. Or would you?"

Later Agnoletta asked Margherita if her will had submitted to her desire and she replied, "It must not."

"And yet does it seem like a good idea to turn down an unexpected gift of Fortune? Who would know?"

"God would know."

"As he knows that your husband has not been a husband to you."

"You are correct that I suffer. But what before was bitter now is sweet. Now let us change the subject."

"As you wish, *madonna*. We are to arrive at Avignon the day after tomorrow. I grow more excited with each step."

"As do I."

"I must say I look forward to being rid of that..."

"You would chase her back into the wilderness?"

"I thought you didn't like her either?"

"Yet she is still God's child. A child, after all."

"Well, she can't enter the pope's city as she is, can she?"

"You are right, I hadn't thought of that."

"Then it seems we have no choice."

"You're right. You must wash the stench off her."

"What!"

"As you say, we have no choice. You must bathe her in a stream and wash her clothes."

"You're not serious. Well I won't do it. I won't, I say."

Agnoletta grabbed the girl without bothering to make herself understood and roughly shoved and dragged her to the stream but when she pulled off her shift and saw the unmistakable curve to her belly she drew back as if struck and cried, "Oh dear lord! Do my eyes deceive me? You are pregnant?" She curved her hands in front of her own belly but the child only blinked. "Who did this to you? Well might I ask. Oh, my poor child." After washing her hair and scrubbing her shift she took her (more gently) by the hand to Margherita who told Tuccio who told Stoldo who told the other guards and the porters overheard and someone informed the count who told the *fattore* and everyone looked at everyone but especially at Margherita whose gender and rank were presumed to somehow give her some special command of the situation. Asked to learn how old she was she told the count, "She says she thinks she's fourteen, but I'd guess thirteen more likely by the look of her."

The other question on everyone's mind was obvious and the conjectures came immediately the first that she had given herself to some peasant in a field and now was paying the price of her unrestrained passion but she was scrawny with nothing lusty about her so incest was next and the one on which everyone settled because any other rape seemed unlikely and the girl wouldn't answer questions about the father (though no one could be sure she understood them). Pity and sympathy were not necessarily the reactions accorded such victims who were seen as irremediably defiled hence revulsion was at least as common and the conjecture that the girl had run away proved to many of the men that she herself was ashamed while the women considered it more likely she was an innocent victim perhaps abused because she was 'simple' and expelled by her family.

For her part she didn't seem to care what the reaction was and as always kept to herself said nothing and played with her kitten but now that everyone knew her condition her strange behavior was no longer so strange so at the next meal it was Margherita who brought her food and when the waif looked up to thank her and they briefly caught each other's gaze she knew there was nothing wrong with her except her circumstances. She returned to her place but kept watching the girl who stared back with the same fixity until Margherita smiled a little and the girl replied with a little smile of her own.

They reached a small city on a river with considerable anticipation that the following day would find them in Avignon until they learned that they had missed seeing the miraculous source of the river in a narrow valley nearby and everyone agreed even the *fattore* that Avignon would still be there a day later whereas it seemed foolish to miss a great natural wonder.

DAY ELEVEN. In the hamlet where they were heading there were no accommodations but they didn't care because the inn the previous night had been miserable the sleeping quarters filthy with old straw a dangerous incident with robbers in which two of the guards had been slightly wounded and in the morning the innkeeper had presented the *fattore* with an outrageous bill. With that behind them everyone was looking forward to the 'closed valley' of spectacular beauty with a miraculous spring at its closed end from which an entire river surged and arriving after an easy hour and a half at its entrance forgot about breakfast as they gazed at the sharp limestone cliffs and the emerald green sparkling river.

Those who could be spared from the mules headed upstream to a pile of boulders on the other side of which was a mountain seven hundred fifty feet almost straight up the base of which had been undermined by the water's agitation. The pool that filled this grotto however seemed completely still as if nothing were happening and it was the incompatibility between this and the white-water river at least fifty feet wide on the other side of the boulders that doubled the awfulness of the mystery; upon seeing it the waif shrieked in terror and ran away as if her life were in danger in fact so terrified was she that when Agnoletta caught up with her and threw her arms around her she was trembling violently.

Bawling something mostly incomprehensible it seemed she was scared of the dragon living in the underwater cave a fear from which the maid was not totally immune for springs were dangerous places sacred when tamed but always mysterious emanations from earth's chthonic realm and in fact later they would learn that there had been a dragon-like monster until the sixth century when a hermit had chased it away to die. When the girl calmed down enough to notice that her kitten was gone she became distraught all over again and ran in all directions calling out its name joined by

Agnoletta who crawled over boulders and up the side of the canyon until it became clear the kitten would not be found; at that point she pulled the child now gently now not so gently toward the departing group and astonishingly the girl's despair rapidly disappeared perhaps because Agnoletta assured her they would get another perhaps because she was accustomed to suffering.

While those who had had to stay with the mules hurried up the path the returning group had breakfast and relaxed in the rising heat beside the refreshing river near the hamlet which without land to cultivate or industry had only a few huts clustered around a primitive little church whose dwellers kept mostly out of sight until an old man drew near to boast that a great Italian poet lived among them. Having understood the key words of his Provençal Tuccio was immediately excited to meet this poet but how would it be possible without an introduction and how would a mere caravan guard albeit noble gain admission? He told Margherita she must meet him whoever he was but unlike him she was not starstruck by poets nor desirous to meet one for she had never read a poem and wouldn't have the first idea what to say but faced with his excited insistence she agreed and the villager was made to understand that the lady would like to meet the poet and proud of his honored resident he agreed to take her to his house to see if the great man was able to receive a guest.

"Where does he live?"

"Right there," he said pointing to a nearby house.

With sudden timidity Margherita said to Tuccio, "What good is it for me to meet this man when you are the one who wishes to do so? I have no idea what to say. You must come with me."

"How can I, dressed as I am? He would never..."

She had an idea and turned to the count who with some persuading acceded to her plan and the four crossed the river to a spectacular site below dramatic cliffs with a castle at their summit which had them gazing in all directions when Tuccio asked the poet's name.

"Francesco Petrarca."

"What? What did you say? Did you say 'Petrarca?' Lord save me, can it be? My God, yes, I remember the name! Margherita, this is he, the poet I—! Don't you remember, this is the one I—!"

"You mean the one..."

"Yes, yes, the one, the very one. Lord save me, what will I—? Oh my God."

Asked by the staring villager if there was a problem the count smiled and shook his head saying, "My squire, who fears no man in battle and no woman in bed, fears great poets," and in fact Tuccio knowing nothing about the man or his poetry was visibly nervous.

"In truth, the man can be difficult," whispered the villager and raising a warning finger said, "Poets," then went inside and reappeared some minutes later smiling but warned they must not take up the poet's time for he was at work. In fact Petrarca was not anxious to receive strangers arriving at his doorstep without notice or introduction but hearing that a beautiful and wealthy noblewoman of inestimable merit from his native Tuscany was passing on pilgrimage and who learning that the successor to the beloved Dante lauded by all Europe lived in this very village... For so the villager had told the story and though the poet's craving for solitude had led him to leave Avignon for this isolated spot his greater craving for fame led him to open his door.

Learning she was Sienese (and setting aside his initial assessment that she was not in fact a beauty till he had appraised her more fully) he mentioned his close friendship with Simone Martini a Sienese who had worked in Siena before coming to Avignon and was shocked to see no sign of recognition. "Alas, of his death three years ago I still mourn. May I ask what you think of his fresco of the *maestà* in the Palazzo Pubblico, a work heralded by so many as a masterpiece?" With still no reaction he assumed his presence made them too nervous for while the count seemed impassive his squire appeared struck dumb while of the lady's obvious discomfort he reserved judgment.

Said the count, "As I am not born Sienese, I cannot share the local pride in having produced such a great painter, but I have had the opportunity to gaze upon this masterpiece. May I ask, did he exhibit the great sensitivity as a friend that he evidently possessed as a painter?"

In answering this question Petrarca told them why he had returned to Avignon as an adult and when he had moved to his present location to escape that impious Babylon and why he'd returned after an extended stay in Italy and how often he traveled to Avignon on necessary errands despite how much he despised that furnace of deceits and that he had recently been offered the post of Papal Secretary which he'd refused with private glee (though he didn't mention the gift of a sinecure in Parma he had not refused) and that he couldn't believe it was already seven years since the Roman Senate had ceremoniously placed the laurel wreath on his head; he also mentioned that he adored gardening despite disliking common people and that from the blessed day he had seen the most beautiful woman in the world he had devoted his life and his art to her consecration. "Her name is Laura. *L'aura* I sometimes refer to her, 'the breeze,' likening her to the incomparable beauty and freshness of a spring day, as the troubadours celebrated it. Sometimes I refer to her as *lauro*, the laurel, both the tree and its leaves, for as the tree she is the wonder and magnificence of the natural world while as the leaves, the leaves enwreathed, she embodies the highest achievement of art, for her beauty and her merit are incomparable, incomparable," and finally he noted how difficult it was to be Europe's most famous poet celebrated in every quarter.

"You must enjoy living here," said the count.

"It was twenty years ago that I first saw my muse. For twenty years have I written of her, in that task am I still active, you may see my current rhyme as yet incomplete there on my writing table, I was at work when you knocked, yet in recent years I have written three works, one for my eyes alone on the decision to be miserable and how to reverse it, the others extolling solitude."

"What a beautiful house," said Margherita, "and the setting, how—"

"Here I remain alone, and as Love invites me, now rhymes and verses, now I gather herbs and flowers. In a valley closed on every side, which is cool comfort for my weary sighs, I arrived alone with Love, pensive and slow."

Believing himself in the presence of greatness in the temple of Love Tuccio was able only to gawk and Petrarca thinking him vulgar was ungraciously condescending until Margherita informed him that this young man was steeped in the poetry of the troubadours and dedicated to fine love; and knowing Tuccio was dying to hear a poem she asked if he would honor them with a brief recital to which he agreed with feigned reluctance after allowing them to beg three times and after enforcing an extended silence to create the requisite mood he recited not a single poem but a medley.

"Because singing, the sorrow disembitters itself..." he began and paused. "And almost in every valley/ booms the sound of my heavy sighs/ that obtain evidence of the painful life..." he said sighing audibly before continuing in a slightly more energetic register, "But much more than ever/ of my sweet and bitter enemy/ there is need that I speak,/ though she be such who exceeds all speech. This one who with her gaze thoughts steals/ opened my chest and my heart took with her hand,/ saying to me, 'Of this make no word,'" and there he fixed a sharp stare on the count who stared back on Margherita who looked away discretely and on Tuccio who held the gaze only a moment before pretending to sink into deep meditation.

Having briefly exited Petrarca returned inside himself where he located his somber mood and recommenced intoning, "So weak is the thread to which follows/ my heavy life/ that if someone does not aid it/ it will be immediately of its course at the limit... When I find myself from her beautiful face/ so much to be separated,/ with desire being unable to move my wings,/ little is left me of the usual consolation/ nor do I know how long I can live in this state./ Every place saddens me where I do not see/ those beautiful gentle eyes/ that carried the keys/ of my sweet thought while it pleased God,/ and since hard exile worsens my situation more,/ if I sleep or walk or sit/ other never do I call for/ and what I saw since then displeases me./ How many mountains and waters,/ how much sea, how many rivers/ hide from me those two eyes/ that almost a beautiful clear sky at mid-day/ makes my darkness..." An extended moment of silence followed the trailing off of his voice which itself had followed his plaintive cry "How many mountains!" following which he stepped to his table reached for a glass of sweetened wine and tipped into his mouth a restorative sip.

"Alas for me," he groaned returning to his place, "that I do not know in which place turns/ the hope that has been betrayed by now many a time!/ For if there is no one who with pity listens to me,/ why scatter to Heaven so often prayers?" and scanning his audience as if to seek an answer while finding none yet satisfied with his effect he briefly turned to the window turned back and continued, "And if I could make happen that to the holy eyes/ would give some pleasure/ some sweet saying of mine,/ oh me blessed above other lovers!" Here briefly appeared a loving smile like a sun emerging from behind a gray cloud only to be obscured by another as he recited, "What am I saying or where am I and who deceives me/ other than myself and my immoderate desire?/ ...With me stays one who day and night vexes me,/ since with his pleasure makes me turn grave/ 'The sweet sight of her beautiful delicate look.'" He walked to the window that looked out across a kitchen garden to the river and beyond it the hamlet and the hills as though she might have been outside waiting for his hopeful despairing look so she could return the look and thus bestow on him a moment of joy and a month of doubt; then he returned to his place of recitation collected his thoughts and continued.

"Lovely eyes where Love makes home,/ to you I turn my frail style/ slow by itself but great pleasure spurs it... Oh hills, oh valleys, oh rivers, oh woods, oh fields,/ oh witnesses of my solemn life,/ how many times did you hear me call Death! ...Happy the soul that for you sighs... Alas, why so infrequently/ do you give me that from which I never am sated,/ why not more often/ do you look at how Love of me makes torment...? I say that from time to time,/ your mercy, I sense in the middle of my soul/ a sweetness unusual and new... Wherefore if any good fruit/ is born of me, from you comes first the seed;/ I to me am practically a dry land/ cultivated by you, and the quality is yours altogether." He sighed languidly eyes turned inward looked at his writing table and sighed looked upward through the ceiling sighed again then slowly lowering his head looked down in thought.

"I think..." he began in a low voice as though talking to himself, "If up there/ whence the Eternal Mover of the stars/ deigned to show His work on Earth,/ are the other works as beautiful,/ may it be open the prison in which I am locked/ and which from the path to such life keeps me!/ Then I turn again to my usual war,/ thanking Nature and the day that I was born/ that have destined me to so much good,/ and her who to so much hope/ raised my heart..." He wiped a tear and continued, "Because I see, and it displeases me,/ that my natural gift to me has no value/ nor makes me worthy of a so dear glance,/ I make an effort to be such/ who to the high hope is suitable/ and to the noble fire with which I fully burn."

Suddenly he seemed to hop out of his persona to the table and scribble a note read it make a change and read it again then taking his time returned to his recital to say pensively practically muttering, "But as best it can satisfies itself/ my soul hesitant and vague," then fully arrived declaimed, "How many times did I say/ then, full of fear,/ 'She certainly was born in Paradise!'" only to fall back into lassitude as if his energy were spent. "For to my tired eyes/ always is she present, whence I am all consumed by desire,/ and thus with me she stays/ such that another I never see nor to see do I yearn,/ nor the name of another in my sighs do I call..."

And as if marshaling the last of his vigor he proclaimed, "Love... you have the arrows and the bow,/ do it by your hand, not with sheer yearning, that I die... Oh world, oh vain thoughts!/ Oh my strong destiny, for what does it put me forward? ...Waiting am I that he shoots the arrow/ the final shot who gave me the first... My song," he concluded addressing his poetry, "motionless in the field/ I will stand, for it is dishonor to die fleeing..."

FRANCESCO. If Francesco was capable of love his foster mother was the one person to whom he could express it for though she had raised him for only a couple of years till he left home at fifteen he came to think of her as his mother and had always made sure she had no financial concerns her only complaint being that he didn't visit her enough. In fact rarely did he visit even when she became blind and frail in her seventies yet clinging to life and able to manage with considerable help from neighbors; when he did come to the hamlet only a short distance beyond the city walls she had him sit beside her so she could touch his arm when he spoke.

About herself she had nothing to say but expected him to talk at length about himself and Margherita and down to the least of the servants and about the least domestic occurrence and if he fell short she prompted him with endless questions about the minutia of his household's economy but there were no longer any questions about children. Those had ceased once it had become clear there would be none at least from his wife for though he assumed she could not possibly know about his relations with servants since he never so much as hinted at the subject he underestimated the efficacy of gossip which reached the hamlet more often than him and she was too fastidious to let slip what she knew.

In his business she had no interest only asking about it politely in a way that invited him to answer briefly though she was proud of his success especially that he had accomplished everything without any help from family (having no family to provide any) but cared nothing about his riches; about his conduct she would have cared but assumed he was not involved in anything devious or dishonest and certainly nothing to do with usury and whenever he visited she spoke of his rectitude as though saying it made it so or might inspire him to make it so. At her age having learned a thing or two about how worldly affairs were conducted among men she would not have been surprised to learn that the record of his activities was not as spotless as he implied but she would have been shocked and so preferred not to hear it. She would not for example have wanted to know that when he had learned the wheat crop was failing in the Sienese *contado* he had bought up Genoese supplies nor that she herself had been the source of that tip nor to hear him cursed in front of the village church as a cold-hearted merchant ruthless and heartless; she might have hoped his motive was the sincere desire to prevent famine without wanting to know his asking price which would have revealed whether it was that or the chance to turn a fast profit.

For his part he could not help but brag about his success after all if not to one's mother then to whom for he was naturally full of pride no doubt too appreciative of his shrewdness though not smug or supercilious but generally offering the appearance without the substance of modesty. "Since God has granted me more than I deserve," he often said as a way of reassuring her whenever she asked him (which was whenever she saw him) when he intended to enjoy what God had granted him and whether his financial affairs were in order; always he answered 'soon, very soon,' as soon as some deal was completed and when in turn he would ask her a dozen times whether she had everything she desired a slight wave of her hand dissipated such a silly question.

Chapter Seventeen

DAY TWELVE. The waif had slept on the stone floor of the little church like a baby in a cradle without so much as a rag beneath her though Agnoletta had offered her better than that to provide a bit of cushioning 'for the baby' she had said but the waif just lay down in silence and closed her eyes with a contented smile and when next they looked at her she was fast asleep.

"Asleep she looks even younger than she is," remarked Agnoletta.

Margherita replied, "In here she is home."

No one knew how old the church was but everything about it suggested a distant past unknown to the age of gigantic magnificently decorated cathedrals with spires rising hundreds of feet brilliant stained glass and monumental statuary; this tiny edifice had no statuary and no windows save a small one without glass at each end little decoration simple construction with a curved barrel-vaulted ceiling about twenty-five feet above the floor supported by two Roman pillars that it was said had been taken from the pagan temple that previously occupied the site. The altar that consisted of a stone slab and the baptismal font that was a solid stone barrel were said to be as old as the church while the sarcophagus in the crypt dated back to the sixth century and contained the remains of the sainted hermit who had vanquished the water dragon.

To Margherita used to the splendor of Siena's cathedral this church was pathetic even in comparison with the little churches she had found charming along the pilgrim route whereas to the waif it might as well have been a cathedral and Margherita watching her with amusement had begun to her surprise to feel some of that mood invade her. She who had been taught to measure religious devotion with size and ornamentation and complexity of design wondered if in its very primitiveness there might lie more not less holiness more mystery more of the drama of direct participation.

It had been Agnoletta's idea to bring the girl into the church with them as it had been the night before when they had stayed in a convent but then she had refrained from suggesting it out of timidity and had instead left her in the stable with the porters which as it happened had been fortunate because it was she who had awakened at the entry of the thieves. There was no longer any question of sending her off but that raised the question of what to do with her in Avignon toward which the caravan had gotten an early start for the *fattore* and the count said she could stay with the porters but Agnoletta argued against that with Margherita saying it was improper.

The mountains having disappeared the river meandered in rivulets across an open plain toward the Rhône as if unsure of the proper path with the caravan following the one that led to Avignon Tuccio and Margherita riding beside each other as usual but oddly quiet glancing often at the water as though it carried their thoughts. When the wall came into view the road became the street of the cloth dyers accommodating a foul if necessary occupation but hardly the approach to the papal seat one would have expected (though as Petrarca had claimed not out of character) and they held their noses past ramshackle dwelling-workshops and expanses of drying cloth to enter the city through a simple gate.

The first needs were to secure the goods and stable the animals toward both of which they were directed by the customs inspectors the latter (and the inn that went with it) outside the century-old wall which the overcrowded city had considerably overflowed. The impatient tourists were eager to get their first look at this booming city which in the four decades since the papacy had moved here from Rome had grown from about five thousand with a Dominican convent and a fledgling university to a European center six or seven times that size.

Swirling around the pope were five hundred or more court officials with twenty cardinals each having a luxurious palace and a huge retinue occupying dozens of dwellings either in the city or across the river; these were served by an army of diplomats tax collectors and couriers all served in turn by merchant bankers who facilitated both the vast wealth of this clerical elite and its desire for luxury goods like gold cloth and furs tapestries and paintings precious stones and spices and on and on.

And to this center from across Europe came emissaries and seekers of every description it took but moments in its overcrowded streets to sense the drive of the place that was in the eyes the sweat the unapologetic bumping of shoulders and the clarion calls of resplendent delegations mounted and haughty forcing their way. Of course Siena too had its importance and its opulence its display and its self-regard so no one was overawed by this but what was distinctive was that this was supposed to be a holy city or at least a city of holy people but everyone knew how far short of that standard Rome had fallen so here too there was no great shock even among the offended; what there was was the excitement of being far from home yet among Italians who leading Europe in banking and commerce dominated the city and having available anything money or ingenuity could acquire.

DAYS THIRTEEN TO SIXTEEN. When Margherita had presented the waif at a convent as a foundling under her protection and asked if she might be received the nun extended her arms toward the girl saying, "Is she not like a certain other young woman, pregnant and on the road, in need of shelter?" Meanwhile the count having presented himself at one of the palaces and the *fattore* using Francesco's letter of introduction at the substantial house of an Italian merchant were meeting to discuss how Margherita was to be chaperoned in the city so in the morning when she exited the convent Tuccio and Stoldo were waiting; for it had been agreed she could not be left alone in a city whose ostentatious wealth created flagrant crime and further that Tuccio would be her guard because it would be impossible to keep him away and he could be counted on not to be distracted from diligently protecting her and with him of course went Stoldo.

For the *fattore* this was either the worst or best arrangement but he simply could not make it his concern and still engage in the kind of commerce Francesco and he had discussed which would keep him going every waking minute; if she behaved properly his concern would prove groundless and if she disgraced herself he could renegotiate better terms against a threat of publicizing her behavior but for the present he would dedicate himself to the enormous commercial opportunities surrounding him. The count was also of two minds about the arrangement but needed to maintain morale and Tuccio was his only man who saw more opportunities in the woman than the city; so either the youth would have his fun and give the lady what she wanted which would not go well for future employment or they would behave properly and save his reputation.

Margherita's present concern was to obtain clothing for the girl who was temporarily covered with something the nuns had found so the first task of the day was to find a pawnshop since no tailor could work quickly enough but while she had no trouble finding the street of pawnshops behind the papal palace what she found as expected were mostly fine gowns that in any case were too big for such a small girl. The only alternative was a tailor and while women of her station didn't visit tailors she didn't see any alternative and was asking directions to their street when politely interrupted by an elegantly dressed woman who proposed that if they came to her house she would have her tailor summoned immediately. Seeing Margherita inspect her she explained that she visited pawnshops on occasion looking for bargains and leaned in to whisper as though they were already friends, "Perhaps precious jewelry pawned by a cardinal's mistress in need of quick cash."

As they were walking to her house Agnoletta exclaimed, *"Madonna,* she has spoken, her name is Piera!"

"Your name is Piera?" asked Margherita gently but the girl who had met her eyes only once could not bring herself to do so again. "'Piera,' that's an Italian name. Are you Italian? Where is your country?"

"Madonna," exclaimed the maid in a loud whisper, "is it possible? That she walked over the Alps?" but Margherita noted that she didn't speak Italian.

"Will you tell us the name of your village?"

"Is she simple?" asked the hostess.

"Assuredly not. But much abused as you can see."

Arriving at a luxurious home near a cardinal's palace the hostess said she felt certain she could find something appropriate around the house and immediately summoned a servant who brought a pile of items several of which could be made to fit with some needlework (and could be let out over the coming months as necessary); then she ordered refreshment while the alterations were made so it was over fine goblets that the two women exchanged the rigorous courtesies of introduction and the careful pleasantries of initial conversation. This concluded and the clothes brought to the girl who at first was afraid to don them but soon was grinning for the first time the hostess proposed that Margherita stay as her guest adding, "Of course your maid and the girl are also welcome, should that be your wish." She did seem very nice and was from Prato near Florence and her accommodations would be superior to the convent's but Margherita knew she would inevitably be drawn into social rounds and thus taken away from Tuccio with whom she had been planning to spend long days exploring the city's notable sights but the more she declined the more the woman insisted.

Here was a strange turn of events for she had a letter of introduction to a merchant with whom Francesco did business which originally she'd intended to use to gain entree to some of the six hundred Italian families mostly Tuscan living in Avignon a more cosmopolitan city than Siena and far from her husband's surveilling eye. The idea had arisen as part of his attempt to get her to travel with a caravan a bribe in effect and she had taken it but obviously had had no idea how different her desires would be when she actually arrived for which the simple escape was not to use the letter but now here she was caught in the same net by another hand. "My robe is dirty and sweaty," she feebly objected at which the hostess dispatched a servant to procure a new one and Margherita saw her plans her expectations her hopes and desires for Avignon all of which involved Tuccio disappear with her hostess's ignorant friendliness.

When she despairingly told him what had happened however he refused to be dismissed saying his orders were to accompany her at all times which gave her the idea to report with feigned embarrassment that the men had informed her they answered to her husband not her and had orders to accompany her everywhere and further if they reported to him that she was not spending her days in holy devotions there would be strife when she returned. "Perhaps you are more fortunate in your husband, but mine..."

"They are all the same," replied the hostess with a wide smile, "and that is why we must be more clever than them. Leave it to me, I will have you in church so much your husband will be amazed at your devotional stamina, for we can entertain ourselves there as well as anywhere!"

Margherita was close to despair when this came to her: "If only that were possible, but alas I must be alone, for so my husband ordered. As you see, he would not even let me join a group of pilgrims. He is quite severe in his views," and suppressing a smile she returned downstairs to tell Tuccio she had rescued them though the day was lost with the first half already gone and the hostess determined to introduce her to noblewomen she knew who belonged to merchant families.

When they were reunited in the morning it felt like liberation though in fact she had enjoyed herself immensely visiting the wives of Avignon's commercial elite and had learned what she never would have otherwise about the city's vast commercial operation known as the papacy; Tuccio was completely uninterested but listened politely to tales like the one of great mounds of gold and silver coins in the pope's palace no sooner counted and stored than replenished until he found an opportunity to introduce the subject so much on his own mind which was Petrarca. Once beyond the state of shock following their departure from his house he'd been flooded with thoughts impressions questions and longed to share them with her who for her part was also perplexed and fascinated. "Remember how, when he was finally finished, he just stared? That was odd!"

"He asked nothing about us, as courtesy would require. Is it possible with poets the usual rules don't apply? On the other hand, how would he have reacted had he learned I am a merchant's wife and not the cousin of a count?"

"He would have ignored it. He is a poet, he can read your soul."

"Then he read my complete ignorance of poetry."

"Mine too, I fear. But we are not ignorant of love." They had never been alone more than a brief time or when they needn't worry about being surprised by someone whereas now they could promenade about the city without a care. "Do you think Laura exists?"

"What a question! If not, he is mad, no?"

"He claims he first saw her in 1327. If she was fifteen then, the youngest a girl could be and attract the passion of a man, then she is thirty-five now. She could well be forty, forty-five, fifty, yet he still writes of her as though she were as he first saw her."

"So you think..."

"I wonder if she exists as an actual person. There could very well be a particular woman who inspired him, it's even possible her name was Laura. If so, does he truly love that woman or the ideal she represents?"

"You think the poet's heart and mind have conspired to dream her?"

"Yes. One who happens to be exactly as described in the troubadour songs. Songs which the *giullare* told me are over two hundred years old."

"You do not think a woman could be as he describes?"

"Perfect in beauty, perfect in intelligence. Pure of heart, conduct above reproach."

"Not that. Someone worthy of suggesting that."

"At the time I had no reason to think Laura was not as real as you. Afterward what has nagged me was the airy way he spoke of her. If she does exist as you do, he has certainly cultivated an ambiguity on this question that cannot be resolved."

"Why do you care?"

"I must know if I am to learn from poetry how to love a flesh and blood woman."

"Certainly it's easier to love an ideal. Maybe that's why he holds her reality in suspense. I think he knows that even if there is a woman named Laura with beautiful eyes and the rest, the Laura of his poems has a higher reality."

"Which is why the extent to which the lower exists is irrelevant. Let the ambiguity persist if it suits his poetic ends so well."

"But didn't you say just now that you need to know?"

"I did, and so I contradict myself."

"Perhaps it doesn't matter."

"Perhaps you are right. Yes, of course you are right. It is sufficient that the poetry be true."

"Do you find it to be true?"

"Oh yes! I see by your face you're not sure. I can't imagine a poet writing more finely about love at a distance. His entire life seems dedicated to it. That's why I would like to know if, when he peers through his window, an actual woman might appear."

"Obviously you and I do not love at a distance. When we embrace or..."

"The actual distance is irrelevant."

"You mean to say it is a way of loving. Yes, I have experienced that."

"Are we losing it? When we duck into an entryway while Stoldo and Agnoletta screen us from view..."

"Yet was it not you just three days ago who..."

"I confess. But he has inspired me anew."

"To seek a love without pleasure."

"To seek a love that is not merely pleasure."

"Did you not see how miserable his love has made him? If that is *fin'amor*..."

"He loves a phantom. I love a woman. I want to know whether *fin'amor* is for phantoms only."

"He may believe his ennobling is all the greater for its lack of reward."

"Yet love entails suffering, does it not?"

"For suffering I need not seek love, for I had it in abundance before I began this pilgrimage."

"Look at Agnoletta and Stoldo, how they hold hands, let themselves be pressed against each other by the throng, all looks and touches. How long before it is we who screen them from view?"

"You fear there is no distinction between their pleasure and ours."

"You do not?"

"You are right. For my salvation, if not yours, there must be one."

Not only did the pope own the city having purchased it from the queen of Naples he was the sole reason for its ascent and whatever one could see and whatever one was not allowed to see expressed this and thus by day three as they toured the city's sights Tuccio was forced to confront his attitudes not just toward the Church but toward religion. They came upon a cardinal's palace recently constructed a huge edifice that filled the entire area of what had been a neighborhood its inner courtyard lined with luxurious arcades they could glimpse through a gap in the massive gate; the same archways were found in the side chapels of the large church up the street also recently built of which Tuccio and Margherita made use of one Stoldo and Agnoletta another while Piera prayed on her knees at an altar to the Virgin Mary.

She who had no interest in the city's structures or operations beyond the fact that they were the Church was content to pray and as the mystery of her story persisted Margherita was intensely curious to learn it while the waif resisted numerous attempts by her and others to get her to talk but as the pair drew closer she kept trying saying, "Weren't you ever frightened when you were alone on the road? Even at night? Wild animals, a vicious dog..." but she only shrugged. All that could be gotten even by Agnoletta with whom she was closest was that she put her faith in the Virgin Mary but even that little was celebrated in the circumstances because it established that she understood and could converse reasonably and with some effort be understood.

When they came to another church Margherita entered to pray confess and take communion and asked Tuccio if he would do the same to which he agreed after some hesitation recalling his pledge to join her pilgrimage; meanwhile Piera prayed beside them but when they sought a priest for confession Margherita eagerly Tuccio hesitantly she hung back shaking her head in fear.

What were the sins Tuccio confessed
Will not be told but can be guessed.

Wandering into the university quarter the next day they found themselves facing bookshops a sight they had never before seen though Siena had a university and each thought how difficult it must be to read the grand books they saw displayed but how sumptuous they were. The binding presses the smells the stacks of loose pages waiting to be bound in cramped low-ceiling rooms they could only guess at what recondite learning must there be contained as they stood in the street mesmerized watching scholars in gowns enter and leave with tomes under their arms Stoldo and Agnoletta waiting bored but trained to patience.

When a bookseller seeing them staring wide-eyed invited them inside they followed passively into a tiny space where after courtesies were exchanged they stood awkwardly looking around without saying a word until finally he said, "Now then, how may I be of service, my lady?" and after another awkward silence Tuccio asked if it would be possible to see a book. "Of course, of course, entirely possible, allow me to ask the subject of your interest," and after another awkward silence he asked if he could show them a book of his own choosing at which the bookseller now as confused as they pulled a book at random off the shelf and opened it before them on his table Tuccio staring in admiration Margherita more uncomfortable than ever because being in Latin she couldn't recognize a single word.

Desperate Tuccio heard himself say, "Would you happen to have a volume of the poetry of Petrarca?"

The bookseller's eyes quickly lit up and just as quickly dimmed and said, "Alas... Petrarca, now you're... Not on the shelf unfortunately. I may tell you that I no longer keep his poems on the shelf because he is constantly revising them, as well as adding new ones to the collection. He came in here himself once, the great poet laureate, stood right where you are now and demanded that I remove his book from my shelf, rip off the binding, and make a number of corrections and additions."

"He was here?"

"As I say, sir, right where you stand. A melancholy disposition if I may say so, but perhaps that is the price of genius." Tuccio was crestfallen. "But of course I can make the book for you. Nothing to it, all we—"

"Unfortunately tomorrow is our last day here," said Margherita. "As you can see, I am en route."

"Yes, of course, lady, I see that most plainly. Alas..."

"Could you have anything by tomorrow? Nothing bound, of course, nor a whole volume, just..."

The bookseller asked how many poems they required to which they asked how many there were. "Last I heard he was closing on two hundred. He told me if he lives long enough he won't stop till he reaches three hundred sixty-six. It seems that number, being all sixes, has some significance for him. For Dante of course it was nines." It was agreed he would have a copyist start right away and if they would stop by the following afternoon he was confident he would have something for them. "Were there any particular...?"

"Use your judgment," said Tuccio the bookseller nodded knowingly and he reached for his purse.

Outside the two grinned at each other like children causing Piera to ask Agnoletta why they were so happy indeed they were so happy it didn't bother them that the cost far exceeded anything they might have imagined Tuccio exclaiming, "Think what a whole volume must cost!"

"Who knew poetry was so precious?" replied Margherita.

They had been to the pope's palace several times but it was only on day four that moving with the crowd along the street toward the unique entrance they found the gate open though heavily guarded thereby getting an unrestricted view of the vast palace built expressly for the popes though apparently insufficient since an extensive addition was underway and impressed only by its stolid mass Tuccio couldn't resist muttering, "Who's he afraid of? This fortress could withstand multitudes."

Margherita was occupied with the sight of a crowd of pilgrims evidently expecting to go inside being organized by guards and when Tuccio noticed he suggested she join them but she hesitated;

reminding her of her disappointment not to be blessed by the bishop of Siena he added, "How can you forgo a chance to be blessed by the pope?" and when still she hesitated he said, "Why do you hesitate? You should go. Should your husband ever condemn your pilgrimage you will tell him the pope himself blessed it."

"I doubt the guard would let me pass."

"Offer him enough he'll let Satan pass."

Reappearing she shook her head and explained that she had gotten no closer to the pope than an antechamber vast and splendid though it was and after a long wait the group was blessed en masse by a functionary; consoled that surely the pope couldn't bless everyone she replied, "That was an expensive blessing," and as they left the area added, "Now I can't tell my husband the pope blessed my pilgrimage."

"Then you shall say it was blessed in the very palace of the pope."

"If I do, I'll be sure not to tell him how much it cost."

Wandering through the adjacent cathedral they discovered when leaving that they had lost Piera and finally found her in a side chapel near the entrance gazing intently at a large statue of the crowned Virgin standing with a stem of three roses in one hand and baby Jesus against her hip in the other and so enchanted was the girl practically rapturous that they couldn't bear to drag her away. Waiting Margherita began to observe the statue and realized that though she must have seen hundreds of such representations this one was particularly beautiful the gentle curve of the body with thrust hip to support the baby their expressions the gesture of the baby grabbing her headscarf the bright yet gentle hues and the statue's placement in a large rounded niche backlit with candles she found herself sincerely moved. Turning away at last she was surprised to find Tuccio standing nearby also gazing and when she whispered, "Do you see it?" he nodded.

Above the cathedral was the impressive bishop's palace which was more attractive than the pope's but they passed it with only a glance to arrive at a massive jagged outcrop near the riverbank on which people liked to walk except Piera wouldn't approach within a certain distance telling Agnoletta its spirit was too strong. "You mean to say you can feel it?" she whispered. "What does it feel like?"

From the rock they could view an expanse of the great river

with a large island connected to the bank by a stone bridge of which everyone in the city seemed proud and they decided to cross on it despite the cost even Piera though she had to be coaxed tightly clutching Agnoletta's hand; partway across Margherita signaled to Tuccio and Stoldo to stay back as she took Piera's other hand and the three paused to gaze at the water then she said, "You know you could tell us if you wanted to. No one else would know."

When the girl made no response Agnoletta said, "You know you're not the only one. It happens all the time."

"Must I say, *madonna*?"

"Not if you don't want to. Wouldn't you feel better if you did?"

"I don't want to."

"We know it wasn't your fault."

"Of course not," said Agnoletta. "If somebody in your village... Your family even." The girl's face remained blank. "We've heard stories, haven't we, *madonna*? There was that nobleman who went to a village at night to a woman's house and demanded that she open the door and when she did he dragged her outside and cut off her head, and then he seized a girl of fifteen who was being raised by the woman and took her by force to his palace and raped her for two weeks before they caught him. And there was another girl who after she was raped, when her brother came back and found out what happened he killed her. And that brute who raped his niece who was a young girl and a virgin, it was out in the forest, and he did it other times too until she became pregnant."

As it seemed she might reply they waited patiently but when she spoke all she said was that she didn't have something anymore and they finally realized she was saying she didn't have morning sickness anymore.

Chapter Eighteen

BLOG POST #11: Saint-Gervais-sur-Mare to Murat-sur-Vèbre. Stage: 10. Stages remaining: 60. Distance: 27.5 km, 17.1 miles. Cumulative distance: 250.0 km, 155.0 miles. Remaining distance: 1,401 km, 868.6 miles. (This is a virtual pilgrimage in the sense that I'm not really en route to Compostela, but I am really walking the miles.)

I look at the elapsed distance and think, "Oh my God, I really walked a hundred fifty-five miles." Then of course I look at the remaining distance and think, "How the heck am I going to do that?" I've walked a considerable distance, yet I feel like I've just gotten started on this thousand mile walking tour of my life.

For five days since Saint-Guilhem-le-Désert I've been walking in the mountains. For the last two I've been in the Parc Régional du Haut-Languedoc, which is incredibly beautiful. It's not just the beauty and the quiet and the ruggedness, it's that this is wilderness, at least the closest thing we have anymore. In the fourteenth century, which I spend a lot of time trying to imagine these days, pilgrims walked through real wilderness, wild lands completely outside human control. Nobles might own them, governments might claim them, but no one controlled them. You have to work your imagination to try to feel what that might have been like, how it might have affected the ideas and attitudes people had, the big ideas, the fundamental ideas, the ones that are so big and so basic that one tends to not even notice them.

For all that, the route I'm on is controversial, at least for some. Yes, the medievals traversed wilderness, but not by choice and not here. That last claim we can't be sure of, but it seems highly likely. It's amazing how little we know about the actual routes pilgrims (travelers generally) took and what the experience was like. Specifically, where would they have gone from Saint-Guilhem, on the route I'm on, or would they detour back to the highway from Montpellier? Remember, it was a real wilderness, not a simulacrum, where you were totally on your own without any communal support in terms of food or shelter or assistance with danger or even a chance to replace your sandals if they tore, and you were in direct confrontation with it, not just the torrents that roar down from the higher lands to the north but the bears and wolves that flourished in such environments. And if you were a true pilgrim you had nothing to defend yourself with but your staff and no food or water but what you could carry in a little satchel and gourd. A saint, a mystic, a hermit, the mentally deranged might try it, but everyone else, it seems clear, would have preferred the relative safety of a main road dotted with settlements.

So I keep thinking about the distance *(real and figurative) between the hiking trail I'm enjoying so much and the actual route pilgrims would have taken. And as I think about it the more I realize it's not just a choice between danger and safety, difficulty and convenience, but between solitude and community. Now, a lot gets said about those two terms in the context of pilgrimage, but most of it, it seems to me, fails to mention a crucial term, which is love. Love is mentioned, but it's generally love of God (and where it extends to love of oneself it seems to entail forgiveness), not love of others. Yet the desire to love and be loved is a fundamental need and so becomes a fundamental drive like the need for food. Both are essential nourishment.*

So much of modern pilgrimage seems to be about solitude and I have come to believe that it is valued precisely for its opposition to normality, that its purpose is always to join or be joined. It's a strategy for a more radical participation. And this participation is always framed in love. So I've been thinking about love between people, and that has naturally led me to romance.

[Discussion of romantic love. Mention that romantic and holy love are related and that this is probably why the language of each so often suggests the other.]

Well, that's enough philosophizing for one stage. Check out the images of this incredibly beautiful region.

Shortly before posting this Tiffany had met the professor at the Westfield Garden State Plaza shopping mall in Paramus New Jersey meeting closer to home to have more time together and in a mall to be in a large crowd far enough away to avoid being recognized. She was a big shopper but she wasn't there to shop rather to discuss pilgrimage though why she was so drawn to that subject she still didn't know and also the Middle Ages because the professor had made that subject fascinating with his passion for obscure facts and minute details though he warned, "There's no money in it, you know. It's literally worthless in this culture."

"That's part of its charm. When I was in college there'd be a charismatic professor who could get so excited about a line in

Horace, say, and you'd get excited too. Suddenly it seemed interesting or beautiful."

"But not important."

"That too. It would turn out that some ancient poet was speaking to you directly, about something you really cared about, as though the distance between you didn't matter. That's you for me. I love it that you care so much, that you make me care. And the money thing? My whole life is money. I love it that when I'm with you I'm in a world where value is not computed that way."

"At the same time you believe that yours is the important one, the real one. My world is nice to visit. I know you're just a tourist there. In a way, all my students are tourists. But you're sincere. And you're not just a student. And you're extraordinary. I think that's why I've been counting the hours till I could see you again."

"Really?"

"That and the fact that you're so beautiful." After she kissed him he told her he had brought her a bilingual edition of the lyric poems of Petrarch a fourteenth-century Italian living in southern France. "I wanted to bring you a gift and I thought of this. It's a big volume, I know, but don't worry, I marked the best ones."

"Did you really?" He nodded shrugged smiled awkwardly. "What does it have to do with pilgrimage?"

"Love? I wanted you to have them."

"They mean something to you."

"I'd like it if they meant something to you. Pilgrimage and romantic love flourished at the same time, which might or might not be a coincidence. The pilgrimage to Compostela from across the Pyrenees enters the historical record in 930 with a monk from a south German abbey called Reichenau. The first documented French pilgrim is 951, Bishop Godescalc of Le Puy which, note, is a starting point of one of the four French routes. Troubadour poetry, where romantic love is celebrated for the first time, appears in the early twelfth century, but it appears fully formed in every way, so we know it must have started earlier. And get this, the first known troubadour was Guilhem de Peitieu who was count of Poitou and duke of Aquitaine where our best candidate for author of the *Pilgrim Guide* lived. And the dates are almost the same, the poet dies and the PG is written within ten years of each other."

"God, I love that. You see how exciting you are?"

"Do you know how beautiful your face is right now?"

He said that romantic love had come down to the

contemporary world unchanged the simplest proof of which was that people still loved Petrarca (as he called him) and he urged her to read the original even if she didn't know Italian (his own knowledge, he said, being limited) so she could get a feel for it which would be aided by her knowledge of Roman lyric poetry and Latin. Asked about the origin of romance he said there was no satisfactory explanation because it appeared out of the blue and was unlike anything that preceded it though one could make limited connections with Ovid whose first-century erotic poems were known in the early Middle Ages though he was attracted to the idea that it might have been part of what he called the vast cultural transfer from the Islamic to the Christian world noting that Spanish Muslims penetrated southwest France as far north as Poitou during the period when troubadour poetry was probably developing.

He also told her that romantic love and holy love were cousins if not siblings which was why at least in centuries past the language of each so often suggested the other and noted that this was true even for the physical dimension of romantic love.

"Physical dimension?"

"Not in Petrarca, but it's all over troubadour poetry, which can be quite frank—hence the claim for the Ovid connection."

"Would you read a poem to me?"

"Not here. The dissonance would be too jarring."

"I'm sorry, I didn't know where else to meet. It does give us more time together."

"Which I appreciate. Oh what the heck, let's do it."

They found a place with plastic plants where they could sit together and he selected the shortest poem in the entire cycle of three hundred sixty-six. "You might recognize this as the tale of Diana and Actaeon from Ovid's *Metamorphoses*." He read the eight lines first in Italian then English which compare a man spying on a shepherdess washing her veil in a pool with the young hunter spying on the beautiful goddess bathing naked and when he finished her eyes widened.

"Whoa!"

"Not easy to be sure. But the best poems are marvelous, which is why I made a selection for you. Maybe at some point we'll find a place more conducive to reading love poems."

"Highly rarified ones. You said the troubadour poems were more..."

"They are and we can read them, but this one rewards close study. Impossible to do here. You might come to love it, as I do."

"We'll come back to it, okay? Promise, I really want to."

He told her the word 'romance' originally meant a story and that the contemporary term was *fin'amor* literally 'fine love' or 'refined love' and that the Petrarca poems cataloged with obsessive repetition his fine love from a distance of a beautiful young woman he might never have met who might well have been a teenager and also might well have not existed. Naturally scholars still debated whether Laura was an actual person and if so who she was an attempt not dissimilar from trying to identify the author of the *Pilgrim Guide*; but Tiffany questioned the value of this debate which seemed as academic as any could be since the answer would reveal nothing about the meaning and beauty the professor claimed for the poetry or even the poet's imagination. In rebuttal he cited the debate over the identity of Dante's Beatrice except there most scholars considered it settled that she was Beatrice Portinari a rich banker's wife who lived near him in Florence but she claimed that this failed to account for the nature of fiction and the professor noted with a great smile that that comment marked her entry into disputation with him.

"Is that bad?"

"It's wonderful. Welcome." Did it support her claim or his, he asked, that the name 'Beatrice' came from the word 'blessed' as 'Laura' could mean 'the breeze' a poetic image of *fin'amor* from the troubadour tradition of which Petrarca made extensive use?

After watching the crowds Tiffany suggested they pretend they were on the pilgrim route bound for Compostela and it was the fourteenth century and they had entered a large town with a crowded marketplace where vendors were hawking their wares everything one could need or want and there were many pilgrims visiting the holy sites and buying religious souvenirs and for a while the pretense worked as they strolled along the hall and when it faded he announced that he had finally received the facsimile of the Compostela manuscript.

"Oh my God, why didn't you tell me?"

"I wanted to give you the Petrarca first, and then one thing led to another."

"Have you had a chance to look at it yet? Of course you have."

He said he had immediately turned to the last of the songs

that followed the *Pilgrim Guide* whose rubric referred to Aimeri Picaud of Parthenay and whose text referred to a pilgrim from his region; studying the script he concluded that it was very close to that of Hand One who wrote books one through five moreover the decoration of the initials was similar to those appearing elsewhere in the manuscript. Furthermore the decorators insofar as they can be identified were active during the crucial period which not only indicated a close association between the scribe and decorators of the songs and the five books but supported the conclusion that Aimeri Picaud of Parthenay wrote both the songs and the *Guide* and very possibly the entire *Codex Calixtinus*.

"That's great! That is great, isn't it?"

In the absence of direct proof, he said, it was about as good as it could get but he would reserve conclusion till he had collated all twelve manuscripts.

"But still, that's very good work, isn't it? No one else has done this, right?"

"When I have completed the project, I will be able to make that claim."

"Come on, make it now. You're breaking new ground."

"I suppose I am. Thanks to you."

"We make a good team."

"Wouldn't it be wonderful to see the original? Just to see it, to be there in the cathedral."

"Let's go."

"You're not serious."

"I'd like to be serious."

"Serious about going to Compostela or serious about going with me?"

"Who else would I go with?"

They entered a movie theater and sat in the back row and when Tiffany emitted revealing sounds and the couple a few rows in front of them looked at each other and turned around they left and sneaked into another one; afterward arms around each other they left the shopping center which neither could tolerate any longer and got in her car where he said, "Where can we go, how much time do you have?"

"Not much. Maybe we should just talk?" She asked if he had ever thought of remarrying.

"Not in the context of an actual woman. In the abstract, yes. I had two children, Morgan was six when she lost her mother. But for years I didn't see anyone and then for years I had nothing to give and then I settled into a lazy uncaring and got used to being single."

"You must have been lonely."

"Maybe I was. Maybe I am. I have my work, which you know fills my life. I have my children. I have friends, a social life."

"Female friends?"

"There are ways to assuage loneliness. And of course there are needs, desires. Those can be assuaged, too."

"As we have just demonstrated."

"Indeed."

"So you haven't been completely alone. There've been opportunities."

"With women? My dear, I work in a place where there are thousands of women. God knows how many I pass every day and many of them are attractive. Some sit in my classroom." He noted that while sexual liaisons with students were of course no longer allowed that didn't make them any less attractive and the ban didn't extend to female faculty; but, he said, few women faculty were single and he detested the idea of having an affair with the wife of a colleague. "I don't see myself as a marriage breaker and I loathe the prospect of a messy relationship."

Tiffany thought, "What does he think might happen with my marriage? But I don't want to think about that either."

Seeing her face he said, "To answer your unasked question, yes, here we are. I would be a cad not to ask myself what I might be doing to your marriage. My feelings for you are obvious and that is precisely the problem. One says, 'I would never hurt her,' but what might do that is one's very presence and removing yourself is the one act of which you are surely incapable."

Tiffany said she didn't want to talk about herself for the moment rather she wanted to know more about him and his cryptic reference to needs and desires. "Does a man who teaches about monks live like one?"

"I think I've already touched on that subject."

"Touch more."

"Why do women crave details? In my experience men generally prefer not to know where their women have been before they met."

"Talk."

"As you command, my lady. So my desires, my fantasies if you will, have been directed more toward the sexual than the romantic. This has led me to more casual relationships, preferably off campus, conferences being a perfect design for such needs. The women are educated, bright, and if one is reasonably attractive and willing to sleep in my hotel room instead of her own, where's the harm? If there's a husband, he's far away, a total stranger, and is probably doing the same himself. So long as she's attractive, I'm not too particular about age or type. Willingness is the main criterion."

"You've never met anyone you found...?"

"How many of these encounters do you think a man who looks like me has had? No, you're the first. In ten years since Jessie died, you're the only one."

"You must have loved her very much."

"She was the love of my life. You've heard the expression *amour fou*, 'crazy love?' That's what it was."

"She was very lucky."

"No, I was." He noted that *amour fou* did not arise in troubadour poetry so much as the romances like the tales of Tristan and Isolde where the madness or folly of love was a constant motif; then he asked if the moment during which she didn't want to talk about herself had passed and if one might now inquire about her own love life to which she responded that she had nothing special to say except that she hadn't married out of *amour fou* and he said, "Yes, I got that impression."

"How? Because of us?" He shrugged. "Maybe that's why... I must be needy in a way I haven't acknowledged. Please don't think Bob and I don't love each other. If he knew about this... We're really good. So I ask myself why am I needy? It surprises me."

"Does it scare you?"

"I don't think so. Maybe I should be scared of that."

"We all need love. It's as fundamental to our condition as food. Not to be flippant, but how many people eat the same food every day? I'm not trying to justify anything, only to understand the impulses we all have."

"You never did, when you were with Jessie. You said so."

"I never wanted to cheat on her, but that doesn't mean that when you encounter a woman you find attractive, that you don't fantasize. Maybe women are different. But everyone craves love, and love is huge, and comes in many varieties. Don't you think so?"

Tiffany said that as late as well into college she had had romantic hopes dreaming of a perfect husband as girls do but by graduate school was willing to settle for a good marriage. "Decent guy, good earner, not too weird. I got that and, I guess, having gotten that I didn't pay much attention to whether I was fulfilled."

"If you could eat as much of your favorite food as you wanted, would you be fulfilled?"

"Is that what you think is going on with us?"

"I don't know what's going on with us. Well, that's not true. I've already told you, in ten years you're the first."

"The first what?"

"The first woman I really want to be with, and really miss when I'm not with her." She nodded and when asked what that meant said it meant she felt the same; he said he would be remiss if he didn't inquire about Bob's situation given that the previous time they were together she had reported difficulties with his job.

"Thanks for asking, I should have told you earlier, things are going well. He didn't get fired. We were pretty sure he wouldn't, they'd be crazy to let him go, but anyway he got past that and spent two frantic weeks lining up a new position, which is really amazing to get repositioned so fast. And now, last night, after only a week learning the new job he comes home breathless about some fantastic idea which he can't discuss with me."

"Sounds good."

"He's totally excited about it, says it's a game changer, so I guess so, yes."

Bob had quickly found the firm's CDO management operation deficient because with investment returns having cratered as security prices declined there was heavy dependence on management fees; these were based on the value of assets under management ('AUM') and the rate charged and not only had asset values declined but the rate because of competition from new firms having entered the business when it was more lucrative with the result that fees had declined by as much as half. Yet with the hedge funds gone and the remaining operations under heightened pressure to increase earnings he saw the CDO managers trying to increase fees so he said to his boss, "Boosting AUM might hold the line, but won't really move the ball forward. And where does more AUM come from when a lot of our activity is buying our competitors' securities so they'll buy ours as real money investors get harder and harder to find? What if I could kick up earnings by banging a few heads in the CDO manager space?"

As he searched for the new route to a vice presidency he saw the rationale for firms like his to do everything but knew the biggest returns went to investors not managers so he looked for an opportunity to reignite investment returns by involving the managers more closely with the trading desk; if he could make a deal he would neither structure it nor select the collateral nor trade the security but he would be the one to make it happen with the result 'firm wins big, Bob wins big' but what was the deal? At lunch with colleagues someone disparagingly remarked that a competitor's CDO had 'headed south' as soon as it appeared saying, "Couldn't have tanked any faster if they had designed it to fail, the shorts made a killing," and he immediately realized that there was no difficulty doing just that because performance depended on the selection of collateral and that was precisely the CDO manager's role; by the time he was back in the office he knew the biggest opportunity was in shorting.

By 2006 the MBS market had settled into a typical arrangement for the parceling of CDOs whereby the highest-rated tranches were retained by the underwriting firms the lowest were bought by hedge funds and the 'mezzanine' tranches between them were repackaged into other CDOs but another side of the market had grown to significance that made investments based on the expectation that certain CDO prices would fall not rise. This practice entailed use of the MBS market's other main innovation the 'credit default swap' (CDS) which combined aspects of an investment and insurance an arrangement that enabled Wall Street to argue (successfully) to the securities regulators that it was insurance and to the insurance regulators that it was a security; that a similar security called a put option had been actively traded since 1973 (and was regulated) didn't seem to matter.

The original purpose of the CDS was to enable an investor to reduce the risk of a CDO it owned declining in price (the insurance aspect) but it was quickly realized that since a CDS could be bought and sold like any security (the investment aspect) it could also be used to bet against a CDO that an investor didn't want to own a practice called 'shorting.' It was also realized that 'synthetic' CDOs could be created out of CDSs instead of being collateralized by pools of mortgages which had distinct advantages: Not needing to purchase and store mortgages eliminated the costs of holding them including the risk that they might decline in value yet the expected investment returns were some fifty percent higher; meanwhile they could be custom-designed referencing any MBS desired and could be created more quickly and easily and finally a single MBS could be referenced by an unlimited number of synthetic CDOs.

Bob had always been aware of this though the hedge funds had mostly used shorting to reduce risk but now he recognized that the synthetic CDO market was booming precisely because of increased interest in shorting. Because a CDS was a contract between two parties an investor could take either side and thus with a synthetic CDO there was a 'long' side benefiting from a rise in price and a 'short' side benefiting from a decline; what caused a growing number of hedge funds to invest more and more on the short side was that the housing market was continuing to deteriorate in both sale prices and mortgage quality especially in markets like California and Florida. This had been a boon to CDO managers needing ever more securities to manage but Bob saw a much bigger opportunity and so the salesman who had earlier proclaimed 'we're a screaming bargain' to entice new money into his hedge fund had suddenly dedicated himself to shorting; but could he convince his firm to design a CDO specifically for the purpose of shorting and then short it?

Knowing how close that came to violating securities law he knew he needed to be extremely careful and for that reason had not even spoken of his idea to Tiffany but first thing Monday morning he pitched the idea to his boss though of course not in those terms rather he talked about their common knowledge that CDOs generally had large exposure to the most overheated housing markets and that the time had come not just to hedge risk but invest more heavily in shorts. Once he had agreement on that point he described a hypothetical situation in which the firm as manager selected CDSs from a portfolio presented by an underwriter and then subsequently the trading desk learning that an outside investor had taken a large short position in the CDO independently decided to short it also. The manager said that was an interesting hypothetical though it was unlikely to occur without collusion among parties that would have to be disclosed to potential investors some of whom would invest long; but if somehow such a CDO came into being without collusion he would be very interested to hear about it.

Since dozens of hedge funds were by this time heavily

involved in shorting and Bob already knew many of them it took little time to find one willing to discuss the hypothetical situation that very afternoon in a noisy bar away from Wall Street which was great news because he needed a third party to discuss the hypothetical with an interested underwriter and someone besides his own firm to make a large short investment should the CDO ever come into being. The underwriter could then approach his firm in the usual arms-length way and if it wished could give it a portfolio from which it would then make selections in its usual independent way without any knowledge of involvement by an outside investor with the underwriter; a few days later a call came from an underwriter seeking a manager for a synthetic CDO the deal was quickly approved and the managers went to work.

When Tiffany and the professor next met it was at a hotel where he said he loved her and she said the same; she said it was lucky she hadn't taken his medieval saints seminar and he gave her a bilingual edition of troubadour poetry saying he'd made a point of not indicating the most interesting poems. She said she had reached the end of the jagged wilderness and would soon enter the smooth lands of Gascony once covered with virgin forest but since replaced with crop fields and pasture punctuated with tame copses home to nothing larger than foxes and rabbits and beautiful little towns; she also said everyone loved Bob's idea though he still would not tell her what it was except that the reason he couldn't sleep was because it was going to be fantastic.

Bob did everything he could to facilitate the fastest possible underwriting with breakfast meetings and dinner meetings and meetings on the sidewalk by a food vendor anyplace noisy and off-site where hypotheticals could be discussed between independent parties until at last the CDO was ready and investors came in mainly on the long side except for one which took a huge short position and then Bob's own traders independently discovering an opportunity also took a huge short position which quickly made a lot of money and Bob became vice president and to celebrate he insisted on flying the family first class to an exclusive luxury resort in the Caribbean.

Chapter Nineteen

FRANCESCO. While most merchants remained local in their activities familiar with their customers comfortable with their guilds' rules taking small risks in expectation of small profits others traded over long distances across many boundaries adapting to foreign markets learning foreign customs languages currencies operating as both merchant and banker in both retail and wholesale and taking great risks while mitigating them by diversifying enterprises and partners. While these latter including Francesco belonged to the same guilds as the rest they were estranged not just economically but socially even morally for while they all had shops in the city he also had operations in Avignon (where he had opened his first branch) Pisa Florence Genoa Majorca Ibiza and Valencia and was in the process of opening one in Barcelona. Yet what distinguished him from the elite merchants was their vastly greater wealth partly because they were heirs to operations that went back generations partly because they functioned as large family businesses but significantly because being of the high nobility their connections gave access to inside deals and their great wealth supported riskier hence more lucrative ventures thus they could increase their capital at rates considerably greater than him.

It was amazing how many Sienese families had grown wealthy through commerce given that a city of fifty thousand mostly poor could not enable such wealth rather what did it was huge amounts of capital invested in far-flung operations from the Black Sea to the Atlantic from north Africa to northern Europe making the city (like its major competitors Florence Pisa Lucca Genoa and Venice) at once a single commercial conglomerate and an imperial capital. As Francesco hurried to his meeting past one massive palace after another he noted that while the city was already studded with them that very fact indicated the possibility of more.

Yet it was not a palace he coveted nor to sit among Siena's magnate families nor necessarily even citizenship which was hereditary unless conferred for individual merit all of which would embroil him in the city's fractious politics and the clawing obligations of civic acts as well as the personal rivalries he had so far mostly avoided rather it was simply to increase his wealth and for that he reasoned he must be admitted to the Mercanzia. This was the city's elite guild of leading merchant bankers many noble who enjoyed governmental privilege and favor the one that supervised all the others even the powerful wool guild while its court held unique sweeping powers indeed the guild effectively controlled the city's commercial operations even the legal rate of exchange with the florin.

Paradoxically however he must become wealthier before anyone would consider admitting him and there were only two ways to do that either over time by the gradual increase of capital or more rapidly by taking greater risks; the first was what he'd been doing his genius having been never to let greed possess him never to commit too much to any one venture or person to stay away from risky loans despite their tempting interest rates and never to trust anyone. "If you transport by land, transport by sea. If you trade in Avignon, trade in Valencia. If you sell cloth, sell arms, if painted coffers, then spices. If with this man, then with that one, and if you hold florins, hold ducats and pounds;" thus he'd advised himself but now he thought, "I grow old and have no sons. Time wanes by the day. Do I challenge Fortune, risk ruin against honor?"

Of course merely to decide was insufficient he must find the opportunity and he was confident he might have though the same palaces that encouraged him cautioned him because they were fortified castles with crenellated walls and towers and living quarters high above the street and the towers would have been even higher were they not regulated by the commune in effect the magnate families agreeing to a self-imposed limit so as not to be forced to raise their own towers ever higher. That the recently completed Torre del Mangia of the Palazzo Pubblico had been exempted from the height limit was a show of civic pride and political faith in communal government but provided scant reassurance given the frequent bloody *vendetti* among these families over the past few years.

The San Gimignano market had been dominated by Florentine merchants but recent spectacular bank failures among Florence's premier banks had created an opportunity for the Sienese to move in or at least so the Mercanzia thought; but knowing it would be difficult to dislodge their rival and often enemy they sought to enlist the aid of merchants whom otherwise they would not have deigned to notice and thus was Francesco di Marco invited to meet with some of the guild's consuls among the most powerful men in the commune.

The proposal was enticing for it opened a path to membership in the Mercanzia possibly even citizenship and beyond that public office with a potential return on investment far exceeding his most successful ventures but of course the risk was commensurate for he was being asked that is required to advance much more capital than he had ever before put into any single venture also he worried about the politics even of a seemingly patriotic campaign. That the fabric of Siena had been badly torn by factionalism was evident even in this meeting in terms of who was there and who wasn't and he could only wonder what the response might be of those who were absent some of whom were no less powerful for as an outsider he had no way to find out no one to consult Lapo could not help him here in fact he could clearly hear his advice to get out of the way yet it was awfully tempting.

Tempting although he knew that the nobility even those who had gone into commerce would always despise men like him whose bourgeois ethic of accumulation and prudence conflicted with its concept of public virtue that entailed the frank possession of wealth and generous expenditure on public display without regard to income. Generosity an essential trait of the noble character was largely foreign to his who was thus seen as greedy and parsimonious while with respect to small merchants with whom he felt more comfortable he was seen to offend the tradition of moderation in his display of a large house fine clothes titled guests he had even acquired a crest to put over his doorway thus a boastful vain man.

What excited him about the streets of palaces which he now passed in reverse as he returned home was not so much their ostentatious wealth and power as the commercial opportunities that nourished them for he simply loved money and nothing interested him so much as the pursuit of it; and unlike the fortunate ones who lived in them all he'd achieved he'd achieved alone a taverner's son who'd married a nobleman's daughter if one in straitened circumstances the daughter of a condemned traitor. So proud yes he thought but with little interest in pretending to nobility with its airs and claims and obligations its political striving and military ambitions and in any case he lacked the time since he was always working; as for those public acts of generosity he gave alms God knew how he gave alms and if he decided to join the campaign maybe he would underwrite a public building knowing how the commune honored such civic virtue but then he thought, "Be careful, Francesco, for you well know what happens to those on the losing side." It took thirty-two workmen six days to completely dismantle the palace of an exiled noble.

He had known as a boy he wanted to become rich and within a year of losing his family to sickness had moved from his village to Siena dreaming unlike almost everyone else of a future different from the universal expectation; and though he knew he could never make his fortune where he would always be the son of a tavern-keeper he didn't go there to get rich he went there to get his start and he apprenticed himself first to one shop then another learning observing listening. When he heard some merchants returned from Rome bragging of the great opportunities offered by that 'corrupt and prosperous city' he never hesitated he sold his meager inheritance a small parcel of land to have a suit of clothes made and provide some initial capital then set about ingratiating himself with a Tolomei one of Siena's most powerful and wealthy merchant-banking families whose cluster of palaces he passed in the Banchi di Sopra near the Piazza del Campo. One day he waited in the courtyard there for hours till someone came out to speak with him briefly and a few months later having wrapped a few belongings in a sack he attached himself to a Tolomei-led company of merchants to set off for Rome he on foot they of course all mounted but he didn't care if need be he would have run the entire way he was fifteen.

At twenty-three he was doing well at twenty-six was established in partnership with other Sienese which he accomplished by dealing mainly in armor which he sold to any buyer even both sides of a conflict; at twenty-eight he opened a shop and four years later was a partner in three of them dealing in a large variety of goods including silks and spices from the Far East. Later he sold salt (a precious commodity) opened a currency exchange dealt in silverware and artwork exported luxury items for women opened a tavern a cloth shop while his main shop offered silver belts and gold wedding rings household goods of all sorts saddles and harnesses altar cloths priests' vestments religious art and more and in all this he was usually his own wholesaler sometimes he even manufactured his own goods.

It wasn't till he returned to Siena a rich merchant and opened a 'central house' (and took a young wife) that he began opening branches in other cities. Further expanding his variety of goods he imported lead alum and pilgrims' robes from Romania spices and slaves from the Black Sea English African and Spanish wool salt from Ibiza silk from Venice leather from Córdoba and Tunis wheat from Sardinia and Sicily oranges dates wine and bark from Catalonia; to Paris he exported silks embroideries and jewels armor and leatherwork in return bought enamels inlaid in gold painted cloth for bed curtains and wall hangings and there was more much more.

More recently he had become active trading in loans mainly buying them at discounts from face value and holding them to maturity though they could be resold if a buyer could be found at an agreeable price. Loans could be bought when the owner needed cash or saw a better opportunity considered it too risky or wanted to diversify; when Francesco's partner in Avignon wrote about an opportunity to get into this lucrative type of investment he had consented providing he diversified his holdings controlled the firm's total exposure and of course negotiated a satisfactory discount. In fact he had been considering this for some time as a way to keep capital invested when trade was slow due to a local political upheaval an outbreak of hostilities or an attempt by competitors to drive the Italians (or the Tuscans or the Sienese) from a certain market and it could also be a way to avoid a special tax assessment.

Once he'd decided the Gimignano campaign was too risky the decision to open a bank came naturally because its high expected returns would grow his wealth quickly and its prestige could make him a candidate for the Mercanzia. Opening a bank as opposed to engaging in banking activities as he had already been doing amounted to publicly offering to provide deposit accounts and loans to those with whom he might have no other commercial dealings while of course it entailed a commitment to maintain physical security of money and adequate capital to meet the bank's cash flow requirements.

As his competitors at least the Italians were doing this he believed he must too and while the Sienese might have lost their dominance they were still prominent though of course his would be a modest operation; he entertained no fantasies about competing with a Tolomei or a Gallerani the big firms were all extended family operations whereas he was alone (his wife's family he held in low esteem) though be it said he already had financial dealings with correspondents in Paris Bruges London Montpellier and elsewhere. "Loans to magnate, merchant, or prelate at, say, thirty percent interest, fully pledged in both property and the usufruct thereof... That is usury, they say, for which I shall be damned, but those who say it as often as not are first in line to borrow and even lend themselves. So long as I later repent sincerely, double my alms..."

As expected however the reaction of colleagues was negative not least his notary's who emphasized his distaste by using the pejorative term for a usurer saying, "Would you announce yourself to the world as a *caorsino*?"

"Have not the Venetians determined that money placed at interest with a bank known to accept it is not subject to the ban on usury?"

"'A bank *or other establishment*,'" he clarified. "To open a bank is to invite attention."

"Perhaps, but it is also to attract more money." Lapo sighed and his eyes saddened. "What? I know that sigh, that look."

"My friend, do you not already have enough money?"

As they were in fact friends with sincere mutual affection Francesco allowed himself to shout while Lapo who knew better than try to match Francesco's rages waited for it like a sudden thunderstorm to abate; he might not have done that however had he realized Francesco's anxiety was equal to his stubbornness and that his temper reflected the first at least as much as the second for as he walked home past the duomo and noted how poorly the new construction was going that was to transform the current cathedral into one massively larger doubt swarmed him like mosquitos. He thought, "Am I who has succeeded by balancing ambition with caution to toss the latter away? I who live in dread of bad news, of being defrauded by a customer or *fattore*, who have placed no faith in the stability of any government or the honesty of any man, am I now to leap into the dark?" For one who had made his fortune by unceasing vigilance a life he knew to be weary but successful was a bank a mad idea or the logical next step?

DAY SEVENTEEN. The route south was flat and open the rocky outcroppings on the western side rounded and smooth the dry midsummer heat not unpleasant and for the first time Margherita had a child and a man she loved a family though an odd one with a sixteen year old husband and a thirteen or fourteen year old daughter while Tuccio at sixteen had a daughter a few years younger and was shortly to become a grandfather. A family nonetheless happy and tasting freedom and they cared for each other looked out for each other shared intimacies even from Piera occasionally a look a touch a word; entering Avignon Margherita had been a woman in love whereas leaving she was that and a mother but only in Tarascon when she refused to follow the caravan did the change emerge fully.

The plan had been that if they reached Beaucaire while the fair was still running they would set up a table and as it happened there were a few days left presenting a commercial opportunity the *fattore* had no intention to bypass for while the greatest fairs were in Champagne he had heard this one was well attended. Fairs were great public commercial events attracting caravans of merchants from near and far the attraction being their unique features for they were blessed by the Church literally blessed in opening ceremonies and protected and facilitated by rulers great and local who granted safe conduct passes and special privileges such as exemption from certain taxes. Special security forces and courts were on hand to maintain order and adjudicate disputes moreover by decree and treaty the merchants traded in complete freedom with guarantees against seizure of money or goods or bodily coercion even for debts in fact the fairs were sanctuaries of international trade with reduced tariffs and legal certifications of contracts and with free and open trade in money and credit at rates allowed up to thirty percent.

They were always crowded with customers large and small retail and wholesale from peasants to nobles jostling before the tables to inspect merchandise haggle over prices and strike bargains but the other great attraction was the continuous reveling not just crowds applauding marvelous street performers but open carousing gambling and prostitution and the caravan was already heading for the ferry in Tarascon when Margherita told the *fattore* she would not be crossing the river.

"Not crossing the river?" She explained that the fair was

antithetical to her pilgrimage and she didn't want Piera exposed to the reveling. "But... You must cross the river."

"Why must I?"

Both endowed with a propensity to anger the conversation followed the predictable path its volume sufficient to be overheard which caused the count to join the field though he said nothing while the fighting lasted; when they were wearied and bruised sufficiently to pause the *fattore* told him what he already knew and Margherita repeated her reasons as he listened impassively frankly surprised at her rebellion at least its directness which seemed to him to touch on boldness if not audacity. Polite as always he asked if he might discuss the situation privately with the *fattore* with the goal of finding a mutually satisfactory resolution and later returned to say it had been agreed that if it were her wish she might remain at the convent in Tarascon in her usual company and with that and a farewell he turned to lead the caravan to the river when Margherita said she required her purse. He stared nodded left and returned with it then turned again while she with the rest of her company watched the caravan proceed to the riverbank where the *fattore* out of earshot began to engage with the ferryman.

As the costs of food and lodging at fairs were fixed by regulation he assumed the ferry toll would be as well and so was shocked to hear how much the man asked who insisted that the regulated price applied only on the Beaucaire side of the river and that he asked no more than what was customary; the *fattore* who doubted both claims but found no authority to whom to appeal was forced to negotiate from weakness while kicking himself that he hadn't accepted the bridge toll at Avignon which might also have avoided the problem with Margherita. As he crossed the river and proceeded to the fair he was furious on both counts for no one hated to be trapped in negotiation more than him and he knew that had he refused her demands her anger would have been even more ferocious as she denied his authority and asserted her noble rank and might even have threatened to send word to Francesco that his new *fattore* was a cheat who had robbed her of her purse.

While there was as he had convinced himself in Avignon the possibility that her conduct could be turned to his advantage there was also the opposite possibility for who could say how a husband would react to such news; meanwhile he would have war and who could say the count would not decide his behavior lacked courtesy and condemn him for it? But if Francesco were to react as he would hope then his position would be enhanced in which case he had done well because the count could testify that he had sternly advised her to comport herself properly while he was away at the fair; rather than fear it then he should look forward to learning when he rejoined her that she'd been caught in adultery.

Then he need only pen a letter sadly but dutifully informing Francesco that despite his best efforts (to which the count could attest) his wife had been unfaithful to him and had not only violated the sanctity of their marriage and her pilgrimage but greatly interfered with his ability to engage in commerce. He considered adding that to his proposal for her to return to Siena she'd replied that if his wish were to be free of her she would gladly continue her journey in the company of a certain caravan guard; he was also unsure whether to conclude that unfortunately it was necessary to reevaluate their agreement but since one couldn't plant and harvest at the same time decided it might be better to wait and instead close on flattery and a reminder that he had steadfastly tried to refuse the position of chaperone.

"Who am I to send, her mother, an aunt?" Francesco had shouted. "They are too old for such a journey. Would you prefer that?"

"Can't your notary find someone?"

"Who, an old nun?"

"Perhaps you should go yourself."

"You know that's out of the question. I'm shocked to hear you even suggest it."

"Surely someone can be found. For a suitable fee."

"No doubt, no doubt, but am I to entrust my wife to a hireling? I would not trust her to a priest."

"She has a brother, if I recall."

"Two. One a wastrel, to whom I am periodically importuned to rescue from some financial misfortune. The other has obligations, work, family."

"We all have obligations."

"He told me to talk her out of it. Don't you see, there is no one else. I'd have no alternative but to let her hazard the road without protection. A bunch of women, who she tells me will be setting out."

"I see your dilemma, Francesco, but do you really think your wife would be safer in the company of some two dozen rough men, far from home?"

"I am not happy about it, but would it be better to trust her to the honor of brigands? You see, I have no choice. If you deny me, I have nowhere else to turn. I must fear for my wife even more than I do already."

The *fattore* knew his negotiating position was weak since Francesco was putting up the bulk of the capital but became strong when it came to determining the amount of the cash fee to be paid in full in advance.

Margherita's group watched the caravan disembark into an open field on the north side of town and proceed to the fair watched in silence until it disappeared and afterward until she said, "As we are on pilgrimage, we will visit the religious sites of the town."

"Two of us, my lady, are not on pilgrimage," said Stoldo, "and with your permission would be off," and permission granted the remaining three watched the pair head downriver toward a thicket grinning and waving watched in silence until they disappeared and afterward until she said, "Shall we go to church?" They walked slowly toward the nearby town gate careful not to touch whereas normally they would have held hands and where normally would have been affectionate smiles were sideways glances; every look every word no matter how banal no matter how many times said before became different became exciting but also frightening in the way of an imminent thunderstorm when one has no shelter. The changed light puts all objects in high relief the air becomes sweeter the trees shake and low clouds move quickly across a sky here dark with intent there bright with insouciance and no matter what one might have been thinking it is the coming storm that now fills the mind; perhaps the land is starved for rain parched with drought yearning for moisture but with relief may come powerful gales lightning strikes felled trees streams in flood fragile crops drowned in a sudden surfeit of what they most desire.

The count had ordered Stoldo to supervise his young friend reminding him that if the lady unlocked the portcullis and Tuccio entered the castle there would be unhappy consequences for everyone but Stoldo was more intent on everyone's pleasure including the lady's if the master were cuckolded intent also on his own because everyone knew pleasure must be enjoyed when available for like a clear shot in a hunt the chance was fleeting. There was no pleasure however for the two crossing the short span to the gate with slow step each unable not to glance back at the bushes each trapped in silence knowing there was nothing to stop them from following and that such a chance might not come again but that not every opportunity should be seized; this silence began their discourse.

Aha! As there is discourse on love at the midpoint of the *Divine Comedy* so is there discourse here (of a sort).

Suddenly Tuccio grabbed her hand and pulled her toward the bushes and at first she followed because he said, "Do you not realize that though we are on Earth we are yet in Paradise and that much is lawful there which here is not lawful?" (*Paradiso* Canto 1)

But she stopped him saying, "You know I want to as much as you."

"Then what stops us? Are we not free?"

"If we follow their example, we will end up as they will."

"Satisfied?"

"For a time, yes, until that very satisfaction creates desire for more and thus becomes dissatisfaction."

"Why might we not satisfy that desire as well?"

"We might, but we would have condemned ourselves."

"To happiness?"

"To misery."

Just inside the town's circular wall the church was not just impressive but beautiful and interesting and when they turned to it Piera was the one who pointed to the heads of sheep goat cow and donkey smiling down at them from above the entry portal. The church was dedicated to Saint Martha whose body lay in a sarcophagus in the crypt and whose story was told by one of the church's canons. Friend to Jesus and sister of Mary Magdalene and Lazarus as described in the gospels she fled persecution in Palestine after the Resurrection with her siblings and others in a boat without sail or rudder landing at the place that became Saintes-Maries-de-la-Mer following which Lazarus became the first bishop of Marseilles while Mary Magdalene retired in penitence to a grotto near La Sainte-Baume. Martha was living in Avignon when the inhabitants of Tarascon having heard of miracles she had performed called on her to deliver them from an amphibious monster the Tarasque that lurked in the Rhône frightening the population and devouring beasts and men; after subduing and delivering it on a leash to the townspeople she lived with them for the rest of her life in a little house surrounded by pious women and there she died and was entombed. A church was built around her sarcophagus which quickly became a destination for pilgrims notably Clovis the first Christian king of France in the year 500 and that church became the crypt of a much larger one a thousand years later which had recently been substantially reworked in the current style with a more open interior.

"Is he dead?" asked Piera.

"Who?"

"The monster. You said Saint Martha delivered him."

"We then slew him. Too bad you won't be here next week, her holy day is July 29, you could have celebrated with us."

"We will be sorry to miss it," said Margherita.

"Father," said Tuccio, "will you hear our confession?"

They remained in the church inspecting whatever could be inspected before exiting into the blinding mid-day sun where they remained beside the church and Margherita said, "I see clearly now that love motivates both what is best in me and what deserves condemnation."

"There is nothing in you to condemn."

"Did you not witness my lust?"

"Is desire necessarily lust? Why is it not love?"

"If it is love, does love not impose duties, strictures, discipline, even as it awakens generosity, kindness, and beauty?"

"Then after all you reject fine love? You do not believe that love is ennobling?"

"I believe I am a better person for this pilgrimage, and knowing love, which I never knew before, is the cause. Therefore you are the cause because love must have an object."

"Then you do believe love is ennobling."

"But what of desire?"

"Can there be love without desire? Is that not like fire without heat?"

"I asked the priest about that. He said that without desire the will could not move. Therefore the intellect must determine what to desire and how much, for there lies the possibility of sin."

"I do not understand such talk."

"Nor I. But I think Saint Martha taught me that peace lies in the conquest of uncontrolled passion."

"Would you be a saint?"

"I would not be a sinner if I can avoid it."

"Even at the cost of a life without joy?"

"I do not believe I would be happy living in sin and I have

seen how little separates me from it. I will love and desire you because I do love you and this desire is as natural as hunger. Even saints have known it. But the moment I surrender to it I become less Saint Martha and more the Tarasque."

"Do you not know that you are in Heaven? And do you not know that Heaven is all holy and what is done here comes from good zeal?" (Paradiso, Canto 22)

She turned into the street and the others followed because the way was narrow but when she turned a corner and kept going he grabbed her arm to ask where they were going and when she didn't answer said, "Mita. I can stand much, but not this. Why can we not love each other the way we are meant to love?" She stared at his heaving chest but said nothing and suddenly he grabbed her hand and headed back toward the gate but after a few steps she refused to continue.

"We cannot go to the river. Don't you understand? We cannot." Again he grabbed for her hand but she drew it back and began to cry.

"Mita, we are free. We are in Paradise. There is no one to stop us." She shook her head but eventually stopped crying and then he pulled her gently and she went along but when the gate came into view she resisted and he pulled harder and she yanked her arm free.

"No!"

"Come!"

"I said no!"

"Mita."

"Is my honor worth less than your gratification?"

"There is no dishonor here, only love."

"You are not such a fool as to believe that."

"Then I am a fool. But a fool who is mad with love for you."

"That is what this is, madness."

"Then so be it."

"It cannot be. It cannot be."

"Only come with me and we will learn what can be."

"What a fool I was to take up with one so young!" she said glaring at him and he grabbed her arm roughly and yanked her toward the gate but when Piera started shrieking they stopped immediately and Margherita threw her arms around her but couldn't calm her; the girl struck her unintentionally as she broke free screaming hysterically and throwing herself against a wall and might have hurt herself had Tuccio not forcibly restrained her.

People gathered to stare until the paroxysms and the howling stopped and the girl went limp in Tuccio's fierce embrace and when she was calm enough they walked to the riverbank to sit side by side watching in silence until Margherita announced that they could not stay in Tarascon and rising quickly to her feet strode back to the church with them in tow to approach the group of pilgrims that was still there.

Chapter Twenty

DAY EIGHTEEN. After the papacy moved there Avignon (rather than Arles) became an assembly point for Italian pilgrims to Compostela where those who had gone over the Alps met those who had come up the coast but whereas in Avignon Margherita had had no desire to join them that had changed; and though the women she'd met in the church belonged to an all-female group and found her traveling arrangements distinctly odd they welcomed her maid and especially the pregnant half-starved waif she had met along the way and taken under her protection. Even her two men of arms were accepted with thanks for the security they might offer especially as one was committed to pilgrimage and thus they launched themselves upon the way in what amounted to a parade since this company of pilgrims was large and festive. Piera as possessed by joy as she had been the previous day by terror practically danced down the road while Margherita was overjoyed to feel a true pilgrim at last though she had spent a miserable night after Agnoletta had related intimate details of her tryst and Tuccio who had also passed a night of torment found himself able and willing to be a pilgrim.

They had even discussed obtaining a robe for him but had rejected the idea since for his primary task he needed to stay armed and though Stoldo remained mounted in the interests of security the others walked their horses and thus was traversed the short distance to the famous abbey of Montmajour in a marsh on the edge of the vast wetlands of the mouth of the Rhône called the Camargas. From the time the abbey had been built on a rock promontory the monks had been gradually draining the marsh so that land had progressively become available not just for agriculture but burial (the first graves were holes hacked into the rock) but though someday it might be possible to walk to the abbey it was still necessary to cross by boat. To meet the need as the monastery had been a major pilgrim destination since acquiring a piece of the True Cross over three hundred years earlier it maintained a ferry service and waiting their turn they were all excited (except Stoldo who would stay with the horses).

The relic was initially housed in the crypt of the abbey church but soon a separate chapel was built a short distance away to accommodate the traffic a structure stunningly beautiful in its elegant simplicity built in the shape of a Greek cross (which Margherita was excited to notice) a central square surrounded by four equal semi-circles with a narthex on one side an entry chamber to serve visitors. "It's beautiful, isn't it," she whispered and to herself she said, "Am I truly in love or merely desperate for affection, dalliance, pleasure? Would I suffer for love, sacrifice for it? I confess I am desperate, yet I swear I love this youth with whom against all imagining I have become pregnant with love. For him would I suffer and sacrifice, I am sure of it."

"It is," replied Tuccio who in fact was moved by the chapel. "One would have guessed something vast. It is but a reliquary which holds its burden well," and to himself said, "Fifty-one days on the pilgrim trail I become a pilgrim and what confronts me but the Calvary Tree. Am I truly in love or infatuated with the idea? I would suffer anything, sacrifice anything, not for love but for love of her. If that is not true love, then I am worse than a fool."

DAYS NINETEEN AND TWENTY. The entire group stayed the night a few miles from Montmajour in Arles where the festive mood continued at the pilgrim hostel of the Confraternity of Saint James and the next morning at that extraordinary city's most famous Christian site the Alyscamps a necropolis originally pagan but Christianized in the fourth century and filled with thousands of ancient sarcophagi. Dante referred to it in canto nine of his *Inferno* a fact of which Margherita and Tuccio were unaware but its fame and allure were apparent in the large numbers of pilgrims wandering its long lanes punctuated with chapels and churches that had once lain astride the Aurelian Way the Roman coastal highway.

They gazed at funerary inscriptions they couldn't read and bas reliefs which acquired with age and location a significance that could not actually be identified but the most eerie attraction was the early twelfth-century church of the resident priory which seemed ancient in its primitiveness almost bereft of adornment its roof supported on four most severe circular columns at least ten feet in diameter. It felt like a cave and in the transepts was as dark as one and from it a monk appeared who unbidden told them stories about the Alyscamps such as when Saint Trophime first bishop of Arles in the third century wanted to bless the necropolis Jesus himself appeared leaving behind the imprint of his knee and Tuccio liking the man suggested that Margherita ask him to hear her confession.

"Why not your confession?"

"I don't have anything to confess right now."

"What makes you think I do?"

"You always do," he replied grinning.

She agreed to do it on condition that he went first and then was shocked when he came out so quickly saying, "I told you I don't have anything to confess." Piera laughed as Margherita went inside to find the monk waiting at the base of the stairway beneath the altar where she took her place at his feet facing away as was the custom and immediately confessed to having salacious dreams.

"How are they salacious, my child?"

"I dream of voluptuous pleasures, father. Not pleasures I have experienced, but pleasures I wish to experience."

"Pleasures with a man?"

"Yes, father. And when I wake up the pictures in these dreams do not go away. Wherever I turn, they impose themselves, with the desires that accompany them."

"What sorts of desires?"

"The desires that accompany the pleasures."

"But of what pleasures do you speak? Men and women engage in many pleasurable activities together."

"These pleasure to which I refer, father, are those men and women share in bed. When they lie together and take their pleasure of each other and experience joy."

"I see."

"All day long, at any time, as I say... In the full solemnity of the mass, when prayer should be most pure, obscene pictures of these pleasures totally captivate my soul. That is why I am here."

"But you say you have not yet experienced these pleasures. Rather you..."

"I desire them, yes, father."

"You desire them."

"I know I should be trembling for my faults, father. Instead I sigh after untasted pleasures. Even in sleep they leave me no peace."

"I see. You are widowed, I presume."

"No, father, but my husband is far away in Siena. And in any case..."

"He does not, shall we say, perform his... Adequately, let us say."

"Exactly, father. And I fear that words escape me in my sleep. Words that make clear the thoughts of my heart."

"I see."

"And I fear there are movements of my body that also betray..."

"Yes, yes, hmm, hmm. This reminds me of nothing so much as what the saintly Eloisa wrote to her beloved Abelardo, perhaps you have heard of that most famous couple in love, when they were living separate monastic lives. I may say that there there was a certain literary... What she writes, you see, reproduces a confession Saint Augustine himself made in book ten of that eponymous work. Are you miserable as she was?"

"I wish I were, father, but, alas, I have never been so happy."

"So you do not, as Eloisa did, cry out in the words of Saint Paul, 'O wretched man that I am! Who shall deliver me from the body of this death?'"

"Not at all, father."

"Hmm, hmm. How often do these..."

"Every night, father. Sometimes several times a night."

"Several times a night, hmm, hmm. And have you experienced any... moisture or, shall we say... wetness?"

"Yes, father, I believe I have sweated a great deal."

"No, I refer to a certain other... wetness."

"Do you mean...?"

"I do."

"I... I..."

"You must make full confession, my child."

"Then, in truth, father, I do believe there has been wetness."

"In..."

"Between my legs, father."

"And these motions of your body... You did say there have been motions of your body?"

"Indeed, father, I cannot lie still."

"What motions have there been?"

"My head rocks from side to side."

"Have there been any other motions?"

"Yes, father, but I am too embarrassed to describe them."

"You must make full confession, my child. You can tell me everything."

"If you insist, father."

"It is not I who insists, but—"

"My thighs, father."

"What about your thighs?"

"They..."

"They what?"

"Do I really have to say?"

"Your confession must be complete."

"They seem to part of their own accord, father."

"Hmm, hmm. Now, when your thighs part, what happens next? Does your hand, for example..."

As this was going on she'd begun to suspect that his breathing was getting heavier soon she had no doubt and as she continued felt his legs pressing against her back then his hands on her shoulders until suddenly he interrupted to say that given the nature of her confession they should move to a more discreet location. "Let me help you to your feet," he said and abruptly slid his hands through her armpits and around to the front grabbing her breasts then led her into a part of the north transept that was quite dark and once there began to paw her and finally tried to embrace her and when she walked out he called, "But my lady, we haven't yet determined your penance."

From the door she replied, "Thanks to you, father, I just made it. I'd say now you should make yours," and indeed he returned to the transept and made his own penance.

"What happened?" asked Tuccio seeing the look on her face.

"I confessed, as we agreed."

As they were leaving the Alyscamps one of the women noted that this was the beginning of the Via Tolosana the Way of Toulouse that would take them far beyond Toulouse to a pass over the Pyrenees where they would join the Camino Francés the French Way across northern Spain and when asked if she would continue with them all the way to Compostela Margherita sadly explained her circumstances at which the woman said, "We have come far, now we go far. When we arrive and turn back, we'll again have far to go."

"Do you ever fear it?"

"I pray for strength," she said smiling and Margherita loved that smile.

Though Stoldo and Agnoletta would clearly have preferred to entertain themselves in other ways even the profane entertainments were to be found among the pilgrims and since Arles was much larger and more crowded than Tarascon there was much more need for vigilance therefore the five stayed together in the sea of pilgrim robes with Margherita and Tuccio in a heady mood insouciant and joyous and sharing the general enthusiasm. Tuccio surprised himself as he shared stories and asked questions telling Margherita how friendly it was but there was no religious awakening and he would have been the last to regard himself as pious yet knew himself to be dedicated to worthiness which went to the heart of many a pilgrimage. As for the other thing he knew that Arles too had a riverbank and the intensity of his urge ebbed and flowed but he understood though he sometimes wished he didn't that his quest required him to resist it and find diversion and focus on the less physical aspects of love for which there was no better vehicle than religious observance.

For the rest of the day they celebrated with the pilgrims who promenaded around the city's wonders notably the Roman coliseum virtually intact and by far the largest structure in the city yet with attentive architectural detail all in gleaming white blocks; but this most spectacular vestige of their pre-Christian past they regarded with desultory interest and left impressed but unmoved wondering why as had happened practically everywhere else its stones had not been taken for other structures. In contrast the friezes and statuary of the cathedral's facade which they visited the next day fascinated all of them Piera of course but Agnoletta too and even Stoldo who thought himself immune to such things discovered he was not while Margherita knew she was in the presence of an artistic treasure as she tried with some success to identify narratives and figures a game to which Tuccio was drawn though he had little to contribute.

One of the large friezes showed a devil perhaps Satan with horns and searing eyes holding a man upside down under each arm their heads at his groin with his legs splayed and between them seated on a large serpent a naked woman full breasted pushing his thighs apart with her arms her head in front of his pudendum the message here so obvious no one said anything. A complementary frieze showed a man being lifted to Heaven by angels and saints while a man gazing up from below prayed with raised palms and God the Father gazing down from above gestured to the world with open hand; below this was a free sculpture of a placid pensive man resting his cheek on his hand seated between two growling lions each with a set of claws on his legs presumably mauling them in fact several sculptures showed men being mauled or eaten by lions while others showed them as guardians and there was also a ram with great spiraled horns and a shepherd's bell around its neck. Complementary to the pensive man was another but this one quite disturbed judging by his stare yet rather than being flanked by mauling lions there were angels and above more angels flocks of them trumpeting the good news some of them falling backward in their exuberance.

"Adam and Eve!" cried Piera pointing to a frieze showing them in the garden at the moment of shame the serpent coiled around the tree; it was Agnoletta who identified Mary in bed in the manger Joseph seated beside her with a crutch and a baby swaddled in a wicker basket two cows happily resting their heads on him though both adults looked worried.

"Is all this not trying to make us feel fear?" said Tuccio. "I don't feel fear."

"Nor do I."

"Still, it's wonderful. Which one is your favorite?"

"I would say the man between two lions."

"Even though they're goring him?"

"I don't think they are. I like the look of him."

"I like baby Jesus with the cows," said Piera.

Agnoletta chose the angels blowing their horns because they were announcing the happiest of days Stoldo the devil because, "If I don't, who will?" he laughingly shouted and Tuccio chose the ram and lion supporting the roof because they looked helpful and content. When they returned to the hostel for supper the *fattore* and the count were waiting and the expressions on their faces were as expected given that upon learning in Tarascon that Margherita had gone to Arles they had set out immediately and en route discussed what to do about a situation they both regarded as dangerous for everyone. The *fattore* had shared his idea for gaining additional compensation to which he argued they were both clearly entitled but the count had argued forcefully that such a move was too dangerous and since the *fattore* had already been considering the same it wasn't hard to dissuade him.

"We expected to find you in Tarascon."

Stoldo and Tuccio relied for their defense on the fact that they were at the lady's service not the reverse with Tuccio going so far as to claim that with regard to the *fattore* the same relationship held while Margherita noted that she had never promised to stay in Tarascon and that in any case where was the harm since they had found her without difficulty and everyone was safe. What disturbed them was not that she was right but that she was becoming more and more independent seeming to care nothing for their judgment let alone their authority and was traveling openly in the company of a man neither her husband nor chaperone.

"Do you think the youth could be pried loose?" the *fattore* had asked. "Could you not simply order him to break with her?"

"Of course. How likely do you think it that he would heed such an order, or even could? He has the madness, has had it for weeks and is beyond recovery. He is young, nothing can be done. Try and I fear they would disappear in the night and we would have to chase them."

"Then do we not have no alternative but to pry loose the lady?"

"As the woman has the same madness, therefore would I guess the outcome the same. You know the story of Abelardo and Eloisa. She writes in one of her letters that what was most astonishing about her love was that it turned into a madness. The same is said often of Isolda's love for Tristano. After all, something has to drive a married woman to defile her honor in a spectacle of illicit affection."

The *fattore* noted that in both love and insanity the soul seemed possessed there was as much pain as pleasure and they were impossible to explain saying, "Do we not ask, as in fact we are asking now, 'What has come over them?'"

"Indeed. Abelardo was too distracted to perform his duties."

"Then must we not consider more robust measures? I wonder if you could send the youth home."

"He would refuse. Those ordered to escort him would refuse. The rest of my men would refuse to move. And who's to say what the woman might do?"

As everyone stared at each other Tuccio requested permission to speak and said, "*Signore*, as we are now united and will not again be divided, might we not simply continue as before?"

As they'd approached Arles across a nearly featureless landscape the one point on which the count and the *fattore* were certain was that the caravan could not simply continue as before and therefore as nothing could be done with the youth something must be done with the woman and the only possibility they could see was to persuade her to return to Siena. The *fattore* wondered if the best hope of achieving that was to send them both home a crazy proposal the count nonetheless considered but in the end found it like the *fattore*'s other ideas too risky.

"Why not? Let her husband deal with her."

"Would you confront him at once with his wife's infidelity and her lover?"

"What's that to us?"

"He will hold us responsible. And in that will not be totally wrong. Where's your compensation then?"

"All right. Let us think. Suppose she were induced to go without him, how might that be accomplished? The coast road might be quicker."

"Too dangerous. Especially if my men are split."

"Suppose we hired more men?"

"Ones you would trust with your life?"

"I have it! Have your men take her to Marseilles and put her on a ship to Genoa. There Francesco could arrange for more guards, send them if need be. I could stay profitably employed in Avignon till your men returned."

"And on ship who would protect her? And what if, God forbid, it were taken by pirates, would you have her sold into slavery in Tunis?"

"Every path has its risks, including the one that lies before us."

"But at least we go together, a sturdy band as you have witnessed." He shook his head. "Francesco. Foolish man, who evidently doesn't know his wife of fifteen years, do you know he told me she would give up the journey before the Alps?"

"I can assure you the man is anything but foolish, though of course, as the proverb says, 'A fool can't see past a fly on his nose while the sage can't smell his own fart.' As I am not a sage neither would I be a fool and so I hope I summarize our predicament correctly when I say we are stuck like a fat man fallen into a skinny barrel."

"It is as you say."

"Then we can expect nothing for our trouble but more trouble."

"Unless somehow, against all hope, one of them sees reason."

The count asked Margherita if he might have a word with her privately and said, "Please know, *donna*, that I bear you no ill will, truly I do not. I have a task to perform, that is all. Now we both know that one of my men, the youngest and one whom I have raised as if he were my son, is madly in love with you and you have responded with feelings of your own. Do I speak fairly thus far?" She nodded. "Then I believe it is not discourteous to ask what your intentions are in this regard." He waited politely. "*Donna?*"

"My hesitation, *signore*, is simply that I do not know. This has never happened before."

"And you do not feel in control of the situation." Again she nodded. "And I assume you have sought guidance, in prayer and confession and so on."

"Many times."

"Then let me ask whether I might be of service. Put another way, is there anything you would like me to do, any assistance or intervention? You see my concern is that we would all come to harm if this situation were to proceed on its current course, all of us. You above all. So..."

"In truth, *signore*, I know not how to reply. Were I miserable, disconsolate..."

"I would not disturb your joy, *madonna*, I might even envy it, but we have an expression, 'Know you how to temper,' referring to one's desires."

"*Signore*, I have tempered my desires all my life. My husband in his wisdom forced me upon your caravan, now there is in this very hostel a group of women bound for Saint James who have invited me to join them, but my husband has forbidden this and in any case I will tell you honestly that I will not leave Tuccio for I love him as he loves me. I say this without blushing because my marriage vows remain intact. I have learned that while marriage can constrain actions it cannot restrain feelings. Love exceeds it. The priests speak of marriage, only the poets sing of love and so as the priests will not instruct me, the poets must."

"Then what would you have me do?"

"As you say, your assignment, nothing more."

FRANCESCO. Francesco owned many plots of land the largest no more than twenty acres but none pleased him so much as the first parcel he had acquired a modest farm bought from Margherita's family located near a spring said to have healing powers. From these came all the necessities of his table and hearth and much of the desirables excepting only the delicacies that had to be imported but they served the additional purpose of recreation for he loved nothing more than to throw off his fine robes and don the coarse woolen tunic of a peasant to pitch into the work beside his laborers with nothing more pleasing than trampling his own grapes. Not for him a castle or country estate he loved his little farm which he affectionately called The Hedgehog (Il Riccio) though this did not impede him from haranguing his managers and workers relentlessly with insulting disrespect for he believed them to be irredeemably lazy on one hand and inveterate cheats on the other who must be scolded and accused at every turn lest one be robbed even more.

Fortunately for these employees he spent little time there because it was hard to find a free hour hard in typical times if he could be said to have typical times but especially hard now that he was up to his chin in work to launch his bank. To complicate his affairs if it could be said that his affairs were ever uncomplicated he had received word that a Venetian ship had been wrecked at sea carrying cargo of a merchant who had purchased it partly with a loan from him and though he had some recourse to collateral he had no doubt the loan would have to be substantially discounted.

This news especially coming when it did led to one of his periodic bouts of envy in which even as he acknowledged that the magnate bankers suffered losses including the ruin of the largest banks in Siena years ago and more recently in Florence he still saw plenty to envy in the opportunities available to politically connected banking families. What came to mind were loans to the commune which could be 'voluntary' or 'forced,' both paying substantial rates of interest indeed rates on voluntary loans as high as sixty percent and if any loan could be deemed usurious surely he thought that was it for where was the risk or loss of use? Many of these loans had terms of only thirty to ninety days and if one were a large enough lender to negotiate terms which was typically the case one received public land and castles as sureties plus the income they produced (the usufruct) plus fees for managing them!

DAY TWENTY-ONE. The women who had conducted Margherita to Arles had left the day before but there were many pilgrims on the road so for the short flat stage along the arid northern edge of the Camargas wetland the festive atmosphere and camaraderie continued which made Margherita and Tuccio feel that though bound to the caravan they belonged to a larger group with a larger purpose. The mood carried right to the abbey church in Saint-Gilles a town made wealthy by pilgrims both en route to Compostela and local for Saint Giles buried in the crypt was a much revered hermit said to have arrived by raft from Greece; and everyone crowded in front of the church partly for Sunday mass and to view the precious relics but also to view the wonderful facade which had the same iconographic sculpture as Arles but the ensemble was larger and in Margherita's judgment more expressive.

"More expressive?"

"Look at the gestures and the facial expressions."

"Didn't we decide yesterday that these sculptures are trying to instill fear?"

"We did, but today I see there's more to it. There's awe, there's yearning. Love. It teaches." As she spoke Tuccio inspected the sculptures approaching some for a closer look. "I think the sculptors have an impossible task. They're trying to describe the physical and moral nature of the world, including the parts beyond our senses. Beyond our intellect even."

"Yes," he said stepping back to take a wider view, "I begin to see what you mean. Not just what we know but what we struggle to imagine."

"Though we call on genius and art and practice to give us understanding, I would say that what they are trying to describe was never imagined. But we can believe and long to see it." (*Paradiso*, Canto 10)

"And if our imaginings are low against such height, it is no wonder since above the sun no eye goes." (Canto 10 continued)

DAY TWENTY-TWO. The human mass that had moved into Saint-Gilles now set out again for Montpellier but it was two days' journey with nothing to see in the flat desert landscape and nothing to do but talk or sing pray or introspect and there was much of that with Margherita and Tuccio learning pilgrimage songs and never at a loss for conversation. "What would we see," he asked, "if we could go beyond the sun? I would like to ascend in a whirlwind and be instantly in the sphere of the fixed stars. From there I would gaze down through the seven celestial spheres." (*Paradiso*, Canto 22) "I would be with you and together we would watch all the poor pilgrims far below trudging toward absolution or improvement."

"Would we be happier watching than trudging?"

"How could we be happier than we are now?"

"We would be closer to God."

"I feel closer to God now, in love with a beautiful woman of great merit, walking with pilgrims to Compostela... And as today is the festival of Saint James, I feel his presence. Do you regret we couldn't stay in Arles for the celebration?"

"If I could not be there, where I imagine the confraternity's pageant will be elaborate and the banquet lavish, then it seems fitting to be here in this wilderness."

"I think so too. This parade is our spectacle. How many of us must there be on the pilgrim route, a thousand miles long and more, all seeking."

"Yet don't you feel it is just we two?"

"I would embrace you now if I could."

"I would have you do it if I could."

"Then let us embrace. Do you feel my arms around you?"

"Do you feel my lips on yours?"

"I am burning."

"If I flame you in the heat of love beyond the measure that on Earth is seen, so that I vanquish the valor of your face, do not be amazed." (*Paradiso*, Canto 5)

"I am amazed. I am filled with wonder and completely vanquished."

"Not so completely that you would not vanquish me."

"May you be vanquished, lady. Most thoroughly and forthwith."

"And filled with something besides wonder?"

"Most certainly."

She told him about her confession in the Alyscamps and how the monk had compared her to Heloise and after they had had a good laugh they talked about how a tragic story had become the butt of low comedy about how their love for each other had survived so many adversities as they remained devoted. They imagined the agony of living in the same place but separate monasteries and discussed the one exception to their chastity of which the actors had made so much which was the time they met in her convent and unable to stop themselves copulated in a corner; and they were adamant that their love must survive that they must avoid the fate of others for as Margherita said, "we must never become miserable like Isolda and Tristano and go to our deaths in longing."

Tuccio noted that they were already avoiding the mistakes of those others who began in wild copulation whereas "we restrain ourselves from ceding to our desires and thereby retain not just our honor but the safety of our love."

"When I hear you talk with such nobility, my love for you exceeds all bounds."

"My love for you, lady, is so great the very idea of bounds is inconceivable. That is why I would lie with you if I could."

"As I would with you. Do you remember how embarrassed we were at the performance?"

"I was not embarrassed because my love for you was already too intense to be bothered, as a horse is not bothered by a mosquito."

"Liar! You were fidgeting as much as me."

Chapter Twenty-one

Four months after Bob was promoted his firm not his unit but the entire bank was precipitously sold over a weekend for a small fraction of its current market value to avoid complete collapse the endpoint of a decline well underway when he'd gotten promoted that resulted directly from exposure to the MBS market; it was announced on a Sunday evening just before the Asian stock markets opened to prevent complete collapse. When the employees arrived for work the next morning they were formally given the news though many had already heard it but those who'd heard it were as shocked as those who hadn't though the bank had been in serious and steadily increasing trouble for months; in fact it was not the only one for even while Bob was still feverishly working on his specially designed CDO other firms had been forced to declare large operating losses proceeding directly from their MBS operations.

Merrill Lynch one of the major players in all aspects of the MBS business had declared a huge quarterly loss that stunned investors who had recently been alerted to expect one about half its size with much of the loss coming from the firm's holdings of 'super-senior' tranches of CDOs that is those with the highest credit ratings believed to be extremely safe. Ten days later Citigroup another major player announced an even bigger loss on its mortgage-related holdings and also said its total exposure was enormously greater than what it had announced three weeks earlier.

Merrill Lynch's CEO resigned with a gigantic severance package Citigroup's amid concerns that he had lost control of the firms' operations and that its audited financial statements did not fairly and adequately present the firm's capital position. Citigroup had more than two thousand operating subsidiaries and a balance sheet that omitted more than a third of its assets and liabilities a situation made possible by the massive deployment of 'special-purpose entities' like the one that employed Bob that were separately incorporated (normally in an 'off-shore' tax haven) and capitalized with a tiny amount of equity and a large amount of debt. On close inspection it was determined that while the bank had been reporting its exposure to subprime mortgages at two percent it was in fact more than a third of its entire capital.

The very week Bob got his promotion his bank announced a large decrease in the value of its mortgage-related assets a direct result of its recent bailout of his unit following the bankruptcy of its hedge funds and this was causing investors to scrutinize its finances ever more closely. By this time it was entirely dependent on one-day loans of fifty to seventy billion dollars for which it was increasingly required to post more collateral and pay higher interest rates and even then more and more potential lenders declined to lend since the firm was now almost thirty-eight dollars in debt for each dollar of assets; by March 2008 the entire bank was so heavily in debt that it had enough cash on hand to operate no longer than about a week.

There was no crisis no precipitating event no malfunction or crash in the MBS market just an accumulation of concern about low-quality mortgages and the securities they collateralized; but it wasn't just that vast amounts of MBS investments were still being held by Wall Street firms but specifically the firm's near-total lack of liquidity causing a complete and constant dependence on overnight loans not just to hold those securities but conduct all its operations. Thus it was extreme leverage arguably an unnecessary feature of the MBS industry that was the proximate cause of the firm's demise because with every drop magnified thirty-eight times it had no capacity to absorb declines in securities prices; but even then it might have survived had it followed its own business plan for like the other Wall Street firms its claim was that it was in the moving not the storage business meaning that it sought to distribute securities rather than hold them yet hold them it did in gigantic amounts.

In a noisy bar well across town from Wall Street three low-level professionals in one of the firm's MBS units had met to discuss the latest of the rumors that for months had been circulating in the informal employee networks that served the need to know what was happening in the absence of dependable information. One of them believed the firm couldn't survive much longer on its current path another that the concerns if not the problems were exaggerated and the third didn't know what to think but what united them in a place where they could speak freely was that they were anxious to discuss recent developments and trusted each other to keep whatever was said confidential; said one, "I think Mister Veepo knows something. Why else does the unit's biggest cheerleader suddenly go over to the dark side?"

"If he thought we were going down, he'd jump ship."

"Maybe he is."

"Maybe he knows he's got time. If we're going down, who knows how soon? Anybody here know how much working capital we've got? I'm guessing not much, but what do I know? Maybe Mister Veepo knows."

"Or thinks he knows."

"He just got his promotion. You really think he'd leave now?"

"What better time? He's riding high. Why wait till some shit hits the fan?"

"He knows something. He's management now, he's privy to some of the financials."

"Monthly production, overhead. That won't tell you much."

"How about never mind what Mister Veepo might know, how about what the fuck is going on?"

A silence fell because it was not knowing that had brought them together so they drank beer till one said, "What if nobody knows?"

"If they know, they won't tell us."

"We know that no sooner does Bob's sucker CDO hit the Street than it starts to sink."

"Bit of an exaggeration, but yeah."

"Anybody on the long side is screwed, right? So what a coincidence, the first time we go short on one of our own products it pays off big-time."

"And Mister Veepo gets his promotion."

"Shrewd move, you have to give him that."

"But what was the move? His CDO was built to fail, right?"

"Good question."

"The market's not what it was, we know that. You can't just pile up some subprime, put a triple-A sticker on it, and watch the money roll in."

"That's been true for a while. The question is are we near the end?"

"No way. A market this big doesn't just go away."

"It's not the market I'm worried about, it's us. Shorting a sucker CDO might be sweet, but our net position is long. We need prices to go up, not down."

"Forget about Bob, the issue is the firm's financial position."

"There's no point arguing over that because we don't know the answer."

"We know it's costing us more and more to roll our paper every night."

"We know lenders have walked away."

"We think we know."

"The rumor's as bad as the fact. Once the Street stops taking our paper..."

"Never happen. We just pay more, that's all."

"That's all? How long does that go on?"

"Both of you calm down. Question: Who's worried? You see investors worried? Credit agencies? Regulators?"

"Do you know how many hedge funds are short now? Dozens, maybe hundreds."

"You can't have a short side without a long side."

"Maybe, but you can have a long side without a short side."

"Not in synthetics you can't."

"Off topic again. In any market somebody will bet against it, so what?"

"So what is when short interest gets so big you have to wonder."

"Do you really see a Wall Street bank going down? Come on."

"Ever notice how after some preventable disaster it seems obvious, but no one saw it coming?"

"I presume you're shopping your resume. Well then, what are we talking about?"

"Maybe we should be shopping our resumes."

"And tell the world we're in deep shit?"

"I still say you're exaggerating."

"Anybody here think our hedge funds would go down like they did? Eighteen billion dollars, poof! Anybody see that coming?"

One night when they were getting ready for bed Bob told Tiffany about a rumor that was circulating that a major lender had threatened to discontinue its loans and said when she asked who it was, "Not the point. The point is someone threatened to walk away. We can't operate without loans."

"Is it a big deal? I guess it must be or you wouldn't be mentioning it."

"It's not a big deal if it's just a ploy to ratchet up our costs but, one, raising our costs is not what we need right now and, b, so long as this trend doesn't continue and maybe get worse."

"Which you see happening?"

"The rumor's flying for a reason. Everybody knows our borrowing costs have been going up, that's not news. So why the rumor?"

"Okay, why the rumor?"

"That's what I'm a little concerned about. You want positive buzz, not this." She watched him. "It would be nice to know if it's true or not, but they're keeping it below the radar. Haven't been able to find a thing on it and obviously nobody's talking."

"Except everybody's talking."

"Exactly, which just makes my job harder. I have to say, a lot of the fun has gone out of the job."

"Since when?"

"I don't know. It creeps up on you."

"You finally get your promotion and..."

"It's not like it was, what, a year ago, two years ago. Maybe it's because I see more now, but people just seem more— management, I mean—I don't know, edgy."

"How so? You haven't..."

"There's a tension around the place that seems different. My job's always been a pressure cooker, I don't mind that, heck, I thrive on it, you do too, it's our world, right? This is different. Anyway, sorry to unload on you."

"So you're okay?"

"Of course."

"How worried are you?"

"Not so worried that I haven't been thinking about what I'm going to do to you when we get in bed."

"You're so romantic."

"That's me, Mister Romance. So what do you say we get in bed and I'll show you how romantic I am."

She thought, "It was just a short time ago he could barely wait to get me in bed. No one else has ever looked at me as he would," however she was not thinking about Bob but the professor and she did not think it in her bedroom but driving home from a hotel. "I loved how he undressed me, how he unbuttoned my blouse and put his hands under my skirt. I quickly learned to dress that way every time." For some five months they had been meeting in hotel parking lots where he invariably arrived first with an overnight bag and they registered as man and wife each time at a different hotel feeling foolish at first and nervous not knowing how such matters were arranged; at first he thought, "The hotel people have to know, she's so much younger than me," but later he thought, "So what if they know, and why couldn't we be married, we love each other," and in the elevator they could barely stay apart there were no preliminaries and once in the room they began.

At first they pretended they had to check out early because there'd been an emergency but later they didn't bother they even enjoyed watching the faces to see how well people pretended they didn't know what was happening. "The sex is still great," he thought and she thought the same, "even if it's not like the first times. How could it be?" They would lie in bed side by side when they couldn't make love any more and have their discussions that way just so he could caress her from time to time to feel her nakedness beside him and sometimes they would caress each other between their thighs and there would be sighs.

Their time was always cut short by Tiffany's need to be home in time to give Kiley supper a ritual she would never have dreamed of missing and one which the professor would never have thought to deprive her no matter how much he would have liked to stay till he could recover his vigor and mount her again. Lack of time controlled them not enough for sex not enough to talk and when eventually sex and talk didn't fill the time there was not enough to go somewhere just to get out of the room and act like a couple who did more than copulate and talk about the meaning of things.

He told her she was only the second woman he'd ever loved and that it had come as a complete surprise it never having occurred to him when they met that he could fall in love with her that that was something that could still happen to him who had avoided entanglements in fact dreaded them and would happily have remained celibate were it not for sexual desire. She said she too was shocked to find herself in love even more shocked to fall for an older man and a scholar of esoteric subjects but he had released something in her she hadn't known was there and she who'd thought she was satisfied with her life had found herself desperate for his company for his attention and then for his gentle and patient ministrations. Neither admitted that with the initial phase of love waning they were becoming anxious about the next what it would be like and what it would mean for the future of their love.

Perversely the passage of time and the lack of time created the necessity to fill time but she still loved to have him read to her because he would alternate between the originals and the always inadequate translations and explicate images and themes as he read from the troubadours and Dante's lyric poems and Petrarch also the romances of Tristan and Isolde Lancelot and Guinevere; he even read Yeats' "The Song of Wandering Aengus" and other poems to demonstrate that nothing had changed. "Think about that, not just the essence but the whole cultural construction we call romantic love has survived intact through six, seven, eight, nine centuries of profound cultural change. And don't think it's because romantic love is universal, because it's not."

When Tiffany and the professor declared their love her enthusiasm for pilgrimage surged and with the passion she had found in love came the excited desire to pursue pilgrimage more fervently; so being still far from Compostela in her virtual journey she resolved to increase the tempo of her stages and it was a suggestion of the professor's to avoid the tedium of trudging through snow and ice in uncongenial surroundings that made it possible for her to do this through the simple stratagem of walking on the treadmill in her basement. "Why not?" he asked rhetorically, "it doesn't seem any more 'virtual' than what you're already doing."

"No," she replied, "it doesn't," in fact she was amazed she hadn't thought of it before because it saved all the time spent planning and commuting to the staging points and she could even watch travel videos of southern France on her laptop as she walked; as to the fact that it might be even less authentic than walking outside she said, "What could be more meaningless and boring than those stages I put myself through? The meaning is surely in my head or nowhere. As for authenticity, there's nothing authentic about virtual pilgrimage, but it's that or nothing."

What increased her efficiency even more was an exercise bike an idea that came to her fairly soon though she initially resisted it as beyond the limit of acceptability even for virtual pilgrimage; for she knew the pilgrim hostels along the routes gave priority to walkers and frowned upon bikers and sometimes even refused to stamp their 'credential' cards necessary to obtain the certificate of pilgrimage called the *compostela*. "A pilgrim walks," she insisted looking forward to the day when she could honestly claim to have walked every step of her thousand mile quest; but then she disputed the idea that using a bicycle automatically invalidated the effort knowing from the professor that in centuries past many pilgrims went on horse or mule even though all were expected to walk. "Some of them at least surely were honest pilgrims and not just tourists or runaways," she thought and the professor agreed; still she wondered if they wrestled with their consciences and so after wrestling with hers she bought an exercise bike thereby completing no less than sixteen stages in five months versus twelve in the preceding fifteen.

At the same time both the professor and she were enthusiastic about the foundation for he had joined its Academic Advisory Board (as its sole member) the previous summer in time to help with the design of the second grant cycle and its announcement in September. That Bob had questioned her decision to continue this very expensive project had not affected their excitement to work together since his objection which was entirely concern for the cost had been halfhearted given that at the time he was flush with his brilliant idea that was going to get him his promotion at last; and then he'd gotten it and was flush with success till March so he had no significant financial concern. Privately he still thought she was spending an awful lot of money indulging her latest enthusiasm but since neither he nor she realized how much of her enthusiasm for the foundation was really for the professor he didn't want to get in her way and this left the lovers alone with their excitement during this period with little to do except review the applications as they arrived.

Arrive they did for the Foundation for Pilgrim Studies now had an eminent scholar in the field working closely with it as academic advisor to build it into a reputable and recognized sponsor of high quality research; and since he knew where when and how to publicize the foundation's fellowship and lent his name to its website and promotional materials it was able to find and attract applicants far beyond what Tiffany had been able to accomplish on her own. The lovers however did not review any applications at their meetings which they preferred to reserve for activities they could perform only in each other's arms and in any case review was a task mainly for the professor; and other than this there wasn't much to do till after the application deadline in mid-February when they would select a winner.

By March however Tiffany's enthusiasm was waning quickly and not just for the foundation as she suddenly found herself all but unwilling to go down to the basement to do stages no matter how efficiently and wondered at this decline in enthusiasm. Noticing how it had earlier surged as her passion for the professor had surged and admitting that that had considerably diminished recently it seemed there was a connection; thus did she come to believe that the unknown reason for her interest in pilgrimage was a hidden desire for love and that the purpose of her pilgrimage was to search for love.

If that were the case and if her love for the professor and his for her were cooling to the point where their love could become cold then she wondered what the point would be to complete the journey and commit herself to a foundation only to see her life return to where she'd started with an acceptable but unsatisfying marriage and an absence of real love in her life; that is she wondered what the point would be to complete a pilgrimage that was a failure or a delusion and finance a foundation that was no longer of interest. Alternatively she wondered perhaps hopefully if she wasn't greatly exaggerating what was merely a resurgence of her ineradicable concern for the authenticity of virtual pilgrimage and the irreducible tedium of biking on an exercise bike in a basement which ordeal she then had to transform in her blog into a wonderful adventure crossing France.

In Bob's life too March was not a happy month but in his case due to the situation at work which had suddenly it seemed become fraught with difficulty as his bank's business practices were increasingly questioned by suppliers and customers until it became impossible to operate. Besides banks declining to renew loans customers especially hedge funds had become reluctant to use its brokerage services fearing that in a liquidity crisis the firm would be unable to return their cash and securities yet two weeks before the precipitous sale of the firm at a giveaway price inspectors of the Securities and Exchange Commission found 'no significant issues' with its liquidity situation. A week before the firm collapsed they suddenly became concerned when its liquidity pool began to rapidly evaporate in the face of panic by counter-parties to loans and securities transactions caused by the public announcement of a credit agency that it was downgrading fifteen MBS's issued by one of the firm's special-purpose entities; and though the firm was able to roll over its loans another day the SEC worried that this would not continue.

Indeed by Wednesday a third of the firm's cash reserves had disappeared but with the bank still able to roll over its loans and 'no notable losses sustained' the SEC in reply to an inquiry from the Federal Reserve Board concluded that the capital position of the firm was 'fine.' Whatever 'fine' might mean the firm was no longer able to do business normally for example it had just offered the best bid to buy a relatively small MBS position from a hedge fund holding the securities at Goldman Sachs which then refused to allow the transaction saying it did not want to become a counter-party to the firm; and although it eventually consented the news of its rejection of a routine trade had become public.

The firm's CEO went on television to claim no knowledge of the incident and rhetorically ask why rumors started but later that day his firm paid over a billion dollars in calls for more collateral from a hundred forty-two counter-parties to securities transactions; meanwhile lenders who had already tightened the terms of their overnight contracts demanded yet more collateral and after close of business some of them said they might become hesitant to provide a further rollover the next day. On this third to the last business day of the firm's independent existence the chairman of the SEC told reporters his agency was monitoring capital levels 'on a constant basis;' that night the firm's CEO telephoned the president of the New York Federal Reserve Bank to discuss possible 'flexibility' in its financial arrangements should the lenders fail to renew. By the next night Thursday most of the firm's cash was gone and it informed the SEC that it would be unable to operate normally on Friday even though executives and regulators maintained that it was solvent its problem being liquidity not capital; indeed the SEC chairman would later testify before the Financial Crisis Inquiry Commission that at all times during the firm's final week of operation it had a capital cushion well above what was required.

When the firm's CEO personally requested a large line of credit from JP Morgan's CEO it was denied on the grounds that that firm too had significant exposure to the MBS market so it seemed the problem was not just liquidity but capital as well; nonetheless when he again spoke with the president of the New

York Fed he insisted his problem was liquidity just liquidity not capital. With the Secretary of the Treasury brought into the discussion the New York Federal Reserve on Friday morning arranged a large loan through JP Morgan but the three major credit agencies lowered the firm's credit rating and by the end of the day it was out of cash and its stock had lost almost half its value in public trading. After the markets closed the CEO was informed that the JP Morgan loan would not be available after the weekend which gave him till Sunday night when Asian markets opened to find a buyer for the firm since it could not conduct business without the loan; and so on Sunday evening JP Morgan publicly announced a deal to buy the firm for two dollars a share which was less than three and a half percent of what the stock had been worth on Friday morning though a week later it would raise it to ten.

For Bob as no doubt for everyone it was a week in hell with more time and energy spent dealing with unverifiable rumors and claims than getting work done for example calling contacts not just up and down the Street but in financial centers all over the world less to transact business than try to glean information and even more assess attitudes because when a firm was in trouble the feelings of customers were more important than any financial data. After a few days of this it began to dawn on the firm's employees if not those responsible for the firm that their jobs might be in imminent risk of dissolution and as it did the calls were increasingly about the possibility of moving to a competitor and Bob as usual was among the first to make this transition and among the best to hide his anxiety beneath his charm.

Though he like everyone around him was infuriated by the refusal of Goldman Sachs to allow a routine trade for a modest sum an act which might have done more than any other to jeopardize the very survival of the firm he didn't allow his anger to cloud his judgment that of all the places to land a new position Goldman was possibly the best and later he would wonder whether it had entered into his judgment that Goldman was best positioned to weather whatever storm was coming because its former CEO had left to become the current Secretary of the Treasury. He like everyone tried desperately to extract some reassurance reading sentences into every word as they surreptitiously watched their CEO on television try desperately without looking desperate to deny what everyone knew and minimize what everyone feared; and he like everyone vilified the chairman of the SEC as they read his press statements that attempted to show that rather than wake up the second before disaster struck he had been vigilant the entire time. 'Where has the SEC been the last ten years?' they griped forgetting that they themselves had cursed it whenever it made the least attempt to do its job.

As each demand arrived for more collateral the news heavily freighted with embellished facts and exaggerated claims spread at the speed of voice and keyboard as everyone searched for a conclusion to the story alternative to the looming one; finding none they worried less about doing their jobs and more about keeping them. The brave hope was, 'We'll make it, we have a large capital cushion;' the two responses were first, 'Would you liquidate the firm's assets to pay daily operating expenses?' and second, 'With all the accounting gimmickry does anyone really know how much capital we have?' As a result everyone including Bob went home Friday believing everyone else would spend the weekend furiously making calls and emailing resumes so he planned to do the same angry with himself for having accepted till now the common refrain: 'Who knew anything like this could happen? The Street has gone crazy, this is triple-A paper.' In fact he had already spent most of Friday calling around as he had no doubt the managers were doing who were closeted in their offices the whole day emerging from time to time just long enough to bark orders.

He didn't actually lose his job for another three weeks three weeks during which he did everything he could to make himself attractive to the new managers from JP Morgan three weeks of anxiety frustration and calling everyone he knew on the Street about a job but in the end he was pushed out the door with a decent severance package and as far as he was concerned a large sign around his neck reading 'unemployed.' Understandably he didn't react well when Tiffany announced she was keeping her appointment with the professor even though he had no way to know she was lying when she claimed the reason was because they had to select the new fellow since the deadline was in ten days for while that was true it omitted that the professor would make the selection and more significantly that no foundation work would occur during the rendezvous. Kiley who was now five and had absorbed the ambient tension as children do began to complain about Tiffany leaving and as is generally the case in such situations no amount of reassurance or promises of the rewards to be received when she returned did anything to placate her.

This rendezvous nothing would deter her from attending would be the first from which she would return home disappointed aware of the diminution of passion much as they both had tried to enliven it and as she drove she wondered if the professor was driving as distractedly as she was. Having heard on the news about the fall of Bob's firm he had emailed her to ask about him but all she could say at that point was that they were crossing their fingers; now her first utterance after embracing him had been that he had just lost his job. "Forgive me, I have to ask, since we're about to award a second fellowship, do we have a concern about the foundation's funding?" She shook her head saying Bob's skills like hers were not limited to one security or market and so were easily transferrable to a new job which she had no doubt he would find quickly as he had the last time thereby lying by telling the truth because what she tried not to betray were her own doubts about her commitment to the project.

Chapter Twenty-two

DAY TWENTY-THREE. Their joyous mood was unchanged untroubled by the late July heat or the monotony of the scenery which remained the same though they had left the Camargas with the transition to the new landscape so gradual as to be undetectable; Tuccio bantered in the usual way with the other guards and Margherita looked after Piera who never complained and rarely spoke and watched the world approach at a mule's pace with wide-eyed wonder while Agnoletta and Stoldo had little to do with each other in the open landscape under the sun's glare.

"Are we still among the fixed stars in the eighth of Heaven's nine spheres?"

"That we are, lady most dear."

"Nay, there is one lady more dear. Let us gaze upon the mother of God. Let us gaze upon the shining brilliance of the choruses of heavenly souls that ring her and sing her praises, and her Son whose presence is with her. Can you do that?"

"I can so long as you are there to guide me."

"Then you must look straight at me with unwavering eye, able to endure my smile without turning away. Can you do that?"

"As you see, lady, I can indeed, though never before was I able to do so, so radiant was it in comparison to my poor vision."

"But now you must take your eyes off me and turn back to the heavenly spectacle."

"I do so, lady, though your beauty be so great as to bind my eyes as before it blinded them, but only in my desire to serve you." (*Paradiso*, Canto 23)

"Is it not the grandest sight you have ever seen?"

"It is, lady. And I marvel that it is I, a poor pilgrim, who sees it. Each soul shines with a brilliant interior light."

"That is the light of heavenly love, of which our love is part."

"Then I would know how long it will last."

"However long be the festival of Paradise, so long our love will radiate around itself such garment." (*Paradiso*, Canto 14)

DAYS TWENTY-FOUR THROUGH TWENTY-SIX. A popular joke about Montpellier had it that once there was a peasant who took his two asses to the city to collect manure for his fields and found himself in the street of the spice merchants where exotic spices from the Far East were ground all day long and no sooner did he get a whiff than he fainted dead away. A crowd gathered and lamentations were heard crying, "Lord, have pity! See here a dead man!" but no one knew what to do until a gallant youth of the neighborhood who happened to pass that way stepped forward to offer to revive the peasant for a modest fee which was quickly donated by a generous townsman whereupon taking up the man's pitchfork he stabbed a juicy piece of manure and held it to his nose. First he was seen to inhale weakly then to take a normal breath and finally his chest swelled and he rose to his feet pronounced himself once again in fine shape and declared to all assembled that never again would he try to pass down the street of spice sellers.

When one of the porters told this joke the others immediately understood that the *fattore* was its butt likened at once to the rich haughty merchants whose precious powders stank in the nostrils of an honest man as their vile usury stank in the nose of God and to the manure-collecting peasant because he was a peasant and they likened his commerce to gathering shit for they had come to dislike him more and more for his rude treatment of them. What would they have thought had they known that in fact Francesco had frequent dealings with an Italian importer of spices whose main house was a few streets away (with a branch in Paris) and that the *fattore* would be calling on it that very afternoon?

The caravan would be staying a few days for the *fattore* to engage in trade Montpellier being an important commercial city and not only for its internationally reputed spice industry supported by research at the university whose medical faculty was generally recognized as the foremost in Europe but already he needed to engage Margherita on the important but delicate question of where the caravan would be headed once it departed. Would it proceed on the pilgrim route as Francesco had led her to believe or divert to Barcelona where she had always known he was ultimately bound which he was hoping since Francesco had insisted she would quickly tire of pilgrimage? The issue arose now because it was here the road west to Toulouse diverged from the coast road south to Barcelona and he put the question as delicately as he could the count impassively beside him.

The count assured her that from Barcelona the *masnada* would be at her disposal to join the pilgrim route in Catalonia and the *fattore* interrupted to say there would surely be pilgrims to the great shrine from there but Margherita said, "The great route and the pilgrims on it may mean nothing to you, but to me everything."

"Everything? To the exclusion of your husband's wish?"

"My husband never gave me cause to believe I was not truly bound for Compostela. If I had anything to gain by pleasing him I might consider this proposal. As it is..." The *fattore* who hated the prospect of the long journey with all the time and resources wasted was angry at Francesco for not having dealt properly with his wife and scolded himself for having assured the count the man was not foolish. "A pilgrimage is not just the end, it is the way, and I intend to follow the way."

"Is there not more than one way?"

"I have heard there is," she acknowledged, "but none that goes by the route you propose. A route is established for imaginative as well as practical reasons."

"A very long route."

"Perhaps God should have placed Compostela closer to Siena."

"It is just, *madonna*, that we were wondering... You have already visited numerous sites, some of which are pilgrim destinations in their own right. And so, one can't help but wonder, the vast distances still before us, all of which of course must then be retraced..."

"You would like to know why I insist on walking so far?"

"Of course no one disputes the holiness of the sanctuary. But with so many..."

"Because it is so far. Can you understand that?"

"I can, *madonna*," interjected the count, "though I myself have not been farther than Assisi. Tuccio's father goes there every year to thank the saint for his son's good fortune. But Compostela, that certainly deserves high praise. May I ask where you find the courage to face the vast expanses of wilderness ahead?"

"In faith, *signore*. The substance of things hoped for." (*Paradiso*, Canto 24, quoting *Hebrews* 11:1) "Do you now wish to question me about faith?"

"Indeed, *madonna*, I might do just that some day, to learn how my own which is weak might be strengthened. I give you my word I will accompany you to the shrine if that remains your wish. Please forgive us for hoping you might reconsider or at least agree to go via Barcelona."

She was more shaken by the count's courtesy than the *fattore*'s rudeness but Tuccio reassured her that the call to pilgrimage preceded the call of lucre and though he didn't say it he felt superior to her husband whom he found lacking in all nobility thinking, "For all his show, he's a stranger to the least refinement of character and deserves nothing from his wife, neither her respect nor her submission." It disturbed him to imagine her sharing his bed and the more he imagined it the more disturbed he became until Stoldo concerned for the health of one whose youth required an outlet for his natural potency announced that the time had come to consider alternatives.

"You're offering me Agnoletta? Are you crazy?"

"She's complaisant."

"She's my lady's maid."

"So? It wouldn't be the first time for such an arrangement."

"Do you really not comprehend that I am in love with the lady and that she loves me?"

"I comprehend the first, but as to the second I must say, my friend, there is more to love than talk. The whole *masnada* agrees that if the master's wife freely and openly takes up with one of us, she should do what courtesy requires and deliver what she proffers." Tuccio warned him not to say another word and Stoldo knew the look well enough to comply but after the anger subsided he tried to make light of the whole affair and announced affably that that very evening when they returned to the inn he would pay the wages of a magdalene of Tuccio's choosing and when Tuccio shook his head he was honestly shocked saying, "By the love of all saints, what's stopping you?"

"The love of one woman. You don't need to understand."

He asked Margherita to give him another reading lesson and with the sheaf of poems they had purchased in Avignon the five walked outside the city to a dry meadow of scattered brush and shrubs and the occasional dwarf tree where three of them settled in a small patch of shade while two went off a discreet distance. Tuccio and Margherita lost themselves in kisses until Piera asked if they were going to read poetry when laughing Margherita opened the sheaf but the first two they found too difficult to understand so it seemed merciful that the third had only eight lines until she painstakingly read it and found the same difficulties.

> Not to her lover more Diana was pleasing
> when by such luck completely naked
> he saw her in the middle of the icy waters,
>
> as to me the shepherdess alpine and harsh
> set to immerse a pretty covering
> that from the breeze the lovely and blonde hair encloses,
>
> such that she made me, now when it burns the sky,
> all tremble with an amorous chill.

"Are you sure that's right? It doesn't make sense. 'It burns the sky?' What burns the sky?"

Going through the poem carefully they saw how modifiers could be separated from what they modified and the natural order of speaking could be reversed and necessary words could be omitted and words or phrases in one line could relate to something else several lines away so that "it burns the sky" meant "the sky burns" and line four referred to line one and line one was a rearrangement of "Diana was not more pleasing to her lover," to which "than the shepherdess was to me" referred; but they wondered who Diana was or the mountain shepherdess or why a shepherdess would be wearing a veil of all things let alone why she would be washing it or why if the sky was so hot everything else was so cold or above all why there was no mention of Laura.

In this arduous way they noticed that the word used for 'immerse' was *bagnare* which suggested 'to wash' but also 'to bathe' which led to the recognition that the first two stanzas presented parallel images the first of a woman bathing naked the second of a woman bathing her head covering and each of them observed by a man. Having seen the parallel they wondered what it meant which led them to examine its disparities for example that the man in the first scene (who remained unidentified) was described as the woman's lover whereas the man in the second (the poem's protagonist) merely experienced an erotic shiver; but above all they wondered why the first woman was completely naked and immersed while the second had removed just her head covering and was washing only that.

Margherita said, "The second scene is more chaste," and suddenly Tuccio saw her in a stream on a burning hot day that seemed so long ago having left her book on a rock to wade into the cold waters to bathe her feet and in so doing had raised her robe; and remembering he relived the feeling that had shaken him at that instant and changed his life and she asked, "Did you just tremble?"

"This poem is about falling in love," he replied. "You're right, it is more chaste. But that very fact makes it more highly charged."

"You must explain that."

"The second man was no less pleased than the first with what each saw. So when the shepherdess bared her head and revealed her blond hair it struck him like lightning. Love's arrow. It's *fin'amor*. She must have been beautiful, and to see just her hair, her face, her eyes... Remember how the great poet talked about Laura's eyes? He didn't need to see more."

Margherita's eyes widened. "It's more chaste yet. He didn't have to see her body because he fell in love with her soul. *Fin'amor*."

"And the beauty of her soul was expressed in her physical beauty. I understand!"

"But a shepherdess?"

They consulted the text. "Alpine and harsh," read Tuccio proud to read the words. "What kind of shepherdess is alpine and harsh? If a man falls in love, what kind of way is that to describe his beloved?"

"Blond hair! It's Laura. What shepherdess has blond hair?"

"You're right! The *giullare* sang a song about a beautiful shepherdess. She turns out to be a nobleman's daughter."

"That's it. She is noble."

"And 'harsh' because probably she has rebuffed his advances."

"'Alpine' because she keeps her distance from him."

"She is huge in his imagination and daunting."

"Of course, she is Laura. I wonder who Diana is."

"Must be someone from one of the old tales."

Both were elated to have so far penetrated a poem that for all its severe brevity seemed dense with suggestion and implication and packed its own erotic charge albeit in a most refined way; and their elation was increased when they noticed that the phrase *l'aura* which they had read 'the breeze' could also be read *Laura*.

The next day the *fattore* again took time away from his commerce to confront Margherita with the count beside him but this time attempted to pressure her by stating that the caravan was never bound for Compostela and that if she insisted on going there the losses would be enormous; and despite her resolve she was shaken because try as she might she couldn't be certain he wasn't telling the truth much as she doubted Francesco would sink to that level. She repeated that she had done everything to dissuade her husband from forcing her to travel with a caravan but he had insisted as was his way therefore he must bear the consequences; and she thought it worthwhile to note that Toulouse was a great city where surely there were opportunities to make money.

"Perhaps, but before and after Toulouse there are none."

As they argued two issues became conflated one diverting to Barcelona and from there continuing to Compostela the other not going to Compostela at all which the count corrected saying, "The issue, *madonna,* is the route. Yesterday you defended the Via Tolosana with an argument of some merit, but I did ask you to reconsider and so now I ask whether it is your contention that Catalonian pilgrims en route to Compostela first cross the Pyrenees in order to make the crossing again beyond Toulouse."

"I would doubt it, though I do not know."

"If we continue on the Via Tolosana and cross the Pyrenees we then follow the Camino Francés west across Castilla León to Galicia. I ask whether Spanish pilgrims to the east do not head west to join that route."

"As I say, it seems likely."

"Then..."

"You have failed to argue why I, who am not in Catalonia and have no reason to go there, should do what you no doubt correctly claim the Catalonians don't do, which is to divert myself from the straight route."

Despite himself a rare smile escaped. "Allow me to argue it now, for it is quite simple. The diversion we propose would seem to do you little or no harm while it helps us greatly."

"Helps you? I see how it helps him, but why you?"

"By 'him,' do you mean your husband?"

"I mean him whom my husband hired as chaperone."

"It helps me because it is easier to protect you alone than you plus an entire caravan, laden with valuable goods and as matters stand bound for wilderness. You have already seen what lurks in such desolate places and what might occur."

She paused shaken again and said, "I sincerely regret that. But once more I—"

"We know," snapped the *fattore*, "but do you mean to say you are completely indifferent, not just to the extensive losses your husband and I will incur—possibly to my ruin, by the way—but to the danger to which you will expose not just yourself and the youth who loves to declare his willingness to die for you, but his friends and his lord, not to mention the girl?"

To this she found no reply and making none they smelled victory and pressed their advantage until breaking a long uncertain silence she said that regarding financial losses she couldn't speak for the *fattore* but regarding her husband she had long believed that his commerce had taken him much too far down a dangerous path to damnation and that she had always intended to implore the apostle once she reached his tomb to intercede for him and save him from himself. It was then the *fattore*'s turn to be shaken though he hid it well knowing that two arrangements condemned as usury by the Church and the king of Aragon who ruled Catalonia he himself would be employing; one was the *cambio a termine* the 'exchange at the end' which deliberately deferred payment to conceal interest by exploiting currency fluctuations the other the *cambio secco* the 'dry exchange' which was a loan disguised as a commercial transaction involving phony accounting.

"Regarding everyone's safety," continued Margherita, "I must pray to Saint James for forgiveness for any harm I may cause and hope no actual harm will befall anyone."

"Hope? Is that your strategy?"

"Surely it is as great as faith."

"In church perhaps. Was it hope that delivered us from the brigands or was it the ingenuity of the count and the prowess of his men?"

"Can you swear we owe nothing to the baron of Galicia?"

"It is plain," said the count, "that the lady possesses great hope, I at least have seen no greater, which allows her to leave Egypt in this life and see Jerusalem." (*Paradiso*, Canto 25)

Tuccio waiting for her asked, "How fare our *lauzengiers*?"

"Poorly, for they fail in their efforts to interfere with our love of this pilgrimage." She asked if he thought she possessed great hope for she couldn't tell whether the count had been serious and he replied that she did indeed for surely it took that and more to set out on the journey she had chosen in the way her husband had imposed. "I don't think I ever thought about it before. You too have great hope."

"I have never thought so."

"Clearly you possess it, for what is great love if not great hope?"

"Then you feel my great love?"

"You know I do."

"What is the difference between love and great love?"

"I don't know."

"Is Petrarca's love great?"

"It strikes me as bizarre. Does he hope his love will be requited or does he simply enjoy his obsession? Does Laura, assuming she exists, know he exists?"

The poet's obsession affected Tuccio deeply but he wondered about the poet's misery retaining the image of him gazing out the window during his recitation forgetting his guests as though she might have been out there and told Margherita how moved he was by a passion whose intensity was almost frightening.

"I thank God I am not that woman," she replied shivering in the heat for she suspected it was not love at least not only love for love she had learned must always involve a giving a losing it must go out from itself whereas this felt to her only taking a retreating within a soul that would rather destroy than risk itself. "To actually be that woman would be terrifying."

"Terrifying perhaps to be that man."

"How does love become that terrible?"

He wondered if perhaps the poet's misery was feigned because alongside the obsession he sensed an odd detachment both in the man and the poem and wondered if maybe in him fine love was too refined lacking the sheer joy and pain of uncertainty or rejection expressed in the troubadour songs; yet he recalled the *giullare* had called him Italy's greatest living poet and thought, "Of course I who can barely read two words cannot presume to judge his poetry." He did however feel competent to judge him as a man and wondered why if he loved her as he claimed he didn't go to her and declare himself concluding that it must not be that kind of love rather a kind that somehow existed in and for itself a kind that however great it made Petrarca as a poet was not for a rude soul like his; it occurred to him that what Petrarca lacked might be the gaiety of the troubadours and when he suggested to Margherita that they strive to amuse themselves more she said they should buy a different book.

"What kind of book?"

"One more gay."

"Can you afford it? I surely can't."

"Your purse or mine, either way it is my husband's. Let us go."

Unlike Avignon Montpellier had one of the greatest and most famous universities in Europe rivaling Paris Bologna and Oxford so they were quickly bewildered by the plethora of shops and more bewildered still when in the first they were politely informed that the title they'd requested the *Story of My Calamities* by Abelard was in Latin. Not knowing this was a most unhappy book they asked in a second shop for an Italian translation and were told one existed only in French and in a third that of course an Italian translation could be produced but not overnight and the bookseller asked if he might suggest another title that might interest them, "for as it happens I do have a version in Italian of a most popular romance concerning a great knight you no doubt know as Signore Lancelotto." Thus did they exit the street of booksellers who purveyed a vast arcane literature in medicine theology law astronomy linguistics logic philosophy and literature ancient and modern with a slim volume neither illuminated nor bound that amounted to but a tiny portion of a vast compilation of tales that had appeared in French prose a century earlier under the title *The Romance of Lancelot of the Lake* and ever since had been immensely popular.

The third day Margherita found herself again before the *fattore* and count who informed her that this would be their last in Montpellier yet still they did not know where they would be going in the morning to which she replied that she found that odd given that she knew where she would be going.

"By that," said the count, "I presume you mean you intend to remain on the road to Toulouse."

"I can't imagine I gave you any reason to doubt that."

"In fact you did not. It is only that we were hoping you would discover mercy among your virtues and dispense a little in our direction."

"Failing which," interjected the *fattore*, "we would find it necessary to be harsh."

The count raised a hand. "You mean to say your soul is pointed at Compostela."

"I believe you already knew that."

"Indeed, but I would know who turned your bow toward such a target."

"In truth, *signore,* I do not recall since so many speak of it. Rather I would say I was aimed at it by arguments for the good, which is the alpha and omega of love and kindles love, for I found both lacking in my life." (*Paradiso,* Canto 26)

"Do love and the good not embrace mercy?"

"Surely they must, *signore.*"

"Then should not one who pursues love and the good be merciful?"

"It seems the question almost answers itself."

"Then, *madonna,* may we call upon your mercy now and ask you to accommodate our need to go south from here, not west."

"You may if you wish, but there is no need, for surely you are free to go where you please and have no need for my consent."

The *fattore* unable to restrain himself further exclaimed, "It is not your consent we seek, rather your... Your... If you will not behave yourself properly, I tell you I will this very hour send a courier to your husband to tell him what has happened and the real reason why you insist on continuing such a long journey."

"The real reason?"

"Need I be more explicit?" She made no reply other than to glower at him and he glowered back panting trying to keep silent but failing. "If you force me to face ruin I will have no choice but to demand a much higher share of the partnership's profits—which I might say are already considerable thanks to me. That means less to your husband, less to you, is that what you want? I bid you speak, woman!"

"Then I shall send a courier myself telling him that you address me like the vile peasant you are, that you are nothing but an uncouth greedy schemer who has probably cheated him and he was a fool to trust you. A fool again for disparaging my pilgrimage and three times a fool for pushing us together. As for my behavior, you may write what you wish, the count who is a nobleman can assure him that I have disgraced neither him nor our marriage."

"Not disgraced? You may pretend innocence but everyone else knows otherwise. Not disgraced? You may as well seize the youth's purse in the public square."

Speechless she slapped him with all her strength.

Rubbing his cheek he continued, "Ask anyone if you dare. Ask the count. Ask your lover."

She looked at the count looked away a silence reigned until he said, "My apologies, *madonna,* I had long hoped to avoid this. Nonetheless, now that the general circumstances have been made clear, may we depend on you to start for Barcelona in the morning?" Margherita turned to stare at him and slowly shook her head and he asked the *fattore,* "As the lady's chaperone, do you have the authority to bring her with us against her will?"

"You wouldn't dare," she hissed.

"I think you know I would if I believed the situation required it, even as I recognize the power of your love. No doubt in its rapture you believe your mind whole and sane and free, you live in joy and the world is full of wonder, but perhaps you still perceive that glimmer of reason that would show you the profound unreason that subjugates and possesses the mind. In that hope I ask again if you will come with us tomorrow to Barcelona."

"Thank you, no, we shall continue on our own."

"A woman, her maid, and a pregnant girl?"

"You said it yourself, I have great faith and hope and love. 'And the greatest of these is love.' And it is a fine love that evidently neither of you understands."

"On the contrary, *donna,* it is you who do not understand."

"Tuccio says to inform you that in the event you leave me, he will accompany me to Compostela, come what may."

"He would defy my orders? More, my wishes?"

"I asked him that. His words were, 'Of course not, I would ignore them.'"

Tuccio could see even before she reached him that she had been greatly tested and took her in his arms but not a single sob escaped though as he released her she gripped him tighter but later she said, "Why is it that when I look at you all my confusion disappears?"

"Because you know I am the one true and certain thing in your life."

She told him they should go to Barcelona for his sake because otherwise harm might come to him which angered him because he said she should know he didn't fear harm to which she replied that she had seen his courage but would not be the agent of his downfall a statement he dismissed. He said she should not trust the count's promise to take her to Compostela not because he was dishonorable but because he might be under orders from Francesco to abbreviate her voyage by any means necessary not excluding deceit a grim warning against which surprisingly she smiled saying, "That's the first time you have referred to my husband by name."

"Margherita, consider: No one wishes to go as much as us. And can we say for sure the *masnada* won't be needed in Barcelona? Besides, everyone detests your husband and would see us happy. I beg you, return to the count right now and tell him we will adhere to the Way no matter what," but she said there was no need for that was what she had said.

Still the rest of the day was not pleasant for something bothered her which she would not divulge even to him it was only later in the convent that she asked Agnoletta whether she alone believed she had remained faithful to her husband by not consummating her love and no sooner was the question asked than she said, "I see the answer on your face. What a fool I have been."

"Everyone who loves is a fool. The more love, the more foolish."

"Not foolish merely. You believe I have as much as committed adultery. I say the words but I don't understand. If love is ennobling, how can it be impious? I believe Tuccio was sent to me, not to test my faith, but express it. As by this pilgrimage I express my love for God and seek His forgiveness, not just for my own sins but my husband's, I express fine love in the only ways available. The heart of fine love is that love between a married woman and an unmarried man—even physical love—can be pure when it elevates the spirit above the mere pleasures of the flesh, when it is worthy of God's praise. Are the poets wrong?"

"Need I remind you that from the beginning I have encouraged you to follow your heart? I know nothing of fine love, but I say so long as the master doesn't find out, where's the harm? And don't they say it's a sin to spurn a gift from God?"

"I haven't heard it's a sin."

"Well I say when God sends you a gift it's wise to accept it. You said yourself he was sent to you. And a very nice gift it is. I bet his pestle can pound your mortar a lot harder than your husband's." At this Margherita couldn't help but laugh. "And how long has it been since the old man mounted your saddle? And," she added in a whisper, "you know you can't get pregnant."

"But... do you not fear sin?"

"I fear sin exactly as much as I believe in the forgiveness of sin. Better to repent than regret I say. Sin today, repent tomorrow. And the priest who absolves you is no doubt teaching the 'Hail Mary' to half the women in the parish, you know it as well as I do. If he squints, half the brats in the parish squint." Margherita fell silent then asked if the *fattore* would not tell her husband to which Agnoletta said it would mark him as a failure. "He has good reason to keep his mouth shut. The count won't say anything because he considers himself above the master and the others won't because they're below." Margherita pondered this. "Have you heard the one about the fat old abbot who eyes the beautiful young thing standing helpless before him and thinks, 'Why not take my pleasure when I can, given that I will always have as much grief and trouble as I wish?' If they can do it, why not us? And you know the saying: 'A sin concealed is half forgiven.'" (Boccaccio, *The Decameron*)

Chapter Twenty-three

> Oh joy! Oh ineffable rapture!
> Oh life complete with love and with peace!
>
> (*Paradiso*, Canto 27)

DAY TWENTY-SEVEN. West of Montpellier they entered the *garrigue* which they had first encountered three weeks earlier but now traveled through its rugged beauty of limestone and semi-arid vegetation spare and sharp-edged with dense thickets of stunted oaks and junipers scattered around an open landscape of dry loose sharp-stone soil sprouting aromatic shrubs of thyme lavender rosemary sage and wildflowers. Except the *fattore* who knew he'd been bested it put the men in a good mood and they filled their lungs with the morning scent jubilant over his defeat especially by a woman which they also saw as Tuccio's victory over the master and were content to go to Compostela and not risk having their employment shortened while Siena endured troubled times; this was probably true for the count too who in any case was as usual unperturbed while Agnoletta was having a good time with Stoldo and Piera was more than content to remain atop her mule especially with her belly swelling.

Margherita and Tuccio were in heaven feeling like the caravan was accompanying them rather than the reverse thus in a sense more fully on pilgrimage and even more confident in their love and the certainty of having a long journey together and though Margherita was confused about what she had discussed with Agnoletta she was elated to see that no one was angry or scornful on the contrary she saw only smiles. "If we have been in Paradise we must now be in its highest sphere. Look down and see how high we have ascended." (*Paradiso*, Canto 27)

"I cannot believe my eyes. I am in Paradise thanks to you."

"You are my guide, despite your youth."

"No, you are the guide. You the pilgrim."

"No, it is you. Thanks to you, my pilgrimage is an ascent, not just a journey. How high we have climbed! I'm so glad you are here with me, safe from Siena's dangers. I tremble to think what might have happened to you with your hot blood in the middle of those street brawls."

"Do not think of it. Siena is far far below. I can hardly see it. We are at the summit of Heaven and I know no reason why we may not remain here."

"The world is so sunk in cupidity that no one can see beyond it. Fidelity and innocence are found only in children. (Canto 27) I see that now so clearly, the more as it is so far below. Just look at Piera. Is she not..."

"The world will never change."

"Fortune will turn it around. True fruit will come after the flower." (Canto 27)

Not only had Margherita kept the caravan on the Toulouse road she had made it detour to a holy site that no pilgrim would miss so after stopping for refreshment at an abbey in the *garrigue* they continued on an old 'devil's bridge' across a river gorge to its brother abbey founded by Saint Guilhem a cousin of Charlemagne which like Montmajour possessed a sliver of the True Cross. Not having visited Montmajour the entire caravan was naturally eager to see the relic which the count made possible and at the *fattore*'s turn Tuccio made sure he learned that many of the pilgrims there were bound for Compostela then said to Margherita, "The church is beautiful, isn't it. In a severe, primitive way. I'm so glad I became a pilgrim, I never expected it to be like this."

"Nor I," she said. "Nor I."

Several hundred feet above the village across a ravine on top of a cliff he noticed a small chapel and said, "Now there's dedication."

"Look, there's another one against the cliff."

"I don't even know how you'd get there. Fervor is amazing, isn't it?"

"The scenery perhaps inspires it, because I've never seen anything so... The river gorge we crossed, with the water rushing over boulders and jagged mountains all around..."

Said Piera, "Everything is like silver in the sun."

DAY TWENTY-EIGHT. The abbey was large enough to have attracted a hamlet but there was no inn so the caravan had to sleep outside yet no one minded because they could stay inside the fortified wall and the setting was so extraordinary that upon rising everyone gazed at it thinking, "After all, there is something to travel besides drudgery." Stirring yes but with the day's destination on the other side of what looked like a nearly impenetrable wilderness there was the question of the route; while the porters were loading the mules the count asked Margherita what she proposed and was relieved to hear that rather than go overland due west over peaks and across river gorges inhabited only by wild boar wolves and bear they could follow the road that wound through the valley through four villages. "Don't worry," she said, "everyone says it's an easy stage."

"I never worry," he said but nonetheless ordered scouts and reminded his men to keep a sharp eye because for all the road provided in food shelter supplies repairs care for sick and injured plus the company of others and easier going this looked like brigand country; the beauty was extraordinary which settled an awed quiet on everyone but a crowd of pilgrims stayed close to the armed men and when the caravan stopped for breakfast beside a rushing stream so did everyone else.

Tuccio asked Margherita what they would see if they saw God, "because surely this is His country if any is," and she replied that she had never thought about it before but Piera said she had seen the Virgin Mother once walking in a meadow picking flowers and Margherita asked if she meant in a dream.

"No dream, I saw her. Maybe here I'll see Jesus."

"What about God the Father?" asked Tuccio and they decided that if He could be seen at all He would appear only as a blinding point of light in the highest Heaven. (*Paradiso*, Canto 28)

He stared here and there as though expecting to see something miraculous stared up the gorge for a long time before saying, "We should head up there, tonight maybe. There will be more of these streams. We should steal away in the dark and escape. There's enough moon to see."

"What are you talking about?"

"Running away."

"Why would we do that when we have just won a major victory?"

"To be together. We have a delightful pilgrimage ahead of us, but at its end what becomes of us? We could follow one of these streams into the hills."

"And then what?"

"Hide. A few hours' lead would be sufficient, we could disappear into this rugged land. We'd go on foot, we could follow a track horses couldn't take, they'd have to continue on foot, but they'd have no will and we'd be running for our lives. A few days at most, they'd give up, the *fattore* would insist. They'd turn back for Barcelona and we could continue to Compostela."

"But we're continuing there now."

"But afterward we wouldn't return to Siena, we'd go somewhere else. Anywhere but there."

"You sound so serious. You're joking, right?"

Suddenly he smiled and said, "Of course I'm joking."

Piera watching him closely asked, "What about me?"

"Do you want to come with us?" She nodded gravely. "You're carrying a child, could you keep up?" Again she nodded. "Then you shall come."

"Except," said Margherita, "you're jesting."

The new cathedral they reached was impressive for the reliquary of its revered bishop-saint but their contemplation during Sunday mass was interrupted by a monk who unbidden began to speak about his priory in the mountains east of the city with the usual intent of persuading Margherita to visit and Tuccio interrupted to ask how far it was.

"A short way."

"A long way," said a nearby priest. "All the way up and then some. Hours of climbing."

"We don't have hours," said Margherita, "but thank you for inviting us."

"Could we spend the night there?" asked Tuccio.

"Of course."

"Why would we do that?" she whispered. "We'd have to return in the morning while everyone waited."

"Mita," he whispered back, "we crossed seven streams today. Seven."

The monk sensing an opportunity launched a full description of his priory's attractions but seeing that even his gross exaggerations failed to hold their attention noted, "Had you stayed on the proper route you would now be in the priory church of Saint-Michel de Grandmont. One errs in taking the easy way instead of God's way."

Margherita said she had it on good authority that she was on the pilgrim route and all the other pilgrims had evidently believed the same. "No other route was presented as a possibility. No one mentioned your priory."

"As there is more than one way to God, there is more than one way to Compostela. But is not the straight path the best?"

"We saw no path, only obstructions."

"Of course, the straight path often appears that way."

"First he argues that there are many paths, then only one," said the priest.

Tuccio noted that if the pilgrim route followed the straight path it wouldn't have led to Saint-Guilhem in the first place. "We go there for its attractions. You have spoken of yours. Surely there is something more?"

"In fact there is..." He described the three types of prehistoric megaliths that dotted the priory fields the tall narrow uprights some carved into elongated vertical rounded shapes the chambers created by two uprights and a capstone some of them underground with small entrances and the boulders carved with a long deep slit narrow in width and gently curved. "Those last we call 'bowls of the devil,'" he said adding that no one knew what these mysterious formations signified but all agreed they were sources of power. "In particular the chambers have curative properties, such as for skin ailments. The erections have a power of fecundity."

"These erections," said Tuccio, "could you describe them in more detail?"

"I'd rather not," said the monk, "but I can assure you all the rocks have long since been exorcised, so you need not fear demons. Some claim to have seen fairies at sunset, though I myself, alas, have never seen one of those fair creatures."

"Does it not sound extremely interesting?" he asked Margherita staring.

"Tuccio, no," she whispered.

When the monk was gone he said, "Perhaps I am rash. As I said yesterday, you are my guide. As for him, does he truly not know what they signify? Should I tell him?"

DAY TWENTY-NINE. The route took them over passes and through ravines in a landscape not of the ferocious beauty of the limestone crags or the spare beauty of the *garrigue* but the luscious beauty of rolling hills and green everywhere; the rough country was still there but out of sight to the north and west detected by the streams that still slipped their way downhill three of which they crossed before stopping for refreshment. Here Tuccio spoke again about running away saying it would be better to go to Compostela another time they should first save themselves moving by night higher into the mountains and then beyond eventually to Paris where there were many Italian merchants where he could find work or they could go farther perhaps to Bruges or even farther than that to the north or east into German lands anywhere far away where they were not known and could never be found.

"You're mad."

"Yes, I'm mad, mad with love, the count himself diagnosed my illness, I have been shot in the heart, I will die without you."

"My dearest one..."

"Who knows how long we will be in this country? Each stream we pass is an opportunity lost. I believe God sent you to me, I believe this pilgrimage is a gift. We are as far north now as we will be and the moon wanes yet shines still, is that not a sign? And Piera still able to travel."

For the first time they discussed their future together which looked profoundly unsatisfying once back in a Siena become a prison with no bars but jailers everywhere; meanwhile the irony of reflecting on future misery in a time of joy and of jail talk when they had won their freedom was not lost on them and Margherita said, "Perhaps it is only now we are free to see our situation. But dearest one, let us not be miserable when we should be most happy."

"I am most happy. Happiness greater than what I feel is inconceivable."

"For me too. Let us preserve it."

"That is what I propose."

"By fleeing?"

"By being together forever." After a long silence she asked if he was serious and he replied, "Only nod and I will prepare."

She was afraid to move and when she spoke said, "God knows, I would not hesitate to obey your order, even if you said we must throw ourselves into a volcano, as Eloisa said to Abelardo. As she said, if my heart is not with you, it is nowhere."

"Then you have no heart, for I do not possess it."

"Listen, it beats beside yours. My one and only, do not make me miserable when I am most happy."

"I would sooner die."

"Then I beg you, let us consider this calmly, as we considered whether or not to consent to Barcelona," and she asked how they could get away undetected how they could acquire provisions and carry them without a pack animal what might happen if they were caught how they would present themselves to the world.

"What does that mean?"

"Are we to be husband and wife?"

When he did not reply she suggested that they enjoy their months of pilgrimage in the safety of the caravan and think of escape when they returned to the Alps. "Piera will have delivered, it will be easier for her to travel."

"With a newborn. In winter."

"We would wait for warmer weather."

"Mita, who knows what will be? Fortune favors us now."

"You speak of permanent exile."

"You speak as if our exile would be voluntary. Do you not see we have no choice if we are to be together?"

"Tuccio, we should consider carefully. I did not simply decide one day to set off on pilgrimage."

"The question is whether we will be together. My answer I already know, I would know yours."

"There may be another way, less dangerous."

"Name it."

"We must think."

> "Your voice assured, bold and glad,
> let sound your will, let sound your desire
> to which my reply is already decreed."

(*Paradiso*, Canto 15) Thus does Dante's ancestor urge him to ask what is on his mind and soon he will prophesy his exile saying:

> "You will leave everything beloved
> most dearly; and this is that arrow
> that the bow of exile first shoots."

(*Paradiso*, Canto 17)

"Exile is the opposite of pilgrimage. I fear it."

"So long as you are with me, I fear nothing. Speak, Mita," he beseeched but she did not reply.

At the town where the river became calm the count called a halt for the day thinking to find there whatever they might need but upon learning that a few hours ahead was a spa with baths he decided to continue and they easily covered the remaining distance following the river into a wide straight long valley. It was in a lovely setting with tame mountains nearby to the south and served by a priory located right beside the road an unusual location suggesting its purpose was to serve travelers which promise was quickly redeemed as everyone was helped to the century-old baths; after a sheltered location was found for the caravan the porters who couldn't believe their good fortune told tales including this one:

Once there was a king who longed for a son and at last one was born but the physicians said he would become blind if ever he saw the sun so he was raised in a cave by monks where he fasted and prayed all day and learned nothing of worldly things. When he turned sixteen his father commanded that he be shown the world so he was dressed in finery and taken to the city where he was struck by the magnificent palaces and churches nobles splendidly dressed with caparisoned horses and all the wonders of a great metropolis; and of each thing he saw he asked the name and so when he came upon beautiful women leaving a wedding he asked what those things were called. "Those are demons that seduce men," he was told and when his father asked what he'd found most wonderful he immediately replied that above all he loved the demons that seduce men and asked for one to be brought so he could play with it.

"It does not play as you imagine," said the king.

"Then I will feed it."

"Its mouth is not where you think, and it requires a special sort of food."

"Then I will find its mouth and give it that special food. Please, father."

The king ordered that he be shown more fine things weapons and armor gold and jewels and the boy was told he could have whatever he wished but no matter what he was shown all he wanted was one of those demons. (Boccaccio, *The Decameron*)

Tuccio and Margherita inspected the primitive little church with its sparse mystical images and strange numerological markings which a monk helped them understand beginning with the tympanum above the west door which instead of the usual frieze depicting the Last Judgment displayed a Maltese cross a crucifix reduced to a four-pointed star within a circle the rays triangular which together produced the numbers three four and twelve representing God (the Trinity) the world (with its four directions) and their proper relationship through the Church (of the twelve apostles) and all within the all-encompassing unitary and perfect one of a circle. The interior was given to the number five with five sections of pillars and arches and five ribs holding up the curved roof above the altar which the monk said was difficult to explain but had been told five represented Man with four limbs and a head five fingers and five senses. The altar was a stone slab across a massive cubical stone block the sole decoration a little face on the wall behind the altar the face of Jesus staring wide-eyed and back to back with it on the church's exterior was a head of a demon the same size and never had Margherita seen images so paired and the message moved her.

The tympanum over the south door had no sculpture no narrative no saints or savior just numerological markings made of inlaid black stones with a circle containing four black triangles pointing toward its center in the form of an X surrounded by two staggered concentric circles of eight black rectangles and around this in a larger arc a half circle of sixteen black triangles again pointing inward and Tuccio asked what it meant.

"Notice that as the black pattern points inward, the inverse pattern in white points out suggesting another Maltese cross. The X is the Greek letter *chi*, the first in the word 'Christ.' Now look at the carvings just below. There are ten, nearly but not quite identical. What do you make of them?"

"I can make nothing of them."

"Ten panels of the crucifixion, why not twelve as is customary? Man has ten digits, ten is a perfect number, true enough, but ten is an unusual number on a church, as is five. These panels are not pictures, they are illuminations of the *chi-rho* symbol, *rho* being the second letter in 'Christ.'"

"It's still a mystery. What does it signify?"

"A mystery, exactly. Mystery is the heart of life, but I will tell you what I think. Fours and eights are associated with birth. Four represents the earth, eight the greater existence beyond earth, sixteen even more so. Baptisteries, you may have noticed, are arrayed in fours and eights. This door leads in to birth—or re-birth—and out to the cemetery, the mystery of death. Ten is a difficult number in this setting, but once associated with the crucifixion, whose mystery is the solution of mystery in the presence of faith, we can see its obvious relationship to human life, perhaps the possibility of perfection of life by means of the savior's sacrifice."

Nearby was a small full-length figure of a man who appeared to be displaying a satchel and staff and she asked if it was a pilgrim.

"Some say he is our patron saint but I like to think he is in fact a pilgrim since we serve so many."

"Tuccio, we are on the right road."

DAY THIRTY. When they heard of the great boar hunting to be found in a nearby gorge a day of recreation was declared to the delight of everyone except the *fattore* and the men merrily sauntered farther into the wide green pleasant valley till coming around a bend were confronted with the stunning splendor of craggy white mountains under an intense blue sky. A bit farther they came to a torrent and unloaded the mules nearby in a discreet location whereupon they divided into hunting parties and everyone not assigned to the first watch headed up the gorge including the *fattore* who took a pike in search of small game while the women were instructed to stay near the guards for safety.

The first to return was Stoldo who by prior agreement led Agnoletta away while Tuccio persevered but Nico could see his interest was not hunting and with a gesture sent him back where he found Margherita and Piera sitting by the river; they made their way uphill through forest and a fair amount of greenery though the terrain had boulders everywhere and Tuccio said they might see wild mountain sheep perched on impossible ledges though probably not before evening. When Piera fascinated by the torrent sat to watch he led Margherita into the woods where they embraced and found themselves on the ground but she pulled away with her robe already raised crying, "I have given you my heart, my mind, my very breath. Would it not be a poor addition to add my body, which in thought is already yours? Of what little consequence could be our physical joining when our souls are already conjoined?"

"That was well said, lady, but does nothing to calm the pounding of my heart. Tomorrow we can repent most sincerely, but right now I cannot conceive that we are fashioned in such a way that we must forever act against our nature."

"Stop."

"I cannot. Your beauty exceeds all measure, not only of everything I can imagine, but truly I believe that only its maker wholly enjoys it." (*Paradiso*, Canto 30)

"Had I a fraction of such beauty I would have known it long ago. Yet it is the sweetest lie I have ever heard."

"Beauty is not just physical. Is not the greater beauty the inner light that makes bodies glow?"

"Then after all I am not beautiful?"

"Let me show you how beautiful you are."

"My dearest one," she sighed but pulled away when Piera was heard approaching.

"Never mind, it is nothing she won't have seen before."

"Please stop."

She discovered them sitting apart breathing heavily and looking from one to the other catching neither's eye she asked, "Were you fucking?"

"Not yet, thanks to you," said Tuccio.

"Thanks to the apostle," said Margherita, "who at the last moment has saved us for our journey."

They continued uphill Tuccio furious for letting his passion distract his will and exclaimed, "Saved us indeed," then in reply to their stares explained that they need only continue to the top of the gorge and keep going. "Everyone is dispersed, distracted. They won't miss us till evening. We couldn't have asked for a better chance."

"We have no food."

"Food is all around. What do you think everyone is doing?" They continued in silence until he said, "So, do we go?" There was no answer. "Remember the Republic of the Escartons? I've been thinking we should go there. We'd be free citizens and with all the merchants coming to the trade fairs I could find employment."

"Are you proposing that we attempt to hide on the main road to Italy?"

"I thought about that, that if word ever got back to Siena your husband could send men to kill me and take you back, but then I thought we might come to some arrangement or threaten him. I remember you told me about a woman who said she preferred to live with a pirate who had abducted her and her husband accepted it."

"That was a tale."

"One I dare say with truth behind it. I do not fear your husband and you have shown that you don't either. Besides, he need not find us, it is a rugged and isolated place and we could change our names."

"So rugged and isolated you might not find sufficient employment."

"Then I will work in the silver mines. Do you remember the silver mines below Briançon? An abbey had a hospital there."

"You would do that?"

"I would do anything to be with you."

"Tuccio..."

"Do you know that when the republic was created the oven tax was eliminated? My father has to pay that cursed tax."

In the end however they returned downhill and by the time the men returned with the catch butchered it and got it onto spits over a huge fire it was evening so the count decided to spend the night there except after the feast the women were conducted the short distance to town to find appropriate accommodations; there they found the other pilgrims while Tuccio returned to his mates to sleep in the open and maybe see wild mountain sheep perched on impossible ledges.

Chapter Twenty-four

When Tiffany confessed the sudden draining of her enthusiasm for stages the professor who had encouraged her to go indoors now encouraged her to return outside hoping neighborhoods might now seem attractive with the daffodils blooming and the forsythia and magnolias and dogwoods and cherries but even so she was not anticipating the stage with pleasure. A week later she was walking from Maubourguet which she knew was the site of a twelfth-century priory whose church still survived in a village which itself lay in the middle of a lush farming region flat and placid but which centuries ago would have been an island in the land of Gascony surrounded with virgin forest all but impenetrable making it dangerous especially from wolves and that contrast seemed to symbolize the current state of her mind if not her life. She also knew that with the forest gone one could look to the south to see the Pyrenees which this time of year would be mostly covered with snow but would gradually cede all but their highest peaks to lush greenery and that too seemed an applicable metaphor.

The neighborhoods were indeed pleasant even the air was perfumed with lily of the valley but no matter what she did to transfer that ambient beauty to the spirit of pilgrimage she couldn't help musing about the apparent link between her enthusiasm for pilgrimage and love for the professor and why she loved two very different men and what was happening with her affair. That it was changing she knew but where it was going she didn't; yet they had been happy in each other's arms the week before and though much of the exploration had passed she still loved his touch her orgasm as intense as ever and afterward as he kissed her she said she loved him. Their love was grounded in intellectual discovery the pleasure of friendship and erotic gratification a relationship of exploration and so the concern was natural that each had discovered about the other all there was to discover; a love real but not powerful and thus perhaps not sustainable for the river of love requires a strong flow to reach the sea meanwhile the picayune details of his research which had once fascinated now bored her while he had always known that her world of finance held no interest for him.

To her he was a scholar to him she was a success for that they would always admire each other but love needs more; in pursuit of whatever that might be they pulled mightily upstream for where the current like a mother had carried them in its strong arms for where it was enough to have roses and champagne poetry and proclamations for when they could lay in the bed of the boat the whole time writhing like snakes oblivious that the current was slowing. For them not the danger of love the wounding the folly and madness rather they sought comfort preferring happiness to adventure relying on the sun of erotic novelty for heat; but comfort becomes dull and novelty is transitory while even sexual excitement requires constant refueling.

As she walked past noisy lawnmowers and herbicide warnings on little flags her musing became a dream that they would go together to Maubourguet to walk the stage she was pretending to walk now and when they came to a dense copse on a rise above the fields they would leave the path to find a private spot where the ground was soft to make love. She imagined the scene vividly imagined that to ignite his fire she pushed him against a tree and opened his trousers on her knees and later beneath his grunting weight would pant and moan and finally scream; but then in her daydream Bob appeared and it seemed he had seen them and in his rage beat his head against a tree but she calmed him with assurances and then she was alone again with the professor who told her all about Gascony.

Stepping off the curb into an intersection the side mirror of an approaching car struck her arm with sufficient force to throw her into a spin and with the heavy pack on her back she lost her balance and fell awkwardly in the road; the driver braked hard and leaving the car in the middle of the street ran to ask if she was all right then seeing she wasn't called nine-one-one then stood there immobile not knowing what to do. Tiffany was clearly dazed not moving despite the painful position of her body and only dimly

aware of the crowd that soon formed alert only when someone tried to help her and she screamed, "Don't move me!" but while people debated whether to try to make her more comfortable she managed to gingerly untangle herself and lay back on the asphalt against her pack and someone kneeling beside her said, "Don't worry, the ambulance will be here in a minute."

She was taken to the emergency room at Saint Barnabus Hospital where she waited hours to be treated during which time her arm swelled and despite her efforts to keep it immobilized against her chest the ice pack did little to help the searing pain which made the wait seem interminable; nonetheless she managed to retrieve her phone to call Bob who of course was upset and told her he would be there right away and against her objection that she didn't want to frighten Kiley said, "I'll see if I can leave her next door."

"Don't worry, I'm okay."

"You don't sound okay. How long have you been there?"

"I'm not sure."

"I'm coming. I'll find someone to take Kiley."

"I love you."

"I love you too."

She held the phone in her hand a good twenty minutes before calling the professor who of course was upset and told her he wished he could be with her and kept asking if she was all right and said he loved her; she said she loved him too and wanted to go to France with him saying, "Let's walk the pilgrim path together. I want to arrive at some medieval church after a day's walk and gaze at the statues with you beside me."

"When do we leave?"

"As soon as my arm heals."

Kiley for whom it was late when they finally got home was angry in her incomprehension and though the neighbors had fed her demanded food which she then refused to eat and they had a difficult task to give her a bath and put her to bed and afterward Bob said, "I know this is not the time, but..." He started by saying that he had tried to be patient with what he called her current obsession but had had no idea when he'd suggested a virtual pilgrimage that it would become such a big production and take precedence over other activities that seemed important like spending time with her daughter and said he had tried to accept the long hours evidently required for the stages and the meetings with her professor but... "What do you two do all the time, anyway? How much work could there be? Is he like your guru or something?"

Referring in code to love Tiffany wrote in her blog, *I haven't said much about being alone. I confess I assumed I wouldn't be alone. I imagined there would be lots of pilgrims on the Way and that my problem would be getting time by myself, not confronting solitude. But it didn't turn out that way. There may be lots of pilgrims but the Way is long, we're stretched out over long distances.*

You can make friends at the hostels and walk the next stage together, assuming your walking speeds are reasonably comparable, but it's amazing how often that's not the case. People are just really different and pilgrims especially have things going on inside that they're processing (or trying to process), so a lot of them prefer to be alone or just end up that way.

Same thing in the evenings. The conversation at the hostels may be just the kind of trail talk you crave, but for many it isn't. There are those who seek something more personal, more intimate. And let's face it, most people (and pilgrims are no exception) are prepared to do more talking than listening. So while there's talk, more often than not you find yourself wishing you could get into a conversation with someone where you would really get each other. Just one person, a soul-mate, where you wouldn't be talking about blisters and coffee deprivation.

To be honest, when I realized I might be facing a thousand mile trek alone, I was pretty nervous. But I told myself to take one stage at a time and not worry about what might happen down the road. Be in the present, right? Some pilgrims write about abandoning themselves to the Way, letting go, surrendering. That's a lot easier to do when your fingers are pried loose by circumstances, not so easy when you're just trying to convince yourself that that's what you should do.

The road is life, right? That's a pretty trite metaphor, but when you're alone on a long pilgrimage it's not a metaphor at all, it's literally your life. It's not easy. It can be scary. I bet if you ask pilgrims what they'd most wish for to ease their journey, it would be a good companion.

What's odd about this—well, maybe not odd, just new—is that solitude is a distinctly modern feature of pilgrimage. In the Middle Ages it would have been unthinkable for almost any traveler to set out alone, not only because it was too dangerous (especially for a woman), but more fundamentally because being alone unnecessarily was unthinkable. Do you know the desire for solitude was a sign of insanity? Either that or a mystical calling.

To herself she admitted that she was tired of writing the blog which continually required her to research what she would have seen had she really been walking the stages a project that at one time had been fun and after all involved little work since all she had to do was download items from 'what to do in...' websites. It also required her to keep thinking of interesting comments to make about the sites but especially about pilgrimage which initially could be mainly questions and speculations and uncertainty but eventually (she assumed) for her sake if not her readers something satisfying was required in terms of answers conclusions insights discoveries and they were not appearing. She kept thinking that surely there was something interesting to say about getting hit by a car on pilgrimage but nothing that seemed worthwhile came to her and there was also the inescapable fact that her blog had failed to attract any following with few hits and a total of one brief (indeed inarticulate) comment.

Because she couldn't drive she had to postpone her next meeting with the professor but she was not entirely disappointed even as she acknowledged with some distress that in fact there was much she wanted to discuss with him; also with her arm in a sling she couldn't walk any distance comfortably even without a backpack and therefore couldn't do any stages for at least six weeks probably two months and in this case she was greatly relieved because she was drained of all motivation. She saw the spurt of stages over the autumn and winter as due more to willpower than desire and at this point considered her pilgrimage moribund with forty-one stages left; therefore she berated herself that she hadn't even reached the Pyrenees and at three hundred ninety-six miles wasn't even halfway in fact by her calculation was only thirty-eight point seven percent of the way to Compostela.

Regardless of the circumstances this forced suspension of her pilgrimage or termination if that's what it was gave her the opportunity to redress the time away from Kiley who was now overjoyed to go on voyages of adventure with her mother visiting children's art classes at the Newark Museum and story hours at the Millburn Public Library and they went to the Short Hills Mall to buy dresses and had pizza and ice cream. Bob didn't mind being left alone because he was busy with his job search which wasn't going nearly as well as the last time when he'd been able to get quickly repositioned in the same unit at his firm because this time many of the non-technical people had been fired throughout the organization either because they were seen as non-essential or because JP Morgan already had enough of its own. Not all of them however could have been as productive as him so he felt he had legitimate cause to believe he'd been singled out for termination because of his close association with his boss who as one of the main players in the firm's MBS game had caused major losses; ironically however his boss had been allowed to keep his job at least for the present presumably because he possessed valuable non-public information about the firm.

He was trying the usual places on the Street and most doors still opened to him but to his shock there were no calls for second interviews forcing him to experience real unemployment for the first time; when Tiffany seeking to reassure him said he needn't worry because they could easily live on what she was earning he wasn't pleased and even less pleased when she reminded him that one of the two deals she'd been pursuing had earned a substantial sum. "You'll find something soon, you'll see. You're a survivor, remember?" He nodded. "Maybe you should broaden your search to independent firms."

"You mean hedge funds."

"You make that sound like..." She could see from his face he thought hedge funds no matter how big were the little players his firm had used as underwriting subcontractors and ready customers for the lower-rated MBS tranches. "I'm getting that you don't see yourself in that space."

"No offense, hon, but can they support my sales volume? I mean come on."

"Your own funds did. Anyway it seems pretty clear the banks are downsizing, not hiring."

"Really, I had no idea." In fact despite his frustration at the delay he kept thinking he'd find something soon because he still believed the MBS market was fundamentally sound and like his boss he had stores of inside information about his firm's investments that would be valuable to a competitor especially now that counter-parties were scrutinizing every piece of collateral; and that combined with what he knew to be his expertise and self-promotion skills more or less supported his confidence if not a cheerful mood. Recognizing that last he soon apologized for his outburst and tried though often failed to be less unpleasant around the house; so when Tiffany announced her next meeting with the professor he asked if she was comfortable enough to drive and suggested she take public transportation since he was under the impression they were meeting in New York and when she said she was worried about being jostled he offered to drive.

"What would you do all that time? And what about Kiley?"

"Hey, I'm just trying to be a good husband."

"And I appreciate it. But I know you'd rather work on your job search."

"Why do you have to go anyway? You made your next grant, now what? Do you sit and talk about pilgrimage the whole time?"

"Something like that."

"I still don't get it. Pilgrimage, you?"

"I don't understand it myself. The professor says I don't need to, that lots of pilgrims..."

"So he is your guru."

"In a way I guess."

"Hey, whatever floats your boat."

A month after the accident she could drive even with the cast though her arm was still tender but her earlier ambivalence about seeing the professor had tilted more toward the needy side so she had arranged to meet and no sooner was the door closed than they began caressing each other and got on the bed where because of her arm certain positional adjustments were required and soon they climaxed and kissed passionately. "I missed you," she said.

"I missed you too."

She told him about the argument with Bob the day of the accident and soon their discussion was itself testy and he learned immediately to be careful because when he asked helpfully if she wanted them to stop seeing each other temporarily she interpreted the question as a desire to be uninvolved in her marital predicament. "You just breeze in, have a good fuck, and breeze out?"

"I think you know that's not true," he said but his very calmness angered her because it looked like detachment; yet he knew that were he not calm it would anger her more because she would feel attacked from both sides.

"I wish I knew what I was doing. Why do I love you?"

He asked if she didn't think it might be possible given that there had only been the one outburst from Bob for them to simply continue as before especially since they had been discreet meeting only once a month and never staying late; in response she only shrugged and he waited. "I think he knows," she said and still he waited. "Are you going to say anything?"

"Whatever I say seems to upset you. I love you."

"You don't just love fucking me? Older guy, younger woman?"

"It's true, you're young and beautiful. If you were old and ugly would I feel the same? Assuredly not. I tell you this in hopes that you will believe what I say next, which is that when I watched you in The Cloisters, which I think was when I fell in love with you, when I saw how entranced you were..."

"You saw Jessie."

"I like to think I saw you. Occasionally you remind me of her. Not often, but occasionally. She was wonderful, you're amazing. I'm twice blessed."

"Really?"

"Tiffany, have you ever heard me lie to you?" Finally he saw her shoulders relax. "Why do you think he knows?"

"I don't. I'm worried that he suspects, because how could he not? Anyone could see how depressed I was coming home from the ER. All he had to do was check my phone to see that I called you. Why would I call unless, you know."

"To cancel our meeting?"

"From the ER? He keeps asking what you and I do together." The professor nodded. "It seems so obvious to me that I'm having an affair. He does tend to be self-absorbed, though, especially these days."

"If he never finds out, your marriage simply continues as if there were no affair."

"How could he never find out?"

"If he's not suspicious..." He shrugged.

"Impossible."

"Why? So long as you don't glow when you return home."

"I'm pretty sure I don't glow."

"Then how would he know?"

"I don't know! It just seems..."

"People have lots of reasons to avoid the truth."

"Thank you, professor."

"How do you know he hasn't had an affair?" She stared into space and finally shrugged. "There was a guy in the English Department, a well-known novelist, whose wife had an affair with his personal assistant for eight years and he never found out."

"How do you know?"

"It came out after he died. He was kind of an ass, lots of people would have been happy to sully his reputation."

"They could have made it up."

"His widow insisted it was true. The hot poker is that he had taken the teaching job on condition that his friend be hired too. He thought he was his flunky."

While he could not have known all the reasons for Tiffany's anxious frustration the professor recognized that it derived in part from the fact that their relationship could not be more than it was and that the room which had been their paradise had become a cage from which she longed to escape but they had so few hours together and the need for discretion was constant and thus the natural progress of their love was constrained. When he presented her with this analysis she agreed complaining that they could never socialize with friends he could never meet Kiley they couldn't even cook a meal together and as if to dramatize her imprisonment she crossed to the window to gaze at the parking lot and then returned to sit on the edge of the bed and watching her he realized his frustration was the same. Pacing the room he suggested that they might be able to go to an afternoon concert together though she might get home on the late side but then they would have just enough time for the concert and nothing else; he said he would love to take her to the opera and Saturday matinees at the Metropolitan Opera began at one o'clock but the performances took so long she wouldn't get home on time and of course there wouldn't be time for anything else.

"We couldn't anyway, because you never know who might see me."

"Maybe if we were in a posh hotel in the city instead of these places. I have no idea what it costs but I'm prepared to be gallant."

"It's a thought, but it would take most of my time to get there and back. We'd barely have time to fuck and check out."

"We could find a really good restaurant and have lunch like we used to."

"And do what, talk about the Middle Ages?"

"I was under the impression you rather enjoyed that."

"I did. I loved it. But now I want to do something else."

"Shopping? I'd love to help you select a dress or an outfit."

She saw he was serious and as she pictured him commenting on how (wonderful) she looked as she stepped out of the dressing room regretted that they couldn't even do that because how could she come home from a meeting that was ostensibly to work on the foundation and discuss pilgrimage carrying shopping bags? "I can't even meet Morgan."

"In principle you could. I didn't realize you wanted to. Do you think it would be a good idea?"

"Why wouldn't it? And by the way, how come you never talk about Louis?"

"Are you frustrated that I don't talk more about my children? I could bring Morgan. But then, you know..."

Recognizing he had to do something or else their rendezvous would be wasted or worse he said, "The new fellow's research proposal is really intriguing, isn't it? Funding it is a real coup for the foundation, you'll see." With his own fellowship ending in a week he began to tell her about his research but seeing that though her mood had lifted she was still preoccupied he summarily announced that though he had not yet completed the analysis and collation of the manuscripts he had two research assistants working with him and expected to have it completed fairly soon; in the meantime, he continued, he had plans to publish an article in a scholarly journal and beyond that an exhaustive monograph for which he had already approached a few university presses. He concluded by saying, "So though I may not have entirely met the terms of our contract I hope you will believe as I do that the fellowship was more than worthwhile;" and then it occurred to him that she could tell her husband that though the fellowship had ended the research had not and thus they would continue to meet because of her interest to hear about it. "Is that a good idea?" he asked.

"Yes," she said.

"You're still glum."

She couldn't bring herself to tell him how the tide of her enthusiasm for the entire project had ebbed but suddenly her mood changed and she said, "Rather, no. I'm not glum, I'm not a glum person. Let's have fun."

"What shall we do?"

"Tell me something terribly interesting." The professor moved to embrace her but she repulsed him saying it wouldn't be time to have sex again for another hour but quickly apologized saying, "I'm acting horribly. Please do tell me the latest about your research."

"I hope you realize it's a remarkable thing you've done, starting a foundation. Do you?"

"Tell me about your research."

"Let's talk about the foundation. Let's talk about the

Academic Advisory Board. The problem for the next several years is that no one interested in receiving a fellowship would want to disqualify themselves by serving on the selection committee. We now know that plenty of scholars are interested in the fellowship and I have no doubt that each year there will be more. It's how to get through this transition period, because once we have a pool of laureates we'll have little trouble creating a real board. I have no doubt of that because Pilgrim Studies is an emerging field. You could not be more bored with this monologue, could you?"

"No," she lied. "Really, Mark, I can't thank you enough for all the work you've done."

"Hopefully our current fellow will agree to serve next year when her fellowship ends. And so on. But I've been thinking about how we might accelerate the process."

"How?"

"By inviting scholars who themselves don't work in the field but are not unsympathetic. As with any new field, there's no dearth of skeptics, but I'm confident I could interest a few who are sympathetic. Eminent scholars, by the way. Not all full professors, but one or two I'm thinking of are emeritus and something like this might interest them."

"Mark, that's a great idea." He studied her. "It's a great idea. I love it." She went to him and embraced him and they both had a sense that a troubling moment had passed perhaps even a crisis and she hoped that the tide having ebbed might now rise.

Later he said he had read her last blog post with particular interest. "You weren't entirely writing about solitude, were you?"

"No." He kissed her. "The fact is I haven't experienced solitude. That whole blog post was a lie."

"I don't think so. If you substitute 'in love' where it says 'alone' at the beginning, the full meaning is revealed. Which is why I wonder what brought you to publicize such private sentiments."

"You're the only one who knows."

"You could have just told me."

"I don't know why." She fell silent before saying, "Is anything really private? If it is, can we stand it?"

"You're saying pilgrimage is a public display of need. That's very interesting."

"What isn't pilgrimage?"

He kissed her again. "You've come a long way."

"Three hundred ninety-six miles."

"I think you know the real miles are inside you."

"That's the problem. I've never once felt that I was doing something holy, whatever that might mean."

"You've been searching for love."

"Is that holy?"

"It's an approach to the holy."

"What is the holy?"

"The dimension of life where meaning resides."

"What do you think of my pilgrimage as a search for love? It seems ridiculous. Walking around the suburbs with a backpack? It makes a lot more sense to search for love here with you. We make love, we talk about love..."

"At this point I don't really think I have to tell you that the backpack symbolizes the burden you carry. That we all carry. In actual pilgrimage it's both symbol and utility, just as the staff and pouch once were. In your virtual pilgrimage it's just symbol. Nothing wrong with that. Its meaning is explicit."

"I have nothing to show for my pilgrimage."

"Not true. You have me."

"You're right, I have you. And I do love you. I don't know why, you're even more obsessive than me, but I do."

"And I love you, even though your obsessiveness is inferior to mine. So that must be worth something, no?"

When she got home Bob met her at the door positively glowing and taking one look at him exclaimed, "You got the job! Which one?"

"Lehman. Just heard a little while ago. I was dying to call, but I didn't want to interrupt anything." She wouldn't have taken the call in any case because a little while ago the professor and she had been in the shower washing sweat and other bodily fluids off each other with a lot of soap and a lot of rubbing.

"Mommy," said Kiley rushing toward her, "daddy got a job!"

After she was put to bed Tiffany asked if he'd thought about how they should celebrate and he said, "Funny you should mention it," and told her he'd decided he wanted to celebrate his new position by trying a new position thus putting Tiffany who managed to look titillated in her own new position of having to feign arousal; after faking an orgasm she felt too guilty to fall asleep so after lying awake and listening to Bob's breathing she slid out of bed and went to the television room. She hoped to watch a costume drama in which young newlyweds are on the high seas bound for an exotic land where the earnest man is to take up a diplomatic post when they're shipwrecked and he believes himself to be the sole survivor; or one in which their ship is overrun by pirates and his beautiful bride is abducted while he's left for dead but she ended up watching a romantic comedy about the dating scene for thirty-somethings which was neither funny nor romantic and when it ended she started another.

Chapter Twenty-five

DAY THIRTY-ONE. What Tuccio first noticed upon setting out was that the river they had been following and into which the gorge drained turned out of sight to the south.

> Had Tuccio known, how pleased he'd be,
> the flow continued to the sea.

While the caravan sought provisions in the walled village he climbed a winding staircase built against a hillside to emerge into a street that took him up to the summit of a promontory inside the right-angle turn of a narrow river; on the ruins of ancient fortifications there was a large priory and there he found Margherita who followed him silently to the edge of the promontory which looked out over the surrounding country and down on an old stone bridge.

"That's a beautiful old bridge," she said. "They call it—"

"Let me guess, the 'bridge of the devil.'"

"Have you noticed that everything here is built of rounded stones? I suspect they were taken from the river bed."

"I didn't come here to discuss masonry."

"They say the bridge is where people go to have commerce with the devil."

"We would have been en route to freedom by now."

"We are en route to freedom."

"You perhaps."

"There is no place in this world, even if we fled to the land of Kublai Khan, where we could live as husband and wife. Don't I already have a husband? Would you ask me to forsake my pilgrimage, my salvation?"

"Forgive me, lady, I thought you loved me."

"How dare you say that to me, who has handed you her very soul."

"You may have it back if you wish."

Fighting back tears she stormed off too soon to see him fight back his own and as he waited for her to return she waited for him to chase her and it was he who yielded saying, "You know very well I don't seek marriage, only love."

"Tuccio. Never, God knows, have I sought in you anything other than you yourself. I never expected a matrimonial alliance, this was neither my pleasure nor my wish. And if the name of 'spouse' seems more holy and stronger, the name of 'lover' has always seemed to me sweeter, like that, without wishing to shock you, of 'concubine' or 'courtesan.' I have seen marriage, I do not desire another. I prefer love to marriage, liberty to attachment. God be my witness, if an emperor had judged me worthy to be his wife, I would have found it more precious and dignified to be called your whore than his empress, for one is merely Fortune, but virtue in the other." (Letter, Heloise to Abelard)

"You have me completely confused, Mita, for I have never dreamed of making you my wife, nor would I have you the other. All I wish—all I wish—is for us to persist in paradise. Beyond that I have no thought."

"Without thought it is folly to run. I do not believe there is sin in our love. The poets assure us there is none and I cannot feel any. I could almost say my marriage is sin, because it is a lie."

"Yet to your marriage shall you return."

"Never."

"Then again I say I'm confused. Your thoughts seem jumbled, mine certainly are."

"In children nothing is easier than love. In adults nothing harder."

"Perhaps we try to think too much?"

"Intellect is our gift. Surely one cannot reason too much, only incorrectly."

"I would have said love is our gift and that one cannot love too much."

"Are you sure? Can one love incorrectly? If love is the basis of all, must it not be the basis of our sins as much as our virtues?"

"I believe my love for you is neither sin nor error. You have expressed the same."

"But is love by itself sufficient? Or must it be guided finally by reason?"

"Is anything less amenable to reason?"

Falling silent they gazed down over the narrow promontory at the bridge of the devil.

"If there were a way to unknot our souls from our bodies, would you want that?"

"To terminate our desire?"

"Perhaps our love as it is can take us only so far. With love of a woman, no matter how lofty, comes desire for her. Suppose as your guide in love I were replaced with an old man, what would you do?"

"I should look up into the highest Heaven where you dwell and thank you for having brought me from servitude to liberty and made my soul healthy." (*Paradiso*, Canto 31)

"But would your love make the final ascent to pure spirit?"

"I rather think my frustrated desire would cast it down."

"Might not a purely spiritual object, which a woman cannot be, enable you to experience a purely spiritual desire?"

"When I look to Saint James, or beyond to Him of whom he is apostle, my desire is pure spirit. When I look at you it is not. Do you mean I should no longer look at you? Or, looking at you, see him? The first is beyond me, the second, thank God, is not. The poets sing to me of ennoblement through love of a worthy woman. I believe our love has brought me far and as I have no wish for sainthood have no wish to go further."

"But suppose it were the clarity of the intellect rather than the passion of love by which the soul is unknotted?"

"Then I should remain knotted in joy. What would you have?"

Again they stared at that bridge as if the devil might be there! The devil himself to meet them in a most alluring guise! Were they afraid of being enticed to the other side? Afraid of falling into the rock-strewn channel, borne away by its force, its twisted course, always downhill?

They followed that stream to the next walled settlement and another to the next exchanging barely a word or glance even when parting for the night.

DAY THIRTY-TWO. After a night's sleep it struck them that the generally wide valley they yet traversed had wild and rocky mountains to the north versus tame and sylvan to the south which they interpreted to offer them a clear choice and the means to choose; in fact as the mountains gradually diminished and the route straightened the loss of further opportunities to disappear into wilderness settled them as did the presence of the other pilgrims sometimes quiet sometimes boisterous even singing. By distance this stage was one of the longer but it was easy so as they made their easy way the lovers felt their fears and ill feelings gradually evaporate while their horses naturally drew side by side.

When Tuccio was scouting Piera took his place and the younger and the older proceeded happily beside each other mostly in silence until when they came to the end of the long valley and no mountains could be seen ahead Margherita proposed that after they fulfilled their pilgrimage Piera return with her to Siena and be installed in her household as a maid to which the girl as was her way showed no reaction. "Agnoletta will teach you housekeeping. If you wish, I will be the child's godmother and help you raise it. You will have security and receive a salary as well as a wardrobe and whatever else you and the child might need. My husband will provide a dowry so you can marry."

"Who would marry me?"

"We will find a suitable man to be your husband. Neither a drunk nor a lout."

"A peasant?"

"Is that what you want?" She didn't reply. "There are many men in Siena who work at a craft or in service and want a wife and who for a suitable dowry will take both you and your baby."

"Truly?"

"I have no doubt. If the dowry be sufficient. I will make sure it is."

DAY THIRTY-THREE. Piera asked Margherita how many children she had. "My husband has one. I am barren."

"Then how can your husband have one?"

"He had one with a servant." She said she had refused to have the baby in the house but was reconsidering. "It would be a companion for yours. It would be nice to have children in the house, don't you think?"

"But..."

"Yes, I was very... but the situation has changed. Now I can have a family."

"Tuccio?"

"It will not be easy, but we will find a way." They talked about the coming baby and made plans and Piera smiled.

They were spending the day in the walled city of Castres beside the last of the gorge rivers thoroughly tame when it reached the city which had grown up around a monastery and was principally engaged in weaving and dying cloth and serving pilgrims en route to Compostela; but what distinguished it was that it stood on the cultural border between Provence and Gascony with their distinctive dialects. "We exit, we enter. May it go on. May we continue in Paradise," said Tuccio.

"How far we have come, how high ascended," said Margherita. "I have been unbound, unknotted."

"I have been bound, knotted."

"As have I."

"As have I."

"Would you have the ardor of desire within you finished?" she asked.

"Not I," he said firmly.

"Nor I," she confessed.

"The intellect may be Man's natural gift, but some are more gifted than others and in me it is slight. But I feel the mighty stir of love, therefore would I and must I favor that."

"I could say the same. Yet in me I find the desire to understand that will pester love."

"Perhaps in the end the intellect should fall away, as it might when trying to solve an insoluble problem, if love the mover is to be seen." (*Paradiso*, Canto 33)

"Perhaps. Are we there?"

"You wish to love God. I wish to love God through you, as Petrarca seeks God in Laura. If that is not the purest love, then may my love be impure."

"Mine too, I suppose, for I am no mystic who would see God face to face."

"We are lovers, the poet is our guide. Let us read today."

A porter told this tale: Once a porter died and by chance neither angel nor devil came for his soul which flew up in the sky but could find no guide to the afterlife until finally it saw the archangel Saint Michael carrying a soul with great joy and followed; when Saint Michael passed through the gate of Paradise so did the porter and after Saint Peter joyfully received the first soul he turned to shut the gate and saw the other and said, "Who brought you here? No one enters without judgment. Besides, porters have no place in Paradise."

"You are just a peasant yourself," replied the soul and so began a jousting of arguments because for every blow of Saint Peter the soul had a parry and a return and a crowd gathered to watch the contest; soon Saint Peter no longer joyous told the soul to wait while he fetched the apostle Saint Thomas but he had no more success so together they went for Saint Paul but with the same result.

Now God hearing this decided he'd better join the field thundering, "Why have you entered Paradise without permission?" but to his amazement the soul rather than cower claimed that he had a better right to be there than many in the crowd for they had committed grave sins whereas he had lived a blameless life filled with pious thoughts and good deeds.

"Besides," he said, "you have proclaimed that a soul's stay in Heaven is forever and I would not turn God into a liar."

HELL

Chapter Twenty-six

DAY ONE. In the second line of canto one of *Inferno* which begins the *Divine Comedy* Dante writes that he "discovered himself in a dark wood" and since Margherita and Tuccio will be traversing the vast primeval forests of Gascony throughout Hell it's worth looking at what Dante meant. It is generally acknowledged that the basic idea of the *Divine Comedy* a tour of the afterlife as well as many of its details come from book six of Virgil's *Aeneid* in which Aeneas the hero visits Hades the underworld where he encounters two woods; many scholars note the first but I didn't find one who acknowledged the second. The first near the entrance to Hades contains the golden bough he needs to gain entrance to the underworld and by its geographical position is clearly analogous to Dante's wood near the entrance to Hell; but there the analogy ends for Dante is not seeking to enter Hell nor looking for anything in the forest on the contrary he has lost his way literally and figuratively and is there because "the straight (or right) path was lost."

Naturally we would like to know what this path is but rather than directly reply Dante devotes the entire poem to telling us however he does give a big hint in the word 'dark' (*oscura*) because the second wood in *Aeneid* book six *unlike the first* is described with the same word; this wood is a 'great forest' in which forever wander those afflicted by 'hard love.' When Dante enters not Limbo but Hell proper (in canto five) he first meets those who are punished for the sin of lust and sees Dido with whom Aeneas had a passionate affair and then forsook; now in Virgil's dark wood Aeneas approaches Dido and tries to explain why he had to abandon her (for which she committed suicide) but she won't listen remains silent and finally runs away a marvelous scene but Dante doesn't copy it rather he presents his own in which another famous lover Francesca da Rimini tells her story of passionate love adultery and murder.

How could that be relevant to his noble sophisticated polemical mystical poem? It is relevant because *he links Francesca to Beatrice* the saintly Beatrice who is the love of his life and the instrument of his eventual salvation; in fact he links love in all its aspects not just spiritual but romantic even sexual to the entire project of the *Divine Comedy* in all its aspects not just those that relate directly to love but to philosophy religion and politics indeed the very nature of the cosmos. In the vast thematic structure which Dante creates he begins with the love of a man and a woman and everything that follows proceeds from that.

Dante's mood in the forest is one of confusion writing, "I don't know how I got there," and it is only when he tries to leave up a dark deserted slope that he is menaced by wild animals the third of whom a wolf forces him back toward the forest whereas for Margherita the sense of menace arrived within sight of the walls of Castres which no sooner left than the forest engulfed her tiny procession. Her anxiety was caused not by the seen but unseen and with the caravan on alert the tension was high as if the very absence of menace signified its presence but what also gripped her was anxiety over what would become of her love her very life after the foreseeable end of her journey; for suddenly that no longer seemed a distant future as she moved alone through the forest with Tuccio nowhere near because the count needed everyone undistracted and Piera wasn't saying a word even Agnoletta was quiet in fact almost no one spoke and when someone did it was in a low voice. As Francesca told Dante, "No greater pain than to remember the happy time in misery" (*Inferno*, Canto 5), so did Margherita wonder at how quickly and thoroughly her joy had evaporated like morning dew in summer heat.

> By fearing paradise abate
> So Paradise did Hell create

Though a short stage it seemed long and the little town a few hundred feet long and a hundred wide squeezed around a single street on an oblong mound slightly above the forest floor offered not a single spot where the lovers could find a moment's privacy until they climbed the little belfry built onto the old church and there to their shock found themselves with a direct view above the forest canopy of the Pyrenees sixty miles to the south as grand and forbidding and beautiful as the Alps. Around the mound a short distance the forest had been cleared to provide small fields for tilling and grazing which had the additional virtue of enabling a few seconds warning of marauders human or animal while to the southeast in the middle distance they could see the range of mountains along whose northern side they had been traveling and could see where it descended to the plain and disappeared.

"That's where Provence ends and Gascony begins."

"Do you remember when you first saw the Alps?" replied Tuccio. The day's misery had passed for they were together holding hands embracing kissing squeezed into a corner of the tower. "Do you think they're as high as the Alps? They look it."

DAY TWO. Even the count might have confessed to being unnerved by the dark forest while the *fattore* whom no one doubted was still fretting over losing 'the contest of Montpellier' was naturally eager to reach Toulouse so by common consent the caravan embarked for the famous city a long though not arduous stage but cut short by a mishap with a mule when one of those stolid creatures took fright for no apparent reason and stopped moving. No enticement or beating could induce it to take a step when without warning it bolted from one side of the road to the other battering its cargo against the trees until one of the straps holding the ensemble together was torn loose; fortunately the next hamlet situated at the intersection with a north-south road existed to serve travelers so they were able to obtain the necessary repairs but could advance no farther that day.

"It's the forest," said a porter. "Must have smelled something."

"Then he did us all a favor," said another. "Best not to know what it was."

There was no priest though it was Sunday or even a church just a small chapel where one could make an offering to the local saint and then there was nothing to do but carouse at the inn so Tuccio suggested they go into the woods but Margherita shuddered at the idea and Piera would neither go nor be left; they tried to read in the field but found little heart for Petrarca's intricate poems much less for Saint Brigid's *Revelations* and even the romance of Lancelot and Guinevere they had bought in Montpellier failed to raise their spirits so they stared at the forest and Tuccio said, "Tristano and Isolda lived out there, in a little hut they built. Lived happily as husband and wife. No one could find them."

"Until the king found them after they were betrayed by a forester."

"If only we could have continued to Toulouse today."

"Tuccio, I am losing the strength to continue. Each step we take brings us closer to the end. If my life were to return to its former state, could I still love God? Was the lid on the coffin of my life raised only to be closed again?"

"Have courage," he replied. "Be bold and frank."

"What will become of us?"

"You are the only one on earth with the power to send me away."

"But what if God doesn't will our love?"

"My heart tells me He does, for if love is not God-given, what is?"

"Even carnal love?"

"If God did not want us to love with our bodies, why did he give us bodies with which to love?"

"Is not lust a sin?"

"Is there no distinction between lust and desire? There must be, for no one claims desire is a sin."

"Is it marriage?"

"Perhaps it is desire without love. We do not behave like animals that rut in a field. Love must add something."

"What does it add?"

DAY THREE. Margherita said, "I've been thinking that the heart alone cannot guide love and that this is the difference between desire and lust. What we have that animals do not is intellect."

"What does intellect have to do with love?"

"We are in pain because we have lost the good of the intellect. Let us strive to discover it."

"My intellect tells me that you have great beauty and great merit and thus are worthy of great love, and Love has selected me to offer it. More than that I cannot say. More than that I see no need to say."

"There must be more."

"Why?"

"If we possess this higher power, it must have a higher purpose, no?"

"Is not love the higher purpose?"

"You believe that where there is true love there cannot be lust. Let us hope that is so."

Tuccio placed his hand on hers with a glad face and she was comforted thinking, "Ahead lie secret things. Perhaps this great pilgrim city will save us. Let us not abandon all hope as we enter it."

The enthusiasm of the pilgrim crowds confronted them as soon as they passed through the great eastern portal into what had been the city's main street since Roman times for there large numbers of pilgrims were gathered near the cathedral celebrating little more than their own presence and shared aspirations and Tuccio said, "Do you see how like us they are? All seekers."

"From what I observe you speak true. They all seem to crave betterment and so must have doubts of achieving it."

"The Heaven-bound don't need pilgrimage, the Hell-bound won't profit from it."

"Then we are not the only ones worth saving and needful of it."

"Nor the only ones more hopeful of mercy than justice."

As they looked a long procession of flagellants entered the square chanting as they whipped their own backs while the crowd made way for them and fell quiet and Tuccio whispered, "I would not have believed that life so many had undone."

"I feel like everyone is waiting to cross a great river."

"So they shall, when they leave the city." (*Inferno*, Canto 3)

DAY FOUR. Told by the *fattore* to expect a lengthy stay while he plied his trade Margherita and Tuccio immersed themselves in rededicating their pilgrimage the three days of wary progress through the forest when they had been more apart than together having weighed on them so there was joy simply to be together and this joy mixed with the seriousness of their purpose. He tried to match her fervor if not belief in prayer confession communion and resolutions of abstinence figuring that an honest effort could not but be salutary while demonstrating his commitment and in fact she was anxious for him to join her and relieved that he did and showed her appreciation by pulling him into an alcove to kiss him passionately saying, "I have discovered that without you I cannot continue. We must be together. We will succeed or fail together."

"I do not fail. As you are my lady, I shall be your knight." They were in the Basilica of Saint-Sernin the most attractive of the city's pilgrim sites thanks to the efforts of its canons to present day-long devotional pageants and also because its great interior known to be quite similar to that of the cathedral of Santiago de Compostela offered arresting exhibits. These included twelfth-century murals beautifully painted statues of apostles and a two-level crypt featuring a piece of the True Cross a large reliquary of Saint James the Apostle the remains of the third-century martyr Saint Saturninus (contracted to 'Sernin') and priceless relics donated by Charlemagne so the lines were especially long and they spent the entire day there. "How large the crowds, how much desire is here. I shall read hope in it and let pleasure seize me rather than great sadness for surely there is much merit here."

"Truly a forest of pilgrims. The forest through which a lost soul wanders becomes a forest of lost souls."

"I wonder how many are rescued from this Limbo of high expectation."

"No mortal could say, but I believe that those whose hope is strong will try hard and as a reward live happier lives." Asked how much progress they had made she said she could measure only by the degree to which her heart was filled with love and asked how full it was said it was completely full.

"Mine too. Then we are saved, no?"

"All I know for sure is that our pilgrimage continues and our task is to follow the Path."

"Then lead me out of the quiet to the breeze that trembles." (*Inferno*, Canto 4)

DAY FIVE. As the word *oscura* provided a link in canto one between Dante's dark wood and Virgil's thereby indicating at the outset that the grand theme of the *Divine Comedy* is love so the word *punto* links Francesca to Beatrice; now both are beautiful women but whereas the first is a lustful adulterer whose story is the climax of *Inferno* canto five the second is perfect in spirituality the woman who as Dante's guide in *Paradiso* constantly admonishes him to stop staring at her and pay attention to his salvation so why would he link them? *Punto* in the first instance identifies the 'point' when Francesca and her husband's brother Paolo reading a tale of illicit love between Sir Lancelot and Queen Guinevere succumbed to their sexual desire: "...but only one point was it that overcame us;" *punto* in *Paradiso* canto twenty-nine refers to the point of light that is God's presence in the Empyrean Heaven at which Beatrice stares fixedly but at which Dante cannot look at all: "...fixed on the point that had overcome me;" so not only does 'point' occur in both lines but a point that *overcomes*.

Inferno canto 5 is fifth from the beginning of the *Divine Comedy* while *Paradiso* canto 29 is fifth from the end; the second quote is line nine with nine (and multiples of nine) being a number associated with Beatrice throughout the poem while the first is eleven lines from the end of the canto which is tantalizing for whereas we shouldn't expect it to be the ninth since only Beatrice is Beatrice still the eleventh is close enough to suggest an intentional link; and note also that while Beatrice is the most important person Dante the pilgrim meets in the afterlife Francesca is arguably the first.

Linking these women would seem to also link Paolo's love for Francesca with Dante's for Beatrice which is quite a significant pairing since Paolo's love was sexual and sent him to Hell while Dante's is supposedly non-sexual and earned him a visit to Paradise (albeit via Hell and Purgatory); but I think Dante is going much further seeking *to unify all love* as the grand theme of his poem. Love Beatrice tells him (in line eighteen which at twice nine is a number of significance) is at the heart of creation and metaphysically inhabits every substance; furthermore Dante uses imagery that is arguably sexual to describe this and while there is probably little imagery that could not be deemed sexual the metaphor of a bow and arrow the pervasive medieval metaphor of the instrument of love can be judged conclusive.

It should be noted that Paolo's love was not merely sexual for he really loved Francesca and though they were sent to Hell what is their punishment but to be in the mildest circle *bound together for all eternity* and flung about by strong winds (presumably the winds of passion) which as hellish punishments go is pretty good. Despite being in Hell the lovers are presented sympathetically effectively blessed with faint condemnation and Dante the pilgrim expresses pity for them so great he faints; and how do Dante and Beatrice move through Paradise but by the action of wind and what would be his most fervent wish but to be bound to her forever.

As this day began for Margherita and Tuccio they were determined to continue their honest efforts to refine their pilgrimage and so went straight to church first thing in the morning to start praying such that by noon they were quite satisfied with their own sincerity and by mid-afternoon confident that their pilgrimage had been reestablished on a higher plane. To cement their moral gains and give themselves an earned respite from their

devotional rounds they decided to read together from Saint Brigid's
Revelations and this time unlike their halfhearted effort a few days
earlier resolved to persevere despite the work's flat style sluggish
pace and dry subject. They were in the abbey church of La Daurade
a monastery within the city walls on the banks of the Garonne large
enough to have a dormitory for women pilgrims where Margherita
was staying so it took but a few minutes for her to fetch the book
whereupon the three of them went to the riverbank in search of a
pleasant spot to read.

She opened the volume to set aside the sheaf of Petrarca
poems and the slender romance stored within its pages and turned
to the place where they had left off scarcely a few pages from the
beginning but then impulsively turned to the middle of the book
where they dutifully struggled through the text she reading haltingly
while Tuccio sounded out letters. What a monk looking up from
his labor in the field would have seen was a woman in pilgrim robe
reading a pious book to a young couple newly wed (judging by the
girl's swollen middle) but a point came when they were overcome
by fatigue and could no longer pay proper attention either to the
text or their pious reflections and at that point it seemed
appropriate to take a break from religious rigors and turn to the
slim volume that lay on the ground beside them. Said Tuccio,
"Surely we bought the romance to read it and what better occasion
than now, when our souls are fortified?"

Crossing the river on the toll-free bridge provided by the
monastery they exited the city walls and followed the road to the
far end of the fields cultivated by monks to find a secluded spot
where the forest abutted on two sides and Tuccio said, "We are in
Paradise again. Open this one in the middle too."

She began to read and quickly it became clear she was reading
about a clandestine meeting between Sir Lancelot knight of King
Arthur and Queen Guinevere his wife in which the two talking of
this and that but mostly of love gradually moved closer and closer;
a few times she stopped reading and they gazed at each other with
wide unblinking eyes but once she stopped to exclaim that she had
just realized the distinction between lust and desire. "The sin of
lust is not desire, it is submitting the intellect to desire."

"I do not care about that now."

"You must, it is crucial."

Sighing he asked, "Are you saying that the sin is not physical
desire in itself but the failure to master it with intellect?"

"Exactly. The sin is not the mere presence of desire but the absence of intellect."

"Fine. But again I say I do not care about that now."

She returned to reading but Tuccio was no longer sounding out letters and when she stopped again they gazed at each other the color draining from their faces and when she read that Lancelot kissed Guinevere on the mouth he reached over and all trembling did the same and she read no further. They could not stop they were caressing each other their motions ever more flagrant until Margherita asked Piera to return to the hostel to get something and though first she ordered and then she begged the girl only shook her head.

"Then stay here," ordered Tuccio impatiently, "don't move," and rising took Margherita by the hand and hurried into the woods but when his breeches were open and her robe was raised Piera threw her arms around him; he pushed her down roughly but she attacked again wordless but shrieking and in the end the lovers were panting with frustration angry and lurching as if buffeted by winds and he bowed his head so long she asked him what he was thinking then burst into tears. "Is not desire supposed to be sweet?" he complained loudly then shouted at Piera, "Who are you to interfere? You had your pleasure." In response she fell like a dead body falls. (*Inferno*, Canto 5)

FRANCESCO. There was a wealthy merchant in Siena who had a nightmare vision of a coming plague a plague unlike anything ever experienced that would soon devastate vast populations across Christendom unless there were sufficient timely repentance which led him to suddenly abandon his fortune go preaching throughout Tuscany and found a small religious order modeled on the Franciscans that was joined by members of Siena's magnate families. He was the same age as Francesco and though they had never been partners because his social position was higher he was known to him as a member of the Mercanzia Siena's guild of elite merchant bankers and one of those involved in the contest with the Florentines over San Gimignano; when Francesco learned of his renunciation he dismissed it as a failure of will but when he fell seriously ill with a fever and required bleeding he remembered it and when he recovered and was making offerings at every altar and doubling his alms he couldn't get it out of his mind.

Still a lifetime of catalogued rationalizations rushed to his aid such as that the Church was forever condemning usury while approving numerous commercial arrangements and high rates of interest and asking who would give to the poor if not the rich. His whole life he'd endured firebrand preachers condemning merchant bankers as the worst of sinners and friezes over the entrance to every church showing them dragged by demons to waiting cauldrons and many a time for the good of his soul he had even gazed at them himself and attended the open-air sermons for one didn't achieve his success without a thick skin; he told himself, "Preachers love to look stern and thunder feverish warnings about the risks we run, since nothing holds a crowd like fear, but God knows we are all sinners, He doesn't expect us to lead blameless lives, that's why He offers us absolution."

He could always contend that the condemnations were not directed at him but at others who did things far worse than anything he had even contemplated thinking, "I am not like them. The things they do..." and on the occasions when anxiety got the better of him he could always acknowledge his sin and thanks to the Church purchase his return to righteousness.

His notary had justified his wealth on the grounds that it was a worldly loan to be repaid therefore so long as he repaid it either during life or by his will at death there was no sin or at least his sin was forgiven and that was a handy justification even more so the claim that one's good fortune was a reward granted by God for virtue. Lapo never went that far but there were those who did who wondered aloud why they in particular had been chosen by God for their good fortune if not that they deserved it saying, "Fortune repays the merchant's virtue and piety," and, "Wealth comes from above and one should thank God for it, not refuse it;" but confronting his own death had unnerved Francesco in a way that had never before happened. However hard he reasoned he could not avoid the conclusion that an irreducible problem persisted with trying to justify commerce and banking which the endless argumentation tried to minimize if not dismiss which was that in and of themselves they required justification.

The argument that rhetorically asked who would give to the poor if not the rich was made above all by Franciscans and Dominicans whose mendicant orders were installed entirely in cities where all merchants lived and thus were often the beneficiaries of legacies left to 'the poor;' however the argument was not made by their great theologian philosophers rather local friars whose convents stood to gain so Francesco wondered whether this was an honest argument or an attempt from self-interest to whitewash moral turpitude. Never before had he lost any sleep over such ruminations but now he did; many times he had said to Lapo, "Man is a dangerous thing and danger lies in dealing with him," but this had always been a way to calm his mind to maintain his shrewd and careful effectiveness to remind him to diversify his investments in places products and people in sum it was a self-caution and by the unceasing vigilance it aroused he had made his fortune but now he acknowledged how weary he was.

He found himself truly worried for the first time as though he had emerged from his fever to find himself in a dark place and overcome at the point where he saw the necessity of confronting his moral condition for he was no longer one who in the middle of his life could complain that he had lost the straight path; was he however like that other to settle a life estate on his wife and give away the balance of his fortune to spend the rest of his days begging?

Chapter Twenty-seven

Bob knew when he joined Lehman Brothers that it was confronting the same concerns about the adequacy of its liquidity and capital as his old firm and had immediately after its collapse faced such financing difficulties that it had to borrow from a new lending facility of the Federal Reserve; he was also aware that market observers identified it as the next big worry among the four remaining large investment banks due to the same risky combination of highly leveraged MBS holdings with very short-term debt. He remained convinced however that such concerns were greatly exaggerated and took considerable comfort in the fact that the firm was increasing its liquidity substantially while reducing its real estate exposure and raising new capital while marginally improving its debt position; this optimism made it all the more jarring when just two weeks into his new job the firm announced a large loss its first as a public company and as he watched the stock price plummet he couldn't help but wonder if he'd made a mistake.

He didn't say anything and Tiffany didn't either causing him to hope she hadn't heard the news but a few days later as they were going to bed she asked in as neutral a tone as possible if he was okay and that's when he knew she knew and he said, "You heard." The stock price had plummeted again when it was announced that the firm was replacing its chief operating and financial officers. "Not great, obviously." She asked again if he was okay and shrugging he said, "I won't pretend my confidence hasn't taken a hit," for he prided himself on what he regarded as the quality of his judgment.

"No," she said.

"No what?"

"You didn't make a mistake. The market's tough right now. We'll get through it."

"Everyone's so damn jittery. These stupid scary headlines."

"Like I say."

What she really thought she kept to herself and a week later it was reported that four financial institutions having 'trading issues' with Lehman had reduced their exposure to the firm which distressed Bob but none of it was on display when they visited his parents and when having no knowledge or suspicion of problems on Wall Street they grilled him on his new job he assured them he was still on track to become CEO of a major bank. As he talked he periodically glanced at Tiffany but she maintained her fixed smile as usual during these conversations interjecting supportive comments where appropriate until Kiley abruptly redirected the conversation by announcing, "Mommy goes on pilgrimage."

"What was that, darling?" asked her grandmother and she repeated it. "I don't understand. Did she say 'pilgrimage?'"

"Pilgrimage is when you walk to a place because you really like it. But I don't like it because mommy goes away too much. She talks to a professor. Do you know what a professor is, grandpa? It's a teacher who knows all about something."

"Yes," said Bob quickly his own fixed smile already installed, "Tiff's gotten interested in pilgrimage to this place in Spain, which is really interesting, it turns out thousands and thousands of people are doing it, it's not necessarily a religious thing, it's just become like this thing. To do. It's all over the internet."

"Well I'll be," said his father. "What next, don't you wonder."

"But mommy doesn't go to Spain," said Kiley.

"Oh," said her grandmother.

"I'm writing a blog," said Tiffany. "You pretend you're touring a certain area and then you write about it as though you really are. It's fun."

"Oh," said her mother-in-law.

"Isn't that interesting," said her father-in-law.

As Bob undertook the task of explaining her pilgrimage which his parents had just heard mentioned for the first time precisely to avoid the discussion which was now occurring because Kiley was no longer too young to say anything about it Tiffany's mind wandered into another topic; as she listened to her in-laws' questions and watched their faces she was thinking that she wouldn't enjoy sex with the professor so much if Bob didn't fall asleep on top of her when he was done without regard to how that left her. "Well," she reproached herself, "he doesn't do it all the time. But," she countered, "he does it often enough. When I have sex with Mark I know he's thinking about me. With Bob it's like he's thinking about work. Or he's too tired to think about anything but sleep." As she heard Bob acknowledging that she had been on pilgrimage when she'd broken her arm she thought it was unfair to be so hard on him when he was under so much pressure. "Even if he were a better lover, having sex with Mark would still be..." No, she concluded, it would be unfair to blame her adultery on Bob.

"On whom would you like to blame it," asked the professor, "yourself?"

"Who should I blame, you?"

"Does someone have to get blamed?"

"It's adultery, Mark. 'Wow, you went on a pilgrimage, what did you do?' 'I committed adultery.' How does that sound?"

"Would it be less true to say you found love?"

"Adulterous love. And please don't remind me that in the Middle Ages that was considered the only true love. At this point it sounds like a pick-up line." They were side by side in bed naked and sweaty which caused the professor to hope the open contradiction between her words and actions would be resolved in favor of the latter and that indeed seemed to be the case as she arose to don a light bathrobe paced the room a few times absentmindedly and turned on the television to a soccer match which she then ignored; the professor watching from the bed asked if they should take a shower and go somewhere and she said, "Yes, let's find a bar and watch a baseball game."

"I didn't realize you were a fan."

"I'm not. I want to go to one of those real New Jersey joints. They'll have lots of beer on tap and when I ask for a white wine they'll look at me funny."

"How will we find one?"

"I have no idea."

"Okay, Jersey joint it is. They won't look at you funny, though. Lots of women drink white wine."

"Okay, let's go to a cocktail lounge and discuss the foundation."

"Now that's a good suggestion, because I've got a couple of ideas I'd like to put forward."

"Excellent. Let's manage our affair in a very sophisticated

way." She removed the bathrobe and let it drop to the floor. "Ready for your shower?"

It wasn't easy to find an attractive place for a casual drink in fact they never found one but just accepted the last place they saw so as not to waste more time and Tiffany determined to be happy but no sooner did the professor indeed start talking about the foundation than she was reminded that her interest in it had somehow been lost which required her to feign interest with nods and appreciative smiles. With the second grant cycle now underway he had turned his attention to the third which would begin with the next announcement in September and he had two ideas for which he sought her approval the first that the grant cycle be changed to begin September first instead of June first on the grounds that this would better accommodate the academic calendar. "It's a small item, I know, but I think it would be helpful."

"That's good then. Anything we can do to make it more..."

"Then you agree?"

"I'm in your hands. Well, I was in your hands."

"It means a one-time three-month delay in our board recruitment."

"If you're okay, I'm okay. What's your other idea?"

"Moving the start to September gives people more time to get ready. Line up research assistants, for example, committee obligations."

"I get it, what's next?"

"My own research would have ramped up more quickly if I'd had more time to prepare. In other words we keep the same application calendar, we just change the grant calendar." Tiffany nodded appreciatively. "My other thought..."

Tiffany couldn't locate her interest in the foundation but when Bob continued to question this very expensive project she defended it on the grounds that the professor had said it was making a significant contribution to important work and as its reputation grew it would emerge as a major player in an exciting new field; as for the money she reminded him that it came from her deal bonuses with the implication that she was free to spend her own money as she wished and after the tax deductions they could easily afford it and still have everything they wanted.

"What about that second home?"

"If you want it so bad, go ahead."

"I thought you wanted it."

"I'm thinking this might not be the greatest time to make a big jump into the housing market."

"Are you kidding? Mortgage terms are unbelievable. No money down? Interest only? Rates are low. Or is this about my job situation?"

"How do you feel about your job situation?"

"I feel great. How do you feel about it?"

"You left out that asking prices are unbelievable. Wherever we look it'll be a seller's market. Have you seen what real estate is going for on the Jersey shore?"

"Tiff, I do this for a living, remember? But you didn't answer my question. Are you worried about me?"

The professor's other idea was to extend the next fellowship's eligibility to European universities and research institutes where there was currently more work being done on pilgrimage than in the US. "Extending our reach to Europe would build the foundation's importance and prestige."

"An international foundation." He nodded. "Again, any downside?"

"Don't see any."

"Let's do it."

When they were back in the car he said, "Why do I get the impression that you're not very enthusiastic about your own foundation? Did I do something wrong? I'm asserting myself too much, aren't I? I think I said 'our foundation,' I shouldn't do that. Believe me, I know very well that this is your project and above all your charitable funding."

"It's your project too. At this point you're doing most of the work."

"I'm just trying to help."

"You are helping. You made the second grant happen. Look how many applications we got, that was all you."

"And yet..."

"I'm very thankful for everything you're doing, Mark, believe me."

"There's something else you'd like to say and I'd like you to feel you could say it."

"It's just my ambivalence, that's all. You know all about it."

"I'm not sure I do. Are you referring to the foundation or our relationship?"

"If they're separate, I don't know where the dividing line is.

You became my pilgrimage. Without you, I don't have a pilgrimage."

"You don't have to be without me."

"Without a pilgrimage do I still have you?"

"What are you saying? I'm in love with you. You're not walking for me, are you?"

"I don't know who I'm walking for. I don't mean that, forget it." She fell silent and he waited. "I think what I mean is that I'm in love with you too, and I don't know what to do with that."

"Could we just love each other?"

"That's the question, isn't it?"

They sat in the car not having anyplace to go or rather they had been intending to return to the hotel but neither wanted to do that; Tiffany said that if they were in France they wouldn't have to go anywhere because they'd be there and the professor suggested that if there was a church they could visit it and pretend but she wasn't aware of any Gothic reproductions like Saint Patrick's and there wasn't enough time to go to New York. He suggested a park as it was a beautiful summer day but she said she didn't know this part of the state so they sat in the car in silence for quite a while until he suddenly said he would drive somewhere.

"Where?"

"Somewhere. I don't know this part of the state either. I don't know any part of this state. I'm not even sure I know where I am. But I don't want to spend our precious time together like this. Maybe we could go to the movies. What do you think?"

"Do you want to?"

"Sure."

"No. Do you want to?"

"Not especially. I want to have a good time with you. I want us to be happy together. You look miserable, how can I help?"

She shrugged then said, "What have we done, Mark?"

"Fallen in love?"

"That was crazy."

"Love can be like that. It's not predictable or safe."

"Are you going to lecture me now on the nature of love?" He shook his head and kept silent. "I think I might be done hearing lectures." Still he kept silent. "I think I might have made a big mistake. Am I really in love or was it just infatuation?" And still he said nothing. "I keep asking where has my enthusiasm gone, for the stages, for the blog, the foundation... for your lectures about the

Middle Ages? Maybe it was a fad, like I told you I've been known to do that. Maybe I just had a crush on you. And still you say nothing."

"I can't tell you how you feel, I can only say how I feel. With me it's not a fad. I'm certain of that, I have no doubts, none."

"Okay, let me ask you this: If I weren't married, what would you do?"

"Do you mean would I ask you to marry me?" She looked at him. "In a heartbeat."

"Liar."

"You're right, I'm lying. I probably wouldn't. I love being with you. I love being with you. But if I'm honest I have to admit I treasure my independence. I've been alone ten years, I've gotten used to it."

"And there we have it."

"That's crap. Excuse me, but that's crap. What do we have? If you were single, we could be together all the time, and I would love that, don't tell me I wouldn't, I don't tell you what's in your mind, don't tell me what's in mine. We could do everything together. Cook breakfast together, watch something stupid on television together, just because we feel like it. I would give anything for that, but it's not going to happen, so why are we arguing about it?"

"You know, if I'm honest, I have to admit that I never really believed your research proposal."

"Wow, you really want to..."

"It's true, I never did. Since we're being so truthful with each other. I mean what's the point of identifying the author of the *Pilgrim Guide*—assuming it's possible, which it isn't, but never mind... How would knowing the author enable you to determine whether the four routes were his invention or even whether he exaggerated their importance? It makes no sense. Even if you could name the author, that's all you'd have, a name, a few biographical tidbits. Not enough to draw any conclusions, to decide any important questions. I remember we once had a discussion about the relevance—or irrelevance—of determining whether Dante and Petrarch wrote about actual women. It's the same here. Whether or not the author had a secret agenda, what difference does it make to deciding the authenticity of the four routes? Does anyone imagine they were a complete fiction?"

She continued: "You say there are many indications that the author may have had a secret agenda and therefore the text cannot be accepted uncritically, but from what you've told me you have no way to link your doubts and suspicions to the specific claims about the routes. Suppose the author did invent the idea of the pilgrim routes having starting points, whatever that might mean. Does it follow from that that the routes themselves were also inventions? Of course not."

"Is this really what you want to discuss? Really? Well then, am I allowed to defend myself? Thank you. The criticisms you make of textual analysis would have merit if we medievalists were not usually confronted, as we certainly are here, with an extreme poverty of source material. If, for example, we had records of pilgrim traffic or even a way to infer it, it would be no great feat to reconstruct the routes taken by pilgrims. If pilgrim hostels or inns for travelers generally still stood, again we'd have concrete data, but they have all but completely disappeared without a trace. Even the great Roman highways are in many places obliterated. Think of archaeology. A pottery shard is discovered and from its style and physical location scholars attempt to reconstruct a lost culture. So, yes, we tend to read much into the tiny bit of data we have, and there is always the danger of reading too much, and even more frustrating, no reliable method to decide how accurate one's reading has been. The *Pilgrim Guide* contains the only reference we have found to the four routes. Which is more likely, that every other reference has been lost or that the author invented them?"

"It's the only reference to any routes. The fact that you have only one surviving data point tells you nothing about the value of that data."

"That's very good. No, really. Now you're thinking like an historian and you see the problem one faces. What does it mean that the *Pilgrim Guide* is a unique find? If it's not merely an accident of survival, wouldn't that suggest that there wasn't much interest in reading about the routes? Yet we know that at the time pilgrimage to Compostela was very popular. Thus the inference that pilgrims already knew the routes or could easily learn them from the many local confraternities that promoted the cult of Saint James. Why then does even a single guide exist unless its author had something to promote? And when you consider that a great many, probably most pilgrims were illiterate, one then has to consider the PG's intended audience."

"What makes you think the author had a secret agenda? You can't just say, 'The book exists, therefore the author had an agenda.""

"Enter textual analysis. Do you want to see what we medievalists have to do so people can believe they, quote, 'know' the Middle Ages? I'll give you just a taste of the sausage. Why does the author devote so much attention to Saint Eutropius while ignoring Saint Martial, even though we're certain of the importance of the latter in the twelfth-century liturgy of the cathedral at Compostela? Why is there no mention of the route from Paris to Orléans and almost none about sites in Spain? Why is nothing said about Cluny, whose monastic order practically established the Compostela pilgrimage and where, according to its colophon, the codex was mostly written? Why does the author make much of rival claims to the relics of Saint Giles and not say a word about the authenticity of the relics of Saint Mary Magdalene at Vézelay? Why does he emphasize the importance of not moving valuable relics just when plans were underway to transfer a major relic of no less than the apostle James himself from Compostela to Pistoia—at least if we accept the veracity of the P manuscript? I could go on. My monograph will go on, with an exhaustive analysis. And discuss the different hands that wrote the extant manuscripts, and the illumination styles. This is the picayune minutiae of my trade, this is what we do. This is what you have bought with your foundation. Maybe now you're sorry. Maybe you'd like to discontinue it."

"I don't know what I want to do."

"Well, before you decide, you might want to consider that sometimes it's impossible to know in advance what knowledge will later be gained by ascertaining an important fact."

Tiffany looked out the window. "I'll tell you something else. I hate your emails. Mostly you write about how you can't wait to fuck me again and then you say something about the Middle Ages."

"Are you serious?"

"Do I look serious?" she said turning.

"I think you're conflating love and sex."

"You taught me that in the Middle Ages there was no distinction."

"I taught you that there was no distinct vocabulary for recreational sex, but that doesn't mean people didn't have it, if only in fantasy. The *fabliaux*, *The Decameron*, *The Canterbury Tales*—"

"I get it, I get it."

"Then please don't accuse me of not loving you. If I just wanted to screw I wouldn't have to drive to New Jersey. But you know that, I know that you know that, so what are we fighting about? I'm no happier about our circumstances than you are."

"You are. If I told you I was leaving Bob you'd kill yourself."

"Then it's fortunate you haven't the slightest intention of doing that. I'm sorry my emails are insufficiently impassioned. When I tell you how beautiful you are and how I can't stop thinking about you and how much I love being with you, I will try to be more literary." There was a long silence during which they turned away and turned back several times. "Am I allowed to note that you too have your obsession with knowing the actual route, which somehow adds authenticity to your pilgrimage? We're both obsessive. Maybe that's why we're drawn to each other."

"Will your monograph say who the author was?"

"Alas, no. What it does do, however, is eliminate certain conjectures and suppositions that have been advanced while defending the strongest candidates based on what we know. Without additional data, alas, we may never know with certainty the identity of the author."

"My emails are no better. I don't want to call you 'darling,' I want..."

She began to cry and he tried to decide what to say or do until he said what was on his mind which was that he too was disappointed that his research hadn't achieved more than it had but he didn't think the situation warranted tears and Tiffany burst out laughing even as she was crying and he put his arms around her and kissed her and they embraced. She said there was a time when romantic declarations were made on good stationery which were saved and cherished whereas currently one pressed 'delete' on a picture of a trash can and she assured him she still loved to hear him talk about the Middle Ages. "It's exciting the way you revive those old texts, that's why I majored in classics."

"Let's face it, romance is intoxicating. And intoxication is temporary and so inevitably one experiences the loss of elation. Thank God for sex."

"I'm not here for sex."

"I know you're not," he replied quickly. "You think I don't know you could do a lot better than me if you just wanted to get laid?"

"You're very good for me."

"As you are for me. You're the second best thing that ever happened to me."

She pinched him and they kissed again and suddenly she threw her arms around him. "I'm sorry," she whispered.

"Don't be. Like I said, I'm disappointed too. If only I could have named the author."

"Stop," she said sweetly.

"I'm disappointed too like you are. Marriages are hard, why should affairs be easy? When it's love and not just sex. Maybe even harder than marriage. No?"

"I think I got angry because I'm afraid. I don't want to lose you."

"You won't lose me. I will never abandon you, my lady, my dearest one, my sweet precious. I wish I could express how much I love you. I..." It excited him that a woman he considered so impressive found him impressive and that was why her criticism had frightened him so much but now that she'd confessed it was just her own fear he was overflowing with tenderness and affection and hadn't the slightest doubt he would love her no less did he not find her beautiful and had she not given herself to him and had he not for months been stroking her naked thighs for she was intelligent and energetic and accomplished and interested in serious topics and besides, he concluded, she laughed at his pale jokes.

"Remember when I asked you what holiness is? Well, you're that part of my life, the dimension where its meaning is." It excited her that a man she considered so wise found her wise and that was why her doubt had frightened her so much but now that he'd confessed he too was disappointed she was overflowing with tenderness and affection for a middle-aged man who took her seriously and helped her who ratified her interests and concerns and made her feel valuable and for months this man who could not love any woman like his dead wife had been loving her the only one despite a campus full of attractive women able to capture his heart and that was why each time he collapsed on top of her with a final grunt she held him tightly and told him she loved him.

"What you just said? That's what I wanted to say but didn't know how." He kissed her passionately.

"You're not so bad."

"I could be better."

"Most men could. Maybe that's why they wrote romances." Though they had already showered they rushed back to the hotel with just enough time to do what they wanted although there wouldn't be time to shower again which violated one of Tiffany's rules of prudence and on the way they happily discussed the pilgrim routes because whether or not any were official in some sense or traditional neither had any doubt that pilgrims like all travelers would seek the highways not just for the relative safety and ease of travel and services (such as they were) but the desire for company. "No one would want to travel long distances alone, never mind the dangers."

"And even if one were in a large party, being on a highway greatly reduced the likelihood of getting lost or diverted."

"Which was no doubt a problem for pilgrims in the Middle Ages as it still is. It's the number one complaint. Everyone complains about well-intentioned locals who with complete conviction send you off in the wrong direction, and when you're walking with a heavy pack... I think I've mentioned that before."

"There's another reason why medievals would have been at least as interested as we moderns in having pre-established routes, which is knowing that one was not simply walking down a road but going somewhere important on a shared and thus purposeful path. I'm going to argue that in my monograph and I learned it from you."

"You really did?"

"Why not? I've never been a pilgrim myself. If there's one major failing we historians have, it's not making sufficient use of imagination. Especially these days when—"

"Thank you, professor, now if you would just keep driving. Turn right at the light. Which reminds me of something else. Unlike now, when pilgrims don't tend to visit sites along the way, it seems like they used to stop all the time, and even go off the main road, like to Saint-Guilhem, right? And there were probably more places to visit along the main roads, don't you think?"

"Indeed, because there was a two-way process of maintaining a route close to certain sites while establishing important sites near a route. This was certainly true in Spain, where I think I mentioned I did research."

"What about the old Roman roads? I can't remember if we've talked about that."

"Not enough scholarly attention has been paid to their condition and use in the medieval period, but again that's a function of an insufficiency of data. We can sometimes use satellite imagery to locate a section of road, but that doesn't tell us when and how it was used."

"But wouldn't medieval highways tend to be in the same places?"

"Absolutely. And that is certainly a factor in the four route controversy."

"Turn left here and then right at the light and we're there." They smiled as they passed the desk burst out laughing in the elevator and turned to each other in the room and when they were done and saying their goodbyes in the parking lot Tiffany said she would like to know more about the professor's children and next time maybe he could bring a photo album.

"Would you like to see pictures of Jess?"

"I'd love to. And I'll bring pictures of Kiley."

"What about Bob?"

"Really?"

"I thought I should ask."

"We can leave Bob out of this for the time being."

"Fine. Would you believe I just told Morgan we never fight?"

"What brought that up?"

"We talk about you. You're no secret to my children, but Morgan, well someday you'll meet her and you'll know what I mean when I say not much gets past her, at least when it comes to her frumpy old dad. So she asked, out of the blue, she asked if we ever fight. And of course I said no. 'Never?' she said. When I asked why, she said that means I'm in love. She said every relationship has disagreements and if we never fight then it means one accedes to the other, and she thinks I would only do that if I were in love. So what does it mean that we had our first fight?"

"That she's wrong. When you're in love everything is terribly important. Especially if you're having an affair. Speaking from my vast experience with affairs."

"I'll tell her we had our first lovers' quarrel."

"And that we're more in love than ever."

Chapter Twenty-eight

DAY SIX. As nothing feeds desire more than its starvation and nothing creates bitterness more than frustrated pleasure Margherita and Tuccio strode back across the river and parted with barely a word.

Imagine their shame! Undone by a romance! They could not even look at each other!

In the morning she quickly rose and left the priory anxious to avoid him though she need not have worried for he was to sit in the inn to get drunk and stare at the prostitutes; unable to focus she wandered the streets with Piera who refused to be left behind although her presence was embarrassing until somehow knowing the right moment she took her hand and Margherita squeezed it and they found their way to the Dominican church whose architectural severity suited her desperation. Recently completed after more than a hundred years its lack of exterior adornment made it seem especially massive and its rigorous simplicity if not harshness so moved her after Saint-Sernin's embellishments that she circumnavigated the entire convent the first created by the order and enormous though right in the heart of the city such that by the time she passed through the drab entrance she was sobbing.

Inside she was again moved to see that the interior lacking transept chancel or crypt was simply a nave with a double span supported on a central line of columns which with the high ceiling and all the windows communicated massiveness and openness to her who turned to Piera to say, "I'm going to be here all day, are you sure you don't want to return to the priory?" but the waif shook her head. The nave was notched on both sides with shallow chapels where she could find small altars at which to pray and make offerings and with Piera never leaving her side went from one to another to plead for guidance until pleasantly interrupted when the friars filed in from the cloister to sing the office of *terce*; she found it beautiful and holy and cried again and when they were done they dispersed throughout the church and she asked one to hear her confession which she made fully despite her shame.

Before Tuccio became drunk he came to his senses and got himself out of the inn whereupon he wandered the streets to clear his head and occasionally eye pedestrians though never sure whether his hope was to see her or not to see her; but when he heard the hour tolled he headed to Saint-Sernin where he got in line for the crypt and prayed at the reliquary of Saint James saying, "I need your help, saint, for I am confused. I am not a monk, I have not left the world, I am a man of arms but nobly born though my nobility is slight, but I would be a knight and have vowed to act nobly. I am in love with a lady of great merit and she is married but I have been assured that this is no bar to our love, in fact I have been told that here lies the greatest love for it is not encumbered by property or alliances or birth, I love this woman solely for herself and would gladly die for her love if need be, and we love each other more than I can say for I am a plain man and no poet, but I can tell you that we desire each other as nature ordains and would lie together as husband and wife, and even this I am told is not a sin so long as our love is pure, yet we feel shame. Twice now we have succumbed and twice been thwarted or perhaps delivered and I have no doubt she at this very moment is praying as I am, for we fear we have wandered from the straight path and are lost in a great dark forest, and so I ask you even though I am not devout, not even observant, I have sinned, but I am trying to improve, to be worthy, and so I beseech your help for without it I don't know what will become of me or, far worse, what might become of her."

When those waiting forced him to move he lost his concentration but pacing up and down the nave he found narrow so far below the ceiling said to himself, "If I were in fact now in the cathedral at Compostela, how would I wish to look back on our holy trip and would I be beside my lady or will I have become hateful to her?" and when he saw a priest he asked to have his confession heard. Afterward he ducked into a side chapel where he wouldn't be jostled or distracted until like one who having fainted regains consciousness he became aware of his surroundings looked around almost in bewilderment and lurched to the exit to hurry to

La Daurade but not finding Margherita threw himself into the city going from one pilgrim site to another; but there were so many pilgrims and places they could be and the streets were so jammed with traffic he gave up and instead inspected the city's gates going from one to another and then returned to La Daurade to wait and when he saw her said, "You should not have gone out alone without protection."

"I saw yesterday how you protect me," she replied but apologized immediately saying, "I should not reproach you for loving me as no one ever has, especially since what happened was my wish as much as yours."

"You are right to reproach me. I failed you. I failed myself."

"Where have you been all day?"

"In church."

They went through the gate to a more discreet location and he apologized to Piera saying he had acted ignobly and would never again strike her. "Thank you for staying with my lady. I will be like a brother to you, you may depend on it," and to Margherita he said, "I fear for our salvation if we try to continue in the same way, for my desire for you is so strong I do not think I can resist it any longer. We must go a different way. Perhaps now you can see that."

She told him she had been in the church of the Dominicans which was very beautiful more for what it omitted than what it contained and said she'd found peace there adding, "I agree with what you say," and when she asked if he was angry with her he knelt and bowed his head and afterward she asked how the priest had reacted to his confession.

"He said I could try forever to justify adultery and fornication but I would never solve the problem that they require justification, instead I should give myself to God. But I already did that when I pledged myself to you. What does a priest know about love?"

"Yet might he not be right?"

"I considered that. If I had to stop loving you I would have to kill myself, which is a sin, so either way I'm a sinner. I'd rather sin by loving you. And if the problem has no solution, then perhaps I am free to stop worrying about it."

"Yet you said..."

"We must leave the path we are on. I know you don't want to, but only then can we be free to love each other. We are not blameless but sinners like everyone else who wish to know love."

"You say I don't want to, but I do, for I too see that we cannot continue this way. But how are we to continue? What is to become of us now?"

He said that when he was in church he'd realized that no one knew where he was. "Tomorrow too, no one will know where we are. We'll have a full day's head start because no one will miss us till evening and they'll have to wait till morning to come after us."

"Are you talking about running away?"

"I looked, there are many routes out of this city, they won't know which way we've gone. And this time we can ride and carry provisions."

"Tuccio, is this the different path of which you spoke?"

"It came to me that this is the best opportunity we've had. Think of it, completely surrounded by forest. We just have to get out of the city without attracting attention. I can arrange for the horses, Stoldo will help and he'd never betray me. I'll wait for you out of sight, you and Piera should leave separately, that way if the count asks the guards at the gate no one will have seen us."

"Tuccio, please tell me how this is a different path."

"If we select the route by lots the count will be least likely to pick the same, but even if he does we can stay ahead with a day's head start, and after a few days they'll abandon pursuit for the *fattore* will be anxious to start for Barcelona. That's the only route we must avoid."

"You're proposing—again—that we run away. Then are we to give ourselves to fornication, as Eloisa did with Abelardo? If we follow their way, will we not reach their end?"

"They stayed. They should have run away. Tristano and Isolda stayed, yet they were never happier than when they were hiding in the forest."

"Are we to spend the rest of our lives hiding in the forest?"

"No, in the kingdom of Prester John."

"The kingdom no one can locate? The one that may not exist?"

"If it exists, I will find it. If it does not, we have the rest of Christendom to find a new home."

"You insist on believing we can live an ideal. I love you for that, but..."

"Now I am confused. What did the priest say to your confession?"

"I did not confess to hear what he would say, rather what I

would say."

"And?"

"I wonder whether this ideal of fine love can actually be lived. Isn't the meaning of 'ideal' that it is beyond life, a vision perceived by life's eyes?"

"It is beyond life if we put it there."

"You truly believe that."

"I don't have to believe it, I know it. I feel it, I experience it. People talk of belief in God. What good is belief? You either know God or you don't. Same with love. What is God if not love?"

"But surely all love is not the same. As you speak I see pennant-waving towers of earthly love, but when I look inside myself as I did today I see the much larger church of heavenly love, which we may call love of God, but isn't it love of one's own soul which is a sketch of God? What the priest said to me is that salvation is not found in the arms of one's lover, but in the breath of the Holy Spirit."

"Does the one necessarily exclude the other?"

"Think of Petrarca back in his closed valley struggling with passion. I must say, for me fine love is more like that and less like your *giullare* entertaining crowds in the public square."

"Then you have changed your mind about love."

"Tuccio, we cannot fuck our way to God."

"I do not speak of that, but of love. You yourself said desire in and of itself is not sinful."

They fell silent.

DAY SEVEN. Tuccio could not let go of his idea to flee the insupportable confines of their circumstances and resolved to convince Margherita rose before dawn and was waiting at the priory gate when she emerged but she said, "Look at me, do you see that I love you? Do you see that I would run with you to the end of the earth if I thought that would solve our problem?"

Eventually he nodded but insisted, "I will speak of nothing else till I have convinced you you are wrong."

"Then let us speak little. Rather should we listen." La Daurade was adjacent to the main street which was always crowded with traffic and probably had been since the Romans built the city but they hardly noticed anything till they had traversed it to reach the cathedral near the eastern gate where they were confronted with the most misshapen and perhaps ugliest church they had ever seen; she proposed that they leave immediately but he wanted to inspect what he called a monstrosity because after all it was a cathedral and thus must have some meaning. When it became apparent that it was constructed of two incomplete churches each with its own axis of alignment and its own architectural style she asked him again to leave but he said he wanted to see the inside so they went in and confirmed that the interior made no more sense than the exterior; they also saw its gaudy emphasis on elaboration rather than elegance and again she said, "Please, Tuccio, let us leave."

"Willingly, but is there no lesson here? This is an episcopal church of the Church, surely the one speaks for the other."

"Tuccio," she pleaded starting to sob and went outside where he consoled her and they walked back up the street; when she was calm she said there seemed to be two kinds of churches the kind where as much as possible was included and the kind where as much as possible was excluded and asked, "What does that mean for us?"

"I think it means that we can stay or we can go, either way we can love each other, it's still the Church. But if we go and forsake its trappings, we may better grasp its essential message. In fact, by leaving its confusion and ugliness we may live in its beauty and simplicity."

She reminded him that they had once agreed to ask Saint James for guidance when they arrived at his tomb but he replied that he had already spoken to him the previous day which was what made him see that escape was the better option.

After a long silence she said, "Don't you see our only hope is to continue this pilgrimage?"

After a long silence he asked, "What did you pray for, yesterday?"

"Patience. I want to believe as much as you that our love is pure no matter how it may look to others, but you yourself said true faith is knowledge, not belief. If we can reach Compostela without succumbing to desire we may be saved."

"If, maybe... Tomorrow night we could lie in each other's arms and gaze at the heavens like Tristano and Isolda."

"And possibly commit a mortal sin."

"Then we shall repent."

"Sincerely?"

"Most sincerely. But I remain convinced our love is not sinful. I cannot believe that God would have put us together if He did not wish us together."

"Even though the Church..." She knew that no sin was beyond forgiveness providing the repentance were sincere but feared sincerity might be lacking for Heloise she had heard had been unable to repent indeed unable to curb her anger at God; still she wondered if it would be so terrible to follow her heart and ask forgiveness for her weakness.

"The Church, we are told, is God's house on earth, but who says so? The Church! And from everything I have seen and heard, you have only to cross that house's threshold to catch the stink of corruption. I say we listen to God."

"You mean listen to your heart."

"Yes, for that is my link to Him."

"So is your mind."

"My mind tells me the same."

As they continued along the busy street whom should they accost but a troubadour entertaining a crowd and of course they joined it but the performance soon ended and after he had collected his modest pile of coins Tuccio handed him another and asked a question that drew him into conversation and he said, "I see you are a man who knows his poetry, will you be attending the contest?"

Thus did Tuccio learn about the Council on the Joyful Wisdom (*Consistori del Gai Saber*) a recently created organization dedicated to reviving and perpetuating troubadour poetry which held an annual contest. "I didn't realize the poetry required reviving."

"There has been much loss since the depredations, when much of the art and many of the artists fled across the Alps and Pyrenees to sunnier lands. The art lives but alas not as well in its original home as it should."

"To what depredations do you refer?"

"The crusade of the north against the south, of course. The French slew us as heretics in our thousands. Then our lands passed to their king. You didn't know this?" Tuccio asked whether he believed the *gai saber* provided real knowledge of love that could be applied to living or was just a poetic ideal and the man didn't hesitate to reply that without any doubt it was the former.

"What we mean to ask," said Margherita, "is whether lovers can actually live by the rules of love promulgated in your poetry—and if so, what of the Church which condemns *fin'amor* as sinful?"

Again without hesitation he said, "The rules of love are

promulgated in our nature and revealed in Scripture, not by us poets and certainly not by the learned doctors of the Church. Since the Church has declared the people of my country its mortal enemy I will not defend it. As for us poets, our subject is sacred, whether it is love of the Virgin Mary or fine love of a noble lady of great merit and beauty."

"But what of physical love?"

"When a man and woman, both worthy, each cognizant of the other's merit and pledged to each other, give and take pleasure, is that not a true marriage? What does a high lady whose heart is chaste owe to a lord who has bought her for her dowry, who mounts her for sons and takes his pleasure with her maidservants?"

Later that day still excited by the discussion Tuccio left Margherita at the priory to have supper at the inn promising to return so they could talk more about the morrow but he was met by the count who sternly announced that the caravan was leaving in the morning saying, "After you've supped, tell the lady to be ready and return immediately to guard the goods, which are again in our custody."

He was devastated she enormously relieved seeing it as almost a miracle to be rescued by the *fattore* of all people for why would he suddenly abandon his commercial opportunities after announcing his intent to remain? "I don't know," said Tuccio, "but we will never have an opportunity like the one we have squandered."

DAY EIGHT.

> Handsome sweet friend, well can I in truth you tell
> that never was it that I was without desire
> since you it suits that you I keep for fine lover;
> nor ever was it that I was not having desire,
> handsome sweet friend, when I often was not seeing you;
> nor ever was it ever that I repented of it,
> nor ever was it, if you went away irritated,
> that I was having joy until you were returned;
> nor...

(Sole surviving fragment of a twelfth-century woman troubadour known as Tibors.)

When Margherita crossed the river to exit through the western gate and passed the field where she had gone with Tuccio she dismounted and told a porter to take her horse because henceforth she would be walking and the count tersely but politely asked what she was doing; she said she was rededicating herself to pilgrimage and he reminded her of the constant danger; she said some dangers were worse than others and he said she was endangering the entire caravan but she insisted and he returned to his place with a grim expression avoiding the *fattore*'s look and when Tuccio returned from scouting they argued.

Everyone was in a foul mood not least the *fattore* who considered himself robbed in Toulouse where he had gotten into a dispute with the customs official over the tariff on his goods which had turned bitter in the absence of an agreement and finally serious when he'd been threatened with arrest unless he paid; having no choice he paid but said he would leave 'this iniquitous city that preys on foreign merchants' as soon as he could load his goods and have nothing further to do with it ever. As they penetrated deeper into the vast forest to the west and south of Toulouse he grumbled about his ill fortune while Margherita talked to herself thus:

"Have I misunderstood you, God? If not, then I am utterly confused, for how am I to understand that the greatest joy contains a seed of bitterness which will grow to destroy it? That the road to the sanctuary of your apostle is the road to misery? And if misery, then no doubt to damnation, for what could my misery mean but that my happiness was not your reward for faith and courage but the devil's snare? But how could that be, are the poets lying? Are women never to know real love but only the love of duty, when they are bound in marriage as girls to strangers who may prove incapable of affection?

"I beg You to take my hand for I am lost. Perhaps I failed to understand pilgrimage, perhaps the Way is a purgatory in which we are made worthy. Is this misery a trial to help me find virtue? But when the suffering born of misery feels no different from the suffering born of joy, how is it to guide us? I do not understand. I walk this path in blindness now.

"Perhaps in my ignorance of love I do not recognize its signs. The poets do sing of the misery of separation, perhaps there is also the misery of being together; or perhaps what we feel is in fact the misery of separation because we are not really together, for how can we truly be together when our love has not been consummated, is that not the measure of separation? Can it be You are telling me... Can it be? See how my heart leaps at the very thought! Perhaps that is it. It must be it, because a pilgrimage must be a road to joy, since it brings us closer to You, otherwise what meaning does it have? Surely joy, not mere pleasure but the true joy of pure love, surely that must be a more reliable guide to what is right than misery.

"But no, that cannot be, for after we have known each other completely, then what? Within two months we will reach Santiago—what then? This path to salvation is a road to misery ever greater. This is not purgatory, it is hell."

That night she slept on the stone floor of a little church while the caravan warily camped outside in a clearing in the forest except the count was received at the small castle that presided over the village where he was told about a terrible illness that could kill an entire population. "Suddenly you are sick. In a day you're bedridden, the next at death's door, and the third turning stiff."

"Have you seen this plague?"

"Don't see much here. Heard of it from a traveler."

"From where?"

"Somewhere I never want to be."

DAY NINE.

> All night I turn and I toss...
> more suffer I pain from love
> than Tristan the lover...
> Oh God, would I were a swallow
> that flew through the air
> and came in night profound
> there in her dwelling...
> Beautiful body with fresh color,
> great pain you make me suffer.

(Bernart de Ventadorn, troubadour)

"Please ride," said the count as they were setting out but Margherita shook her head and without a further word he turned his horse and started; Piera too would have walked but she insisted she stay on the mule for the sake of the baby and Agnoletta too was told to remain mounted while Tuccio seeing this said nothing and rode forward to scout talking to himself thus:

"Are the poets swindlers? I believe I have been given false coin, for where is the joy in love? Have I not done everything required of a worthy lover? Though I burn with desire, I remain pure. I admit it has been a struggle but after all isn't that what a test entails? Never have I forced my lady to consent to what we both desire, and will not so long as there be doubt in her heart about its rightness, for what she does she does of her own free will. Nor have I gone with another when I could have; instead I have suffered, I have endured—and I have been happy. And happily would I endure twice the pain of frustration if that is what joy requires, but what do I learn but that the path we thought led to joy leads instead to misery. I am confused. Have I been wrong about everything from the beginning?

"I know that I love her with all my heart and that she loves me and beyond that I know nothing. I can stay on this road, but I no longer know where it leads; and when we complete our journey, then what, never again to see each other? To pass in the street and wish each other good day? That is torture and I will not submit to it. Either this way leads to happiness or I will seek a glorious death in battle.

"I am not pious like her. My faith, if I have any, burns faintly and till I met her I never felt its heat. Now I feel it slightly, unless of course it is the fire of love. Then I have been consumed by it, feeling nothing else these weeks and what paradise it was! But where did it go? We never left the road, yet somehow strayed so far neither of us can see it nor knows how to return."

In Auch the ancient capital of Gascony they were drawn to the public square by the beat of a drum where they found a storyteller reciting tales of Tristan and Isolde punctuated with interludes on a flute; in one tale they met because as usual Tristan could not control his desire and after having had their pleasure fell asleep in an orchard where they were discovered by the king her husband and his evil dwarf who had long suspected they'd been meeting secretly but hadn't managed to catch them. While the king went for witnesses so he could have the pair burned at the stake Tristan told Isolde he must depart to save her whereupon to the storyteller's chant they declared their undying love for each other and Tuccio noted that there was no mention of her going with him and wondered why but there was no explanation; later at the inn he again eyed the prostitutes and this time went with one.

DAY TEN. The forest continued unbroken excepting a few openings that offered a brief respite when the caravan entered them but greater despondency when they left for this was a virgin forest of ancient trees with a tall canopy that blocked the sky and little underbrush stunningly beautiful but eventually unnerving as one longed to be done with its sameness and its threat. They were traversing an area of new towns created for foresters farmers and artisans under the protection of a local lord established with a charter of rights and regulations for the purpose of settling the wilderness and clearing the forest the towns architecturally organized around a large central square where merchandise was produced and sold; standing in such a square with the forest pushed back beyond reassuring fields and the town noisy with activity one could feel briefly liberated.

As the caravan relaxed a little and took refreshment and strolled around the square of a town pretty with half-beamed houses and a lovely church Tuccio and Margherita remained tense he staying close to Stoldo she to Piera and Agnoletta such that when they exited through a large stone gate and were quickly ingested by the forest again everyone's mood but theirs quickly reverted as surely as the massive wooden doors swinging closed every night. They alone were relieved and asked about this Tuccio told Stoldo, "I have learned that for the noble lover pain becomes his pleasure."

"Why anyone chooses to be a noble lover I cannot imagine. Do I suffer from love, does Agnoletta? I say let me be ignoble!"

"Have no fear my friend, you have achieved it. As for me, let me be gay!"

> Well is it proven and accepted
> how valiant I am and accomplished...
> A hundred ladies I know who each would want me...
> Ladies I kiss and knights upset.

(Peire Vidal, troubadour)

In the town where they were to spend the night there was a church with a tower which he climbed to get above the forest and there again was the expanse of the Pyrenees like a wall beyond the undulating plain which he stared at long till appearing suddenly beside him was Margherita and they embraced with silent ferocity; later at the inn he drank and watched the prostitutes.

DAY ELEVEN. Seeing that their predicament was neither of their making nor did they seem to hold the solution Tuccio convinced he was going insane survived the day as he rode alone improvising nonsense songs while Margherita walked twenty-two miles without speaking; at the end of this interminable stage was a town called Maubourguet with an inn where he got drunk and fell asleep at the table and an old monastery with a plain drab church where she prayed till she fell asleep without supper beneath a night gone dark with just a sliver of moon.

> Another day, another day
> another day of forest way.

Chapter Twenty-nine

DAY TWELVE. After they'd been on the road several hours the land rose for the first time since entering Gascony a few hundred feet and steeply enough so that the path laced sideways rather than run straight up and down but more significantly for the first time they heard wolves; there was no mistaking that eerie terrifying howl which on first occurrence brought everyone to a halt. The count after waiting continued forward and when the howling was heard again the caravan kept moving because it was not close but for Tuccio who was alone it was different for after he too had stopped in a natural first reaction and then continued he saw a band of wolves cross the road in front of him.

They raced across his path as if in pursuit of something seeming not to notice him so after having paused again he started forward a second time and when he reached the point of crossing he gazed as best he could in the direction they had gone and elsewhere and saw nothing but trees; soon however he thought he heard snarling and then he was sure of it and then he came upon them tearing at the carcass of a large deer so intent on their meal that again they seemed unaware of him or at least uninterested. Concerned that if he continued the wolves having finished might turn upon the caravan he retreated and waited until it grew quiet and when next he reached the spot the carcass lay mostly bones and hide and the wolves were gone.

For a while he advanced without detecting anything but then entering a burnt-out clearing the result of a lightning strike he saw them and they saw him and turned to face him forming a skirmish line like soldiers and growling approached slowly heads low; he watched and dismounted slapped his horse into a trot back to the caravan found a spot to his liking backed by a large tree and drew his weapons sword in the right dagger in the left. His gaze seemed unfocused body relaxed as he waited seemed not to see the unwavering stares of eyes close-set drawing nearer with measured silent steps; they spread out as they drew close Tuccio stock still except his eyes until the moment before they attacked he erupted slashing two of them before they reached him and when a third leapt at him he stabbed it with his knife in the belly and it fell away howling piteously.

After the first bloodletting they backed away the one he'd stabbed lying on its side bleeding howling and whimpering its body trembling and jerking violently; of the two he'd slashed one was badly wounded the other less so but both though bleeding still confronted him with vicious eyes; his own eyes were also vicious now slightly narrowed sometimes focused sometimes not. The two younger wolves that had hesitated the first time were now circling with the others and again he waited and when the older pair attacked he slashed at one and thrust at the other wounding it mortally but the first rebounded and came at him again joined by the two younger ones and one of them leaping closed its jaws on his sword arm. He managed to stab it with his knife twice with rapid thrusts but though it had little fight left it held on growling and jerking its head violently tearing at him as he turned to face the others which paced around him; unable to free his sword arm from the wolf's jaws he feinted with his dagger at one and then another holding them back.

When Stoldo and Nico leapt off their horses and began slashing he turned and thrust his knife through the wolf's neck and then into its side repeatedly until its jaw's grip loosened and released; behind his back he heard the others limp away howling piteously then his mates were around him asking how badly he was hurt inspecting his bleeding arm looking for other wounds. "Are you hurt?" they kept asking but he made no reply only looking at them nodding blankly until Stoldo cried, "Say something, by Jesus!"

"I'm not hurt."

"Your arm is ripped open."

He looked at his arm. "So it is," he said and as Nico began to unlace the bloody leather gauntlet his knees went weak and he fell like a dead body falls and when Margherita saw him she screamed.

As he'd been confronting the wolves the caravan of course

had drawn closer until Stoldo and Nico at the head came within earshot and had raced ahead the others arriving at their pace. Though Margherita had managed to stanch most of the bleeding it was clear he couldn't continue so after his arm had been strapped to his chest and he'd recovered enough to ride the count gave the order to return to the monastery in Maubourguet; but with the need to stop several times when Margherita insisted the pain had become unbearable and once when he became so faint he almost fell off his horse it took more hours to return than it had to arrive at a place no one wanted to pass again. When the count as close to scolding Tuccio as he would come asked why he'd dismounted thereby greatly increasing his danger indeed why he hadn't retreated or at least called for help Tuccio replied that he'd dismounted to save his horse and had called for help by sending him back. "Would you have had me lead the wolves to the caravan?"

"I would have had you save yourself."

FRANCESCO. For some years Francesco had let his intention be known to leave his fortune to the poor which he knew to be the only reliable way to save himself from going to Hell but he had never been able to decide on the best way to effect it. A friar had advised him to endow a local convent the one as it happened to which he belonged while a priest had advised him to leave his estate to the bishop to be administered on behalf of the poor by local clergy such as himself and Francesco went so far as to have a will drawn but Lapo hearing of it tried to convince him not to sign it assuring him he knew it to be more the rule than the exception for fortunes left 'for the poor' to be embezzled by unscrupulous Church administrators or used to pay the debts of the bishop or other prelate and if neither then dissipated through mismanagement. Francesco shrugging said that might be the least objectionable way to handle the issue of usury and cited the case of a merchant whose estate had been opened by the bishop's court (thankfully for him in Florence not Siena) to claims of usury by former borrowers some of whom were members of that very court. "Wouldn't you say the Church is less likely to do that if it is the beneficiary of my largesse?"

"No, because 'the Church' is an abstraction while the judges of a court are not. And if they have not personally benefited from your bequest 'for the poor...'"

"Then what do you suggest?"

"Would it be too much to suggest that, as you are obviously distressed by practices you fear usurious, you cease to practice them?"

"As you well know, I do not knowingly engage in usury. My concern, as you well know, is that some priest or monk will find it in my ledgers nonetheless after I am gone and can no longer defend myself."

"Do you think you can defend yourself against the higher judge?"

"That is why I have had this will drawn. It not only gives to the poor, it creates a separate fund whose purpose is known to my executors though the will doesn't elaborate."

"To recompense any victims of usury or unjust practice."

"Exactly. And it pays for two hundred fifty thousand masses to be said in my memory immediately upon my death for the earliest possible release of my soul from Purgatory."

"Then you do not subscribe to the dictum that Fortune repays the merchant's virtue?"

"Stop toying with me! I will not be a mouse to your cat."

"Forgive me, my friend, if I am more concerned for your eternal welfare than you are yourself. If I may ask, why not three hundred thousand? Or have you a written guarantee that two hundred fifty is sufficient?"

"Then make it three hundred, I will pay!"

"But might it not have to be four hundred?"

"Then what would you have me do?"

"Other than put your house in order while you still can? Let me write you a will that ensures your fortune will benefit the poor."

"And not the Church."

"Exactly. You hesitate. Do you subscribe to the dictum that God in his grace has lent you the goods you enjoy during your worldly pilgrimage and that, like all loans, it must be repaid for the salvation of your soul?"

"You know I do."

"Then it must be repaid, must it not?"

"That is what I have been assured I am doing."

"But you did not come to me. Might that be because you feared what I would say?"

"I am here now, am I not?"

"Then let us rectify this all important matter. You hesitate."

"Let me think about it."

"Think all you like, my friend, it will not assuage the anxiety that is tearing at you."

DAYS THIRTEEN THROUGH SIXTEEN. "I'd like to know what you were thinking."

"You're angry."

"Of course I'm angry."

"Yet you didn't ask me yesterday."

"Seeing how you were suffering I was biting my tongue. But why?" Tuccio had barely moved since having his wounds dressed and being put to bed the previous afternoon indeed Margherita who had installed herself beside him had also barely moved nor had Piera though Margherita had finally been persuaded to go to her own bed to get some sleep whereas Piera refused to leave and had spent the entire night on the stone floor of the dormitory that served as a hospital. She repeated her question but he only shook his head and when pressed gave curt vague replies as he winced from the constant pain with the most she could get his repeated assertion that he'd been defending the caravan a claim the count had disputed and which she doubted; it was not totally implausible that had he turned his horse and galloped back to the group the wolves might have chased him but a small pack menacing an entire caravan in full summer when prey was abundant would have been exceedingly unlikely. "Why didn't you call for help?"

"You were out of earshot."

"Yet two men ran to your aid."

"That was later."

"Why didn't you shout then?"

To that he didn't reply perhaps from exhaustion nor to questions about why he hadn't tried to scare off the wolves though later after he awoke he said it was not easy to frighten a pack of wolves; by late morning his arm swollen and inflamed with infection he was mostly sleeping putting an end to the interrogation. The men visited for the entire caravan was staying at the monastery the count as he had done before having explained their circumstances and stated his intention to make a generous donation and Tuccio's half-dead appearance had helped; his groaning while he slept was hard to bear Margherita gazing at him lovingly her eyes welling with tears more than once and when he writhed in pain she would try to soothe him with caresses and soft murmurings about her love.

Once when he awoke he said he was afflicted by a terrible

memory which had entered his thoughts during the interminable journey back to the monastery when he hadn't been sure from one moment to the next whether he could continue and now had come into his dreams a terrible memory about an execution he had witnessed. The information arrived in disordered fragments but eventually she was able to construct it into a coherent story about the execution of a heretic that had occurred when the *masnada* was in the employ of Siena's war captain who was responsible for security both outside and within the city and had been assigned to police the streets.

The victim was one of the so-called Fraticelli ('Little Brothers') who by taking Saint Francis at his word to repudiate the possession of property by those who pretended to serve Jesus had incurred the wrath of their order and the official Church. This particular friar had come to Siena and according to the inquisition had preached in the public square that Christ the Redeemer possessed no property and that He and his disciples had denounced the taking holding or exchanging of goods; and since he had confessed to the charges it had been ordered by the court that unless he recanted he would be taken to the place of justice where his spirit would be separated from his body.

In the courtyard the vicar general of the bishop told the condemned that he was still free to renounce his errors and return to the Holy Church but he replied that he believed in the poor crucified Christ and that Jesus had showed the way to perfection by possessing nothing; the judge then turned his back and he was seized by guards and roughly pushed outside the gate of the bishop's palace where an angry throng immediately began to spit on him and hurl epithets and mockery and scratch and beat him. When ordered Tuccio and the others mounted for the occasion intervened to escort the condemned but the streets were so jammed they could barely advance and when eventually they reached the square they found it equally packed with shouting shoving crowds so that it was all they could do to get him to the stake and push the mob back to a safe distance. "Save yourself, save yourself," was heard from beyond the circle of horses to which he replied with what remained of his voice, "Save yourselves."

Tuccio watched as he was bound and heard a lone supporter shout before being overwhelmed, "Fra Michele, martyr of Christ, remain firm for soon you will receive the crown." When the fire was started and the flames began to rise the condemned was heard singing the Te Deum and when the fire had burned the cords that bound him he fell dead onto the burning timbers the smell of cooked meat filling the air; the crowd grew quiet and then here and there someone shouted that Fra Michele was a saint but when more than a few had said this others shouted them down saying he was a heretic and the tumult grew louder and more violent until brawls erupted and the *masnada* had to intervene to separate the belligerents.

Fever set in overnight which increased during the day as the wounds festered Tuccio writhing and grimacing unable to move because of the pain and Margherita furious with herself for having slept resolved not to leave his bedside again and changed the poultices herself and cleaned away the pus. Mercifully he slept much of the time though it tore at her to hear him groan when he moved in his sleep and she told Piera his condition was her fault.

"No, you are good."

"Good? I tell you this is my fault. All he wants is to love me. All I want is to love him. We should just love each other and be done with it." She fell silent staring into space then stared at Piera. "I do not know if you were made woman by lover or rapist, but no longer a maid you must understand something of what I express." The girl made no reply. "You're getting plump. Are you looking forward to being a mother?" She looked blank and finally shrugged. "If the father is a rapist, don't think about him. Having a child, even in such a way, is a blessing. Or rather, we will make it a blessing. We'll love the child."

"Yes," she said vaguely.

"You'll see, you'll be a good mother, though a child yourself. Had you been properly betrothed, you'd still have had your first-born at a tender age. Don't worry, we'll raise it together. We'll love it."

"Yes."

Margherita turned back to Tuccio watching him seeing his agony shaking her head her chest heaving and said, "What have I done, what has happened to us?" and again turned to stare at Piera saying, "You are too young to know misery. Look at your life, and yet... A kitten becomes your world. I will get you a litter of kittens. But if I lose Tuccio..." She took her hand and the girl clasped hers and stroked it. "They say he is just a youth and he is just a youth, and I a grown woman, old enough to be his mother. And yet he would have me as a wife, not a mother. And I would have him, but as what, a husband? Such a pairing has never been seen. Yet would I have him, therefore as a lover, therefore would I be an adulteress." Piera shook her head. "What? How not?"

"You love him," she said and Margherita began to cry and she put her arms around her.

"I should fear the torments of Hell, but instead I yearn for his embrace. I cannot lose him this way."

"You will not."

"If he dies, I will too. Let the wolves take me too."

Piera's eyes filled with fear and she began to cry and they put their arms around each other and rocked back and forth.

> O sweet breeze that comes from there
> where my friend sleeps and sojourns and lies,
> of his sweet breath a drink bring me here.
>
> My mouth opens from the great desire that I have for it.

(Troubadour, possibly Raimbaut de Vaqueiras.)

"He looks so young," she said. "I'm used to seeing an old man beside me in bed. How can I think of him as a lover when he looks like a boy? I'm not his lover, I'm his mother. This is not adultery, it's incest. This is all madness, isn't it?" Piera shook her head. "It is. Yesterday I asked him what he was thinking, now I'm asking myself. All this time, trying to make sense of his foolhardy childish ideas. Look at him. A child like you." She wasn't angry but had become a mystery to herself thinking, "How strange is love! All I want right now is to be his mother, to tend his wounds," and aloud said, "My madness has made me miserable."

Did not Heloise write to Abelard, "She is the most unhappy who was first the most happy?" Did not Francesca da Rimini tell Dante much the same in *Inferno* Canto 5?

She thought Tuccio was asleep but he'd overheard and said, "Let us die together."

She was startled and several replies came and went unspoken until she said, "To do that is to go to Hell."

"We are there already," he said.

That night he sank into delirium in his sleep moaning and exclaiming fragmentary phrases that could not be fully deciphered but clearly indicated turmoil which made it impossible for Margherita to sleep properly even if she could have on the floor with other patients making disturbing noises and attending monks coming and going through the night so that when dawn arrived she was exhausted and distraught. She implored Piera and Agnoletta to go to church to beseech the Virgin Mother to save Tuccio she herself being too frightened to leave his side even for a moment and they went with reluctance Piera because she didn't want to leave her Agnoletta because she feared she might have to confess; but when they returned Agnoletta urged her to go too to add her prayers to theirs and Piera assured her she knew the Queen of Heaven was listening because as she was praying she felt her touch.

In the austere grey abbey church Margherita immediately fell to her knees praying and sobbing and when she could beg no longer found a priest and confessed to having seduced a boy and driven him to ruin; upon returning Agnoletta informed her he was raving about the wolf attack and sure enough she heard 'howl' in a phrase more of sounds than words followed by similar outbursts in a pained suffering voice. 'Must sacrifice,' she heard but then much mumbling sometimes barely audible sometimes shouted and then, 'Merit... Noble, a noble born...' followed by more about sacrifice and then there was the word 'heretic' and reference to the fire and the smell and again the smell; briefly he became quiet though with tortured face then exclaimed, 'A saint!' though it might have been more a question and then, 'the Church...' followed by 'love,' which she wasn't sure she had heard correctly until he repeated it.

"Tuccio," she whispered leaning in closely, "my love, my friend, please don't worry, this is all my fault but we'll..." She so wanted to caress him but feared the slightest touch might startle him which would be extremely painful with his arm so inflamed so what came instead were piteous moans and sobbing, "My love, my love..."

"Prove," he seemed to reply, "must prove... I too must..."

"Can you hear me, dearest one? You are so brave. You are my knight. You will get better and I will love you as a woman should."

It seemed he did hear for he said, "To run away, childish, coward..."

"A coward? Not you, not you, you didn't run away."

"Run away... Foolish."

She realized he wasn't talking about running away from the wolves but about asking her to run away with him and as she cried she assured him they would be together always for he was her knight and she his lady and their love would forge a way through every obstacle and they would lie in each other's arms like proper lovers the way the old songs said in a meadow beside a stream under a blue sky or all night long in a castle chamber with a lookout to warn them when the *gilos* the jealous husband approached.

> May God the discerning...
> wish, if it please Him, that I and my lady lie together
> ...that her beautiful body, kissing, smiling, [I] uncover
> and that I admire it...

(Arnaut Daniel, troubadour)

When Stoldo arrived she told him Tuccio had been raving about the wolf attack seeming to confuse it with an execution the *masnada* had attended in Siena and asked, "Did something happen there?"

"We watched a man get roasted to death. The fire was as close as that bed there. Have you ever enjoyed that pleasure? The crowd seemed to love it."

"It must have been terrible."

"It is not the dying. We are men of arms after all. I think you know he decapitated one of the brigands in that godforsaken village."

"I didn't know."

"Lopped off his head. He knew better than to put himself at the mercy of a pack of wolves. Why do you think he did that?" As her eyes filled with tears he stared at her with hostile eyes saying, "When a man loves a woman she owes him nothing, but when she professes to return his love... Did he tell you he had a brother who died of fever? He is my brother for I love him as one, and if you have killed him..."

"If I have killed him I will give my own life in expiation because the moment he is gone is the moment I no longer wish to breathe."

"If he were to lose his life I would take yours."

"You would take it with my gratitude, for I will not live in a world that no longer shines on him."

They stared at each other chests heaving his eyes burning hers weeping and for a long time neither spoke until when the heaving settled he said, "Do you have any idea how deeply he loves you? I have tried to talk him out of it, we all have, the count too, but how do you talk a youth out of such love?"

"I do know," she said quietly. "I knew it before this. We have tried to find a path for our love. You may know, perhaps better than he, how difficult that is."

"Difficult? Let me simplify it for you, lady."

> Well should man lady blame
> when too much [she] goes her friend delaying
> for long talk of love
> is great boredom and on a par with deceit.

(Bernart de Ventadorn, troubadour)

"I assure you it has not been boring nor have I been deceitful. I have loved him openly."

"You have openly behaved like a fool and played him for a fool, but you have not loved him. We all await it, lady. Had you given him what he has earned, he would not be lying here."

When she asked what it was that so disturbed Tuccio if it was not the execution itself he replied, "They cruelly murdered a man because he had the temerity to denounce their obscene hypocrisy. If there is justice in the next world like they say then they too will feel the licking of the flames. It was our worst day, no one speaks of it."

By night she was so distraught Agnoletta practically pulled her to her bed where she wrestled with the sleep of the exhausted guilty and when she awoke and saw daylight rushed to his side without washing or brushing her hair; he was still delirious and burning with fever and when a monk arrived in priest's robes and displayed a candle a crucifix and a vial she fainted. It did no good to reassure her that the sacrament of extreme unction could give health to the body as it did to the soul and was thus not to be taken as a sign of imminent death so while he spread a clean white cloth and arranged his spiritual tools she wept uncontrollably; eventually she was composed enough to join the others in prayer as he requested though clasping her hands not gently but frantically and her prayer was more sobbing than words. For the anointing with oil she gently uncovered his body and gently recovered it for the final blessing after which the monk tried to console her but she was inconsolable barely able to stand and not firmly in her right mind terrified that because he was unconscious he had received only conditional absolution.

One by one the men present both guards and porters came to the bed while the monk as he exited whispered to the count that he would return later to see if he could bring some comfort to 'the youth's mother' and the count chuckled wryly to himself as he turned his eyes on Margherita trying to decide whether she deserved compassion for all the men again regarded her with barely disguised hostility and she wasn't too distracted to feel it. There had been talk that if Tuccio were to die they would refuse to continue to Compostela even the count considering this despite having given his word in view of the greatly altered circumstances and taking the *fattore* to be more or less truthful in his claim that Francesco never expected his wife to go all the way. At Tuccio's bedside they treated her as though she were not there and in her grief she made no protest for she was consumed with the fear that either the only man she ever loved was about to die or that he would recover and blame her like the others indeed as she did herself and withdraw his love.

> But I so fear your anger
> totally am I intimidated by it.
> For you I suffer pain and mistreatment
> and my body [is] tormented.
> At night, when I lie in my bed,
> I am many times awakened.

(Raimbaut de Vaqueiras, troubadour)

FRANCESCO. In the *Divine Comedy* Dante gives special significance to the midpoint of each part whereby in *Purgatorio* it's the so-called discourse on love in which he presents his theory of love as the cause of all sin as well as virtue which forms the theoretical basis of the poem's over-arching structure; in *Paradiso* it's a prophecy about his forced exile from Florence the seminal event in his life and in *Inferno* it's the punishment of crimes against nature the most severe of which is usury. Among those who attended the martyrdom of the upstart Franciscan Fra Michele was Francesco di Marco who like many in the crowd was curious to know whether the man would recant before it was too late and though he was not close enough to watch the flames burn the flesh he was close enough to smell it; unlike most others he had a special interest in the outcome and when the man remained recalcitrant to the end actually singing at his own immolation it disturbed him profoundly.

In the immediate aftermath when those who had not come to blows were discussing the event he heard it said that as the condemned was bound to the stake and people had shouted for him to repent he had replied, "Repent yourselves. Repent your usury, your false commerce, your gambling, your fornication." It shook him to his core as nothing else had that the man believed in their evil so strongly that he preferred to die horribly rather than withdraw his condemnation; and then no sooner was he dead than people started thinking he must have been a saint because he had held fast his convictions rather than save himself.

He knew of a trial of usurers in nearby Pistoia which had resulted in at least one being literally branded as a heretic on his chest and thigh in the form of the cross while elsewhere merchants were described as blasphemers and liars even drinkers and whoremongers. In more than one city he had heard of lenders being excluded from the sacraments and denied burial in sacred ground but against all this he had his standard defense that he was not one of those despicable usurers whose thinly disguised loans extorted rates as high as twenty thirty even fifty percent a defense he now feared had been ripped away and as the crowd dispersed he worried that someone would point to him since his occupation was easily identifiable by his dress.

In his mind he saw a rampaging soldier bent on rape tearing the clothes from a helpless victim he even saw a bloodthirsty pack of wolves tear a man to pieces but such was his distress that he wasn't sure whether he was the victim or the marauder. Assailed by such fevered thoughts he fled the square but couldn't bring himself to return to the warehouse where secretaries awaited the resumption of letters dictated to partners suppliers and customers nor to his other warehouses and workshops where employees were making his fortune nor to his house where his wife would certainly wonder what was wrong that he had come home so early so he paced the streets as though on an urgent errand or deep in thought not greeting anyone. Eventually he forced himself to his desk but dismissed the secretaries and stood staring at the wall unable to stop wondering whether Fra Michele had survived long enough to smell himself.

Chapter Thirty

Six weeks after Bob joined the one hundred fifty-seven year old Wall Street investment bank Lehman Brothers two of its major providers of short-term financing both large money market funds announced that they would no longer be doing business with the firm given that it was financing its MBS assets on a very leveraged basis with a lot of short-term financing (just as Bob's old firm had done) and Bob could not help but be disturbed whether or not he was worried. To him it was inconceivable that this firm could go the way of the other even as he admitted he had found that firm's collapse inconceivable; and while he was smart enough to acknowledge that his ability to conceive an event made no difference in terms of whether or not it would actually occur unfortunately when he evaluated the situation he was unable to distinguish between a sanguine risk assessment and a failure of imagination. Soon afterward news leaked that the Secretary of the Treasury and the president of the New York Federal Reserve Bank had arranged for the firm's CEO to talk to his counterpart at Bank of America about the possibility of being acquired but the talks went nowhere because he was not interested in being acquired and Bob was unable to decide whether that was good news or bad.

Mortgage-backed securities he reminded himself were based on mortgages and while more and more of the mortgages were substandard they were being made by hundreds and hundreds probably thousands of lenders all over the country to millions of homeowners; and even if the incentive of issuers to maintain high lending standards had declined as the transfer of liability for loan losses to securities firms had become so easy and lucrative the borrowers who pledged their homes would not have signed unless they were confident of their ability to make the payments. The reasonable conclusion then if one believed that economic actors in large numbers tended toward rationality was that the mortgage business was still sound; and he knew the MBS business was sound therefore the only question was whether there was a prudent limit to leverage and there again he had to believe that the thousands and thousands of highly trained experts on Wall Street and sophisticated high net worth investors could not all be wrong.

Of course he knew in fact was exquisitely aware that concerns had been raised which had resulted in credit rating downgrades lower MBS prices tougher scrutiny of collateral and all the rest the whole point of those actions having been to maintain the integrity and stability of the business so again the reasonable conclusion was that the market was still sound and not the opposite. His CEO then, he reasoned, had probably acted in the best interests of Lehman's stakeholders not just his own desire to keep his job when he had declined to deliver his firm to a competitor at a time when the stock price had been battered in the market because the industry was going through a period of reassessment. Nonetheless Bob knew this didn't change the fact that what was happening was happening and therefore he couldn't avoid the question of whether he had erred in trying to get rehired as quickly as possible rather than seek to reposition himself on the Street; for he had taken the easier path of selling his inside information on his old firm's MBS business rather than the one he always claimed he could take but recognized as more difficult which was to bring his toolkit of skills to a different market. That however would have entailed learning a new business and thus likely a cut in rank if not in pay and he still believed he was on the best path where he had the most experience and something of a reputation and was thus most valuable to an employer precisely because he'd be most successful on the job.

As before he made no mention of these developments but even exploratory merger talks made the news when the parties were major financial institutions so Tiffany saw it and then wondered why he wasn't saying anything; it was after she'd asked three times if there was anything new at the office that he said, "Should there be anything new at the office?"

"I guess I'm curious why you don't mention that your firm might be in play as a takeover candidate."

"Because it's not?" As he watched she waited nodding meaninglessly until after denying that there was a situation then minimizing the situation he admitted that he was in the same situation now he'd been in a few months earlier except with three to four times the exposure to overnight borrowing saying, "We owe two hundred bil just in repos. Do you think I screwed up?"

She shook her head immediately and then there was a long pause before she said, "Well obviously you can't leave now."

"No one would hire me, they'd assume there was some problem and I was it."

"So in a way there's no point talking about it."

"You're the one who asked, remember? I sure didn't ask for this."

"You don't have to shout. I just thought..."

"You want me to say I screwed up?"

"I didn't say that."

"You haven't said anything!"

"I guess I just wanted to know if you're concerned. Come on, you'll wake Kiley."

"Of course I'm concerned, I'm not an idiot. You think if I knew when I took the job what I know now... It's unbelievable, really, I'm barely on board before..." Nonetheless he said he wasn't worried because as he put it, "How could everybody be wrong?"

"So you don't see the market crashing."

"Since when did you become so averse to risk?"

"I'm not averse to risk. I take big risks for a living. But what I am averse to is being blindsided by something I should have seen coming, so that's why I'd like to hear from you that your confidence is still intact."

"My confidence is still intact. How's yours?"

"If you're okay, I'm okay."

From her professional distance it seemed that serious problems were festering like unattended wounds on Wall Street but by inclination and training that inherent risk indicated opportunity for above-average investment returns and in that case the problems themselves need not signal the need for change as long as the infection didn't become something more serious. Thus she continued to trust her husband's judgment but when it came to pilgrimage which had come to embrace the entirety of her own preoccupations there seemed much less clarity indeed the constant menace of confusion. With confusion came doubt with doubt trepidation and so confronted with forty-one remaining stages she felt overwhelmed which was why she hadn't completed a single one in the weeks since her cast had been removed; but after the last rendezvous with her lover who had again managed to inspire her she determined to complete the task she had assigned herself to reach Compostela after a thousand-mile journey alone largely on foot and the rest using her feet to power herself.

The problem however which if not a festering wound was a bad bruise (indeed had it not been a broken arm?) was that determination was all she had left and thus even inspired she was bereft of willpower and could not bring herself to complete a stage either to walk outside or bike in the basement even though the latter she kept telling herself could be completed in a single hour since it was a tiny stage of only nine point three miles. From there she told herself it was only one stage more to Lescar from where she could look straight out from its elevation to the wall of mountain she would then surmount in four stages four stages that in reality were stunningly beautiful and only the last really difficult; but instead of doing a stage she took Kiley to the Short Hills Mall. That evening however filled with guilt and shame after putting Kiley to bed she went to the basement and an hour later felt stupid to have made an ordeal out of such a trivial stage in fact after starting upstairs she returned to the bike and rode to Lescar all of twelve point four miles more and went upstairs feeling triumphant if silly and told Bob he was wrong to think her car accident was a signal that it was time to end the pilgrimage saying, "You see, my head is still in the game."

Nonetheless she wrote in her next blog post, *People ask me, 'Do you really believe the apostle James is buried in Spain when the Bible tells us he was martyred in Jerusalem?' To me that misses the point. Maybe fervent Christians believe it or at least don't dispute it, but I bet a lot of pilgrims are like me and just don't care. Do I think James' disciples could have put his body on a boat in the Holy Land which ended up safely without a rudder on the north Atlantic Coast of Spain? No. Do I think that some eight hundred years later a hermit was advised by angels that the tomb of Saint James was near his hermitage and not long afterward a group of local faithful saw the exact location indicated by the light of a star? No. Do I think the local bishop, having seen the same strange nocturnal light, ordered a dig that unearthed the buried tomb and was (somehow) able to certify that it was in fact that of Saint James? No again.*

But to me the attraction of Compostela has nothing to do with any of that. To me its attraction is that for twelve centuries large numbers of people have walked there, most over long distances in all weather in the most primitive of conditions for the fundamental purpose of becoming better, whatever that might mean in each particular case. Yes, there were and still are other reasons to go, the sheer fun of the adventure for one, but that doesn't diminish the primitive appeal of the place and the idea and the activity.

For me, unable to really go to Arles and walk for two and a half months—there's no way my profession would ever allow that—it has been a virtual pilgrimage, walking around where I live, around New Jersey, and even in my basement, a far cry from the real thing, and yet in my mind and in my heart I have sincerely tried to make it as real as possible. I won't lie to you, I didn't always succeed, in fact I may have failed more than I succeeded. It's the moments of success you cherish. The moments of insight. The moments when what you're doing suddenly feels right.

I have no intention of giving up on my pilgrimage. No way. But the time has come to end this blog, which has served its purpose and maybe provided something helpful to you. That's my hope, anyway. A weird thing about pilgrimage is that we mainly do it alone, and in a way every pilgrim is alone on the Way whether or not they're literally by themselves, yet in a very real way it's a communal activity.

What she didn't say was that she had exhausted her ability to say anything meaningful and furthermore the blog had never attracted any following with few 'hits' and all of one comment; that last she found the most painful aspect of the whole undertaking because it seemed almost cruel. When she had walked outside after a winter in her basement and in her absorbing introspection gotten hit by a car her blog post talked about solitude but it also reported the accident making clear that it had really happened while pretending she'd been near Maubourguet France approaching the foothills of the Pyrenees. She had even gone so far as to imagine that had it happened in the Middle Ages she would have been taken to the monastery there and wondered what medical care or treatment might have been provided and thus (she believed) had made something interesting out of her rather banal experience; at the same time though she felt there was a way in which her experience had not been banal at all that rather it had been in a way the most important moment of her pilgrimage so far. She had also not avoided telling how anxious she'd been waiting for treatment in the emergency room with her arm badly swollen and discolored and the pain pretty intense and not knowing how bad it was and for all these reasons was shocked when the post received not a single comment.

"Surely..." she thought and in that moment realized that no

one cared about her blog except her and maybe the professor that all this time she'd been talking to herself entertaining herself only and she found that that was not sufficient and as a result she lacked the will to continue in fact she felt embarrassed even humiliated and wished she could expunge the entire blog; what bothered her most was that she had identified herself in each post as executive director of the Foundation for Pilgrim Studies. When she saw the professor waiting for her patiently in the parking lot not having seen her arrive she threw herself into his arms and kissed him in a way that reminded both of them of the first time she had done that of how shocked they had both been how good it had felt; and now she held him tightly and said, "I can't believe how much I missed you. Why do I need you so much?" In the room she turned immediately and started unbuttoning his shirt and not long after screamed so loudly the professor said that if the hotel didn't know before what they were doing there they certainly knew now; but he knew there was more happening than pursuit of pleasure and worried.

She had already apologized by email for her 'unforgivable attack' at their last rendezvous and he had of course forgiven her while apologizing for any excessive behavior of his own but nonetheless she returned to the subject saying she had re-read the *Pilgrim Guide* and been reminded that all it claimed for the four routes was, "There are four roads which, leading to Santiago, converge into one near Puente la Reina in Spanish territory." Thus, she said, the author didn't claim that there were only four pilgrim routes in France or even that these were the main ones let alone official in some sense and the professor not wishing to delve into all the inferences that could and had been drawn from such a simple pronouncement kept quiet until she asked why he didn't speak.

Whatever else might be said, he replied, the four routes were strategically arrayed to catch travelers from a very large portion of France and well beyond and made substantial use of Roman highways and almost certainly were well used for all travel purposes hence traditional at least in that sense. Tiffany added that having herself made a little study of the Via Tolosana she had found only two possible routes from Italy namely over the Alps and along the coast both Roman roads and both if one was en route to Toulouse leading to Arles. "From Arles to Montpellier there is only one possible route, again a Roman road. From Montpellier to Toulouse, there are two possible routes, one that seems more likely to me beneath the Haut Languedoc, the other via Narbonne across the semi-desert to Carcassonne, both probably Roman roads. Once at Toulouse the route is more or less certain all the way over the Pyrenees and across Spain, and again the Pyrenean route was a Roman road. So I don't see much opportunity for debate over this route at least. But the issue of starting points is entirely different. Would a pilgrim who happened to live near Montpellier go first to Arles so as to start at the beginning?"

"It seems doubtful, doesn't it."

"Highly doubtful. So I think you're right to try to get to the bottom of this. It took me a long time to understand but I finally did. I'm so sorry, Mark."

He tried to make a joke out of it saying she could never be as sorry as he was for getting into the controversy in the first place and to change the subject asked if she had brought photos as agreed with the result that with a combination of gaiety and seriousness they were soon showing each other their families for she had brought a whole stack of photos of Kiley going back to when she was an infant and he pored over each of them.

"It's okay, you don't have to... I just grabbed what I had."

"I'm enjoying this. Your daughter, after all. She looks like you."

"Now I can't say how beautiful she is."

"Yes you can. She is beautiful, like her mother. Is she as cute as she seems?"

"Totally cute. She can be a handful too."

"Wait till she's a teenager."

When a photo of Bob appeared she said, "I know I said I'd leave him out but it seemed weird to deliberately exclude him, so..."

"It's fine." He took the photo and studied it.

"What are you...?"

He shrugged. "I guess I'm checking out my competition."

"It's not competition."

"I know that, that was silly. He seems like a nice guy."

"He is a nice guy."

Unlike her he had a proper photo album and when the pictures of Jessica appeared Tiffany said, "She was pretty. She looks happy. It's not just a camera smile."

"Yes to both," he said. "She had quite an aura about her. I haven't looked at these in a while."

"I like the way you look at them."

"How do I look at them?"

"Like you still love her. It's okay, you've made no secret of it."

"You're okay with that?"

"Absolutely."

"Even if that means..."

"That you could never love me like you loved her? Yes."

"I don't really know, it may just take time."

"I wouldn't want you ever to love her less so you could love me more."

"Really?"

"With her it was crazy love, I think that's wonderful. She was so lucky, and I wouldn't ever..."

"I'm kind of crazy about you too."

"Let me tell you something. Don't you think I feel... I don't know what the word is... that after ten years of not being able to love any woman, you..."

"Sometimes I've worried that part of me was buried with Jess."

"And I love you for that."

"You're not hurt?"

"A little jealous, maybe. Not hurt."

"You would tell me how you really feel, correct? See, that face you just made, that's what concerns me."

"I'll tell you how I really feel, okay? Seeing how much you still love Jessie, it's kind of thrilling."

"Thrilling?"

"It kind of turns me on. Maybe men can't get that, but trust me, it makes you more attractive to women, not less."

"Wow."

"When you make love to me so gently, I can feel your passion and for a brief time I can believe that I've become her."

"You might be right about that."

"And I'll bet you anything those women you picked up at conferences, it turned them on too."

He looked doubtful. "I never..."

"You didn't have to. They could pick up on it." They fell silent and held hands and when they turned back to the photos and a good recent one of his son appeared she said, "Louis is a good-looking guy."

"Don't make me jealous of my own son, okay?"

"Don't be ridiculous. Trade you in for a guy as good as you but hunky and half your age?"

"Yeah, and, what, thirteen years younger than you, so be careful what you say."

"Let's talk about Morgan, because she looks like a real firecracker."

"She is."

"I'd love to meet her. She's as bright as you, right? I can tell. Both of them."

"I'm very proud of them. They're doing well."

"Is Morgan rebellious?"

"She's not contrary for its own sake, but she's definitely exploring."

"Boyfriend?"

"Several. I think she tries them on for size. This one's not enough this, that one's not enough that."

"Good for her."

"Yeah?"

"Sure. She doesn't let them own her."

It was a beautiful summer day and both wanting to get out of the room they found a park online that wasn't too far away and strolled hand in hand commenting on this and that and nothing at all as though they were a normal couple and not on a tight schedule; it was while they were sitting on a bench watching some toddlers play his arm around her leaning over from time to time to kiss her that she told him she wanted to 'suspend' the announcement of the third fellowship and in reply to his controlled surprise said she wasn't sure what she wanted to do with the foundation.

"You've got all of August to decide."

"I don't want you to work for nothing."

"I don't mind. Or do you mean you've actually decided and you're letting me down gently."

"I really haven't decided. It's no secret I'm confused about my pilgrimage."

"You've put a lot of work into this. May I ask if the cost is a consideration? Because if it is... If you do decide to go ahead, we'd need to be ready. So why don't I..."

"You've done so much work already. I feel terrible as it is."

"Don't, please."

"Why shouldn't I feel terrible?"

"Because I want you to be happy."

"At this point the foundation is as much yours as mine. I would hate to take it away from you."

"You've got a month to decide. If it's the money, that gives us a bit of time to—" Seeing her shake her head he fell silent.

"A month from now we'll be together again and I couldn't bear to look at your face after you'd done all the work and tell you I'm pulling the announcement at the last minute. No, Mark, I think it's better this way. If necessary the announcement can appear a few weeks later, we've got a much longer application period now."

"It's true, it's a self-imposed deadline. Do you want to talk about this?" She shrugged in a way that indicated assent so he waited for her to begin.

"Is there any point at which virtual pilgrimage becomes so inauthentic as to be a sham?"

"I don't think I know how to answer that. It sounds like you think you're there."

"Air conditioning, Mark. I mean, come on. You know, you say, 'Well, I can't go to France so I'll walk around New Jersey.' And then you say, 'It's too boring to walk around New Jersey and I don't have time anyway, so why not walk on a treadmill?' And then you say, 'Well, then, why not an exercise bike?' And I did a lot of stages that way and wrote about it as though I was, you know, crossing France. So I go back outside... but then it's hot out and I'm short on time, so back to the bike. And it's air conditioned, and when I get done it's straight to the shower. I mean, where does it end? Does any of this matter?"

"Maybe the answer is that it matters if you say it matters."

"What kind of answer is that?"

"A poor one, no doubt. If you're asking me for a rule, maybe the rule is a pilgrimage is where you go to Arles and walk to Compostela. But that's out of the question, so maybe an alternative rule is you do the best you can. But now you're really on your own."

"That's for sure."

"That seems kind of brave to me."

"Unless it's just an easy way out."

"If there's one feeling you've conveyed about your pilgrimage, it's that it's been anything but easy."

"I don't know, Mark. I can hardly claim... Other than getting hit by a car..."

"Why assume pilgrimage has to involve suffering or be an ordeal? What would you say if you learned that some pilgrims sang and danced the whole way?"

She nodded and said, "Every time I stumble, you pick me up. Still, Mark, air conditioning?"

"Then that's your answer. No more air conditioning." She nodded again and he told himself, "She knew she was going to tell me this all the while we were making love and looking at pictures," and said, "I could walk with you if you want."

She studied him considering his offer and said, "That's a tempting offer, but I think we both know I have to do this alone. Though if you ask me why, I'll tell you I don't know."

"Are we okay?"

"It's not easy to commit adultery without guilt." They sat in silence discreetly checking their watches. "It's pretty here."

"It is, isn't it."

A pigeon landed nearby and they watched it bob its head and she told herself, "Of course I could continue funding the foundation and let Mark run it. He's practically running it now. But that feels like buying his love." He told himself, "The last thing I'd want is for her to keep putting up the money just to please me. But if we could find other donors..." She told herself, "If we were to seek other funding, my continued support would be essential. Without that..." She told him she was worried that the foundation could come between them and asked how he would feel if she continued funding it but withdrew from direct involvement; he replied that he wouldn't want her to feel she had to do that and suggested the possibility of having the foundation continue without her. "It would always be your achievement. You were the founder."

"I really don't know what I'll do at this point."

"That's okay. Whatever you decide. It's just, if you want it to continue in some form..."

"We would need to plan, of course."

"So..."

"Don't do anything for the moment. Give me a little time."

He thought, "It might be possible to subsume our program under the aegis of a larger foundation, but we'd have to come with funding." She thought, "Regarding funding, who better than me to identify potential donors?"

When the time came to leave and they were returning to the hotel he said, "I read your last blog post. It seemed somewhat sad."

"You're probably the only person who could see that. It served its purpose. It was time to let it go."

"Nonetheless..."

"Not everything works out."

"I know you didn't write about it, but I'm wondering if you had a chance to find out what there is to see in Lescar," and when she shook her head he told her where to find an envelope in his bag which contained photographs he had printed off a website of mosaics in the church there and she viewed them with increasing interest. "I thought you'd like them. I thought they were wonderful. So playful and, interestingly, not sacred imagery at all, and yet it's a church. In fact it's arguably the holiest part of the church, at the eastern end, behind the altar from the point of view of the congregation, but in fact in front of it. No doubt symbolic, though it's not obvious what's symbolized. If you like, I could forward them to a colleague who's an expert in medieval iconography. I have you to thank for discovering these, by the way, I had no idea they existed. Which seems odd in retrospect, since they're clearly important."

She told herself, "He knew he was going to tell me this all the while we were making love and looking at pictures," and asked if this was meant to encourage her.

"Does it encourage you?"

"Do you want me to be encouraged?"

"I don't want you to be sad."

"I'm not sad. I'm not a sad person. What I lack right now is what these mosaics have, exuberance. I want to get it back."

"I can't help feeling your uncertainty about the foundation is related to that."

"Of course it's related to that. But I don't want to talk about it now, if that's okay. Wouldn't it be great if we were driving to Lescar right now instead of the hotel?"

"I don't know, the hotel has certain advantages," he said and touched her leg.

As they were saying goodbye she told him about Bob's job situation which she said was a concern for both of them though they weren't really worried. "Markets do this from time to time. Did you just shake your head?"

"This world the two of you exist in. People think my world is arcane."

"Your world is arcane."

"Not yours?" He told her he couldn't help thinking about what she had written in her blog about the story of Saint James. "It's amazing what people are willing to believe, isn't it? You're absolutely right, of course, it seems incredible to us, at least to many of us, that people could have believed in those miracles. But don't we have our own miracles?"

"Are we still talking about Bob?"

"I'm talking about these investments he works with. I'm saying the content of miracles has changed but clearly not our willingness to believe in them."

"I'm afraid you've lost me, professor. What miracles?"

"I'm sorry, I shouldn't have said that. Obviously I'm way out of my depth when it comes to banking and all that. I guess I'm saying that, to me at least, it looks like in his world of mortgage securities, the whole operation seems based on belief and faith."

"I think you're referring to the laws of economics."

"Maybe I am. Like I say, I have no idea what I'm talking about. But the credit ratings, for example. From what you've told me, they seem to be based on little more than belief and faith."

"Okay, I see what you're saying. But I still don't get the miracle part."

"Never mind, it was a silly remark. Not that they are miracles, but that people believe miraculous things can happen. In this case, investors. Anyway, I hope it works out for Bob."

Chapter Thirty-one

DAY SEVENTEEN. Tuccio awoke in the morning drenched in sweat weak and pale with his arm still exceedingly tender but with clear eyes and he ate for the first time in days; sobbing and laughing Margherita fed him from her own hand then rushed to church to thank God and the Mother of God and the apostle James and Saint Martin to whom the church was dedicated then rushed back to make sure she hadn't been dreaming and found him asleep and when Piera said he was very weak she replied laughing, "I know."

He asked if she would read from the book she had brought on pilgrimage, "The one you were reading when I fell in love with you."

"Then you're not angry with me?"

"Why should I be angry?"

"Everyone else is."

"The *lauzengiers*. You should not expect otherwise."

"You should be angry because what happened is my fault."

"No. Everyone now knows how much I love you."

"Please tell me that is not why you did it!"

"It is not."

"When you were delirious the wolves seemed to harry you all over again."

"In my nightmares I heard much howling which filled me with dread and I couldn't get away from it. I have never heard anything so terrible." She whispered that while he'd been delirious she had come to a decision and suggestively put a hand on his leg but to her shocked surprise he shook his head and replied quietly, "No one reproaches a man for plucking the love of a lady if he can. His ardor elevates his merit, but of course it is not the same for her and you must not ruin yourself on my account."

"Was it not you who suggested that if we are sinners we might as well sin?"

"That is not the only foolish statement I have made. That I am a sinner is obvious and like all sinners I am weak. But I would not succumb to weakness," and he reminded her that thanks to her he too was on pilgrimage.

"You do not wish to lie with me?" she whispered and again touched his thigh.

He took her hand and kissed it and whispered, "You know what your touch does to me."

"Then let me touch you. I'll draw the curtains."

"And draw attention. Don't you see, we cannot."

"You are right, we must wait till we are away from here."

"Mita, if we forsake the dream of fine love, what are we?"

"Let us not forsake it."

He sighed. "You are a wonder, Mita. Noble, despite the tawdriness of the life to which your merchant husband has you yoked."

"Has? Rather had."

"For us there can be no life together. We are caught in a predicament of our own making, or rather Love has sprung a trap and we are its prey. There is no possible escape."

"I refuse to believe that."

"Me too. Yet it is so." They stared at each other. "Do you see now what I am saying?"

"You are saying that the same joy that uplifts us is a blow that slays us."

"Yes. The same stab of love that gives so much pleasure does waste our flesh whose bodies will thin." (Jaufré Rudel de Blaye, troubadour)

"I don't think I have ever been so miserable."

DAY EIGHTEEN. When reading from Saint Brigid's *Revelations* failed to console them he insisted on hobbling outside with his bad arm immobilized against his chest to feel the sun and escape the hospital's foul air but it required all his strength indeed he would have collapsed had she not supported him and he complained, "I wish we could see the mountains."

"I'm sure we could from the bell tower. When you recover your strength we will."

"Let us imagine them since we know they are there. And we

will soon be there."

"You wish to continue."

"I will get you to Compostela, Mita. That is the least I can do for you."

"You have done so much for me."

"I have done nothing but ruin your life."

"Do you really have no idea of the riches you have given me?"

"I have failed you."

"If anyone has failed, it is me."

"Then we have both failed."

"You are not yourself. When you are strong again you will not think that way."

Alas for our lovers! How thin love has made them!

The count arriving politely asked Margherita if he could speak privately with Tuccio and sitting beside him against the wall of the church repeated what he had told him earlier that his liaison with the master's wife did not displease him or any of the men for no one liked the master and would be happy to see horns put on his head but added, "It seems however that for reasons known only to you, instead of bedding the woman you have fallen in love with her, a kind of love that abjures pleasure in favor of intense suffering." He spoke of the pain it caused him as well as Stoldo and the others to see him suffer. "And for what? I know this idea of refined love has gripped you like irons, but I too have heard the songs and it seems to me that in the intensity of misguided youth you have neglected an essential element in such love which is its pleasure. The suffering must be sweet. If it were nothing but pain and sorrow, only the insane would pursue it. I will confess I have never experienced this love. I would have doubted its existence had I not seen you find it. But it seems clear to me that what once you found you since lost. This is not that of which the poets sing. This is not even holy abstinence. It is self-destruction. You may speak if you wish."

"*Signore*, I have nothing to say."

Changing his tone he said that he was not yet so old that he could not recall what it was like to be young and so he understood how a woman could loom so large before one's eyes that one could see nothing else. "That is why I ask you, if you love me at all, to believe me when I tell you that this is not the end of your life. You have a long road ahead of you. Many things will happen, you will meet many people."

"Other women, you mean," interrupted Tuccio. "You mean to tell me there will be others."

"I do not say that, because I know you could not believe me if I did. I say to you that this love with this woman is impossible. Not difficult, not dangerous, impossible. It is not an act of prowess. One cannot jump off a cliff and survive. This is such a cliff."

"Tristano did."

"Are you Tristano? Is this a romance or your life?" Tuccio said nothing. "When you see that, when you understand it, you will know what you must do. That will be difficult but you are nothing if not brave. Be brave now. Let us see real prowess, not foolhardy acts."

He had put an affectionate hand on him and risen when Tuccio said, "And if I cannot do as you recommend?"

He stared considered his words. "Cannot? I don't think I have ever heard you use that word."

Tuccio stared back not with insolence but uncertainty finally saying, "You have been a second father to me. The love and gratitude I bear toward you and the others... I do not wish to hurt anyone..."

"Then why do you hurt yourself?"

Sighing deeply he repeated, "I do not wish to hurt anyone. And so I ask you, son to father, if I cannot have your blessing, may I at least... No, that's not it. I know we are doomed. I..."

"If it is noble to die for love—and frankly this happens only in romances but never mind—if it is noble to die for love, it is also noble to... Now I too have gotten lost in my own words." He returned to his place on the ground and the two felt the scene and the day's heat. "You mean to see her in Siena?" When Tuccio shrugged he sighed deeply.

"The prospect of longing for her every moment while knowing she is suffering under the thumb of that..."

"Guarding caravans is not a knight's calling and my hope is that there will be more suitable opportunities by the time we return."

"But the others worry."

"If I cannot find other employment..."

"The merchant will hire others and everyone will be out of work, all because of me."

"Are they wrong to worry?"

"What I do not understand is how I got to this intolerable

place. But, no matter, I will find a way to fight my way out of it."

"As it would be futile to order you to drop her, let me suggest something far easier and more pleasant, to do with her what you surely wish to do and which she no doubt wishes too."

"The poets condone it, recommend it even, but the Church does not."

"The same Church that rails against fornication while keeping mistresses and fathering half the brats in the parish."

"We are not unaware of that."

"And yet..."

"It is not easy to defy the Church. There is Hell."

"You both have plenty of time to repent."

"We have considered that."

"You have considered! You discuss fucking instead of fucking?" He looked at Margherita who was waiting in the distance.

"If our love is impossible, why are you adamant that we should... Ah."

The count shrugged. "Satisfying one's desire has a way of..."

"You are wrong about us."

"Prove me wrong. Save the lady, save yourself, save all of us. Let nature take its course."

"And if we don't grow tired of each other?"

"You will perish with a smile." He rose and left with the nod to Margherita that courtesy demanded.

DAY NINETEEN. Since the return of the caravan to the monastery the *fattore* had been fretting over the lost revenue and added cost the delay was causing him and was seething with anger that "the foolish love of a youth for the most ordinary of women whom he had elevated into a blond heroine" had brought the best opportunity of his life to a halt. He blamed the count for not controlling him whom at a minimum he should not have allowed to scout alone when it was obvious he was muddled by foolish thoughts and desire and went to him to propose again that they turn to Barcelona as soon as Tuccio could travel instead of continuing "a senseless journey to a distant shrine merely because a woman with all the stubbornness of Woman refused to hear reason." The count however took offense at the suggestion that Tuccio's folly was his fault and made his own that the *fattore* had failed in his commitment to chaperone the merchant's wife an obligation he had accepted for reasons known only to himself; and as a result of this unpleasant conversation the *fattore* had returned to scheming for as he reminded himself the *Book of Good Customs* stated, "the first grief is to be harmed by one's enemy, the first joy is to take one's revenge."

He feared entering the hospital but learning that Margherita had come out the previous day he lay in wait until she emerged with Tuccio who refused her support instead insisting on walking by himself which he accomplished with a visible effort; approaching quickly he asked with all the politeness he could muster if he might speak privately with her and barely waiting for consent led her out of earshot to deliver a prepared speech in which he noted several times that he was no stranger to the urgings of the heart. Like the count he urged the consummation of the relationship but unlike him arrived at his point with a multitude of circumlocutions and a more delicate choice of words; his thinking was that if she betrayed his failure to chaperone by seeing Tuccio in Siena Francesco enraged would bring his mercantile venture in Barcelona to an immediate end like the maid who aiming for a mouse breaks a pot. If however she took the bait they would lose interest in each other once the anticipation of forbidden pleasure was replaced with the knowledge (for him) that one cunt was much the same as another and (for her) that a small man had a small dick and so he gleefully told himself, "By the time they're back in Siena they won't abide the sight of each other!"

Margherita said, "You advise your partner's wife to commit adultery?"

"You may recall I advised you not to get involved, but that advice was not heeded." She bowed her head granting the point. "*Madonna*, I am nothing if not practical and it is clear you love this..."

"You may call him a youth if you cannot call him a man."

"This youth," he continued. "As it is clear he loves you. Love, as we all know... What I mean to say..."

"Since we have already sinned in our minds, what further sin to let our bodies have their way?"

They stared at each other until finally he nodded saying, "Who among us is a saint? We do our best. When you get to Compostela, you can seek absolution."

To herself she admitted that he was not saying anything she hadn't already thought a thousand times but wouldn't give him the satisfaction of knowing that. "Let me see if I understand, you after all a wise man of commerce and I just a woman. If I do not take my pleasure with Tuccio you will report me as an adulterer; but if I do, you won't."

The *fattore* sighed shrugged appealed with his hands. "*Madonna*. I am trying to be practical."

"You think we will tire of each other."

"I hope you will find a way to return to the purpose of your pilgrimage."

She glanced at Tuccio who was ready to come to her aid but quickly turned back worried that otherwise he would approach and debilitated as he was confront the *fattore* having already told her his suspicion that he was not just a *lauzengier* but one who desired her for himself. For her part she was desperate not to lose the purpose of her pilgrimage but it seemed inconceivable to her that she could tire of Tuccio rather her fear was the opposite that once having enjoyed him physically she would never be able to return to her former life; in the end she came to an understanding with the *fattore* that if she let nature run its course he would do his best to see that she had opportunities back in Siena to receive her lover.

DAY TWENTY. By the next day the wounds had closed and the swelling had declined as the infection had subsided and if he kept his arm bound he could move normally without much pain; also his strength markedly increased he exercised till he could barely stand and while he rested Margherita read from Saint Brigid whose interminable pieties neither enjoyed but both endured. While of course happy to see this rapid even miraculous recovery his challenging of the wolves was the last straw for the men who had endured what they had come to see as a silly love affair which was yet forcing them to travel almost to land's end to satisfy a woman's whim; and while thankfully the wolves had not killed or maimed their favorite they had made it clear that the time for intervention had come and to the task they unanimously delegated Stoldo.

When he had separated the pair by taking Tuccio to join Nico and the others saying they wished to welcome him back Agnoletta by arrangement opened a conversation with Margherita about love a topic they had already discussed many times but this time there was the unprecedented urgency of what had just occurred that enabled her to ask whether her mistress did not think the time had come to make a certain decision to which she replied, "So you too are here to tell me to consummate our relationship. I suppose this was arranged."

"Everyone is worried and rightly so since Tuccio was fortunate not to have been mauled and eaten."

"Do they think I too am not..." Suddenly she grew pale and had to sit.

Agnoletta told her she had won the admiration and even affection of the men but it was now apparent that Tuccio's very life was in danger and they believed she was the only one who could rescue him.

"By letting him fuck me."

"There are worse punishments. And seeing that you have twice come together for that purpose, at least twice you have confessed to me..."

"None of you appreciates true love."

"You are right, *madonna*, we do not. And this despite the fact that you have tried to explain it to me many times. I do not understand how a woman can love a man as much as you do and not express it in more than words." Margherita said nothing. "For want of your embrace he has almost died. Meanwhile for want of his, are you yourself not dying in a way? If you would not save yourself, surely you would save him. How can that be a sin?" Margherita said nothing. "There is more, *madonna*. I do not speak of it for myself only, but the men are anxious and have urged me to tell you of our concern that when the master learns what is between you he will dismiss all of us from his employ."

"How will he learn of it if no one tells him?"

"You will tell him yourself a hundred times a day, for your unhappiness is written on your face. And if only once Tuccio were to appear and he saw how you look at him..."

"And by giving way to our mutual desire..."

"Admitted, the men think you would tire of each other before we reach Siena, but I do not, I think your only hope to keep love secret from your husband is for that love to make you happy. A woman thwarted betrays herself with every glance, only a satisfied woman can deceive her husband." Margherita said nothing. "Besides, it troubles me to think how you must suffer. Whenever Stoldo and I lie together I think of what you are missing, how frustrated you must feel, still young yet tethered to an old goat who if rendered wouldn't drip a spoonful of sauce. *Monna*, has he not starved you of what all women need? Do you not crave feeding by one so young and virile, a man of prowess? I see in your face what you feel. Do you not see how absurd is this love? For all our sakes including your own—and God knows, his—take him to your bed."

"In a monastery?"

"Then take him outside. Take him in a dark corner. When we leave this place, take him in the forest. Take him standing up, take him bending over, but take him. Everyone will praise you for it, it is your duty."

At the same time that Piera hearing this was shaking her head Stoldo was telling Tuccio, "I love you like a brother and as my younger brother I tell you there will be other women—" but Tuccio stopped him.

"If you love me, do not speak of other women, there are no other women."

Laughing he said, "I can assure you, there—" but Tuccio was shaking his head in a way that made him stop at once.

"I wish to fight to the death defending her. I see no alternative."

"Suppose you simply took her in your arms and loved her. Would that be so terrible? It is not as dangerous and much easier."

"You mock me?"

"I am a blind man groping to find you. Where are you?"

"On the road to Compostela."

"You?" he asked finally. "Or her?"

"I no longer know where she ends and I begin."

"In a way I envy you. But, my God, the suffering."

"Whom do we hurt but ourselves?"

"That is already too many. But there are the rest of us, for we will surely lose our positions once the old miser learns his coin jingles in another's purse. If you love us you will pound the lady as you both deserve. As soon as we leave here, take her off the road and push her against a tree. She will thank you for it. We will all thank you."

"You know we have twice begun. The deed is not just mine to do, my fate is in her hands, I am helpless before my love of her. Call me the most stupid man alive, call me insane, I can do nothing but love her."

"Then love her, by all that is holy!"

"You think I will tire of the fruit once I have tasted it."

"Not once, but when you have picked the tree clean..."

"You are wrong."

Since Stoldo like the others had never been able to see what he saw in her he was in fact convinced that once he had gotten used to enjoying her he would grow tired of her whether or not she tired of him. "Am I? Is one tree that different from another?"

"You don't understand."

"You're right, but I know this, like Nico says, 'Who stirs the pot should taste the soup.'"

DAY TWENTY-ONE. During the night of the eighteenth day of Hell the first day after the fever broke during Tuccio's nine-day convalescence after Piera had fallen asleep and the ward was temporarily empty of attending monks Margherita who had stayed awake arose and quietly drew the curtain across his bed with herself inside; there she drew aside the sheet gently because his arm was still very tender and opened his breeches. The following night she did the same but this time Piera awoke and seeing the curtain drawn peeked inside to see her caressing his erection while he kept his mouth tightly shut his chest heaving beyond his control his eyes bulging; the third night she too pretended to be asleep and so got to watch the whole episode in which Margherita replaced her hand with her mouth and after he had stopped jerking whispered that that avoided the need to clean up afterwards.

The next day he told the count he would be ready to depart the following morning and despite the fact that neither his wounds nor his strength were fully recovered the count accepted the information without question and relayed it to the men who all rejoiced to be on their way and would have rejoiced more had they known Margherita had acted in accord with advice given if not necessarily because of it; she certainly felt better but ironically Tuccio did not.

"How have we forsaken the dream of fine love? Do not the poets sing of physical love?"

"It must be beautiful."

"Judging by the look on your face, I'd say it was. Do you now intend for us to love each other as did Eloisa and Abelardo after the world forced them to remain apart, with bitterness and recrimination?"

"In Auch after the miserable days that followed Toulouse there was a storyteller in the square who told a tale of Tristano and Isolda, and I realized that like them there is no escape from our predicament. The *lauzengiers* will harry us forever and destroy us if they can."

"The *lauzengiers* are unanimous in urging us to copulate forthwith."

"I doubt the *gilos* your husband will share their view."

"I thought you loved me."

"How can you question that?"

"I thought you wanted to love me as a man should love a woman. Do you now wish to become a saint?"

"You know what I want."

"It seems I don't. Did I not bring you pleasure the last three nights?"

"You know you did."

"And would you like that pleasure to continue?" At this her eyes became large and unblinking and he felt the stirrings of the pleasure to which she referred.

"You know I would. Dead am I if your love you deign not to give me, for I don't see, neither can I think, where I might go or turn or stay if you wished me far away." (Italian troubadour writing in Provençal known as Sordello who in the *Divine Comedy* accompanies Dante on Mount Purgatory.)

"But I do give my love. Having you almost die a horrible death because of me made me understand that our love, our fine love, requires me to give my body to you. And you know my desire." Looking around and seeing no one (besides Piera) she put her hand on his crotch. "I wish to possess this part of you too. As soon as we leave this place. You must teach me everything you know. And if you do not know it all, then we will learn the rest together, for my husband has taught me very little."

"Are you trying to excite me?"

"Am I exciting you?" Seeing the look in his eye she asked if his caged bird was fluttering its wings and he moved to grab her but just then a couple of monks came into view.

He repeated what he'd heard from the storyteller about Isolde in her husband's castle living for news of Tristan while he wandered in foreign lands pining for her until they died of grief but Margherita surprisingly replied that if their future were to be bleak then for that very reason they should take their pleasure when they could; he said that might be so but asked if she had considered what it would mean for them to think of each other all the time yet be together almost none of it. They both knew women took lovers she said she would simply become one of them learning the arts of deception including how to meet discretely and asked if he had heard the tale about the noblewoman married to a merchant who used a gullible confessor to unwittingly pass messages and gifts to her lover.

"Unless they are willing accomplices there are never any nosy neighbors or servants in those stories. The man can always pass unseen and unheard in and out of the house using an upstairs window for a door, reached by climbing a tree in the garden. Does your house have a well situated tree whose sturdy branches lead to your window? Do all your servants sleep like priests who have celebrated with the blood of Jesus too much? I hope so, unless all that love-making occurs in stony silence."

"Obviously we would meet somewhere else."

"Where? You cannot leave the city, much less travel. I have no home there. Even if I did, you would be seen and quickly denounced or blackmailed. Do you really believe the *fattore* would help, even if he could from Barcelona—and could you stand to be in his debt?"

"Are you trying to dishearten me?"

"Do you think I sought the wolves to demonstrate my fighting skills?"

"And yet," she thought, "such fine love as that which in my heart enters, I think there never was in body nor even in soul."

"And yet," he thought, "of my body would I be hers, not of my soul." (Arnaut Daniel, troubadour, who appears in *Purgatorio* and in homage to whom eight lines are written in Provençal.)

> Piera of course was standing there
> and looking at them as they turned to stare
> she shook her head at each so slow
> reminding the pair of the champion's bow,
> for what against Love could be more sweet
> than suffering complete defeat?

At bedtime Tuccio told Margherita to go to her own bed and when Piera stayed he told her to go too saying, "You have showed me great kindness, sister, but now I will sleep better knowing you too have a bed," and he embraced her; after staring at him she turned to go with Margherita who sought to explain why it was good and proper for them to complete their love though the girl's opinion was written on her face.

"I don't know what happened to you, but I love Tuccio and he loves me. My husband and I have never loved each other. I no longer care what the Church says about adultery because with so many high clergy violating their own rules I don't see what authority they can have. If Hell and damnation were what they say, they wouldn't sin so flagrantly. Besides, is it not sinful to let a man commit suicide because of me? I care for what's right and now after what has happened it seems it would be a blessing, not a sin, for us to do what all men and women who love each other wish to do. He could have died, I will not risk that again." She added, "I know in Toulouse you pulled him off for love of me but please don't do that again. As your mistress I could order you but instead I ask, for as you will need my help in Siena, I will need yours. You will be our communicant, bringing news of each other and taking messages." Piera said nothing and Margherita concluded by saying, "And if we are not both of us lovers, from another love I do not see that ever is my heart brightened." (Bernart de Ventadorn, troubadour)

Tuccio said to himself, "But he is foolish who acts without restraint and does not hold himself appropriately." (Bernart de Ventadorn, troubadour)

Chapter Thirty-two

DAY TWENTY-TWO. It pleased everyone when Margherita set out on horseback including Tuccio who not sent to scout was free to ride beside her and who having been inside the monastery walls for nine days had almost forgotten how overwhelming were the forest's gigantic trees that all but blocked the sky; when he passed the spot where he had chosen to fight to the death he shuddered involuntarily and Margherita took his hand. His wounds far from healed were tightly bound but occasionally some motion caused a searing pain making the stage which was not short in any case seem endless but ever mindful how long the caravan had waited for him he gritted his teeth and continued.

Of course there was also the pleasure of being beside Margherita as they plodded down the road at a cautious pace but the pleasure was heavily larded with confusion and the confusion with guilt for upon awakening he'd immediately decided he'd been a fool the previous day and had set out with great anticipation only to find he had successfully planted doubt in her mind too and so there was an awkwardness a shyness even that intruded upon their happiness. When the caravan stopped for breakfast however they shared wide-eyed unblinking stares and then she touched him and then they were going into the woods and Nico missing nothing followed while the rest of the caravan fell silent and strained its collective ear; it wasn't long before they heard the telltale cry despite Margherita's effort to muffle herself and everyone immediately grinned including the count and the *fattore* who turned to each other as if they had just won a victory.

The pair that emerged to general applause could not hide their smiling their embarrassment greatly increased when Nico followed to give an antic reenactment of what he swore he had witnessed that omitted nothing and caused an uproar as he portrayed Margherita's progress toward her climax and Tuccio's begging for it to come soon because he could not hold out much longer. "To horse, to horse!" someone shouted and everyone roared again as they mounted and the lovers beamed at each other with the shy joy of young newlyweds.

As the land rose and fell in a series of hills some high and steep a general sense of ease pervaded the caravan the lovers completely absorbed in each other either not noticing the overloud jokes and double entendres or secretly enjoying them; thus no one noticed Piera until when they stopped for refreshment and Nico reprised his earlier performance she began to shriek like one possessed and ran into the woods as if chased by a wild animal. Everyone was stunned never having seen this side of her except Margherita who called after her and Tuccio who chased her as best he could but with one arm tethered he couldn't move quickly so even pregnant she stayed ahead of him until she fell with a loud thud and cry of pain.

She had fallen off a rock ledge and tumbled to the bottom where she hit a fallen trunk and when he reached her she was holding her middle rocking with pain and crying but as he made to gently lift her she erupted with a fierce scream her eyes frenzied and raked her fingernails across his cheek; retreating in pain and a flash of anger he wiped the blood and said, "My God, what did they do to you?" She thrashed her arms and threw herself about shrieking and sobbing and smacked her arm against the trunk oblivious of her safety and might have badly injured herself if he hadn't torn off his sling and thrown his arms around her amazed at the strength of her mania and refused to loosen his grip until at last she was quieted by exhaustion. "Please don't cry anymore," he said gently and later, "Please don't be afraid. You'll see, we'll be happy together," and returning to the caravan Margherita silently inspected his wounds and restored his sling and later in town all three stood at the entrance to the priory church gazing in silence at the fanciful statuary.

DAY TWENTY-THREE. Fortunately it was a short stage and the caravan was most of the way to Lescar when Piera miscarried with extensive hemorrhaging; as soon as Margherita and Agnoletta were able to stanch the bleeding she was lashed to her mule at most half conscious and everyone hurried as much as possible the rest of the way Tuccio taking it upon himself to gallop ahead where he was dismayed to learn there was no hospital but a priest promised to meet him with the local midwife when he returned with the girl. He was at the gate when they arrived and took them to a thatched hovel where the midwife had already prepared poultices and Piera was installed on a pile of straw with only the women allowed to remain. Outside the priest assured everyone she was expert in her art and the rest was up to God then gently but firmly led them away the count and the *fattore* to fine homes the rest to the inn but the men agreed among themselves both the guards and the porters that one of them would go for news at each tolling of the bell whether day or night; Tuccio insisted on being the first but there was no news that day.

DAY TWENTY-FOUR. Tuccio waited on the porch of the small cathedral figuring that at some point Margherita would arrive to pray for Piera waited under the arched entryway so she wouldn't see him till it was too late to turn away. Lescar was built on a hill with the church at the top so from its porch he could look above the town wall to the Pyrenees which presented across his view a facade of jagged peaks like the Alps and with nothing to do he stared at them and when after hours of waiting she appeared he followed her inside without a word but she said, "Please, I am here to pray."

"So am I." She prayed and he tried to pray and when he saw she was done he stopped and outside said, "Mita..."

"I must return."

"At least tell me... Everyone wants to know how she is."

"We don't know yet."

"Is there fever?"

"Not yet," she mumbled and left without another word.

DAY TWENTY-FIVE. When she next arrived she was again unhappy to see him and anxious to get away looking haggard and vexed.

"You look tired. Can I help?"

"You have done enough."

He nodded they stared she went inside he followed and stood across the nave where she could see him and a few times she turned to find him staring and when she left he stayed and outside she turned to see if he had followed.

The *fattore* was ruing his bad fortune counting the cost of a second unnecessary delay and being forced to go fourteen hundred miles out of his way plus the thwarted trading opportunity in Toulouse; knowing that for reasons he couldn't fathom the men had grown fond of the waif and therefore would refuse to leave her while in mortal danger he couldn't help but approach the count to see if first they could leave immediately and second could turn east to Barcelona rather than west to Compostela once over the mountains. As to the first he suggested that some way might be arranged for her to rejoin them when she was sufficiently recovered while regarding the second said he was well aware the lady would strenuously object but judged everyone had no doubt come to share his conviction that "this so-called pilgrimage has become a farce perpetrated by a woman who now openly fornicates with one of her husband's employees."

"How do you imagine the men would respond to your requests?" replied the count calmly.

"That is where I look to your leadership."

"Alas my skills do not include miracles."

"Your men will do as you order."

"My men will do as I order so long as it does not greatly offend their sense of justice. You know as well as me how they would respond to an order to abandon the girl."

"She can be brought to us once she has recovered."

"How?"

"I would happily leave the arrangements to you."

"You are too kind. And the other?"

His frustration showed. "The woman has shown herself to be..."

"Has she? I will not praise her for cuckolding her husband, but I can appreciate her frustration with what are no doubt the rare and inadequate ministrations of that old prune, while admiring her pluck in taking her fortune in her own hands. Whom would you rather have in bed, a shriveled old hag or a piece of shapely ripe fruit?"

"If I may ask, *signore,* is it that you admire the woman or detest her husband?"

"A nobleman learns to respect courage. And I am in her debt."

"In her debt?"

"By withholding herself she almost killed Tuccio, of whom since the loss of my own son I have grown more than fond. Recognizing this she has sacrificed her honor to save him. In that I see considerable merit."

"Does she not merely further her own pleasure?"

"Does she look like she is enjoying much pleasure?"

"Is her current condition not the wages of sin?"

"I wouldn't know, as I am not a cleric. But the men now esteem her for her sacrifice and would not willingly deprive her of the shrine when we are only weeks away. Besides, would we not all benefit from a visit to the apostle's tomb? I would think that in your occupation wearing the shell could be—what is the word?—a credit."

That night there was a full moon and when it rose Tuccio stared at it from the cathedral porch where he stood alone.

DAY TWENTY-SIX. When the midwife announced that the wound was healing well without corruption or fever the news quickly spread and the worry that had besieged everyone ceded to relief; now it was just a question of waiting till she was strong enough to travel but the reaction was very different for Margherita who said, "I'm tired of praying." Gingerly Tuccio reached for her hand and feeling no resistance kissed it though they were not alone in the cathedral in fact a priest was nearby and scowled but they just couldn't care anymore Margherita tearfully lamenting that first she had prayed for him then for Piera now for the baby her baby that would never be.

"Perhaps your prayers were answered," he said. "I didn't die, Piera never even lost consciousness or slid into delirium. Her recovery is assured."

"And the baby?"

He shrugged sadly mostly for her loss but maybe his own too he didn't know. "Who can say how prayers are answered?"

"I'm exhausted from constantly beseeching guidance and never receiving any."

"Remember when we said we would ask at the tomb of San Giacomo?"

"That seems a long time ago."

"Which means we are that much closer."

"Could he not speak to me here?"

"No one knows better than you that the pilgrim's way is long and hard."

"My strength is gone."

"Let's forget everything for now and admire this church which seems to have amazing artwork. Look at the sculpture around the top of this column, it probably has a name, do you know it?"

"I don't know anything."

"Let's look at it. Let's look at all the columns. It's beautiful here."

The priest approached unbidden to say that the original cathedral had been destroyed by Vikings in the ninth century and that this one was begun in the year 1120 and took seventy-five years to complete and Margherita asked, "Why should I care?"

Moving away from him they looked at the sculptured capitals of the columns going from one to another in silence until Tuccio said, "They're wonderful, aren't they? So wild, so primitive." There were fanciful nasty monsters with long rows of teeth and elongated cat-like monsters with protruding spines that might have been friendly or might have calmly bitten off someone's head and weird scaled serpents and lions with huge claws and jaws with people in their clutches their heads inside their mouths and other strange creatures catching people in awful predicaments and he said, "This cathedral is small compared with ours but much more interesting, no?"

Near the head of the church they discovered mosaics in the floor whose childlike playfulness immediately captivated one of them while the other assumed the imagery was symbolic but of what she didn't know; there was a hunter running on a peg leg while shooting a bow another spearing a wild boar a recalcitrant dog tethered to a loping donkey (shouldn't it have been the reverse?) a lion with its jaws around the neck of a goat or gazelle with a second about to pounce from behind and there were large long-tailed birds some underfoot one upside down another swooping from above. "I have no idea what this means," he said turning to her who merely shrugged and when the priest told them the mosaics had been completed two centuries earlier he asked, "But what do they symbolize?"

"Symbolize?"

"The beasts on the columns, horrifying, threatening, their meaning is clear. But this... This is carefree, comical. I have never seen anything like this in a church."

"I have," said Margherita, "but as I was then in Paradise I thought them wonderful." Looking at her quizzically the priest assured them the mosaics could not be more serious but Tuccio looked at them again and shrugged and Margherita asked why they were in a church when there was nothing Christian about them adding, "They're not even religious so far as I can see."

"Let me assure you they—"

"Perhaps they mimic some original in the Roman temple that no doubt once stood on this spot."

"My lady, I assure you there is nothing pagan—"

"To a mind already confused they bring more confusion whereas one comes to church for clarity," she said leaving and Tuccio after apologizing followed her into a side chapel even darker than the nave where he found her crying her back to him and when he touched her shoulder she turned to him stared said, "I don't know anything," and cried again. Gently he drew her close his arms around her but still she sobbed until he lifted her face wiped her tears and kissed her lips and suddenly she was holding him fiercely her lips against his and their embrace changed until unable to restrain themselves her back against the wall he raised her robe in fistfuls as her fingers trembled at his breeches and he slid into her and thrust until the cry of their orgasm reverberated throughout the cathedral but there was little joy in it and they separated in shame.

FRANCESCO. Feeling sorry for himself Francesco thought, "What if I were to die while she's off chasing God?" and no sooner thought than it became impossible for him to continue working so powerfully did its possessive mournfulness snatch him in its claws and flap the air till it was far up in the sky where he could do nothing but pray that the empty-eyed beast that bore him to his doom would not loose its grip. The blackness of night was the worst but during the long days too Death waited for him to strangle on his last breath tainting his half-formed images with menace and terror such that whoever saw him wondered what calamity had befallen him. He was in fact feeling poorly the predictable confluence perhaps of age overwork and the filthy stench of the summer city and had even taken to bed though he had his ledgers brought to him and his secretaries waited at his bedside their writing desks on their laps ink pens and paper at the ready while he allowed himself as he rarely did to be diverted into morbid if not dire thoughts.

"No doubt she would miss me," he continued, "or would she? Of course she would. Yet she might not. I have not been the most attentive of husbands, or appreciative for that matter. For she did maintain this household, a great and unenviable task which by her absence she has enabled me to learn firsthand." He saw her weeping at her loss of him and pitied her for the lonely life she would then have to live which turned his thoughts to the will he had recently had made but had not yet divulged to his notary in which (against Lapo's standing advice) he left the bulk of his estate to the Church; but now fearing that might not be enough to assure his salvation he summoned a priest to whom he repented any usurious activity in which he might have engaged and swore never to return to it should God in his mercy restore him to health.

He knew one could die of inhaling miasma and spoke through a handkerchief both to keep out the foul particles and catch any expectoration of blood that would signal the end; yet it seemed strange to him that he should have to die and leaving everything enter the afterlife naked as a beggar as though his life were not valuable and his death bad luck against which all his prayers were of no avail. He did not appreciate that he was extraordinary at least in that he was of those few who had become something other than that to which they had been born whose life had evolved who by their own efforts had managed to change their social position and perhaps as a result had developed a stronger sense of self than others one that experienced itself as more separate; thus death came harder to him for it was easier to frame death when life was just the lit part of the day and the light was on one not in one whereas he alas had convinced himself of his intrinsic specialness.

Moreover he was unhappy had always been unhappy which he told his secretaries shocking them with a sudden declaration that broke the silence when he said, "Fortune has so willed that from the day of my birth I have never known a whole happy day. You might think as a result one would welcome death, but on the contrary one meets it with bitterness, for only the happy can die happy." There was a fable he knew well for he had grown up hearing fables about the cock which found a pearl on a dunghill and cared nothing for it but hastened after the rotten grain which lay nearby and he thought of it and congratulated himself for having coveted the precious stone all his life while spurning the rotten grain and this led him to wonder whether his epitaph (for he had no doubt he merited one) would fully acknowledge his social contributions.

"Lord," he prayed, "let it not say as does that of a certain merchant of this city who by dint of superior industry and skill managed with your blessing to amass considerable wealth, much of which he generously shared with the people of this commune, and whose tomb was placed at the foot of the high altar in a certain church with an epitaph that reads, 'Here lies the body of the prudent and honorable man So-and-so, citizen and prosperous merchant of Siena who died on such and such a date, may his soul rest in peace.' That I believe is faint praise of a life's achievement and causes me to fear greatly that his poor soul is in Purgatory struggling without the prayers of those yet living. Since by your generosity one may purchase masses to speed one's way to Paradise, I have taken full advantage of your grace by setting aside payment for a hundred thousand of them, but without the recommendation that sufficient prayers provide I worry I may not have done enough, and if that be the case I implore you to look into my heart and see there my good intentions.

"I know I may not be one to inspire great love, but surely the respect one has earned for one's achievement carries weight in the divine scale. There may be those who will carp, 'If he ever rendered a service to Siena, it was only because he stood to profit by it,' but I trust you will recognize there the urging of some old grievance or envy since you know I have always pushed myself to be ever more generous, and if I ever fell short it was not for lack of good will."

Speaking to God like this made him think of Margherita to whom he would have made a similar declaration and that made him wonder where in the world she was and where in her spiritual journey for he had always suspected though he hated to admit it that her pilgrimage was to some extent because of him; by this time she could be anywhere even about to re-enter Siena but if she were still far away he wondered if she could be going all the way to Compostela for he had heard nothing from his *fattore* in months.

He had never actually instructed him not to allow her to go there so confident had he been that the issue would never come to a point but if she had reached Spanish land or were to reach it there to be prevented from completing her mission after having gone all that way he could imagine her anger toward him and now that he might be dying he would have liked to explain himself. He decided to write to his foreign agents against the chance that a letter might find her or at least bring word and he told his secretaries to prepare new letters as he composed his thoughts but as he dictated he ran into difficulties expressing himself properly and the text meandered until in the confusion of justifying himself and mourning the loss of his own life it lost its direction entirely so he had the letters set aside and when his crisis passed he forgot about them.

DAY TWENTY-SEVEN. As Margherita and Piera were ushered by the midwife out of town they looked about furtively and joining the main thoroughfare pulled cowls over their heads relaxing only when they had passed through the gate; left there they quickly strode around a bend and turned into a field to find a protected spot behind a haystack where they rested in silence under midsummer's glare. "You're not too tired?" asked Margherita who studied the self-contained girl until her thoughts turned to the mountains they would ascend when Piera was strong enough the mountains that frightened her in a way different from the Alps challenging her to remain on the pilgrim's way which was so much more than a physical ordeal; for she had no doubt she'd been lost since entering this great dark wood and feared that this might be her last chance to return to the right path but to return to it she must be able to identify it to know it when she saw it.

"The church has wonderful mosaics," she said, "I'm sure you'd like them. Do you know what mosaics are?" and she began to describe them but stopped when it wasn't clear whether they interested her who would gaze into the sky until blinded by the light and Margherita thought, "Of course, she's been in a windowless hut for three days," but when she began to weep Piera took her hand.

Poor Margherita! See how she suffers!

She thought, "I wonder if she misses the baby. I miss it, what it meant for me who tried so hard to get pregnant. We could have wintered with the Italians in Avignon. Perhaps we would have gone via Barcelona, for no doubt there are many holy sites in Spain and why fight with the *fattore* who after all has not refused to go to Compostela? I almost pity him who no doubt rues the day he went into partnership with Francesco. Poor Francesco, he probably expected me home by now, returning full of gratitude to his protection in the meekness of defeat. 'Foolish woman,' he would say and I would agree. 'Yes, how foolish to think that I, a woman, could go to Compostela.'

"She would have delivered the baby in Avignon and I would have found a strong peasant to nurse her, and when the deep snow was off the Alps we would have returned home and I would have said to Francesco, 'I have returned with a baby girl. She is not yours, but she is mine. I will raise her as mine and you will provide for her as though she were yours.' That is over now. I still have Piera, though, and I will keep her like a daughter and find her a husband, which without a bastard child will be easier, even if I cannot pass her off as a virgin. Though there is that tale of a beautiful blond virgin who is tricked into becoming the plaything of a monk, but when this comes to the attention of a noble benefactress she is betrothed as a virgin to a worthy man with whom she lives as a respected wife." She paused to watch Piera who was still deep in her own world. "I would have liked to have a little girl. I would have dressed her in frilly clothes."

When she asked Piera if she was suffering from the loss of her baby she got no reply and asked again louder but still there was no response and she thought, "I suppose I'd be shocked if she reacted with distress, since a girl so young with neither husband nor family, and who was probably raped, would be expected to find relief in having the pregnancy aborted. But it's so hard to tell with her," and the third time she asked she saw her stare at something with intense concentration but seeing nothing turned back to the girl whose eyes were now wide and unfocused and then she got to her feet and took several steps. "Piera?" She took a few more steps and stood transfixed head tilted back. "Piera?" She didn't respond and Margherita afraid to call again watched immobile so as not to disturb her until after a few minutes she suddenly relaxed and turned and she asked what she had seen.

"You didn't see her?"

"See whom?"

"Saint Brigid. You didn't see her?"

"Of course I didn't see her. What are you talking about?"

"Saint Brigid was here."

Margherita studied her. "You're saying you just saw Saint Brigid?"

"Didn't you see her?" After a long pause Margherita asked what she looked like. "Beautiful."

"I mean what did she look like?"

"Like a saint. I saw a star, but not the kind that shines from the sky. I saw a light, but not the kind that shines in this world. I smelled a fragrance, but not of anything in this world."

"Weren't you afraid?"

"It was so beautiful. And then she spoke, but not from a human mouth."

After another long pause she asked, "Did you not wonder

whether it was an illusion?"

"How could it be illusion when it was real?"

"How do you know who it was?"

"She told me."

"In what language?"

"In my language."

"You're saying Saint Brigid appeared to you."

"That's who she said she was." Margherita fell silent staring as Piera silent stared back and then she asked what she'd said. "She told me what the Son says. The Son says that good fruit comes from goodness and bad fruit comes from evil. They grow like fruit from seeds, great goodness from a good seed and great evil from a bad one. Do you know what the heaviest burden is for things that grow?" Margherita shook her head slowly hesitantly. "That's what she asked me. It's a child that cannot be born and dies inside the womb of the mother. And the mother also dies and the father carries her to the grave and buries her with the rotting fetus. Because the mother is the devil's wife, her soul is evil. Her child is the devil's child because sin pleases her, she gets pleasure from it. That's what she said."

"She said that? You heard her say that?"

"She said the mother swells through the increase in sin and she wants to give birth but she can't, God won't allow it. She wants to keep sinning, but God won't allow it."

Margherita kept staring pale with fear and starting to tremble asked, "Are you inventing this?" almost choking and when Piera shook her head asked again almost shouting, "Tell me the truth! I am your mother, you must speak to me with respect. Did she say this or are you inventing it?"

"She said then the mother feels fear because she has no more strength or joy. Worry and sorrow are everywhere. And then her womb ruptures and she despairs, she despairs because she cannot do any good, no good deed—"

"Stop, stop it, she didn't say that."

"She did, and she said she dies blaming God and the devil takes her down to Hell. She said that. She said she's buried in Hell forever with the rot of her sin and the child of her depraved pleasure." (Saint Brigid, *Revelations*) Chest heaving she stopped and waited while Margherita sobbed until suddenly she stopped and the look of her eyes changed.

"Tell me how you got pregnant. You weren't raped at all, were

you? Of course not, why didn't I see it before? Tell me! Tell me!"
she shrieked almost hysterically and shaken the girl fell back but
she grabbed her and pulled her face around but still she said
nothing; later Margherita said, "Why do you hate me? Don't you
see how I care for you?"

"I don't hate you, I love you." Margherita's eyes teared and
when Piera added, "You are my mother," she sobbed again and the
girl put her arms around her and tried to console her.

"Why do you oppose my love for Tuccio?"

"I don't. He is my brother, I love him too."

"Don't you see that when a woman and man really love each
other they cannot live in the world as though they were not living
in the world? We have bodies and they express love as much as the
souls they house—maybe because they house them. How else is
the soul to express itself fully?"

"I only know what Saint Brigid said."

"I don't believe there was any Saint Brigid. You had a waking
dream."

"She was real. She said something else. She said a great plague
is coming, one that will ravage the whole world. She said it was
good my baby wasn't born, because it would have died anyway but
this way it didn't suffer. Millions will suffer, she said, not just
villages here and there." When Margherita asked what she knew
about plague she said her village had been ravaged by it and that
almost everyone had died.

Chapter Thirty-three

"It's a pleasure to meet you at last. Most favorite father has told me so little about you." Tiffany and the professor were back for lunch at the restaurant where they had had their first meetings he as arranged bringing his daughter Morgan in hopes that Tiffany would take an interest in her and thereby maintain her interest in him while she perhaps hoping the same had more than once expressed interest in meeting her with the result that the two of them immediately fell in love. As they took their seats and looked at menus the pair couldn't take their eyes off each other Tiffany because Morgan was so cute a seventeen year old version of Kiley and Morgan because Tiffany was nothing like what she'd expected and within minutes the professor seeing how well his plan had succeeded was grinning as though he had just won a prize.

This was the first time in a year they hadn't met at a hotel and they'd both been wondering how they'd feel about that; as it happened neither minded but there was a certain awkwardness that descended on them as though suddenly they didn't know each other as intimately as they'd believed. "Frumpy old dad is a great lover," Morgan was saying with a sideways glance at her father who responded with an affectionate smile. "I don't have too many memories of my mom, she died when I was six, and it's hard to separate what I remember from what my dad has told me. But the one thing that comes through is how much love there was. They really loved us, my brother and me, and they really loved each other. I mean they really loved each other. When she was gone, that great love of my dad's just kept going. It was like some big hot asteroid wandering through space. And then you came along and attracted it."

"Your father is really a great guy."

"He's the best. That's why I call him 'most favorite father.'"

"You know, he still loves your mother." She glanced at the professor who replied with an appreciative smile. "I wouldn't want you to think..."

"That you're going to come live with us and be my mom? Don't worry."

"What I meant was that..."

"I bet my dad told you you're the first after my mom."

"Morgan," he objected, "she is the first. What are you saying?"

"Most favorite father doesn't like to talk about a certain divorced woman who settled her possessive gaze on him. You know I'm right, dad. I think he tried for our sake, Louis's and mine, to make it work. It didn't last long."

"It never started. I fear most favorite daughter is giving you the wrong impression."

"Oh dear, I guess that wasn't cool." Tiffany looked from one to the other until Morgan said, "Sometimes when I'm running with the soccer ball it gets away from me and I do something stupid. Sorry, dad."

He reached for her hand. "No harm done, honey. At least I hope no harm done." Tiffany shook her head reassuringly.

"Anyway," said Morgan, "that was it till you appeared. Forget what I said, okay? Foul called, game goes on. You did play soccer, right? You must have, all Tiffanys play soccer."

"Morgan..."

"She's right," said Tiffany with a chuckle, "I did play. As did you, it seems."

"Big-time. We did the whole suburban thing. Really, forget what I said, okay? She was still on the rebound from a divorce and was coming on way too strong. I think dad was more embarrassed than anything else. She made us all pretty uncomfortable, like who is this woman?"

"Morgan, I think what would be helpful right now is if you would tell Tiffany that this was not long after your mom died, that Louis and you were children and I was concerned."

"I think you were really distraught, but we were too young to comprehend."

"Half the time I didn't even invite her."

"It's true. Louis told me she'd just show up. Oh boy, Morgan, you really did it this time. Red card for sure, automatic ejection."

"I'm not ejecting you and I'm sure your father isn't either. I'm so glad you came today, I've been wanting to meet you for so long."

"I've been wanting to meet you too. Like who is this masterful woman who swept my dad off his feet? You've made him very happy, you know. Happier than I can remember. When he first told me about you, I didn't believe it. I mean you were so glamorous and I was like uh-oh, what's pops gotten himself into with a woman who's obviously way out of his league?"

Said the professor, "I think this is the moment when I notice I need to use the men's room. I'll leave you two wonderful ladies to say whatever you're about to say in the fervent hope that it won't be totally embarrassing for me when I return."

Both of them watched him leave as though they needed to confirm he was really gone before turning to each other with a sudden awkwardness that caused the conversation to stumble until Morgan apologized again for what she'd said and Tiffany assured her that no apology was needed because they were friends. "Gee," said Morgan, "now you're making me wish you really could come live with us and be my mom."

"I'm too young to be your mom."

"You're thirty-three?"

"Thirty-four. Your father and I are seventeen years apart. If you're thinking that's weird, well I did too at first. But you know, it turned out not to matter. I kind of like that he's older."

"He's really nuts about you, you know. You must really get him because you've been seeing each other for a long time. And you've been sleeping together for a year, so I guess the weird thing worked itself out. That's why I'm thinking this can't be a one-way street, you must kind of love him too. Oh dear, was that another foul about the sleeping together? Don't worry, he didn't tell me. But we women, you know, we can see it on a guy's face, right? They can't hide it. He came home one Saturday after seeing you and I could see how his face was lit. It was don't ask don't tell, but I knew. I was like, 'So how was your meeting?' and he's like, 'Good, good.'" She burst out laughing as if someone had just told a great joke and Tiffany couldn't help but laugh too despite her embarrassment and when they saw the professor approaching they burst out laughing again and he pretended to be worried and asked if he should leave again and they made him sit but he pointedly didn't ask about the joke.

They fell to talking about Tiffany's pilgrimage where Morgan had many questions which she was happy to answer because even more than the professor Morgan was the first person to be intensely curious about what she was doing and desirous to hear all about it and she found descriptions and explanations pouring out of her as if a blockage had been removed. Her last two stages had been outdoors in accordance with her recent resolution that there would be no more biking that she would walk outside no matter how boring or time-consuming and heedless of the weather or how motivated she was because she deemed it the least artificial virtualization of real pilgrimage and so she had no need to feel embarrassed when she explained what she was trying to accomplish even when she lacked full understanding of her own motivations. What she withheld was a frank admission that she had lost all enthusiasm for the project and that at this point (and maybe for some time) was continuing entirely out of determination not to fail at a task she had set herself with perhaps the hope that she might find a way to rekindle her interest and maybe even discover what pilgrimage meant to her.

Because the first outdoor stage was relatively long at twenty miles she started and ended at her front door to save time but even at a brisk steady pace of four miles per hour this was a five-hour stage plus resting time which meant she probably wouldn't get home in time to give Kiley supper so she'd arranged with Bob to bring her so she could feel she was part of it. After a few blocks she was told it was time to turn back and when she refused they walked another and then one more and then Bob insisted and when they turned back she gaily cried, "Bye, mommy!"

"See you at suppertime, pumpkin, I love you!"

Said Bob, "Don't get hit by a car!"

"Thank you!"

On the way home Kiley asked, "Will mommy get hit by a car?"

"No, angel, that was a joke."

"It didn't sound like a joke."

"It was. It's hard to explain, but it was."

"Explain it to me."

Tiffany thought, "If someone asks what I'm doing, will I say I'm on pilgrimage or training for a hike? If I say pilgrimage, how will I explain it, because how could I be on pilgrimage in Short

Hills New Jersey? And how will I feel if they get a bewildered look on their face? Then I have to explain virtual pilgrimage. I may even have to explain pilgrimage. And there's a worse possibility, that people stare at me from behind their curtains. How do I feel about that? Another problem I could solve by biking in the basement. But I've already been over that."

She did her best to imagine she was walking the real path descending from the church steps in Lescar after a final look at the strangely wonderful mosaics to the river below the town and then beginning the four-stage ascent up the river valley to the top of the pass through spectacular scenery of lush hills with always the shimmering rocky peaks beyond that were as unnerving as they were grand. It was however impossible to maintain that level of pretense hour after hour when one was walking the streets of Short Hills remarkable only for the opulence of its homes and the perfection of its lawns and even though she was supposedly walking to the large town of Oloron-Sainte-Marie which was formerly a Roman settlement and later a major stop on the way to Compostela her mind inevitably strayed.

What she saw instead of the playful statuettes adorning the entrance to the former cathedral was Bob's long-suppressed but ill-disguised look of frustration over all the time pilgrimage took from the family though it had been a nice gesture to walk with her so Kiley could see the family united if only briefly and tell everyone that she too was on pilgrimage. For what the decision to walk all remaining stages meant was that after this one was completed he had thirty-seven more Saturdays of absences to expect when he would be solely responsible for Kiley and if she kept seeing the professor it became a year unless of course she used a bike which he implored her to reconsider saying, "You don't have to bike in the basement, you could bike outside. Would that be some kind of sacrilege or something? Do people bike to Compostela?"

Since she knew that in fact some did though there were those who frowned upon it and it wasn't clear how committed to the idea of pilgrimage the bikers were she'd tried to explain that biking took her even further from real pilgrimage than she already was and therefore made it harder to achieve any kind of authentic experience but it was clear he couldn't or wouldn't be persuaded. What seemed to rankle most was not the stages because if there were thirty-seven more stages then there were thirty-seven more stages but what he wanted to know was why it was necessary to pay a monthly visit to the professor as though he were her psychotherapist.

Naturally Tiffany played that last part over and over in her mind especially where he said, "Why do you have to spend so much time with this guy? What do you two do, anyway?" If he were suspicious, she reasoned, he would fish for information but having suspicions and acting on them were very different especially when it came to direct confrontation so she wondered whether it was an innocent request when he asked her to describe him.

"What would you like to know?"

"Where does he teach, is he a full professor?"

To her this suggested wanting to know where he lived and how old he was omitting only whether he was good-looking. "Is he a full professor? I have no idea, but he's been teaching a long time. He teaches at Yale. Did I mention I almost took a course from him when I was there? How's that for a coincidence?"

The next week she went out again but for a much shorter stage so walking from her doorstep she could easily be home for Kiley's supper and nothing further having happened during the week with Bob she was free to imagine that she was now well up the valley yet though the steep mountains were close the pass was surprisingly level. With that stage completed the question then became whether to go out again the following week for as part of her resolution to walk all stages was a commitment to go out every Saturday (except of course when she was with the professor) but in deference to Bob she decided to make a point of taking Kiley for the day and to do this one Saturday per month even though it would further delay the completion of her pilgrimage.

After lunch the plan was to go to The Cloisters but instead of going for the car the women already engrossed in conversation kept walking up the avenue and the professor stayed back to let them speak freely because it was clear they had much to say to each other that was not for his ears. He had after all brought his daughter precisely in the hope that they would become intimate and couldn't have been more pleased to see it happen though he would have been quite surprised to learn that what they were discussing was nothing less than the subject of adultery and they had gotten there after Tiffany as much to make polite conversation as anything else asked Morgan if she had a boyfriend.

"Kind of. Boys want too much, you know? I'm saving myself for divorce."

"Your dad led me to believe that, you know..."

"Yeah. But can I ask you something? Okay, never mind. So there's this boy, right? Who's with this girl I know. I don't know her well, but we're kind of friends. And..."

Before long Tiffany found herself telling this teenage girl she'd known for ninety minutes that she wasn't staying with her husband for the sake of their daughter but because she loved him and loved her family and her home but then she'd met a man who couldn't be more different from her husband and she became attracted to him without even realizing it or knowing why and found she wanted to be with him and loved to be with him and eventually realized that she loved him loved two men.

"And that's okay?"

"That's a big subject, isn't it?"

Morgan who sought assurances on behalf of her father feared that Tiffany was not in love with him at all she just thought so because she was infatuated with him or with the idea of loving two men at the same time and maybe it had something to do with her fascination with pilgrimage since he was an expert on the subject and that she would find that her love ended when her pilgrimage ended. "How do you know you're not having some sort of fling?"

Tiffany knowing she had a history of sudden enthusiasms followed by sudden losses of interest struggled to reply convincingly as she spoke of depth of feelings and the sacrifices and commitments one made in service to love; in rebuttal Morgan asked rhetorically if it wasn't true that the absence of doubt didn't mean a love was true while the presence of it didn't necessarily mean it wasn't. She continued by asking whether Tiffany wasn't concerned that seeing each other just one afternoon a month wasn't sustainable and that therefore at some point she was going to have to make a change either to her affair or her marriage saying, "I guess I don't understand why you don't suffer over barely having any time together, if you really love each other like you say. When I'm in love and can't be with the boy, my heart aches."

"You're asking me if my heart aches." How many times since she'd become interested in pilgrimage had the subject of suffering arisen, she asked herself, and answered by saying that it was equal to the number of times she had wondered why she wasn't suffering and worried that that was a problem with the authenticity of her experiences and attitudes. "You know I recently asked your father about that, not about our relationship specifically, but about pilgrimage. Because you're right that my feelings for your father arose out of my pilgrimage and are bound up with it. He asked me why I kept assuming that pilgrimage had to entail suffering. Maybe it's the same way with love. It's true that romantic love always seems to involve suffering, but is it real suffering, real pain, or is it longing and desire? Because I definitely feel longing and desire."

"For my dad."

"Yes," she replied with embarrassment, "for your dad."

"And I guess we don't pursue this particular line of questioning into too much more detail."

"That would be nice." She was almost on the point of saying that though she had just met Morgan she was already in love with her.

"But can you really continue the way you are indefinitely?"

"Are we talking about seeing your father or..."

"I meant the seeing my father, but now I'm thinking it's the 'or.'"

"Then again it's a big question. And I don't know how one answers it. I guess I can say that I have no idea what I would do differently."

"About seeing my dad."

"About anything. Certainly I'm not happy that I have so little time with your father. We barely say hello before we're glancing at our watches fretting over how little time we have left. He can tell you I've expressed frustration over that more than once."

"Has he?"

"Expressed frustration? Yes." They fell into a long silence until Morgan asked what it was like to be in love with two men at the same time and to her surprise Tiffany burst out laughing and said, "It's like being in love with one man, but twice as much."

"I'm not asking for intimate details."

"I'm not about to provide any."

"But I'm really curious how that works."

"You've never been attracted to two boys at the same time?"

"I don't think so."

"I'm not sure I know what to say."

"But you're convinced you're really in love with both of them."

"I don't think it takes convincing. You feel it."

"Feelings change."

"Again, I don't know what to say."

"For example, when you're in love you want to be with the person all the time."

"If I could I would definitely spend a lot more time with your father."

"Would you marry him?"

"I might."

"But you might not."

"Small detail, he'd have to ask me. Maybe we'd live together. Maybe he'd prefer that we didn't. You'd be a factor, you know, how you felt about it."

"I'd love it. Come live with us and be my big sister." She suddenly hooked her arm around Tiffany's and let out one of her belly laughs and the pair practically danced up the avenue but this didn't change the fact that she was worried about her father getting hurt whether because of Tiffany having a change of heart or the inherent difficulties of juggling a marriage and an affair.

When the professor half seriously asked if they wanted him to take a taxi to the museum Morgan said, "You've done well, father," Tiffany added her own thanks with a smile and Morgan added, "But don't think we're done talking about you yet."

"I didn't know I was so interesting."

"You're fascinating," said Tiffany. "But it's not all about you. It's just not for male ears."

"Especially when two of them belong to one's father."

He promised that in the museum he would keep to another room so they could converse to their hearts' delight and they drove uptown to a place that had special meaning for the lovers since it was there that Tiffany had felt the strong pull of attachment and the professor had fallen in love but Morgan had never been there so to her it was just a museum and one she was not convinced would be interesting. Inside Tiffany said, "I forgot how amazing this place is," but Morgan was not enchanted for so far her intellect had remained uninfected by her father's medieval bug with the result that the objects that filled the museum even the large architectural elements did not excite her as they excited him neither firing her imagination nor delighting her esthetic sense and in any case she had not come to New York to walk around a museum.

Again she hooked her arm around Tiffany's and led her into a room that turned out to be the Saint-Guilhem cloister where she saw nothing of interest even when Tiffany mentioned that this might have been the place where her interest in the medieval world had been fully awakened and that her father had specifically brought her here after she had talked to him about the real Saint-Guilhem which judging by the photographs was dramatically beautiful and had been an important stage on the medieval route to Compostela.

"I'm not sure I get pilgrimage," said Morgan.

"I'm not sure I do either," said Tiffany with a laugh.

"But pilgrimage came first and then my father, right?"

Tiffany studied her inscrutable face and said she had majored in classics at Yale and so must have been ready.

"For what?"

"For everything."

"Can I ask you something? Are you ever unhappy when you get home after being with my dad?"

"Why, is he?"

"Once. He tried to hide it but, like I said, guys are so easy to read. He said it was because of a quarrel."

"Did he say what the quarrel was about? I'm afraid I kind of lost it." They continued in silence. "Was he very...?"

"It can't be easy, keeping two men going."

"You're worried about your father. I can't imagine breaking up with him. He's become so important to me. You're right, though, I can't pretend I'm not married. It's hard sometimes. Can I ask if he's said anything?"

Morgan had thought her father was unhappy either because his relationship was not going well or because it was going very well and he was frustrated by the severe limitations of its circumstances but being a teenager she had quickly concluded it made no difference because either way he was unhappy and therefore was wasting his time with a futile affair. She had not however wanted to confront him with the reality of his life when it was burdening him and then watching him it seemed that the sadness had passed but she knew how girls could act when their boyfriends followed them like puppy dogs and continued to be concerned that the affair was bound to be futile. Given an inevitable conclusion what was the point of pursuing it even if it was making him happy?

"It's hard not to fret about the constraints," continued Tiffany.

"There's an easy solution."

"Not for me. I can't speak for anyone else."

"I don't see my dad breaking up."

"Can I ask if you think he should?"

"Of course not. I just want it to work out somehow."

"Me too."

More than once she had asked her father whether he'd be interested in marrying Tiffany if he could or at least living with her and he always said no which was an answer she couldn't understand. "Then what?" she asked. "This is love, right, not just, you know."

"You're young for this."

"Out with it," she demanded in her irresistible way and he explained that he was satisfied even happy with the arrangement though he wished they had more time together because it was all pleasure and no effort; but she objected that he wasn't one to avoid effort and he admitted that he had gotten used to being single had come to appreciate its advantages and feared that a second marriage or some facsimile would turn out to be disastrous.

"Isn't crazy love supposed to sweep fear aside?"

"Actually *amour fou*, or *fin'amor* which might be the better term here, avoids the issue entirely because, as is the case here, the woman is always married and as is not the case here adultery used to be a much bigger issue."

"I'm not talking about medieval romance. Didn't she sweep you off your feet, take your breath away, make your little heart go ka-boom ka-boom and all that good stuff?"

"Love is more than being taken by someone's appearance."

"I'm not talking about her appearance. I guess you're right, I'm too young for this. Or, to put it another way, this must be some weird middle-age thing."

This was why he asked her from time to time whether she wanted him to remarry because if she did he would make an effort in that direction but if she was really content without a mother then he was content without a wife and therefore it didn't bother him to know that after Tiffany said goodbye she went home to another man and a child he would probably never meet. As he walked around the museum glancing often at his watch he wasn't really looking at anything except his daughter whom he spied occasionally walking through the galleries with his lover like they were fast friends even arm in arm like women did in Europe and it pleased him greatly.

"Thank you for not being a sex bomb," said Morgan. "I can

say that, right? I mean you're attractive and all, but it's good to know it wasn't just body shape that made my dad fall for you. The girls who are too beautiful just drive boys nuts. Do you believe in sexual inebriation?"

This kind of conversational catapulting notwithstanding Morgan knew she couldn't monopolize the whole afternoon and that the two of them would want time together so after looking at her watch she told Tiffany it was time for them to deliver her father from limbo and that she would walk around the park outside and meet them later and the first words out of Tiffany's mouth after she had embraced him were that she was in love with his daughter.

"I'm a bit fond of her myself."

"She is so..."

"It's obvious she feels the same about you."

"I did miss you though."

"Was it worth it?"

"Thank you for bringing her."

They walked through the galleries not quite as aimlessly as Tiffany had done with Morgan pausing from time to time to gaze at this or that object though mostly just to absorb the magic of the place but in the Saint-Guilhem cloister they stopped before one of the pillars whose capital viewed from their angle of approach displayed a primitive head of stark features seeming to peer around a corner its wide eyes staring at nothing. "Marvelous, isn't it." Later he asked if she had made a decision about her foundation and immediately sadness gripped her as if the elation created by Morgan had caused its opposite for she knew that behind his simple question was the fact that the announcement of the third fellowship was due to be posted in two weeks and much work needed to be done unless he had already done it.

"Have you been working on it?" she asked.

"You asked me not to. I'm confused."

She thought: "I know he's anxious to proceed, but I am still torn though Morgan has unquestionably tilted the balance toward continuation, for carried away by my feelings and with money not a big factor why wouldn't I consent, especially when the foundation requires as little of my time as I wish? Is it because a two-year commitment, announcing a grant this September that doesn't actually begin till the following one, seems forever when I am already exhausted by the thought that it will take another year of walking to complete the stages? Yet I can't bring myself to sink the foundation just when it's poised to emerge as an important patron of research.

"If I give the go-ahead I can suspend the grant later, but not without causing serious damage to the foundation's reputation, especially if applications have started arriving. And of course once an award is announced, I'm committed. Is money an issue after all? Does it seem like a lot of money to spend on a personal project and am I really prepared to fund the foundation out of earned income indefinitely? I'm no happier than he with delaying the announcement after he's done so much work to build the foundation's credibility, but a delay of a few weeks won't cause any serious harm, certainly less harm than announcing the fellowship and then withdrawing it." To the professor she said, "I hope it wasn't too weird, walking around by yourself."

Chapter Thirty-four

DAY TWENTY-EIGHT.
> From this it can be seen how is founded
> blessed being in the act which sees,
> not in that which loves...

(*Paradiso*, Canto 28)

Tuccio said everyone knew visions had to be carefully evaluated since not all were trustworthy and in reply to Margherita's point that a warning from the higher world was not easily dismissed noted that it wasn't easily understood either but she replied, "The meaning seemed clear."

"Seemed clear, that's my point."

"I saw her," said Piera.

"I'm not saying you didn't."

"But you doubt it," said Agnoletta.

"Visions should be doubted before accepted."

She observed that the vision or whatever it was could well have been about Piera since she was the one who'd gotten pregnant and miscarried and that this could be true whether or not she'd been raped especially if she'd been taken more than once and had had some pleasure in it. The consensus among the caravan however was that vision or dream it had to be taken seriously because the girl precisely due to her strangeness could not be dismissed and this presented them with a dilemma for they had come to see Margherita's offer of her body as a sacrifice to save Tuccio and therefore at least for his sake if not now also for hers they wanted the love to endure. Piera had been mysterious from the moment she'd appeared and now it was admitted that partly for that reason had exercised a kind of power over everyone as old comments were repeated that no one knew from where she came weren't even sure what language she spoke and above all that she had appeared suddenly out of nowhere beside the road in the middle of the wilderness.

The girl's prior behavior became the basis for opposing conclusions on one hand that the vision was true because it was consistent with what had happened before especially the fit that had caused the miscarriage which till now had seemed bizarre on the other that it was false because it merely expressed the girl's understandable fear of copulation. Furthermore between true and false were intermediate possibilities such as that the saint had in fact appeared but the girl in her youth had failed to comprehend the full or correct meaning of the message therefore her report need not be considered accurate. Since therefore it was impossible to know for sure what had happened some were led to doubt it others to accept that something significant had occurred but where there was unanimous agreement was the belief that if one of them were to be visited from the non-material realm with a portent whether in vision or dream it would be Piera and therefore the more enduring anxiety surrounded the prophecy of devastating plague.

To Margherita it was not possible to walk away from the condemnation with merely a shrug and Tuccio too was affected though less willing to believe that Piera had been visited and less inclined to modify his behavior even if she had; so it was Margherita who fell deeply into cogitation and arrived at the conclusion which seemed to her unavoidable and thereby true that love could not be sufficient. "From the beginning Tuccio has asserted the opposite, and I came to share that belief because it seemed correct to one new to love who had for her only tutor a youth ardent in desire. Now however comes Piera's experience, whatever it was, which makes me see that intellect is also necessary, that it is not enough to feel, we must think. As to what we are to think, did I not stumble on the answer when I noted that we all have bodies? Pure spirituality is a contradiction in terms when applied to people and thus must be at best an ideal condition that supposes a body can ignore itself. And now I see that this is the virtue of *fin'amor*, which seeks to refine us rather than pretend falsely that anyone can successfully deny one's nature."

By such thoughts did she come to consider the possibility that the best way to defeat desire might be with moderation rather than abstinence for after all nothing could kill desire more effectively than sating it even if temporarily while in the alternative passion became a glutton by its starvation; the problem with this argument however was that it contradicted every teaching and led to the absurd conclusion that fornication was acceptable in moderation. Yet she remembered what the old man with the big ears had said on top of the Alps about becoming versus being; wasn't this she thought such a solution to that conflict that put an end to forever trying to become what one could not be to instead be what one was? "'With intelligence you may trust your will,' he said. Well, there is no question what our will proposes and here is intelligence, so perhaps we may trust it." How though could moderation be applied to a healthy male youth and a woman of normal appetite who had been starved her entire woman's life and who were now after weeks of denying themselves the pleasures of intimacy tormented by desire?

If moderation was a wrong turn in her thinking yet she could find no quarrel with her insight that love was not enough that blessedness must be founded in *seeing* that is intelligent understanding; but what use was it if it could not solve the irreducible dilemma that no compromise was possible between love and adultery? Thus she found the taste here very bitter even as she had to admit that Tuccio and she had provided a living demonstration of the insufficiency of love if misery and condemnation were to be avoided and therefore resolved to further ponder the issue.

DAY TWENTY-NINE. Shocked to see how stricken Margherita seemed and dismayed by the looks she'd given him Tuccio was deeply disturbed and after being abandoned at the cathedral without a word had spent the rest of the day lurching about town locked in argument with himself; when the next day he was no better Stoldo and Nico resolved to take him to Lescar's sister town of Pau in search of distraction. With a combination of force and cajoling they induced him to come and no sooner were they out the gate than he began to talk saying, "You should have seen her, she looked ill. And when she looked at me, it was not a look of love. She barely spoke to me and in the end just turned away and left me there."

Gingerly they tried to explain that it was folly to try to understand women for they were fickle by nature and foreign to man but he insisted that she was anything but fickle that she had always been as true and loyal as the two of them but was deeply troubled by a love that made her an adulteress. "Though she has no love for her husband, she takes her marriage vows seriously, as the Church enjoins her to do. For she takes the Church seriously too and trusts it, taking the priests at their word that they speak for God. And when a saint appears..." They hoped there would be a juggler in the square for nothing was so distracting as the antics of those charmers and with Pau larger than Lescar and a more commercial town their expectation was not unfounded but to find one they had to wander the small streets and squares.

They confessed their former hope that by pushing the lovers together they would tire of each other but assured him that because of what they deemed her sacrifice all the men now fervently wished the love to endure. As no one shared Margherita's regard for the Church its hypocrisy had much greater weight in their estimation than hers plus everyone knew her marriage had been arranged so Francesco's children could claim noble lineage; so while they might not accept the poets' claims for fine love they still recognized that everyone would seek happiness and pleasure where they could find it in a cruel world and Nico said, "It adds to her merit that she would not be an adulteress."

Said Stoldo, "You are fortunate to have the love of a lady, even one married to a merchant."

"She blames me for what happened to Piera. Worse, she blames me for coercing her sacrifice. She is right on both counts. And yet so firmly did I believe it was I who needed to sacrifice and that is why I confronted the wolves. I thought, 'Whether I live or die, I will have merit in her eyes and she can measure my love.' What a fool."

"She is a fine woman," said Nico. "She knows you gave her more in those few minutes than her husband could in a lifetime."

"She'll be back, you'll see," said Stoldo. "Love is stronger than the Church."

Had it not been for the miscarriage and vision the men would unabashedly be celebrating the consummation of the love that had prevailed as if a great impediment had finally been removed; they were even more willing to go to Compostela which had seemed pointless so recently for the expectation had been that after they dutifully delivered the lovers to their goal the long voyage home would bring the unwinding of their love and had even speculated whether it would be slow or fast polite or nasty. Astonishingly however they had become fond of Margherita seeing her now as not just a woman of stamina and even courage who had earned grudging respect and not just the woman who had bested the *fattore* in a battle of wits but one who had given her love not quickly not because she couldn't control her appetites but out of love so deep she was willing to risk humiliation to save someone dear to them. They had even begun to hope that a woman married to one of Siena's richest second-tier merchants might prove helpful to Tuccio to all of them to maintain their employment if it came to that and had even discussed how the clandestine love affair might be facilitated when they were back in Siena noting for example that the count maintained a house there but the problem now was Piera.

No one knew why she was so upset by the consummation of love whether terrified about copulation or violently opposed to adultery but her fit could not be dismissed as illness or aberration especially in light of the vision for it was believed the girl saw things others didn't while some even suggested she'd been sent to them for a reason. The vision seemed to confirm that the fit was a clear signal the copulation was wrong even Tuccio admitting it had thrown him into doubt saying, "I know you mock *fin'amor* but I never doubted it, I only worried that I couldn't accomplish its fulfillment given our circumstances. And then we seemed to have been trapped, for *fin'amor* defends adultery in service to true love, but how can it be reconciled with the universal condemnation of the Church? It seems it cannot and so must ignore or defy it, and this I am prepared to do, but Margherita..."

"Suppose the vision were the false raving of a girl suffering the effects of rape, unwanted pregnancy, ostracism, a severe hemorrhagic miscarriage..."

"Maybe insanity," added Nico, "but unfortunately we cannot reject the vision simply because it came through the girl, since we know it is often troubled souls who are the vehicles for such visitations."

"What do you make of the miscarriage?" asked Tuccio gingerly.

Regarding the loss of the baby they said everyone was relieved that a girl still a child herself who played with kittens would not be burdened with motherhood while as to the miscarriage if the vision were a sign then surely it was too and the violence of the abortion was probably a measure of the violence with which the fetus had been engendered.

"Yet she seems as indifferent to its loss as she was to its presence."

"She's always well hidden."

"She's a strange one, I tell you. But look, a juggler. Come!"

DAY THIRTY. When the midwife declared Piera ready for travel the next day a porter noted that she would be in convalescence seven days seven as everyone knew being a sacred number representing the covenant with God so when she indicated her desire to attend Sunday mass everyone followed her into the cathedral and watched her throughout the service though for what reason no one could have said. For the lovers it was so awkward that after the priests were done Margherita signaled to Tuccio to follow her outside to a private spot where she told him she didn't blame him for anything only herself that it was not hate but her guilt and shame that made it hard to be with him; further she said she still loved him would always love him but when he moved to embrace her she withdrew and he said, "Everyone sings the praises of your noble sacrifice including me and respects you now more than ever."

"If the vision be true, have I any choice but never to see you again?"

"What if it's false or its message unsure?"

"I still face the charge of fornication."

"Not among my people. Once, maybe. No longer."

"With pleasure comes guilt and the more the one the more the other."

"Yet so many women do it."

"Real women or women in stories? Has it occurred to you how little time we have left?" She knew that were she really contemplating an end to their affair she would not be mourning the increasingly brief time they had together and recognized her yearning for the embrace of a man who loved her not the motions of a man relieving his need; thus she knew there was no proper way forward that she was damned by two impossible alternatives.

"Do you ever wonder what it is about our love that so upsets her?"

"You know what it is."

"I wonder if we would feel ourselves in such a predicament had she never appeared."

"What she thinks or feels need not concern us."

"Yet you..."

"You are right, I see her as one sent to keep me on the right path."

"You mean since the vision."

"Not since the vision." Yet she repeated that the return to Francesco promised nothing but unhappiness and that each step forward was another toward the end of her pilgrimage a pilgrimage which having seemed the instrument of her deliverance had become that of her damnation; and now she foresaw that the loss of the baby condemned her to raising her husband's bastard. Its loss moreover was making her realize the extent to which it was to have been the centerpiece of her future life for whereas she could be with Tuccio only on occasion she would have been with the baby always she had even come to pretend it would in a way have been theirs would have reminded her of him would have been his presence; moreover now that it was gone she feared Piera would drift away after she married.

"Piera will yet give you a child. You said yourself in a few years she'll marry."

"In a few years."

Tuccio too was struggling. "Your husband surely must travel from time to time. Given that no servant could feel loyal to him they might conspire to allow us..."

"Someone would let the cat out. And the neighbors, once they smelled what was cooking..."

"I could come after dark."

"More desperate encounters like the one we recently had? That is cold comfort."

"And none at all, I admit, for one who dreams of waking beside you in the morning. Still I swear to you, we will find a way. Be happy."

"I have nothing in the world to make me happy."

"Am I nothing?"

"You are everything. Please be as little vexed with me as you can."

"But I am not vexed. I swear to you there is hope for us."

"Weight me with as little grief as you can, for I can no longer bear much. I'm so dejected, Tuccio. This pilgrimage has..."

When she'd asked the midwife about Piera showing no sign of mourning she said it was not uncommon in miscarriage this far into pregnancy for the mother not to show any response for a while. "I wouldn't worry about it, but if it persists... A mother naturally loves her baby, and when she loses it... Try to keep her amused. What does she enjoy doing?"

FRANCESCO. Unable to stop his wife from making plans for pilgrimage despite his order to desist and then unable to dissuade her and finally unable to bribe her with gifts Francesco consulted his notary who while agreeing she was insolent where she should be humble said she was marked by a turbulence of spirit rare in women and therefore recommended careful thought about the consequences of preventing her from going. When he saw however that the merchant was incapable of this and heard him simply resolve to insist more forcefully he warned him, "Would you put your wife's salvation at risk—and thereby your own? Think, she goes as much for you as for herself. And note, she may leave the lion but will no doubt return the lamb."

Despite his best efforts he could not help his difficult friend appreciate his wife's troubled mind much less his role in it as Francesco remained baffled to find her insistent on pilgrimage saying, "And if she must go, why such a long one when so many short ones are possible? And why walk at all when I have offered to buy her an equivalent indulgence?"

"My dear friend, I refuse to believe that you do not see how the cynical payment of a sum that supposedly covers the cost of travel utterly destroys the meaning of pilgrimage, even if the Church in its mercy traffics in such abuses. If she were paralytic, say, perhaps I could see it."

"Yes, in that case..."

"Do you wish your wife to be crippled?" He was as close to anger as he ever got.

Francesco saw it but was not one to back away from a misstep. "Don't be silly. But how am I to manage without her, am I to run my house in addition to my businesses?"

"I will take it upon myself to find you an excellent steward."

"A thief, you mean."

"Francesco, may I ask..." He paused but was unable to stop himself from asking whether he had any love in his heart for Margherita. Normally he would have couched such impudence in circumlocutions knowing the man was not one to speak of love and watched him splutter in his search for suitable phrases like, 'While my daily toil of necessity hardens me to certain...' and 'Yet my heart is not completely...' until gently he raised a hand and there followed the rarest of occurrences a brief silence that allowed him to regain his composure. "My friend, we have known each other a long time. Believe me when I say there isn't a day when I don't recall with gratitude that I owe my life to you, who took pity on a country boy with dreams of studying law. If the law teaches us to see both sides to a dispute it also encourages us to seek a middle way. If this pilgrimage were a legal question I would advise you to pay more attention to a fact I have already noted, that Margherita walks as much for your salvation as hers."

"My soul has recourse to other means—as you more than anyone well know—than abandoning our home for an entire year to, to..."

"I beg you be careful what you say, my friend."

"A pilgrimage, yes yes I understand. And of course I myself have done it. But why such a vast distance when Rome, a holier site, is so much closer?"

"I myself raised that very point."

"But she would not listen. She is stubborn."

Lapo could not restrain a broad smile saying, "Could anyone capable of standing up to you for fifteen years—and a young woman at that—be anything but stubborn? If one were not born stubborn, surely one would become it. Not to mention that stubbornness is not entirely foreign to your nature," and again he smiled with even somehow sincere affection in it.

"I cannot agree to this."

"Then do not. Merely allow it to happen."

"And buy myself a year of turmoil?"

"You will buy it whether she goes or stays, but this way the cost would be lower."

"Perhaps, but still far too high."

"Find a way to lower it."

This he would do by refusing to let her travel with other pilgrims attaching her instead to his caravan which would more than defray her cost and to boot make better speed on the road thereby returning her more quickly; in so doing he often reminded himself, "That Lapo Mazzei is no one to preach, since his own marriage is nothing to crow about. He says, 'I try to love my wife because she is the companion God has given me,' but try all you like, my young friend, you might as well try to make the sun go backward."

DAY THIRTY-ONE. In the midst of positive if brief

celebration to be on the road again and soon out of the interminable forest after two long forced delays (one would have thought the *fattore* overjoyed to go to Compostela) the lovers were at pains to gild their gloom in bright smiles but no one was fooled not even they themselves; Margherita felt herself in a state of complete confusion about her pilgrimage about her love about her life while Tuccio feared their love like an aging knight was losing force and might be unable to overcome its adversaries. The fording of the river at Pau marked the transition into the valley of the Aspe whose beautiful grandeur could be seen through occasional gaps in the trees and whose wetness and morning cool told them that it being now September summer was waning on the mountains' north side.

After a few hours into a fairly long though not tiring stage due to surprisingly little ascent the relief to be traveling again ceded to a pessimism that gradually overtook everyone partly because ahead lay the second scaling of high peaks followed by the deserts of Spanish lands whose aridity the Gascons had described in forbidding terms but also one had to wonder at this point what the purpose was. Piera was as inscrutable as ever and looking at her inevitably reminded one of her vision's harsh judgment and terrifying prophecy; as Margherita looked at her what developed for the first time was fear of reaching Compostela of actually achieving the goal that had cost her so much and this because of what she might learn there for she thought, "Suppose the apostle does speak to me and answers the question I have been intending to ask for months, but the answer is not the one for which I hope?"

"Did you hear that?" exclaimed Tuccio. "I think I heard a nightingale, did you hear it?" but she shrugged disconsolately so he repeated, "I think I may have heard one, but I'm not sure, it was faint."

> How many poets began their songs
> with that for which the sad lover longs,
> those troubadours who of love did sing
> of nightingale that arrives in spring,
> its voice so sweet from the forest deep
> direct to hearts its sweet call does leap,
> so soothing softening cares and woes
> that come from love's most evil blows.

(Based on the first stanza of a song by the troubadour Bernart de

Ventadorn.)

"To hear one now at summer's end in mid-day," Tuccio continued, "surely that is a good sign."

The caravan passed over gently rounded hills continually but barely climbing to arrive at a hamlet that consisted of little more than a hospital for pilgrims run by a monastic order that maintained its headquarters there and they stopped to eat and rest the animals and gather information about the way ahead thankful to find a settlement and even more that no one required the hospital's services. After sitting uncomfortably together Margherita Tuccio and Piera entered a small church to look around and ascend the low bell tower from whose enclosed perch they had a clear view of the jagged peaks and Piera broke a long silence by saying, "It's beautiful."

"The mountains?" asked Tuccio.

"This church. So simple." One of the monks who spoke a Spanish dialect they found difficult to understand had said the centuries-old hospital was part of a network related to the 'reconquest' of Muslim Spain by Christian armies from the north.

"The same wall of jagged peaks as the Alps."

"Impossible to imagine there's a way through."

"I was so happy then."

"And yet you know there is."

"Beautiful," said Piera.

"I wanted the baby so much," said Margherita weeping and when Tuccio tried to caress her she moved out of range.

"There's always a way through," he said loudly and Piera went to her and hugged her while he stood alone staring at the peaks until he too went over and put his arms around both of them.

To complete the stage required four more hours of walking for Margherita who wouldn't even consider riding so it was late afternoon when they reached the twin towns of Oloron and Sainte-Marie which had been one town until destroyed by Vikings in the ninth century but currently one side of the river that ran through the middle belonged to a bishop the other to a viscount; they entered Oloron which to compete for pilgrims with the cathedral on the opposing hill built a church of comparable size dedicated to the Holy Cross though it lacked a relic a fact that no doubt disappointed pilgrims as it did Piera when she entered expectantly and discovered there was no sliver. She insisted on descending the steep hill to the river and ascending the other side where she was again disappointed to discover that the cathedral had collapsed in a fire and though under reconstruction was far from complete; what remained was a bell tower that was an odd construction for a church but well suited for military purposes since it was built over the entrance a stolid construction designed for protection not beauty but open at the bottom to allow access to the porch and that entrance was as marvelous as any they had seen.

Margherita and Tuccio had had no choice but to follow since they could neither stop her nor let her go alone and in fact had no objection to going since otherwise they would not have known what to do with themselves and so they were beside her enjoying the small sculptures that populated the entrance becoming almost gay as they had been long ago doing the same in Tarascon and Arles and Saint-Gilles when they had become a family. As each pointed they examined a monster whose jaws engulfed the head and shoulders of its human victim and the pair of figures crouching back to back in existential dread the semicircle of holy kings with stringed instruments celebrating the divine presence and just below them the ring of men at their various labors (though one was daydreaming) also the noblemen bearded and booted in the upper corners the one on the left with his arm raised perhaps in welcome the other with his fingers over his chin as though pondering some difficult question.

When they tired it was already late the women expected for supper at the nearby pilgrim hostel where Tuccio accompanied them and believing they were reconciled reached for Margherita's hand at the door; when she resisted he grabbed it and telling Piera to go inside pulled her around the corner where under the arcade of the ramshackle houses' overhanging upper stories he pushed her against the wall and embraced her and desperately she returned his kisses saying, "What will become of us?"

"I do not know, but let us face it with courage."

"I know now why you fought the wolves for I would do something like it."

"Do not. I did not face the wolves to end my love, rather to become worthy of it."

"I too want to become worthy of it."

"Mita, you already are. I love you because you are worthy, your task is to remain true to our love."

"Yours is the only one I have ever known, and whatever happens I will never have another."

After many more kisses they parted and Tuccio remained outside the door until he attracted the suspicious gazes of local men dangerous in their fear whereupon he departed with slow step back down to the river and up the steep bank until he reached the ruins of the old Roman ramparts that had once protected this frontier fortress and there he gazed at the river below rushing downhill. This was a very good site for a fortress and he wondered what might have been here before the Romans and before them and before them and all those people he surmised must have had desires and ideals and fears; moving along the top of the ruined wall he came to a spot where there was a striking view of a line of jagged peaks bare rock near the summits forested below and at that too he stared long.

Shepherds who had taken their flocks into the high pastures for the summer had another month before the snows and glacial winds would drive them back down and they slept outside with their sheep; so with few merchant caravans having reason to be on this route the rough inn in Oloron was filled with locals who used it not as hostel but tavern and brothel and a rowdy affair it was with danger not just for the merchandise and the animals but the men themselves who thus had to stand guard the whole night in the barn weapons at the ready. The *fattore* abandoned his bed upstairs for a pile of straw trying unsuccessfully to console himself that for a good part of his life he had not slept on anything more luxurious but he too got little sleep.

Chapter Thirty-five

DAY THIRTY-TWO. The *fattore* got so little sleep that in the morning he got into a shouting argument with the innkeeper over the bill saying that between the bedbugs and the foul smells the carousing and the fistfights he would have done better sleeping on the floor of the church; replied the innkeeper, "Then you should have gone there," demanding payment in full and surrounded by men who looked more than willing to enforce his claim. The whole day his thoughts concerned how insane his venture had become how much farther it was to Santiago than Barcelona with not a commercial destination to be found his sole emotion angry frustration that he was powerless to turn the caravan from ludicrous fantasies toward plain good sense and he lashed out at the count who had spent the night with a local nobleman (though one not decisively wealthier than his neighbors) but apologized immediately when reminded that he a commoner was addressing the count of Sarteano.

Said the count, "As we are both in the employ of the same person, we will treat each other with appropriate courtesy. As to the rest, no one could be more frustrated than me, who finds himself a world away from where he should be, exposing his men to constant danger, yoked as surely as the mules to a load of merchandise that has no market in this wilderness, with no rationale but the maintenance of a love affair with which I was never happy and which now appears to be nearing its inevitable conclusion following what appears to have been the condemnation of a higher power." If they were agreed in their unhappiness they were also agreed in their fervent wish to be done with the whole business as soon as possible and so despite the lack of sleep the count announced a long stage which he said would not entail much climbing having been assured that despite the mountains appearing to block the way the valley wound its way between them rising little till the last ten miles when the ascent became very steep.

They followed the river out of Oloron that Tuccio had been contemplating from the ruins the previous day the intent to cover the bulk of the distance this day and the bulk of the climb the next and so be done with the forests of Gascony even though some had counseled three days; sure enough they were soon confronted by a peak that seemed to block their route but as they approached a way appeared that never strayed far from the river flowing strongly even on this near level ground months after snow-melt. The country was very beautiful with the hills rising steeply on either side but this did nothing to lift anyone's spirits instead silence rankled like bad weather until after many hours they reached a hamlet that turned out to be a place of local pilgrimage a fact they learned from more than one priest bent on donations from travelers especially rich merchants leading long caravans and so annoying were they that not even Piera would take a peek.

They passed some ruins that might have been a seasonal camp for foresters as they followed the river upstream on a route that had become irregular with detours where there was no path along the riverbank forcing them to dismount and make multiple short steep climbs and descents which only added to the grim mood; by the time they approached a tiny settlement the river had narrowed considerably and seemed to have become more rock-strewn despite little change in elevation. Not long after when the path did rise modestly they entered fog and then drizzle so it was almost shocking to see a solitary figure appear on foot who raised a hand in greeting closely followed by Tuccio on horseback who said, "By his appearance I make him a forester, but beyond that I can learn nothing, for his dialect is incomprehensible."

"Speak," said the count. "Who are you and whence and why?"

The stranger willingly complied which quickly confirmed his incomprehensibility but also his harmlessness and the count asked, "Brigands? Marauders, bandits?" pointing generally to their surroundings and the man gestured energetically to indicate that that was not a problem pointing to the mens' weapons and shaking his head then began to pantomime chopping and sawing pointing up toward the heights and finally he pointed to himself and made gestures to indicate that he walked back and forth between above and below. "Hungry?" asked the count pointing to his open mouth and when the man nodded he called for a rest despite the lateness and everyone happily dismounted and he told Tuccio, "See what you can learn from him, he knows the forest."

The youth led the old man to where the women were sitting Margherita barely nodding a greeting before exhausted she lay back and immediately fell asleep for like the men (though for her own reasons) she had barely slept and unlike them had been walking the entire stage; Agnoletta found something to put under her head and sat beside her. Tuccio after watching moved closer and caressed her and then leaned over and kissed her gently on the lips; when she opened her eyes he apologized saying he couldn't stop himself and she should go back to sleep but she blinked away her sleepiness and sat up and the two of them exchanged long looks until she reached for his hand while the old forester observed.

The girl he quickly guessed was the pilgrim's daughter the woman attending her obviously her maidservant but was it possible the youth he had presumed her son was her lover; and clearly she was not the wife of the merchant who had appraised him haughtily as he'd approached nor of the count who looked through her so what he wondered could possibly be her relationship to the caravan? "For one such as myself," he thought, "who has spent much of his life in the wilderness, the ways of the world have always seemed strange. Clearly she is highborn though I would guess not very for her lack of haughtiness suggests a middle rung. And then there is the matter of taking up with a caravan guard and in full view of everyone, but as I say, who can understand the workings of the heart, not me at least. They say there is wisdom in it but if you ask me there's something strange in giving Man a rational mind, a passionate nature, and the will to set them against each other every moment of his twisted life. Wisdom? More like confusion it seems to me."

When Margherita fell asleep Tuccio brought food and drink for the forester and questioned him about the way ahead which was not easy though with frequent repetition and imaginative gesturing he managed to satisfy himself that there were no particular dangers at least not from humans; rearing up like a bear with raised claws the man seemed to be warning that bears were the main danger but he could not believe a bear would menace a caravan at least not this time of year when food was plentiful and cubs were sufficiently grown so he dismissed the warning. What the man was actually saying was that bears were a danger to himself when he traveled alone through the woods which he did constantly as he went back and forth between the logging camp and the village bringing the men news and whatever supplies he could still carry for he no longer had the strength of a younger man and he started to narrate a certain close encounter he had had but stopped when he saw the youth couldn't understand.

With nothing more to be said he fell silent and turned to his food looking up occasionally to nod his gratitude and smile as strangers do who can't make themselves understood while Tuccio watched him eat and admired the stamina of one who at his age and fully laden could still climb the nearly vertical ascent. When he finished the meal Margherita awoke and reached for Tuccio's hand and he observed them with a sympathetic smile and suddenly began to speak about the most spectacular view of the mountains which was to be had by climbing some three miles to the logging camp at the base of the high peaks far above the river saying, "This view is not just impressive for to see it is to come face to face with God."

Seeing their blank faces despite his pantomime he said, "You may think I exaggerate, but I assure you I do not. You may think, you who have come far, that you have seen many such wonders, but I assure you you have not seen one like this. But you would have to go on foot because the terrain is too steep and rugged for horses. I wonder if the lady would be able to accomplish such a feat, but I think it would be worthwhile to try. I will be returning at dawn, if you wish you may come with me and could catch up with the caravan later. I warn you, though, it is a difficult climb, some three miles, did I say that? But you would not regret it, for as I say, you would see God. Let me try to describe it, though who can describe God's face even when he has seen it? Of course if there is fog up there as there is here—and there often is, it comes and goes with the winds—then you would see nothing. It would be there, right before your eyes, but you might as well be blind as try to discern it.

"Once you reach the camp the land is flat and the trees give way to grasses and flowers and you may hear the reassuring tinkle of sheep-bells, for the flocks are still up there in their summer meadows. You cross the meadow away from camp toward a low green mountain for ahead of you, in a completely different size dimension, is a solid white stone mass rising straight up to the heavens. In minutes fog can blot it out, and minutes later it reappears. You cannot believe your eyes. It rises straight up, pointing to Heaven, pure white, not a tree on it." Of course they understood little he said but got the gist and thanked him but said their stage would be rigorous enough without adding a difficult climb and thanking them for the food he nodded with compassion for the profound sadness he saw on their faces and left and when the caravan continued they recognized the path to the heights for it was wide enough to drag down the logs and Tuccio asked if they should have gone.

"How?" she said and later added, "We are off the straight path."

"I know."

"Sadness troubles us."

"I know."

"We don't know where to find rest."

"I know. I feel like you are speaking the words to a song."

She was! She was paraphrasing the third stanza of the same song that appeared in day thirty-one!

"I have lost all hope, Tuccio."

And now she was paraphrasing Dante's *Inferno*! (Canto 3)

"I still have hope."

"You should let it go."

"I can't."

"It's your youth."

Much of the troubadour's poem expresses bitterness at the faithlessness of the lady which betrays both the poet's love and her own and blames this loss of joy on the *lauzengiers* whereas Tuccio was mindful that Margherita had never been unfaithful even in word and the *lauzengiers* having been hostile eventually came to support and even encourage their love which thus in both ways did not fit the mold. This made him worry that it was not fine love after all but the bitterness that characterized much of troubadour lyrics had been absent from their love and that led him to wonder if on the contrary theirs was the finest of fine love proved all the more by their misery in fact he thought perhaps that was why their love might not be possible yet even as he thought those words he determined to refute them. "Am I, as we are poised at last to exit this dark forest and ascend the narrow rugged mountain pass through what we are told has been called the 'Summit Portal' since Roman times, to abandon all hope as we enter the portal? (*Inferno*,

Canto 3) I will not. Give me death, rather."

Soon after passing the turn for the logging camp the caravan arrived exhausted in a foul mood at a hamlet above the river without hostel inn or stable just a small church whose dark interior and hard floor comprised their sole hospitality; there after eating what food they had the count decided that since the porters and guards would have to stay outside with the animals and goods all the men would sleep on the bare earth despite the risk of rain and cold during the night.

DAY THIRTY-THREE. Astonishingly the route was level even as they reached the next settlement but soon afterward the ascent began and quickly the degree of incline increased and increased again and the animals labored and the men dismounted but the laden mules struggled. The pass had narrowed considerably as had the river which was now a rushing rocky stream until they came to a place where the gap was wide enough just for the stream the path cut into the mountainside above it little more than a mule track that would have accommodated with difficulty the wagons of the Roman legions; the mood was grim not at all mitigated by the spectacular scenic drama that enveloped the minuscule caravan moreover cold wet air had settled into the ravine and more than once a porter loudly cursed his mule while the guards heads down yanked on their horses' halters.

One of the mules suddenly went berserk missed its footing near the edge and tumbled into the ravine smashing itself against the rocks and before its load broke loose the weight had caused the shrieking beast to roll as it fell until it thudded to a stop twisted among the boulders in the torrent its blood coloring the water; when they reached it its chest was still heaving its unseeing eyes bulging from their sockets and at a nod from the *fattore* the mule's porter pulled his knife and deftly slit its neck. Merchandise was strewn about the embankment amid broken trunks and cases; the *fattore* screaming orders directed their recovery and searched the area himself to be sure nothing was lost and when it had all been brought up and laid out on the path he inspected every item mourning the painted wooden box that had been smashed and vowing to dry the bolt of cloth that had made it all the way to the water.

By the time everything had been reloaded as well as possible (some of it into the horse's saddlebags some dangling from bits of rope) and the men had rested and taken refreshment hours had passed too many hours the count reluctantly concluded to reach the refuge of Santa Cristina a mile or so past the summit for though he reckoned it was less than ten miles to the top at the rate they'd been going that could take five hours of walking and with the animals even more heavily laden and already tired not to mention the men... So having come no more than four miles he saw no alternative but to turn back and make the final ascent the next day.

In *Paradiso* Canto 33 when Dante is face to face with God all intellect falls away to reveal a love whose only desire and object is God a love pure in that it is devoid of bodily passion and unmediated by the intellect; intellect which is necessary not just to temper passion but instruct it succeeds in eliminating itself as it produces love that is completely refined the ultimate passion which is not the return of passion because it is intelligent. The earlier insight (Canto 28) was that love by itself is insufficient the current one that neither is intellect (being the *foundation* of blessedness not its entirety) that is neither love nor reason are sufficient alone but both are necessary and together are sufficient; at the small rudimentary pilgrim hostel Margherita told Piera and Agnoletta, "I have nothing left. Whatever intellect I may once have possessed is gone."

"What's 'intellect?'" asked Piera.

"I have no idea."

FRANCESCO. Francesco climbed the tower of the Palazzo Pubblico because he was enraged that the Church and so many of his countrymen refused to acknowledge the risk entailed in any investment of money whether in trade or lending including the loans they deemed risk-free and hence usury; for a man his age to climb two hundred eighty-nine feet of stairs was no easy task necessitating many pauses in a stairwell so narrow it barely allowed someone to pass but he was determined by a perverse combination of angry frustration and civic pride. The tower sixteen years in construction had recently been completed moreover its height was made equal to the campanile of the duomo no more but not an inch less to make manifest that the city's power equaled the Church's and he who had spent his life in Siena and had never climbed the campanile wanted to see the view despite the never-diminishing press of work which he justified by intending to weigh a new opportunity as he climbed.

He had considered paying one of his men to make the climb

for him and describe the view but decided that made no sense the view was predictable the experience was all and besides he thought maybe the climb and the view would give him perspective on his life but he didn't gain perspective and instead of working he fulminated. As was often the case it was Lapo his only friend who despite being the facilitator of his ventures was the bane of his moral existence who had urged him to reject the new opportunity saying, "Why open yourself to a charge of usury, just now as the sunset of your long life in commerce arrives? Is there that much money to be made in this dubious venture—and more to the point, why do you need more money?"

As a matter of fact said Francesco to himself there was the potential to make a lot of money but more to the point Lapo despite his daily involvement in the world of high commerce and banking had never seemed to grasp the fundamental point that the quest for ever more wealth was not a function of need at least not the need for more money; nor did he appreciate that at every step of the way people and institutions and ideas and attitudes arose to block the way or at least impede one's progress. Money he was told was nothing more than a medium of exchange and thus the attempt to make money from money was to sell time which was unnatural because time was free and belonged to everyone therefore lending was in and of itself unjust in fact as a theft of time it was a crime against nature and hence God. Why could they not understand, he thought bitterly, that money was not just a medium of exchange at least no longer in the developing circumstances of modern life; more simply why could they not see that even the most benign loan to a close friend entailed significant risk of loss and therefore was entitled to an exemption from the charge of usury?

"Still," it was asked, "How can the mere passage of time create money?"

"Do they not grasp that even when money borrowed is sunk into personal consumption rather than productive enterprise it still promotes enterprise in the maker of the goods purchased?"

"But," they say, "how do ten coins become twelve merely by the passage of time?"

"I am not selling time, I am selling the use of money. Is it not established through the centuries that a man who owns land may keep it yet rent its use? When I lend I merely do the same with capital."

"Can you sell me the use of wine without selling me the wine? When you sell me wine, do you not sell me the right to consume it? Were you to sell me wine separately from the use of the wine, you would be selling the same thing twice, or you would be selling what does not exist, which is a crime and a sin. If you ask for double payment, one for the return of the wine in equal measure, another for the use of the wine, is that not unjust? That is usury." (Thomas Aquinas, *Summa Theologica*)

Why could they not see he thought bitterly his chest heaving with exertion that if land had productive capacity and manufactories had productive capacity then so could money? Why were those 'real' property and money only 'personal?' Why was money only a reward for labor never a producer of it; only what was extracted never what was invested; always an effect and never a cause? "The preachers thunder at me, 'You do not participate in the work of men!' but I work as hard as any man, am I not entitled to payment?" Still panting he returned to the endless stairway and climbed though his legs had little remaining strength and turned and turned as the narrow stairway wound its way up the tower until without warning the bell at the summit began to ring so loudly he covered his ears and stopped climbing again and panted.

"In Venice, I am told, usury is reserved as a charge against abuse of normal practices to collect the approved rate of interest. They recognize that a man has as much right to income from currency as from landed property and as long as his investment entails risk and the return is uncertain, he is entitled to his return. Why can we not do the same?" The bell tolled the end of work at sunset and when the ringing ceased he turned back down the stairs and descended.

DAY THIRTY-FOUR. It was downright cold when the sad bitter party set out and it got colder as they climbed with fog enveloping them and mist heavy enough to soak their clothes and when they reached the neck where the accident had occurred they all stared down at the remains of the mule that had already been found by predators. When they were well clear of it and the mountains parted somewhat to provide a bit of ground the count declared a stop for breakfast which was uncharacteristically subdued but when rain threatened he ordered the caravan en route before the weather deteriorated further and with a groan everyone arose and soon was again trudging uphill. With the path too steep and rough to ride there was no chance of meeting brigands and thus no reason to deploy scouts in fact there was better security in staying together and with no way to separate Tuccio from Margherita he occupied the rear behind her and when the rain fell harder and more steadily and the fog thickened he tapped her on the shoulder and they slowed their pace until a gap opened and then turned and were quickly out of sight.

Piera however had followed them and when they realized Margherita said, "Did I not order you to stay with Agnoletta? You may not come with us this time. Please," but when they turned down the path again she again followed and Margherita took her hands and begged her to return to Agnoletta; as the girl's eyes teared Margherita nodded but Piera shook her head and Margherita pleaded with her until she stopped crying and stared and this time when the pair turned down the path she stayed.

When Nico noticed they were missing he asked Agnoletta in a sharp whisper where they were going and when she turned and he saw she was weeping he told Stoldo and asked if they should pursue them; after long reflection he shook his head and then Piera appeared and they questioned her but she only stared and though it was obvious she'd been crying he still shook his head. "Sure?" asked Nico who stared down the path while the caravan disappeared then at Stoldo whose chest was heaving and when Agnoletta's eyes again filled with tears his did too but in the end he shook his head again and they turned up the path to retake the caravan.

They tethered their horses by the river below the cliff and Margherita asked, "Why here?"

"Because once up that cliff no one can disturb us."

"But the mule."

"Don't look at the mule," he ordered but she couldn't not look at it until it was out of sight as he led her up a very steep path over boulders and around gnarled trees.

> "Hold tight, for by such steps,"
> said the master, panting like a man tired,
> "should one leave so much evil."

(*Inferno*, Canto 34 where Dante and his guide leave Hell by climbing Satan's mountainous body.)

The rain had stopped as suddenly as it started and when at last they'd reached a comfortable perch some two hundred feet above the river the fog had dispersed giving them the most splendid view imaginable of surging mountains of supreme beauty and Tuccio said, "At last we are alone together. And look where we are!" While they watched their arms around each other an eagle swooped across the sky and a vulture and he said, "Remember when I led you up the mountain at Carrara to show you the sea? It was before I'd fallen in love with you, at least before I knew it;" later he broke the silence again to say the caravan was well on its way to food and shelter at the famous hostel of Santa Cristina on the Spanish side of the pass noting, "They will soon be near the top."

"Why do you say that? They still have hours of hard climbing ahead of them. As do we."

"But not yet," he said as he turned and kissed her and after each had undressed the other slowly they took their time and he spread her robe on the ground and she lay down; afterward they lay beside each other naked despite the cold until they began to shiver and then used the pilgrim robe to wrap themselves together and tried to make the pleasure lead them to joy but it would not and even when after kissing and caressing she lay back and they copulated again even after that there was little smiling. As the weather kept changing between fog and clear sky rain and dryness they saw no reason not to stay and try to summon joy knowing full well its refusal was final and with their trying neither noticed that the air was getting colder and colder until they could no longer warm each other and the wind rose and it began to snow.

"I don't care," she said. "I want more love."

"Me too. It's just a squall, it will pass." When it didn't pass they recognized they could become stranded and might freeze to death as there was no way on that cliff which rose above them hundreds more feet to gather wood for fire and even then they'd be exposed on that ledge to the full force of whatever was coming; so they rose and helped each other dress but their clothes were soaked and muddy and chilled them even more till they were shivering uncontrollably and as they struggled he said, "Don't be afraid."

When the squall intensified so they could see no farther than a few feet she said, "Dearest love, kiss me again."

The rocks were snow-covered the path whatever there was of one slippery the river far below and almost straight down and neither could avoid looking for the mule. "Just follow me," he said as he began the descent, "and watch your step."

She thought, "What difference does it make what happens if plague is coming?"

Chapter Thirty-six

Thirty-seven days before Bob's new firm filed for bankruptcy under pressure from federal regulators seeking to avoid chaos in the banking system (which in fact would occur because of the bankruptcy) a mid-level functionary at the Federal Reserve floated a proposal to collect information from the firm to "identify those of its activities that could significantly harm financial markets and the economy if it filed for bankruptcy." He followed up a week later and two weeks after that his office was informed that the Secretary of the Treasury agreed on the need to collect certain information and a week after that he circulated for approval a draft letter that would request the information and it was now nine days before the bankruptcy. Of course the regulators couldn't have known that they themselves would force the firm into bankruptcy but what they certainly knew was that the problems not just with Bob's firm but with the entire MBS industry both its practices and its attitudes had been fully visible for years which raises an interesting question in social psychology namely how close to a cliff do people have to get before they worry that they're heading for a cliff? Nothing new happened at the end rather the MBS business and the financial industry and the system itself simply proceeded by logical steps to the edge of the cliff.

Bob didn't know how close to the end he was any more than his CEO or the board of directors because he like everyone assumed that everyone else knew what they were doing as he was certain he knew what he was doing and not only was he good at it he was outstanding and each day he went to work determined to show everyone how good he was at his job and how smart it would be to give him more responsibility and pay him more money.

Though a smaller fish at the new firm he was excited to find himself swimming in a much bigger pond and it hadn't taken him long to see a way to become a bigger fish bigger than he could have been at the old firm because a bigger pond meant more opportunity and so seven business days before the end when word went round that the firm was going to announce a large quarterly loss due to having to reduce the reported value of certain MBS assets he was busily doing deals making friends and identifying rivals.

No one was worried because they knew the firm was taking steps to bolster capital and there was talk of an investment from the Korea Development Bank or rather some people might have been very worried or everyone might have worried about something but the position of the system as a whole in which all worries as well as hopes and expectations were weighed against each other was one of overwhelming confidence in the integrity of the system and the value of its financial instruments. That Sunday however the nation's two publicly traded quasi-governmental corporations that guaranteed trillions of dollars of home mortgages with the implied backing of the US Treasury were placed in conservatorship and when Tiffany asked Bob what he thought he said, "Inadequate loan loss reserves."

"I think we know that. Why didn't we know it yesterday?"

"Maybe we did."

"Obviously we didn't, otherwise they would have been pulled yesterday and all the investors who bought shares yesterday wouldn't have thrown their money away."

"You know what I mean. The day before yesterday, figuratively speaking."

"Even then. It's not like house prices in many markets haven't been sinking for, what, a year now at least. And the mortgages being written, I mean come on."

"So you're an industry critic now?"

"I'm married to a man whose career is riding on this industry."

"I'm riding fine, thank you."

"Your horse has already been shot out from under you twice."

"And now I'm doing very well thank you on my third horse."

"And what if this one gets shot?"

"Won't happen."

"I sure hope not."

"Since when are you a worrier?"

"I told you before, I don't worry about risk, I worry about unknown risk because somebody didn't do their due diligence properly. It sure seems like that's what happened here."

"No argument there. If the government didn't have its head up its ass—"

"It's not just the government. A lot of smart money just went down the tubes."

"Because of the government."

"Not just because of the government."

"Because of the government. Those two never should have existed in the first place. A for-profit corporation with the implicit guarantee of the Treasury? Then they go into the nuthouse with the taxpayers on the hook. Not to mention the accounting fraud."

"Okay, but there's buzz about trouble at WaMu, AIG, Merrill Lynch. Which I'm sure you know." 'WaMu' was the large commercial bank Washington Mutual a major provider of substandard mortgages AIG was American International Group the biggest underwriter of credit default swaps and Merrill Lynch was a major player in every facet of the MBS business.

He gestured. "AIG, Merrill? Give me a break. I don't know about the lenders."

"There you go. If the loans are dubious, then everything downstream is dubious."

"Not everything. But I agree, you have to do your homework. Have you forgotten you're talking to the guy who took his firm short?"

"Are you really not the least bit concerned that so many mortgages getting written really shouldn't get written?"

"That's my point. Some of them, sure. Why do you think I went short?"

"So?"

"So what? Show me a market that doesn't have excesses."

"So, how might the excesses impact your firm?"

"I don't see that they do."

"If mortgages are riskier than we thought, then MBSs are riskier. And if that's not priced in, then the market is due to correct. Wouldn't that mean more collateral calls, more equity needed? What does that do to your credit?" She thought, "What if the government had decided to let the mortgage companies fail instead of rescuing them?"

Bob knew of his firm's dependence on JP Morgan to provide intra-day credit for the overnight repo loans but he thought, "Why would JPM disturb that? They're collecting nice fees while taking practically no risk."

BLOG POST #1: Arles to Saint-Gilles. Stage: 1. Stages remaining: 69. Distance: 22.0 km, 13.6 miles. Cumulative distance: 22.0 km, 13.6 miles. Remaining distance: 1,629 km, 1,010.0 miles. (This is a virtual pilgrimage in the sense that I'm not really en route to Compostela, but I am really walking the miles.)

[Description of flight from New York to Nice approach over brilliant blue Mediterranean exhilarating glimpses of sheer seaside cliffs with Alps in background emerging from airport into brilliant morning sunshine sleepy but too excited to notice. Tempting thought to explore visual glories of Riviera but no time; taxi to TGV train station fast train to Arles. Gorgeous dramatic scenery surprised how much is arid. Brief description of arrival at small hotel in old city (hailed taxi but told easier to walk) relief that receptionist speaks some English because know only a few words of French (taxi driver indicated walking with two fingers and pointing). Purposely not four-star hotel because of pilgrimage. Caught glimpse of preserved Roman coliseum immediately went out for better look too excited to nap.]

To be honest, besides excitement and jet lag I'm also pretty nervous. For me this is unusual. I have a high-stress job with a lot of responsibility, I make multi-million dollar decisions as a matter of course, and yet the prospect of walking for four hours over level terrain the day after tomorrow has me worried. About what, I don't know. I'm thinking maybe I should have checked into a pilgrim hostel after all. I decided not to because they provide pretty basic accommodation and I figured I'd need a quiet room and a good bed, but on the other hand now I'm alone and feeling alone and regretting it. But there's nothing like a cup of delicious French coffee at an outdoor cafe to lift one's spirits and, spirits lifted, I'm off to explore this amazing place.

[Description of city's sights including Roman necropolis called Alyscamps.]

As I'm leaving the Alyscamps I notice the small marker near the entrance that indicates the beginning of the official hiking route called the GR653, the modern version of the ancient Way of Toulouse from Arles to Santiago de Compostela. This is where my thousand mile trek is about to begin. Here's a photo of it. It represents the scallop shell which we know has been the insignia of the Compostela pilgrimage since at least the twelfth century because it's discussed in a famous book called The Book of Saint James. *If you've heard of the famous* Pilgrim Guide *of Aimery Picaud, that's actually Book Five of this book and it mentions the shells being sold to pilgrims in front of the Cathedral of Santiago de Compostela as souvenirs. The scallop shell has come down to us as the scallops called* coquilles Saint-Jacques, *which is French for 'shells of Saint James.'*

The key point, though, is that pilgrims picked up their shell when they reached Compostela and wore it home as a badge of accomplishment. Nowadays nobody walks home so if people are going to display it it has to be on the way there. Call it a badge of aspiration, but there are those who take exception to giving oneself an award before one has earned it. Upon consideration I decided I'm in that latter camp and have chosen not to acquire a shell until I reach my goal.

Later: I'm setting out in the morning. I can't shake my nervousness, which I really didn't expect. I think it's because I'm alone.

I feel the need to confess that I don't really know why I'm here. Or rather I don't know why I want to be here. I'm not religious, I don't believe that a supernatural being governs nature, I certainly don't believe in sin and salvation (though I acknowledge wrong and redemption). Apparently though—and I say 'apparently' because I wasn't aware of it till I suddenly found myself interested in pilgrimage—I have a feeling for sacredness, the sense that objects and actions in this world can be or become utterly transformed into something supremely significant, beautiful, good. What transforms them? Hard to say. But what transforms a hike into a pilgrimage is the desire to experience sacredness. And the will, because it's not easy. And it's kind of scary.

I suppose that shouldn't surprise me as much as it does. After all, when your goal is to put yourself face to face with transcendence, you shouldn't be shocked if the experience (or the anticipation of the experience) is frightening. What will I see? What will I see out there and what might I see in here?

And yet, where are you? You're on a road, there's traffic, noises, the signs and paraphernalia of daily life, all the things that have not been transformed, that in some sense you're trying to escape. How do you do it? Why is walking a reasonable method, why not dreaming or contemplating beauty or some type of mental discipline? Pilgrims acknowledge that nothing can be discovered at the end of the journey that was not present at the beginning, yet they walk.

I don't understand it. I hope I'm as ready to be tested as I think I am, but I'm also excited. I think it's going to be beautiful. I think I'm going to meet interesting people. After seventy days of walking I'm going to be in Santiago de Compostela and I'll be able to look back and say, "I just climbed over the Pyrenees, I crossed deserts. I walked a thousand miles." And I will be in a place that's sacred because multitudes over centuries have made it sacred.

But I don't know what I will have learned. To find out I have to walk there.

A week after meeting Morgan Tiffany returned to New York with her staff and backpack to which she had affixed an insignia of the scallop shell just purchased from a pilgrimage website and left the car near Saint Patrick's Cathedral to begin her next stage. She sat in a pew surveying the interior to put herself in the right mental state but soon left because the later she got home the angrier Bob would be and began walking on the crowded sidewalks of midtown Manhattan where many blocks and considerable practice were required before she had learned how best to meet the looks and stares at which point began the regret over those who turned away or worst of all completely ignored her with not even a glance. She had a second insignia on a cap she'd also purchased from the website and when a young man who had just passed appeared at her side to ask if she was on a virtual pilgrimage to Santiago de Compostela she looked at him in astonishment and he exclaimed, "That is so cool! I saw the insignia and I thought 'okay,' but then I thought, 'Why the staff and backpack?' I don't know, it just came to me."

She was going to the Cathedral Church of Saint John the Divine which the professor had visited as a student and might have walked through Central Park in fact with over five miles to go after completing her circuit she could have walked all over Central Park but instead was deliberately avoiding it to remain on crowded streets for the entire stage. Bob had said, "Why do you have to go to New York? Does this have something to do with the professor? That guy is starting to piss me off," and in fact the professor had twice offered to walk with her and she had considered it before insisting on going alone but hearing the voice of the young stranger instead of her husband's her gait seemed lighter now.

Pausing only for brief looks at the facade and interior of the gigantic cathedral she continued to Riverside Church the other Gothic revival the professor had mentioned and from there after another quick survey turned back to complete her stage on midtown avenues crowded with pedestrians. Had she actually been in the upper reaches of the Pyrenees she would have been following a torrent toward its source on a rugged path but instead was constantly jostled by oblivious or annoyed pedestrians who banged into her backpack and got their shopping bags entangled with her staff.

"So," she told the professor five weeks later, "I'd have to say, on balance, it worked out pretty well. New Yorkers are tough, though." They were back in a hotel in New Jersey and still in bed after one of their longer sessions reclining side by side against the pillows naked chatting with much to say to each other and they got on the topic of the new fellow whose research on medieval women pilgrims was interesting to both of them and the professor seized another opportunity to remind her that funding a recognized historian who had not previously worked on pilgrimage was a coup for the foundation.

"Let's visit her."

"Seriously?"

"Isn't it a valid function of the board to review a fellow's progress? It's over three months now. I think I could sell it to Bob."

"With everything that's going on?"

"We'd just go for a weekend. Maybe even overnight."

"To California. You really want to travel that much."

"You know what would really be great? To tell Bob about us and have him accept it."

"Now I know you're not serious."

"Wouldn't that be great? Why does it have to be impossible? You're the historian, haven't plenty of married men accepted that their wives were mistresses of somebody else?"

"I don't know about plenty."

"What's the big deal? Sometimes I sleep with Bob and sometimes with you. We could be one big happy family. Kiley would adore Morgan."

"You don't really think you could tell him, do you?"

"Of course not. So let's go to California."

The day after two government-sponsored mortgage companies were seized by regulators which was six days before Bob's firm declared bankruptcy officials of the New York Federal Reserve Bank were notified of a meeting to be held the next day to 'continue the discussion' of how to deal with a failing investment bank and when they arrived they were given a list of the overnight repos Lehman held through JP Morgan which totaled roughly two hundred billion dollars. Most of these loans were provided by ten lenders of whom three had just demanded more collateral furthermore there would be no investment from Korea Development Bank and after the firm's stock plunged fifty-five percent in a day the Secretary of the Treasury convened a conference call with the chairmen of the SEC and Federal Reserve the president of the New York Fed and his own staff to discuss a possible bankruptcy.

The next day Wednesday four days before Lehman declared bankruptcy as large purchasers of its short-term debt securities sharply reduced their exposures working groups at the Federal Reserve were directed to spend *a few hours* on a plan for acquisition or recapitalization and a senior vice president circulated her opinion on another regulator's request for thoughts. That night another official circulated a plan to convene the main lenders on Friday and have the Secretary of the Treasury give them till Sunday night to devise a credible plan to save the firm while the Secretary himself called the CEO of Bank of America to request he consider buying it.

On Thursday morning a Goldman Sachs executive sent an email to the New York Fed saying the situation was "getting pretty scary and ugly" and "the market is getting very spooked" and the situation was "spinning out of control" and in the afternoon the Fed circulated another plan this one to convene the creditors not to rescue the firm but "make plans to cope with its bankruptcy." That night *a little before midnight* a senior New York Fed official notified colleagues that panicked hedge funds had called to say that if Lehman Brothers collapsed so would Washington Mutual and Merrill Lynch and there would be a 'full-blown' recession and so they were 'begging and pleading for a large-scale solution' that went beyond Bob's firm enough beyond presumably to catch their falling investments. Also around midnight JP Morgan demanded that Bob's firm post five billion dollars *in cash* by the opening of business failing which it would cease to provide credit knowing that without it the firm could not survive a single day.

In the morning Friday two days before it would declare bankruptcy Bob's firm delivered the cash; the Treasury Secretary flew to New York for meetings while the chairman of the Fed stayed in Washington in case he had to convene the board of governors to exercise emergency lending powers; the CEO of Bank of America said his accountants had inspected the books and found the assets overvalued so there would be no deal without government assistance. At the meeting in the afternoon the major banks could not agree on whether Bob's firm was solvent the one point on which they agreed being that the real estate asset values carried on its books (reported just two days earlier) were inflated probably to twice their market value in which case the firm had no net worth.

Stage thirty-five which would take her to the top of the pass over the Pyrenees Tiffany completed from the house because Bob had complained so bitterly about the Manhattan stage taking so long but at least she was able to suggest the taxing climb by walking from South Orange village to Old Short Hills Road which was under three miles and mostly not steep whereas the real stage was eleven point two miles and very steep. Still it was more than enough to get winded if one were carrying a fully loaded backpack at a brisk pace fuming over Bob's outburst which if she acceded to it meant she'd have to walk another thirty-five stages around suburban Essex County which she thought was a lot to ask and given that her enthusiasm was gone there was a good chance she wouldn't be able to do it even with the professor's support. The alternative was to ignore him but in fairness she recognized that it was he who'd thought of virtual pilgrimage in the first place and had been more or less patient for a long time and also of course there was the turmoil with his job which was certainly upsetting.

More troubling was trying to decide what he suspected about her relationship with the professor for that it was no longer just professional he had guessed the question was whether he suspected they were more than friends and all this too she narrated for the professor who tried to be encouraging but she complained that if her affair were going to be discovered she wanted it to be more than it was and fretted that they had too little time together to develop shared memories.

"You don't think we have shared memories? Where we first met, the places we went."

"I want more."

"Here's a shared memory. Remember when we went into the movie theater at the mall and one of us couldn't keep her mouth shut when she was being, ahem, stimulated?"

"I want more memories like that."

"What are we waiting for? There's a movie theater right across the road."

"I'm serious."

"So am I."

She said she was disappointed not to have ever come up with an affectionate name for him.

"'Professor' has a certain charm."

"No it doesn't."

"It does when I'm inside you."

"You're in a funny mood."

"Then we both are. I just want to cheer you up."

"I've never even brought you a gift you liked."

"What are you talking about?"

"Don't lie. We both know it."

"Don't worry about it. Even Jess couldn't pick a book for me. Truth."

"Truth?"

"Truth."

"I knew I should have gone with the lace underwear."

"The books I've picked for you haven't exactly been a smashing success. Don't deny it."

"Let's watch porn."

"Seriously?"

She said, "'Oh my,' said the nurse, 'that swelling looks serious.' 'It is, nurse, it's driving me crazy.' 'Well, we're going to have to reduce it. Does that hurt?' 'Not at all, nurse.' 'Oh my, this seems to be making it even worse.' 'Don't stop, it takes a while.' 'You mean this has happened before? Then we can't take any chances. Let me try an oral technique. Don't be alarmed if there's a discharge.'"

He said, "'Now, I'm going to press gently in different places and you tell me if anything feels tender, okay?' 'Okay, doctor.' 'Does that hurt? How about that?' 'Doctor, could you do that again?' 'It looks pretty red, I think we've got an inflammation. Nurse, bring me some of that ointment. Now I'm going to put a little on my finger, like this, and insert it, like this, and you tell me if that—' 'Oh, doctor, oh.'"

On Friday evening the Treasury Secretary gathered the CEOs of the big Wall Street firms to tell them that the government would not rescue Lehman Brothers so a private-sector solution to prevent bankruptcy was the only option and therefore the people in the room needed to develop a realistic plan to limit damage to the system with the expectation that they would take the losses themselves without 'a single penny' in extraordinary credit support from the government. This was discounted by the bankers as a negotiating ploy so when their forensic team reported in the morning that the assets were overvalued by fifteen to twenty-five billion dollars no one offered to provide financing instead the CEO of Merrill Lynch who believed his firm would be next to fail after Bob's met with the CEO of Bank of America and the very next day would agree to be acquired.

To frighten the regulators Bob's firm submitted a document Saturday afternoon describing how default on its obligations would trigger a cascade of further defaults but that night a British bank announced an agreement to buy the firm (minus its overvalued assets which despite their gross overvaluation would be financed by a consortium of other banks) but in the morning canceled the deal because the British regulatory agency had declined to approve it. The problem boiled down to a guarantee that the Federal Reserve wanted the bank to assume but the British regulator wanted the Federal Reserve to assume which it wouldn't do because the potential liability was tens of billions of dollars and furthermore if a run on the firm's assets occurred despite the guarantee the British bank could reject the acquisition and leave the Fed in possession of a huge insolvent bank; but despite hectic negotiations the British regulator refused to acquiesce.

The negotiating team from Bob's firm spent a hectic day digesting each development and trying desperately to convince the Federal Reserve to loosen its requirements for access to an emergency lending facility but it refused knowing that without it the firm could not open for business the next morning instead it said it would like the firm to declare bankruptcy and would like it declared that very night to coincide with another announcement it couldn't divulge which was the sale of Merrill Lynch. The firm's bankruptcy lawyers had prepared a presentation for the Fed's legal counsel to show that bankruptcy would be catastrophic but the parties were at cross purposes because the regulator had firmly decided that Bob's present firm would not be rescued by the taxpayers as his prior firm had been six months earlier while the firm's management was convinced that it would. They believed the government would intervene at the last minute so their job was to remain obstinate while the Fed tried to make them realize that their options were to file for bankruptcy immediately or have chaos erupt in the morning.

Their negotiators left the Federal Reserve offices and returned to company headquarters Sunday night where there was pandemonium with hundreds of employees rushing in and out of offices and the president reported to a stunned board of directors that the acquisition deal had collapsed and the government was instructing them to file for bankruptcy immediately. The phone rang from the chairman of the SEC who had the Fed's general counsel on the line and he told the board the situation was serious and required action; when he was asked if he was directing them to file for bankruptcy the two conferred off the line and returned to say the decision was the board's to make and when the question was repeated the reply was that the government's position had been made clear earlier that day. The president then advised the board that the firm could not obtain necessary funding without government assistance and the board voted to file for bankruptcy at one forty-five in the morning.

Over the ensuing days almost every major American financial institution faced imminent collapse as massive losses spread throughout the financial system either because their operations were so intertwined with already failing firms they couldn't extricate themselves or because investors creditors or depositors en masse tried to retrieve their money. Panic gripped markets and as credit which like blood had to flow constantly and adequately to keep the financial system alive became unavailable markets almost ceased to function not just in the US but internationally and the stock market began a devastating plunge thereby demonstrating that it wasn't till people actually saw the system collapse before their eyes that they realized or admitted the system could collapse.

Having spent an entire week checking news alerts hourly and contacting everyone he could Bob heard about the bankruptcy only when he was getting dressed for work Monday morning and was thunderstruck because he could not believe the Federal Reserve would refuse emergency credit to a major American financial institution. "Tiffany!"

"What's the matter? My God, I thought you'd..."

"They let us go down. I'm done. It's over." He told her the news and they gaped at each other. "I don't know what to do. What do I do?"

"You go to work, what else?"

"My work ended last night."

"You don't know that."

"They shot my horse again. You said they would and I said no."

"I didn't. I didn't see this coming either."

He called her mid-afternoon to say he was thinking of resigning immediately since he didn't expect to last the week anyway and the sooner he started looking for a new job the better his chances (and it felt more dignified than waiting to get fired) but she urged him instead to use his time to start searching since little work was likely to get done anyway. "The longer they pay you the better," she said and he knew what she meant and it turned out to be good advice because by Friday afternoon he had learned that every firm on Wall Street and beyond was too much in crisis mode to think about hiring and after his termination interview he gathered the contents of his workstation into a cardboard box and descended in an elevator crowded with people clutching boxes who said nothing and glanced at no one.

The prior Saturday would have been Tiffany's regular date to meet the professor but Bob had been too distraught not knowing what was happening with his firm and the day after he lost his job she again didn't have the heart to leave him home by himself and in any case he was useless to take care of Kiley but the following Saturday she arranged to meet him even though Bob was still so depressed he hadn't left the house since the day he'd lost his job. When the professor asked how he was she shook her head and the conversation drifted across the troubled waters of the financial crisis with Tiffany saying the economic picture in the country could turn very dark.

"Give me a for instance."

"We're already in a housing crisis. All those mortgages people can't pay? Do the math."

"I told you I'm no good at math."

"People stop shopping so they can pay their mortgage. Many can't pay anyway and lose their homes. Think foreclosure, maybe on a massive scale. Economy slows, maybe into recession, maybe into a really bad recession. Unemployment. The stock market is already crashing, God knows where the bottom is. This could get really bad."

"Are you concerned for yourself?"

"You mean my job? Oh my God! It just occurred to me that if there's a wave of foreclosures, we might want to buy up residential properties. 'We' meaning my firm."

"Doesn't that seem kind of... ghoulish?"

"Once they're foreclosed the family that lost their home is already out of the picture. Somebody's going to buy the house, why not me? Haven't you heard that crisis means opportunity? That's why I'm not worried about my firm—or my own job, there are lots of directions we could go. Fortunately we never got into MBS in any kind of big way, and when we did it was mostly on the short side. Which I never told Bob, by the way."

"So I have to ask. Forgive me for being self-interested."

"You want to know if Bob's out of work for a long time, how that affects the foundation."

"In a word, yes."

"I don't see a problem. This year's funded. By next year Bob will be on his feet again, even if it's not in the same professional space. And if he's not, it still won't matter. That residential housing idea that just came to me, do you have any idea what that could be worth?"

"I have no idea. But sometimes, my lady, you take my breath away."

"Would you like to have sex with me?"

"Very much. But before I do, may I ask if that means you've made a decision about the next round?"

Unexpectedly she became quiet before answering. "If you wouldn't mind getting the announcement ready before I've committed to it..."

"Wouldn't mind at all."

"The weird thing about this crisis? Somehow it's made me more fond of the foundation. Don't ask me to explain it, but..."

A few hours later after showering they took the elevator the few floors down checked out and walked into the parking lot to find the late September air had turned unexpectedly cool.

Postscript

When I was in graduate school I discovered that the typical 'western' recounts a myth, that is a story that appears to be about one thing while in fact is about something more fundamental, conveying secret (esoteric) messages through elements of the story. The key to receiving the messages is to recognize how the story operates on multiple levels; once the key is lost, the story's meaning is lost. Though we have lost the key to our myths, we still love to hear them.

In modern fiction myth appears most often in 'genre' novels, though elements often appear in 'literary' novels. Powerful cultural forces are at work. Pilgrimage, for example, is easily appreciated—not just understood but felt—as *simultaneously* a physical act (a journey), an archetypal structure (the quest), and a metaphor (for struggle, the search for meaning, life itself).

Despite disagreement among scholars about the subject of the *Divine Comedy*, it seems obvious that its subject is love, but love writ large, love in all its forms, personal and social, physical and spiritual. Much is conveyed by use of numbers and I was able to incorporate some of this. Because Dante associated nine with his beloved Beatrice, much of significance occurs in lines and cantos that are nines or multiples of nines and so, for example, days nine, eighteen, and twenty-seven of Purgatory contain particularly significant events. He also stresses midpoints (indeed the first line of the poem refers to a midpoint) and you might find it interesting to compare his *Purgatorio* canto seventeen with my Purgatory day seventeen, and similarly his *Paradiso* and *Inferno* seventeens with my Francesco scenes between sixteen and seventeen in Paradise and Hell.

Dante sometimes draws comparisons by linking cantos of the same number, for example linking one famous woman lover in *Inferno* canto five with another in *Purgatorio* five, and both with Beatrice's commentary on love in *Paradiso* five; in my story similar parallels occur. Also I sometimes create parallel events in corresponding sections, for example as Dante is interrogated three times in *Paradiso* cantos twenty-four through twenty-six, Margherita is interrogated on the same topics on the same days; and there are other correspondences, for example Purgatory day thirty-three is modeled on *Purgatorio* canto twenty-seven.

I realize that my translations do not meet the usual expectations of ease and lucidity. All translators say they have remained faithful to the original, yet their translations usually bury it under the crushing weight of alterations to make them 'readable.' My quarrel is not over how one balances the competing ideals of preserving the original while providing a smooth translation, but with those translations, of which there are many, especially of Dante and the troubadours, that alter, not just words and syntax, not just images and analogies, not just sound and feel and rhythm and flow, but the very meaning of the original.

Let us say frankly that the problems in translating these poets are insuperable and thus one must decide what goals to compromise; therefore one must decide on one's intent, and mine was to refer the reader beyond the translation to try to give a sense of the original. Where, for example, the syntax of the original is *deliberately* awkward, the translation should be awkward.

Therefore my translations seem crude. Sometimes—often, far more often than you have been led to believe—the crudeness is in the original; sometimes the translation is crude because I sacrificed our preferences for word and phrase order where I believed something was to be gained from seeing the structure of the original. Sometimes the meaning of the original is obscure. Where it's obscure because we have lost the exact meaning, one does one's best; but what to do when the obscurity is there on purpose, as it sometimes is in Dante and often is in Petrarch? Would you say, "If that's the way two of the most skilled poets of all time left their poems after decades of labor, works as taut as any ever created (which, by the way, fed my motivation to try my own poor powers in this novel), then that's the way they should be left in translation." I would.